GHOST SHIP TO VENUS

The *Empress of Kolain* was a luxury spaceship traveling from Mars to Venus. But because of its location, it was out of reach of radio waves . . . it was, in a sense, invisible. Therefore, for all practical purposes, the ship was non-existent; and it would remain in that state until it came to life once again upon landing on Venus.

But the *Empress of Kolain* had to be stopped before reaching its destination . . .

So it was up to Venus Equilateral to do something. But how were they going to capture a ship that didn't exist . . . a ship that was hurtling through space some 200 million miles away?

"IN ESSENCE, VENUS EQUILATERAL REPRESENTS THE BASIC PATTERN OF SCIENCE FICTION . . . EXCELLENT!"

—John W. Campbell

Also by George O. Smith:

THE BRAIN MACHINE

*THE PATH OF UNREASON

SCIENTISTS' NIGHTMARES:
The Baffling, the Fake & the Unsolvable

*Published by Ballantine Books

THE COMPLETE VENUS EQUILATERAL

GEORGE O. SMITH

Introduction by
Arthur C. Clarke

BALLANTINE BOOKS • NEW YORK

Library of Congress Catalog Card Number:

ISBN 0-345-25551-8-195

Manufactured in the United States of America

First Edition: November 1976

Cover art by Rick Sternbach

ACKNOWLEDGMENTS

"QRM—Interplanetary," copyright © 1942 by Street & Smith Publications, Inc., for *Astounding Science Fiction*, October 1942.

"Calling the Empress," copyright © 1943 by Street & Smith Publications, Inc., for *Astounding Science Fiction*, June 1943.

"Recoil," copyright © 1943 by Street & Smith Publications, Inc., for *Astounding Science Fiction*, November 1943.

"Lost Art," copyright © 1943 by Street & Smith Publications, Inc., for *Astounding Science Fiction*, December 1943.

"Off the Beam," copyright © 1944 by Street & Smith Publications, Inc., for *Astounding Science Fiction*, February 1944.

"The Long Way," copyright © 1944 by Street & Smith Publications, Inc., for *Astounding Science Fiction*, April 1944.

"Beam Pirate," copyright © 1944 by Street & Smith Publications, Inc., for *Astounding Science Fiction*, October 1944.

"Firing Line," copyright © 1944 by Street & Smith Publications, Inc., for *Astounding Science Fiction*, December 1944.

"Special Delivery," copyright © 1945 by Street & Smith Publications, Inc., for *Astounding Science Fiction*, March 1945.

"Pandora's Millions," copyright © 1945 by Street & Smith Publications, Inc., for *Astounding Science Fiction*, June 1945.

"Mad Holiday," copyright © 1947 by The Prime Press for *Venus Equilateral*.

"The External Triangle," copyright © 1973 by Random House, Inc., for *Astounding: John W. Campbell Memorial Anthology* (Harry Harrison, ed.). Originally published as "Interlude."

"Identity," copyright © 1945 by Street & Smith Publications, Inc., for *Astounding Science Fiction*, November 1945.

To James Clerk Maxwell, whose electromagnetic equations founded the art of electronics and thus made Venus Equilateral possible . . .

And to my son, George O. Smith (Jr.), who may someday work there.

CONTENTS

INTRODUCTION

Like all science and science-fiction writers, I am used to talking glibly in millions of years, but it's very hard to accept the fact that I started reading these stories more than thirty years ago. It seems only yesterday, and I can remember exactly how it happened.

Owing to the war, normal supplies of *Astounding Stories* (*Analog*'s precursor) had been cut off by the British authorities, who foolishly imagined that there were better uses for shipping space and hard-earned dollars. Luckily, before withdrawal symptoms had become too serious, my good friend Willy Ley came to the rescue. He conscientiously mailed me every issue until I was able to renew my subscription on the outbreak of peace.

So I read George O. Smith's "Venus Equilateral" stories within a few weeks of their appearance, and greatly enjoyed them because I was obviously in the same line of business as the author. We were both working on radar, though that name had yet to enter the public domain. There was, however, a slight difference in the size of our hardware. My gear weighed about thirty tons and occupied two large trucks—and was the only sample of its kind ever built. (You'll find the details, more or less, in the novel *Glide Path.*) George's contraptions weighed a few ounces, were a couple of inches long, and were manufactured in tens of thousands. Even more remarkable, they were built to be shot from anti-aircraft guns—not a procedure recommended for delicate electronics equipment. (Especially vacuum tubes, which were all we had in those pre-transistor days.) I can still hardly believe in the "radio proximity fuse," and have often wondered what crackpot invented it. He probably read science fiction.

I imagined that George wrote these stories as relaxation from the serious business of winning the war, and I momentarily expected him to run into trouble with Security. From time to time he skated on pretty thin ice, and in this he was in good company. Everyone knows how John W. Campbell, Jr. (then Editor of *Astounding/Analog*) was once visited by the FBI, and asked if he would kindly desist from publishing stories about the military uses of uranium . . .

Though there had been many tales about "space stations" long before the Venus Equilateral series (Murray Leninster's "Power Planet" is a classic example from the early Thirties), George Smith was probably the first writer—certainly the first technically qualified writer—to spell out their uses for space communications. It is therefore quite possible that these stories influenced me subconsciously when, at Stratford-on-Avon during the closing months of the war, I worked out the principles of synchronous communications satellites now embodied in the global Intelsat system. Appropriately enough, the person who pointed this out to me is another long-time science-fiction fan: Dr. John Pierce, instigator of the Bell Laboratories program that led to Echo and Telstar.

It is interesting to see how George and I, who consider ourselves imaginative characters, both failed to anticipate the truly fantastic technical advances of the last few decades. We both thought that our "extraterrestrial relays" would be large, *manned* structures carrying armies of engineers—as, indeed, will one day be the case. Neither of us dreamed that most of the things we described would be done—within twenty years!—by a few pounds of incredibly miniaturized electronic equipment. And neither of us could possibly have foreseen the maser, that wonderful amplifying device which has made communication over "merely" planetary distances almost laughably simple.

Nevertheless, the problem which George Smith set out to solve remains, and will probably always remain. For short but annoying—and therefore intolerable—periods of time, the sun will block communications between planets and spacecraft. Some kind of repeater station will therefore be necessary to bypass signals around this million-mile-diameter obstacle.

Perhaps it will not be where George placed it, equidistant from Venus and the sun; for numerous reasons, a relay in Earth orbit, leading or trailing our planet by a constant few million miles, might be preferable. It is true that such a position would not be dynamically stable, but then I have always had doubts concerning the long-term stability of Venus Equilateral. Even mighty Jupiter cannot stop his "Trojan" asteroids from drifting back and forth over hundreds of millions of miles of orbit, and anything that approached Earth as closely as Venus Equilateral would be violently perturbed by our planet's gravitational field. However, such wanderings would be of little practical importance, and if necessary could be corrected rather easily by modest amounts of rocket power. Witness the ease with which today's synchronous satellites are kept on station over fixed lines of longitude, at the cost of a few pounds of fuel per year.

There is another respect in which George Smith, I am sure, correctly anticipates the future. Large, manned space stations will certainly not be used merely for communications. They will open up unlimited—literally—vistas for scientific research, technology, medicine, tourism, manufacturing, and even sport. Though not *all* the eventful happenings of the following space opera will actually materialize, you can be sure that still more surprising ones will.

And I hope that George and I are still around, another thirty years from now, to see how unimaginative we both were.

ARTHUR C. CLARKE

Colombo
Sri Lanka
February 1976

Venus Equilateral Relay Station, to give it the full name, was a manned satellite that occupied the libration point sixty degrees ahead of Venus along the planet's orbit. It relayed radio messages among the three inner planets when the sun intervened.

Its usefulness was often misunderstood, since many persons think that the intervention of the sun means the physical presence of the obscuring mass dead in line. This is not so. The sun is a tremendous generator of radiothermal noise, and since communication fails when the signal-to-noise ratio becomes untenable, the relay station becomes useful or at least expedient, long before and long after solar syzygy.

Venus Equilateral and the persons who worked there were first reported as fiction in 1942 in *Astounding Science Fiction* under the title "QRM—Interplanetary," the QRM signal being wireless telegraphers' code, meaning, "I am being interfered with." The report was popular; this was the beginning of a series that ran for three years and through thirteen novelettes.

QRM—International Code signal meaning "interference" of controllable nature, such as man-made static, cross modulation from another channel adjoining, or willful obliteration of signals by an interfering source.

Interference not of natural sources such as electrical storms, common static, et cetera. (Designated by International Code as QRN.)

—Handbook, Interplanetary Amateur Radio League

QRM—INTERPLANETARY

Korvus, the Magnificent, Nilamo of Yoralen, picked up the telephone in his palace and said: "I want to talk to Wilneda. He is at the International Hotel in Detroit, Michigan."

"I'm sorry, sir," came the voice of the operator. "Talking is not possible, due to the fifteen-minute transmission lag between here and Terra. However, teletype messages are welcome."

Her voice originated fifteen hundred miles north of Yoralen, but it sounded as though she might be in the next room. Korvus thought for a moment and then said: "Take this message: 'Wilneda: Add to order for mining machinery one type 56-XXD flier to replace washed-out model. And remember, alcohol and energy will not mix!' Sign that Korvus."

"Yes, Mr. Korvus."

"Not *mister*!" yelled the monarch. "I am Korvus the Magnificent! I am Nilamo of Yoralen!"

"Yes, your magnificence," said the operator humbly. It was more than possible that she was stifling a laugh, which knowledge made the little man of Venus squirm in wrath. But there was nothing he could do about it, so he wisely said nothing.

To give Korvus credit, he was not a pompous little man. He was large—for a Venusian—which made him small according to the standards set up by the Terrestrians. He, as Nilamo of Yoralen, had extended the once-small kingdom outward to include most of the Palanortis Country, which extended from 23.0 degrees North Latitude to 61.7 degrees, and almost across the whole, single continent that was the dry land of Venus.

So Korvus' message to Terra zoomed across the fifteen hundred rocky miles of Palanortis to Northern Landing. It passed high across the thousand-foot-high trees and over the mountain ranges. It swept over open patches of water, and across intervening cities and towns. It went with the speed of light and in a tight beam from Yoralen to Northern Landing, straight as a die and with person-to-person clarity. The operator in the city that lay across the North Pole of Venus clicked on a teletype, reading back the message as it was printed.

Korvus told her: "That is correct."

"The message will be in the hands of your representative Wilneda within the hour."

The punched tape from Operator No. 7's machine slid along the line until it entered a coupling machine.

The coupling machine worked furiously. It accepted the tapes from seventy operators as fast as they could set them. It selected the messages as they entered the machine, placing a mechanical preference upon whichever message happened to be ahead of the others on the moving tapes. The master tape moved continuously at eleven thousand words per minute, taking teletype messages from everywhere in the Northern Hemisphere of Venus to Terra and Mars. It was a busy machine; even at eleven thousand words per minute it often got hours behind.

The synchronous-keyed signal from the coupling machine left the operating room and went to the transmission room. It was amplified and sent out of the city to a small, squat building at the outskirts of Northern Landing. It was hurled at the sky out of a reflector antenna by a thousand-kilowatt transmitter.

The wave seared against the Venusian Heaviside Layer. It fought and it struggled. And, as is the case with strife, it lost heavily in the encounter. The beam was resisted fiercely. Infiltrations of ionization tore at the radio beam, stripping and trying to beat it down.

But man triumphed over nature. The megawatt of energy that came in a tight beam from the building at

Northern Landing emerged from the Heaviside Layer as a weak, piffling signal. It wavered and it crackled. It wanted desperately to lie down and sleep. Its directional qualities were impaired, and it wobbled badly. It arrived at the relay station tired and worn.

One million watts of ultra-high frequency energy at the start, it was measurable in microvolts when it reached a space station only five hundred miles above the city of Northern Landing.

The signal, as weak and as wobbly as it was, was taken in by eager receptors. It was amplified. It was dehashed, destaticked and deloused. And once again, one hundred decibels stronger and infinitely cleaner, the signal was hurled out on a tight beam from a gigantic parabolic reflector.

Across sixty-seven million miles of space went the signal. Across the orbit of Venus it went in a vast chord, and arrived at the Venus Equilateral Station with less trouble than the original transmission through the Heaviside Layer. The signal was amplified and demodulated. It went into a decoupler machine where the messages were sorted mechanically and sent, each to the proper channel, into other coupler machines. Beams from Venus Equilateral were directed at Mars and at Terra.

The Terra beam ended at Luna. Here it again was placed in the two-compartment beam and from Luna it punched down at Terra's Layer, emerging into the atmosphere of Terra as weak and as tired as it had been when it had come out of the Venusian Heaviside Layer. It entered a station in the Bahamas, was stripped of the interference, and put upon the land beams. It entered decoupling machines that sorted the messages as to destination. These various beams spread out across the face of Terra, the one carrying Korvus' message finally coming into a station at Ten Mile Road and Woodward. From this station, at the outskirts of Detroit, it went upon land wires downtown to the International Hotel.

The teletype machine in the office of the hotel began to click rapidly. The message to Wilneda was arriving.

And fifty-five minutes after the operator told Korvus that less than an hour would ensue, Wilneda was saying, humorously, "So, Korvus was drunk again last night—"

Completion of Korvus' message to Wilneda completes also one phase of the tale at hand. It is not important. There were a hundred and fifty other messages that might have been accompanied in the same manner, each as interesting to the person who likes the explanation of the interplanetary communication service. But this is not a technical journal. A more complete explanation of the various phases that a message goes through in leaving a city on Venus to go to Terra may be found in the *Communications Technical Review,* Volume XXVII, number 8, pages 411 to 716. Readers more interested in the technical aspects are referred to the article.

It so happens that Korvus' message was picked out of a hundred-odd messages because of one thing only. At the time that Korvus' message was in transit through the decoupler machines at the Venus Equilateral Relay Station, something of a material nature was entering the air lock of the station.

It was an unexpected visit.

Don Channing looked up at the indicator panel in his office and frowned in puzzlement. He punched a buzzer and spoke into the communicator on his desk.

"Find out who that is, will you, Arden?"

"He isn't expected," came back the voice of Arden Westland.

"I know that. But I've been expecting someone ever since John Peters retired last week. You know why."

"You hope to get his job," said the girl in an amused voice. "I hope you do. So that someone else will sit around all day trying to make you retire so that he can have your job!"

"Now look, Arden, I've never tried to make Peters retire."

"No, but when the word came that he was thinking of it, you began to think about taking over. Don't worry, I don't blame you." There was quite a protracted silence, and then her voice returned. "The visitor is a gentleman by the name of Francis Burbank. He came out in a flitter with a chauffeur and all."

"Big shot, hey?"

"Take it easy. He's coming up the office now."

"I gather that he desires audience with me?" asked Don.

"I think that he's here to lay down the law! You'll have to get out of Peters' office, if his appearance is any guide."

Some more silence followed. The communicator was turned off at the other end, which made Channing fume. He would have preferred to hear the interchange of words between his secretary and the newcomer. Then, instead of having the man announced, the door opened and the stranger entered. He came to the point immediately.

"You're Don Channing? Acting Director of Venus Equilateral?"

"I am."

"Then I have some news for you, Dr. Channing. I have been appointed Director by the Interplanetary Communications Commission. You are to resume your position as Electronics Engineer."

"Oh?" said Channing. "I sort of believed that I would be offered *this* position."

"There was a discussion of that procedure. However, the commission decided that a man of more commercial training would better fill the position. The Communications Division has been operating at too small a profit. They felt that a man of commercial experience could cut expenses and so on to good effect. You understand their reasoning, of course," said Burbank.

"Not exactly."

"Well, it is like this. They know that a scientist is not usually the man to consider the cost of experimentation. Scientists build thousand-ton cyclotrons to convert a penny's worth of lead into one and one-tenth cents' worth of lead and gold. And they use three hundred dollars' worth of power and a million-dollar machine to do it with.

"They feel that a man with training like that will not know the real meaning of the phrase 'cutting expenses.' A new broom sweeps clean, Dr. Channing. There must be many places where a man of commercial experience can cut expenses. I, as Director, shall do so."

"I wish you luck," said Channing.

"Then, there is no hard feeling?"

"I can't say that. It is probably not your fault. I cannot feel against you, but I do feel sort of let down at the decision of the commission. I have had experience in this job."

"The commission may appoint you to follow me. If your work shows a grasp of commercial operations, I shall so recommend."

"Thanks," said Channing dryly. "May I buy you a drink?"

"I never drink. And I do not believe in it. If it were mine to say, I'd prohibit liquor from the premises. Venus Equilateral would be better off without it."

Don Channing snapped the communicator. "Miss Westland, will you come in?"

She entered, puzzlement on her face.

"This is Mr. Burbank. His position places him in control of this office. You will, in the future, report to him directly. The report on the operations, engineering projects, and so on that I was to send in to the commission this morning will, therefore, be placed in Mr. Burbank's hands as soon as possible."

"Yes, Dr. Channing." Her eyes held a twinkle, but there was concern and sympathy in them, too. "Shall I get them immediately?"

"They are ready?"

"I was about to put them on the tape when you called."

"Then give them to Mr. Burbank." Channing turned to Burbank. "Miss Westland will hand you the reports I mentioned. They are complete and precise. A perusal of them will put you in grasp of the situation here at Venus Equilateral better than will an all-afternoon conference. I'll have Miss Westland haul my junk out of here. You may consider this as your office, it having been used by Dr. Peters. And, in the meantime, I've got to check up on some experiments on the ninth level." Channing paused. "You'll excuse me?"

"Yes, if Miss Westland knows where to find you."

"She will. I'll inform her of my whereabouts."

"I may want to consult you after I read the reports."

"That will be all right. The autocall can find me anywhere on Venus Equilateral, if I'm not at the place Miss Westland calls."

Don Channing stopped at Arden's desk. "I'm booted," he told her.

"Leaving Venus Equilateral?" she asked with concern.

"No, blond and beautiful, I'm just shunted back to my own office."

"Can't I go with you?" pleaded the girl.

"Nope. You are to stay here and be a nice, good-looking Mata Hari. This bird seems to think that he can run Venus Equilateral like a bus or a factory. I know the type, and the first thing he'll do is to run the place into a snarl. Keep me informed of anything complicated, will you?"

"Sure. And where are you going now?"

"I'm going down and get Walt Franks. We're going to inspect the transparency of a new type of glass."

"I didn't know that optical investigations come under your jurisdiction."

"This investigation will consist of a visit to the ninth level."

"Can't you take me along?"

"Not today," he grinned. "Your new boss does not believe in the evils of looking through the bottom of a glass. We must behave with decorum. We must forget fun. We are now operating under a man who will commercialize electronics to a fine art."

"Don't get stewed. He may want to know where the electrons are kept."

"I'm not going to drink that much. Walt and I need a discussion," he said. "And in the meantime, haul my spinach out of the office, will you, and take it back to the electronics office? I'll be needing it back there."

"O.K., Don," she said. "I'll see you later."

Channing left to go to the ninth level. He stopped long enough to collect Walt Franks.

Over a tall glass of beer, Channing told Franks of Burbank's visit. And why.

Only one thing stuck in Franks' mind. "Did you say that he might close Joe's?" asked Franks.

"He said that if it were in his power to do so, he would."

"Heaven forbid. Where will we go to be alone?"

"Alone?" snorted Channing. The barroom was half

filled with people, being the only drinking establishment for sixty-odd million miles.

"Well, you know what I mean."

"I could smuggle in a few cases of beer," suggested Don.

"Couldn't we smuggle him out?"

"That would be desirable. But I think he is here to stay. Darn it all, why do they have to appoint some confounded political pal to a job like this? I'm telling you, Walt, he must weigh two hundred if he weighs a pound. He holds his stomach on his lap when he sits down."

Walt looked up and down Channing's slender figure. "Well, he won't be holding Westland on his lap if it is filled with stomach."

"I never hold Westland on my lap—"

"No?"

"—during working hours!" Channing finished. He grinned at Franks and ordered another beer. "And how is the Office of Beam Control going to make out under the new regime?"

"I'll answer that after I see how the new regime treats the Office of Beam Control," answered Franks. "I doubt that he can do much to bugger things up in my office. There aren't many cheaper ways to direct a beam, you know."

"Yeah. You're safe."

"But what I can't understand is why they didn't continue you in that job. You've been handling the business ever since last December, when Peters got sick. You've been doing all right."

"Doing all right just means that I've been carrying over Peters' methods and ideas. What the commission wants, apparently, is something new. Ergo, the new broom."

"Personally, I like that one about the old shoes being more comfortable," said Franks. "If you say the right word, Don, I'll slip him a dose of high voltage. That should fix him."

"I think that the better way would be to *work* for the bird. Then when he goes, I'll have his recommendation."

"Phooey," snorted Franks. "They'll just appoint another political pal. They've tried it before and they'll try it again. I wonder what precinct he carries."

The telephone rang in the bar, and the bartender, after answering, motioned to Walt Franks. "You're wanted in your office," said the bartender. "And besides," he told Channing, "if I'm going to get lunch for three thousand people, you'd better trot along, too. It's nearly eleven o'clock, you know, and the first batch of two hundred will be coming in."

Joe was quite inaccurate as to the figures. The complement of Venus Equilateral was just shy of twenty-seven hundred. They worked in three eight-hour shifts, about nine hundred to a shift. They had their breakfast, lunch, and dinner hours staggered so that at no time was there more than about two hundred people in the big lunchroom. The bar, it may be mentioned, was in a smaller room at one end of the much larger cafeteria.

The Venus Equilateral Relay Station was a modern miracle of engineering if you liked to believe the books. Actually, Venus Equilateral was an asteroid that had been shoved into its orbit about the Sun, forming a practical demonstration of the equilateral triangle solution of the Three Moving Bodies. It was a long cylinder, about three miles in length by about a mile in diameter.

In 1946, the United States Army Signal Corps succeeded in sending forth and receiving in return a radar signal from the moon. This was an academic triumph; at that time such a feat had no practical value. Its value came later when the skies were opened up for travel; when men crossed the void of space to colonize the nearer planets, Mars and Venus.

They found, then, that communications back and forth depended upon the initial experiment in 1946.

But there were barriers, even in deep space. The penetration of the Heaviside Layer was no great problem. That had been done. But they found that Sol, our sun, was often in the path of the communications beam because the planets all make their way around Sol at different rates of speed.

All too frequently Mars is on the opposite side of the sun from Terra, or Sol might lie between Venus and Mars. Astronomically, this situation where two planets lie on opposite sides of the sun is called Major Opposition, which is an appropriate name even though those who named it were not thinking in terms of communications.

The concept of Sol being between two planets and interfering with communication does not mean a true physical alignment. The Sun is a tremendous generator of radiothermal energy, so that communication begins to fail when the other planet is 15 to 20 degrees from the Sun. Thus, from 30 to 40 degrees of opposition passage, Venus Equilateral is a necessary relay station.

To circumvent this natural barrier to communications, mankind made use of one of the classic solutions of the problem of the Three Moving Bodies, in which is it stated that three celestial objects at the corners of an equilateral triangle will so remain, rotating about their common center of gravity. This equilateral position between the sun and any planet is called the "Trojan" position because it has been known for some time that a group of asteroids precedes and follows Jupiter around in its orbit. The "Trojan" comes from the fact that these asteroids bear the well-known names of the heroes of the famous Trojan War.

To communicate around the sun, then, it is only necessary to establish a relay station in the Trojan position of the desired planet. This will be either ahead or behind the planet in its orbit; and the planet, the sun, and the station will form an equilateral triangle.

So was born the Venus Equilateral Relay Station.

Little remained of the original asteroid. At the present time, the original rock had been discarded to make room for the ever-growing personnel and material that were needed to operate the relay station. What had been an asteroid with machinery was now a huge pile of machinery with people. The insides, formerly of spongy rock, were now neatly cubed off into offices, rooms, hallways, and so on, divided by sheets of steel. The outer surface, once rugged and forbidding, was now all shiny steel. The small asteroid, a tiny thing, was gone, the station having overflowed the asteroid soon after men found that uninterrupted communication *was* possible between the worlds.

Now the man-made asteroid carried twenty-seven hundred people. There were stores, offices, places of recreation, churches, marriages, deaths, and everything but taxes. Judging by its population, it was a small town.

Venus Equilateral rotated about its axis. On the inner surface of its double-walled shell were the homes of the people—not cottages, but apartmental cubicles, one, two, three, six rooms. Centrifugal force made a little more than one Earth G of artificial gravity. Above this shell of apartments, the offices began. Offices, recreation centers, and so on. Up in the central position, where the gravity was nil or near-nil, the automatic machinery was placed: the servogyroscopes and their beam finders, the storerooms, the air plant, the hydroponic farms, and all other things that needed little or no gravity for well-being.

This was the Venus Equilateral Relay Station, sixty degrees ahead of the planet Venus, on Venus' orbit. Often closer to Terra than Venus, the relay station offered a perfect place to relay messages through whenever Mars or Terra was on the other side of the Sun. It was seldom idle, for it was seldom that Mars and Venus were in such a position that direct communications between all the three planets was possible.

This was the center of Interplanetary Communications. This was the main office. It was the heart of the Solar System's communication line, and as such, it was well manned. Orders for everything emanated from Venus Equilateral. It was a delicate proposition, Venus Equilateral was, and hence the present-on-all-occasions official capacities and office staff.

This was the organization that Don Channing hoped to direct. A closed corporation with one purpose in mind: interplanetary communication!

Channing wondered if the summons for Walt Franks was an official one. Returning to the electronics office, Don punched the communicator and asked: "Is Walt in there?"

Arden's voice came back: "No, but Burbank is in Franks' office. Wanna listen?"

"Eavesdropper! Using the communicator?"

"Sure."

"Better shut it off," Don warned. "Burbank isn't foolish, you know, and there are pilot lights and warning flags on those things to tell if someone has the key open. I wouldn't want to see you fired for listening in."

"All right, but it was getting interesting."

"If I'm betting on the right horse," said Channing, "this will be interesting for all before it is finished."

Seven days went by in monotonous procession. Seven days in a world of constant climate. One week, marked only by the changing of work shifts and the clocks that marked off the eight-hour periods. Seven days unmarred by rain or cold or heat. Seven days of uninterrupted sunshine that flickered in and out of the sealed viewports with eye-searing brilliance, coming and going as the station rotated.

But in the front offices, things were not serene. Not that monotony ever set in seriously in the engineering department, but that sacred sanctum of all-things-that-didn't-behave-as-they-should found that even their usual turmoil was worse. There was nothing that a person could set his fingers on directly. It was more of a quiet, undercover nature. On Monday, Francis Burbank sent around a communiqué removing the option of free messages for the personnel. On Tuesday, he remanded the years-long custom of permitting the supply ships to carry, free, packages from friends at home. On Wednesday, Burbank decided that there should be a curfew on the one and only beer emporium. "Curfew" was a revision made after he found that complete curtailing of all alcoholic beverages might easily lead to a more moral problem; there being little enough to do with one's spare time. On Thursday, he set up a stiff-necked staff of censors for the moving picture house. On Friday, he put a tax on cigarettes and candy. On Saturday, he installed time clocks in all the laboratories and professional offices, where previous to his coming, men had come for work a half-hour late and worked an hour overtime at night.

On Sunday—

Don Channing stormed into the Director's office with a scowl on his face.

"Look," he said, "for years we have felt that any man, woman, or child who was willing to come out here was worth all the freedom and consideration that we could give them. What about this damned tax on cigarettes? And candy? And who told you to stop our folks from telling their folks that they are still in good health? And why stop them from sending packages of candy, cake, mementoes, clothing, soap, mosquito dope, liquor, or anything else?. And did you ever think that a curfew is something that can be applied only when time is one and the same for all? On Venus Equilateral, Mr. Burbank, six o'clock in the evening is two hours after dinner for one group, two hours after going to work for the second group, and mid-sleep for the third. Then this matter of cutting all love scenes, drinking, female vampires, banditry, bedroom items, murders, and sweater girls out of the movies? We are a selected group and well prepared to take care of our morality. Any man or woman going offside would be heaved out quick. Why, after years of personal freedom, do we find ourselves under the authority of a veritable dictatorship?"

Francis Burbank was not touched. "I'll trouble you to keep to your own laboratory," he told Channing. "Perhaps your own laxity in matters of this sort is the reason why the commission preferred someone better prepared. You speak of many things. There will be more to come. I'll answer some of your questions. Why should we permit our profits to be eaten up by people sending messages, cost-free, to their acquaintances all over the minor planets? Why should valuable space for valuable supplies be taken up with personal favors between friends? And if the personnel wants to smoke and drink, let them pay for the privilege! It will help to pay for the high price of shipping the useless items out from the nearest planet—as well as saving of precious storage space!"

"But you're breeding ill will among the employees," Channing objected.

"Any who prefer to do so may leave!" snapped Burbank.

"You may find it difficult to hire people to spend their lives in a place that offers no sight of a sky or a breath of fresh air. The people here may go home to their own planets to find that smell of fresh, spring air is more desirable than a climate that never varies from the personal optimum. I wonder, occasionally, if it might not be possible to instigate some sort of cold snap or a rainy season just for the purpose of bringing to the members of Venus Equilateral some of the surprises that are to be found in Chicago or New York. Hell, even Canalopsis has an occasional rainstorm!"

"Return to your laboratory," said Burbank coldly. "And let me run the station. Why should we spend useful money to pamper people? I don't care if Canalopsis does have an occasional storm, we are not on Mars, we are in Venus Equilateral. You tend to your end of the business and I'll do as I deem fitting for the station!"

Channing mentally threw up his hands and literally stalked out of the office. Here was a close-knit organization being shot full of holes by a screwball. He stamped down to the ninth level and beat upon the closed door of Joe's. The door remained closed.

Channing beat with his knuckles until they bled. Finally a door popped open down the hallway fifty yards and a man looked out. His head popped in again, and within thirty seconds the door to Joe's opened and admitted Channing.

Joe slapped the door shut behind Channing quickly.

"What in hell are you operating, Joe—a speakeasy?"

"The next time you want in," Joe informed him, "knock on 902 twice, 914 once, and then here four times. We'll let you in. And now, don't say anything too loud." Joe put a finger to his lips and winked broadly. "Even the walls listen," he said in a stage whisper.

He led Channing into the room and put on the light. There was a flurry of people who tried to hide their glasses under the table. "Never mind," called Joe. "It's only Dr. Channing."

The room relaxed.

"I want something stiff," Channing told Joe. "I've just gone three rounds with His Nibs and came out cold."

Some people within earshot asked about it. Channing explained what had transpired. The people seemed satisfied that Channing had done his best for them. The room relaxed into routine.

The signal knock came on the door and was opened to admit Walt Franks and Arden Westland. Franks looked as though he had been given a stiff workout in a cement mixer.

"Scotch," said Arden. "And a glass of brew for the lady."

"What happened to him?"

"He's been trying to keep to Burbank's latest suggestions."

"You've been working too hard," Channing chided him gently. "This is the wrong time to mention it, I suppose, but did that beam slippage have anything to do with your condition—or was it vice versa?"

"You know that I haven't anything to do with the beam controls personally," said Franks. He straightened up and faced Channing defiantly.

"Don't get mad. What was it?"

"Mastermind, up there, called me in to see if there were some manner or means of tightening the beam. I told him, sure, we could hold the beam to practically nothing. He asked me why we didn't hold the beam to a parallel and save the dispersed power. He claimed that we could reduce power by two to one if more of it came into the station instead of being smeared all over the firmament. I, foolishly, agreed with him. He's right. You could. But only if everything is immobilized. I've been trying to work out some means of controlling the beam magnetically so that it would compensate for the normal variations due to magnetic influences. So far I've failed."

"It can't be done. I know, because I worked on the problem for three years with some of the best brains in the system. To date, it is impossible."

A click attracted their attention. It was the pneumatic tube. A cylinder dropped out of the tube, and Joe opened it and handed the enclosed paper to Franks.

He read:

WALT:

I'M SENDING THIS TO YOU AT JOE'S BECAUSE I KNOW THAT IS WHERE YOU ARE AND I THINK YOU SHOULD GET THIS REAL QUICK.

JEANNE S.

Walt smiled wearily and said: "A good secretary is a

thing of beauty. A thing of beauty is admired and is a joy forever. Jeanne is both. She is a jewel."

"Yeah, we know. What does the letter say?"

"It is another communiqué from our doting boss. He is removing from my control the odd three hundred men I've got working on Beam Control. He is to assume the responsibility for them himself. I'm practically out of a job."

"Make that two Scotches," Channing told Joe.

"Make it three," chimed in Arden. "I've got to work for him, too!"

"Is that so bad?" asked Channing. "All you've got to do is to listen carefully and do as you're told. We have to answer to the bird, too."

"Yeah," said Arden, "but you fellows don't have to listen to a dopey guy ask foolish questions all day. It's driving me silly."

"What I'd like to know," murmured Franks, "is what is the idea of pulling me off the job? Nuts, I've been on the Beam Control for years. I've got the finest crew of men anywhere. They can actually foresee a shift and compensate for it, I think. I picked 'em myself and I've been proud of my outfit. Now," he said brokenly, "I've got no outfit. In fact, I have darned little crew left at all. Only my dozen lab members. I'll have to go back to swinging a meter myself before this is over."

It was quite a comedown. From the master of over three hundred highly paid, highly prized, intelligent technicians, Walt Franks was now the superintendent of one dozen laboratory technicians. It was a definite cut in his status.

Channing finished his drink and, seeing that Franks' attention was elsewhere, he told Arden: "Thanks for taking care of him, but don't use all your sympathy on him. I feel that I'm going to need your shoulder to cry on before long."

"Anytime you want a soft shoulder," said Arden generously, "let me know. I'll come a-running."

Channing went out. He roamed nervously all the rest of the day. He visited the bar several times, but the general air of the place depressed him. From a place of recreation, laughter, and pleasantry, Joe's place had changed to a room for reminiscences and remorse, a place to drown one's troubles—or poison them—or to preserve them in alcohol.

He went to see the local moving picture, a piece advertised as being one of the best mystery thrillers since Hitchcock. He found that all of the interesting parts were cut out and that the only thing that remained was a rather disjointed portrayal of a detective finding meaningless clues and ultimately the criminal. There was a suggestion at the end that the detective and the criminal had fought it out, but whether it was with pistols, field pieces, knives, cream puffs, or words was left to the imagination. It was also to be assumed that he and the heroine, who went into a partial blackout every time she sat down, finally got acquainted enough to hold hands after the picture.

Channing stormed out of the theater after seeing the above and finding that the only cartoon had been barred because it showed an innocuous cow without benefit of shorts.

He troubled Joe for a bottle of the best and took to his apartment in disappointment. By eight o'clock in the evening, Don Channing was asleep with all his clothing on. The bed rolled and refused to stay on an even keel, but Channing found a necktie and tied himself securely in the bed and died off in a beautiful, boiled cloud.

He woke to the tune of a beautiful hangover. Gulped seven glasses of water, he staggered to the shower. Fifteen lavish minutes of iced needles and some coffee brought him part way back to his own, cheerful self. He headed down the hall toward the elevator.

He found a note in his office directing him to appear at a conference in Burbank's office. Groaning in anguish, Channing went to the Director's office expecting the worst.

It was bad. In fact, it was enough to drive everyone in the conference to drink. Burbank asked opinions on everything, and then tore the opinions apart with little regard to their validity. He expressed his own opinion many times, which was a disgusted sense of the personnel's inability to do anything of real value.

"Certainly," he stormed, "I know you are operating.

But have there been any new developments coming out of your laboratory, Mr. Channing?"

Someone was about to tell Burbank that Channing had a doctor's degree, but Don shook his head.

"We've been working on a lot of small items," said Channing. "I cannot say whether there has been any one big thing that we could point to. As we make developments, we put them into service. Added together, they make quite an honest effort."

"What, for instance?" Burbank stormed.

"The last one was the coupler machine improvement that permitted better than ten thousand words per minute."

"Up to that time the best wordage was something like eight thousand words," said Burbank. "I think that you have been resting too long on your laurels. Unless you can bring me something big enough to advertise, I shall have to take measures. Now *you*, Mr. Warren," continued Burbank. "You are the man who is supposed to be superintendent of maintenance. May I ask why the outer hull is not painted?"

"Because it would be a waste of paint," said Warren. "Figure out the acreage of a surface of a cylinder three miles long and a mile in diameter. It is almost eleven square miles! Eleven square miles to paint from scaffolding hung from the outside itself."

"Use bos'n's chairs," snapped Burbank.

"A bos'n's chair would be worthless," Warren informed Burbank. "You must remember that to anyone trying to operate on the outer hull, the outer hull is a ceiling and directly overhead. Another thing," said Warren, "you paint that hull and you'll run this station by yourself. Why d'ya think we have it shiny?"

"If we paint the hull," persisted Burbank, "it will be more presentable than that nondescript steel color."

"That steel color is as shiny as we could make it," growled Warren. "We want to get rid of as much radiated heat as we can. You slap a coat of any kind of paint on that hull and you'll have plenty of heat in here."

"Ah, that sounds interesting. We'll save heating costs—"

"Don't be an idiot," snapped Warren. "Heating costs,

my grandmother's eye. Look, Burbank, did you ever hear of the Uranium Pile? Part of our income comes from refining uranium and plutonium and the preparation of radioisotopes. And— Good Lord, I'm not going to try to explain fission-reacting materials to you; get that first old copy of the Smyth Report and get caught up-to-date.

"The fact remains," continued Warren, cooling somewhat after displaying Burbank's ignorance, "that we have more power than we know what to do with. We're operating on a safe margin by radiating just a little more than we generate. We make up the rest by the old methods of artificial heating.

"But there have been a lot of times when it became necessary to dissipate a lot of energy for divers reasons and then we've had to shut off the heating. What would happen if we couldn't cool off the damned coffee can? We'd roast to death the first time we got a new employee with a body temperature a degree above normal."

"You're being openly rebellious," Burbank warned him.

"So I am. And if you persist in your attempt to make this place presentable, you'll find me and my gang outright mutinous! Good day, sir!"

He stormed out of the office and slammed the door.

"Take a note, Miss Westland. 'Interplanetary Communications Commission, Terra. Gentlemen: Michael Warren, superintendent of maintenance at Venus Equilateral, has proven to be unreceptive to certain suggestions as to the appearance and/or operation of Venus Equilateral. It is my request that he be replaced immediately. Signed, Francis Burbank, Director.' " He paused to see what effect that message had upon the faces of the men around the table. "Send that by special delivery!"

Johnny Billings opened his mouth to say something, but shut it with a snap. Westland looked up at Burbank, but she said nothing. She gave Channing a sly smile, and Channing smiled back. There were grins about the table, too, for everyone recognized the boner. Burbank had just sent a letter from the interworld-communications relay station by special delivery mail.

It would not get to Terra for better than two weeks; a use of the station's facilities would have the message in the hands of the commission within the hour.

"That will be all, gentlemen," Burbank smiled smugly. "Our next conference will be next Monday morning!"

"Mr. Channing," chortled the pleasant voice of Arden Westland, "now that the trifling influence of the boss versus secretary taboo is off, will you have the pleasure of buying me a drink?"

"Can you repeat that word for word and explain it?" grinned Don.

"A man isn't supposed to make eyes at his secretary. A gal ain't supposed to seduce her boss. Now that you are no longer Acting Director, and I no longer your stenog, how about some sociability?"

"I never thought that I'd be propositioned by a typewriter jockey," said Channing, "but I'll do it. What time is it? Do we do it openly, or must we sneak over to the apartment and snaffle a snort on the sly?"

"We snaffle. That is, if you trust me in your apartment."

"I'm scared to death," Channing informed her. "But if I should fail to defend my honor, we must remember that it is no dishonor to try and fail."

"That sounds like a nice alibi," said Arden with a smile. "Or a come-on. I don't know which. Or, Mr. Channing, am I being told that my advances might not be welcome?"

"We shall see," Channing said. "We'll have to make a careful study of the matter. I cannot make any statements without first making a thorough examination under all sorts of conditions. Here we are. You will precede me through the door, please."

"Why?" asked Arden.

"So that you cannot back out at the last possible moment. Once I get inside, I'll think about keeping you there!"

"As long as you have some illegal fluid, I'll stay." She tried to leer at Don but failed because she had had all too little experience in leering. "Bring it on!"

"Here's to the good old days," Don toasted as the drinks were raised.

"Nope. Here's to the future," proposed Arden. "Those good old days—all they were was old. If you were back in them, you'd still have to have the pleasure of meeting Burbank."

"Grrrr," growled Channing. "That name is never mentioned in this household."

"You haven't a pix of the old bird turned to the wall, have you?" asked Arden.

"I tossed it out."

"We'll drink to that." They drained glasses. "And we'll have another."

"I need another," said Channing. "Can you imagine that buzzard asking me to invent something big in seven days?"

"Sure. By the same reasoning that he uses to send a letter from Venus Equilateral instead of just slipping it on the Terra beam. Faulty."

"Phoney."

The door opened abruptly and Walt Franks entered. "D'ja hear the latest?" he asked breathlessly.

"No," said Channing.

He was reaching for another glass automatically. He poured, and Walt watched the amber fluid creep up the glass, led by a sheet of white foam.

"Then look!"

Walt handed Channing an official envelope. It was a regular notice to the effect that there had been eleven failures of service through Venus Equilateral.

"Eleven! What makes?"

"Mastermind."

"What's he done?"

"Remember the removal of my jurisdiction over the beam control operators? Well, in the last ten days, Burbank has installed some new features to cut expenses. I think that he hopes to lay off a couple of hundred men."

"What's he doing, do you know?"

"He's shortening the dispersion. He intends to cut the power by slamming more of the widespread beam into the receptor. The tighter beam makes aiming more difficult, you know, because at seventy million miles, every time little Joey of Mars swings his toy horseshoe magnet on the end of his string, the beam wobbles. And at seventy million miles, how much wobbling does it take to send a narrow beam clear off the target?"

"The normal dispersion of the beam from Venus is over a thousand miles wide. It gyrates and wobbles through most of that arc. That is why we picked that particular dispersion. If we could have pointed the thing like an arrow, we'd have kept the dispersion down."

"Right. And he's tightened the beam to less than a hundred miles' dispersion. Now, every time a sunspot gets hit amidships with a lady sunspot, the beam goes off on a tangent. We've lost the beam eleven times in a week. That's more times than I've lost it in three years!"

"O.K.," said Channing. "So what? Mastermind is responsible. We'll sit tight and wait for developments. In any display of abilities, we can spike Mr. Burbank. Have another drink?"

"Got any more? If you've not, I've got a couple of cases cached underneath the bed in my apartment."

"I've plenty," said Channing. "And I'll need plenty. I have exactly twenty-two hours left in which to produce something comparable to the telephone, the electric light, the airplane, or the expanding universe! Phooey. Pour me another, Arden."

A knock at the door; a feminine voice interrupted simultaneously. "May I come in?"

It was Walt's secretary. She looked worried. In one hand she waved another letter.

"Another communiqué?" asked Channing.

"Worse. Notice that for the last three hours there have been less than twelve percent of messages relayed!"

"Five minutes' operation out of an hour," said Channing. "Where's that from?"

"Came out on the Terra beam. It's marked number seventeen, so I guess that sixteen other tries have been made."

"What has Mastermind tried this time?" Channing stormed. He tore out of the room and headed for the Director's office on a dead run. On the way, he hit his shoulder on the door, caromed off the opposite wall, righted himself, and was gone in a flurry of flying feet.

Three heads popped out of doors to see who was making the noise.

Channing skidded into Burbank's office on his heels. "What gives?" he snapped. "D'ya realize that we've lost the beam? What have you been doing?"

"It is a minor difficulty," said Burbank calmly. "We will iron it out presently."

"Presently! Our charter doesn't permit interruptions of service of that magnitude. I ask again: What are you doing?"

"You, as Electronics Engineer, have no right to question me. I repeat, we shall iron out the difficulty presently."

Channing snorted and tore out of Burbank's office. He headed for the Office of Beam Control, turned the corner on one foot, and slammed the door roughly.

"Chuck!" he yelled. "Chuck Thomas! Where are you?"

No answer. Channing left the beam office and headed for the master control panels, out near the airlock end of Venus Equilateral. He found Thomas stewing over a complicated piece of apparatus.

"Chuck, for the love of Michael, what in the devil is going on?"

"Thought you knew," answered Thomas. "Burbank had the crew install photoelectric mosaic banks on the beam controls. He intends to use the photomosaics to keep Venus, Terra, and Mars on the beam."

"Great Sniveling Scott! They tried that in the last century and tossed it out three days later. Where's the crew now?"

"Packing for home. They've been laid off!"

"Get 'em back! Put 'em to work. Turn off those darned photomosaics and use the manual again. We've lost every beam we ever had."

A sarcastic voice came in at this point. "For what reason do you interfere with my improvements?" sneered the voice. "Could it be that you are accepting graft from the employees to keep them on the job by preventing the installation of superior equipment?"

Channing turned on his toe and let Burbank have one. It was a neat job, coming up at the right time and connecting sweetly. Burbank went over on his head.

"Get going," Channing snapped at Thomas.

Charles Thomas grinned. It was not Channing's one-ninety that decided him to comply. He left.

Channing shook Burbank's shoulder. He slapped the man's face. Eyes opened, accusing eyes rendered mute by a very sore jaw, tongue, and throat.

"Now listen," snapped Channing. "Listen to every word! Mosaic directors are useless. Know why? It is because of the lag. At planetary distances, light takes an appreciable time to reach. Your beam wobbles. Your planet swerves out of line because of intervening factors; varying magnetic fields, even the bending of light due to gravitational fields will shake the beam microscopically. But, Burbank, a microscopic discrepancy is all that is needed to bust things wide open. You've got to have experienced men to operate the beam controls. Men who can think. Men who can, from experience, reason that this fluctuation will not last, but will swing back in a few seconds, or that this type of swerving will increase in magnitude for a half-hour, maintain the status, and then return, pass through zero and find the same level on the minus side.

"Since light and centimeter waves are not exactly alike in performance, a field that will serve one may not affect the other as much. Ergo, your photomosaic is useless. The photoelectric mosaic is a brilliant gadget for keeping a plane in a spotlight or for aiming a sixteen-inch gun, but it is worthless for anything over a couple of million miles. So I've called the men back to their stations. And don't try anything foolish again without consulting the men who are paid to think!"

Channing got up and left. As he strode down the stairs to the apartment level, he met many of the men who had been laid off. None of them said a word, but all of them wore bright, knowing smiles.

By Monday morning, however, Burbank was himself again. The rebuff given him by Don Channing had worn off and he was sparkling with ideas. He speared Franks with the glitter in his eyes and said: "If our beams are always on the center, why is it necessary to use multiplex diversity?"

Franks smiled. "You're mistaken," he told Burbank. "They're not always on the button. They vary. Therefore, we use diversity transmission so that if one beam fails momentarily, one of the other beams will bring the signal in. It is analogous to tying five or six ropes onto a hoisted stone. If one breaks, you have the others."

"You have them running all the time, then?"

"Certainly. At several minutes of time lag in transmission, to try and establish a beam failure of a few seconds' duration is utter foolishness."

"And you disperse the beam to a thousand miles wide to keep the beam centered at any variation?" Burbank shot at Channing.

"Not for *any* variation. Make that any *normal* gyration and I'll buy it."

"Then why don't we disperse the beam to two or three thousand miles and do away with diversity transmission?" asked Burbank triumphantly.

"Ever heard of fading?" asked Channing with a grin. "Your signal comes and goes. Not gyration; it just gets weaker. It fails for want of something to eat, I guess, and takes off after a wandering cosmic ray. At any rate, there are many times per minute that one beam will be right on the nose and yet so weak that our strippers cannot clean it enough to make it usable. Then the diversity system comes in handy. Our coupling detectors automatically select the proper signal channel. It takes the one that is the strongest and subdues the rest within itself."

"Complicated?"

"It was done in the heyday of radio—1935 or so. Your two channels come in to a common detector. Automatic volume-control voltage comes from the single detector and is applied to all channels. This voltage is proper for the strongest channel, but is too high for the ones receiving the weaker signal, blocking them by rendering them insensitive. When the strong channel fades and the weak channel rises, the detector follows down until the two signal channels are equal and then it rises with the stronger channel."

"I see," said Burbank. "Has anything been done about fading?"

"It is like the weather, according to Mark Twain," smiled Channing. " 'Everybody talks about it, but nobody does anything about it.' About all we've learned is that we can cuss it out and it doesn't cuss back."

"I think it should be tried," said Burbank.

"If you'll pardon me, it has been tried. The first installation at Venus Equilateral was made that way. It didn't work, though we used more power than all of our diversity transmitters together. Sorry."

"Have you anything to report?" Burbank asked Channing.

"Nothing. I've been more than busy investigating the trouble we've had in keeping the beams centered."

Burbank said nothing. He was stopped. He hoped that the secret of his failure was not generally known, but he knew at the same time that when three hundred men are aware of something interesting, some of them will see to it that all the others involved will surely know. He looked at the faces of the men around the table and saw suppressed mirth in every one of them. Burbank writhed in inward anger. But he was a good poker player. He didn't show it at all.

He then went on to other problems. He ironed some out, others he shelved for the time being. Burbank was a good businessman. But like so many other businessmen, Burbank had the firm conviction that if he had the time to spare and at the same time was free of the worries and paperwork of his position, he could step into the laboratory and show the engineers how to make things hum. He was infuriated every time he saw one of the engineering staff sitting with hands behind head, lost in a gazy, unreal land of deep thought. Though he knew better, he was often tempted to raise hell because the man was obviously loafing.

But give him credit. He could handle business angles to perfection. In spite of his tangle over the beam control, he had rebounded excellently and had ironed out all of the complaints that had poured in. Ironed it out to the satisfaction of the injured party as well as the Interplanetary Communications Commission, who were interested in anything that cost money.

He dismissed the conference and went to thinking. And he assumed the same pose that infuriated him in other men under him: hands behind head, feet upon desk.

The moving-picture theater was dark. The hero reached longing arms to the heroine, and there was a sort of magnetic attraction. They approached one another. But the spark misfired. It was blacked out with a nice slice of utter blackness that came from the screen and spread its lightlessness all over the theater. In the ensuing darkness, several osculations resounded that were more personal and more satisfying than the censored clinch. The lights flashed on and several male heads moved back hastily. Female lips smiled happily. Some of them parted in speech.

One of them said: "Why, Mr. Channing!"

"Shut up, Arden," snapped the man. "People will think that I've been kissing you."

"If someone else was taking advantage of the situation," she said, "you got gypped. I thought I was kissing you and I cooked with gas!"

"Did you ever try that before?" asked Channing interestedly.

"Why?" she asked.

"I liked it. I merely wondered, if you'd worked it on other men, what there was about you that kept you single."

"They all died after the first application," she said. "They couldn't take it."

"Let me outta here! I get the implication. I am the first bird that hasn't died, hey?" He yawned luxuriously.

"Company or the hour?" asked Arden.

"Can't be either," he said. "Come on, let's break a bottle of beer open. I'm dry!"

"I've got a slight headache," she told him. "From what, I can't imagine."

"I haven't a headache, but I'm sort of logy."

"What have you been doing?" asked Arden. "Haven't seen you for a couple of days."

"Nothing worth mentioning. Had an idea a couple of days ago and went to work on it."

"Haven't been working overtime or missing breakfast?"

"Nope."

"Then I don't see why you should be ill. I can explain my headache away by attributing it to eyestrain. Since Billyboy came here, and censored the movies to the bone, the darned things flicker like anything. But eyestrain doesn't create an autointoxication. So, my fine fellow, what have you been drinking?"

"Nothing that I haven't been drinking since I first took to my second bottlehood some years ago."

"You wouldn't be suffering from a hangover from that hangover you had a couple of weeks ago?"

"Nope. I swore off. Never again will I try to drink a whole quart of Two Moons in one evening. It got me."

"It had you for a couple of days." Arden laughed. "All to itself."

Don Channing said nothing. He recalled, all too vividly, the rolling of the tummy that ensued after that session with the only fighter that hadn't yet been beaten: Old John Barleycorn.

"How are you coming on with Burbank?" asked Arden. "I haven't heard a rave for—well, ever since Monday morning's conference. Three days without a nasty dig at Our Boss. That's a record."

"Give the devil his due. He's been more than busy placating irate citizens. That last debacle with the beam control gave him a real Moscow winter. His reforms came to a stop whilst he entrenched. But he's been doing an excellent job of squirming out from under. Of course, it has been helped by the fact that even though the service was rotten for a few hours, the customers couldn't rush out to some other agency to get communications with the other planets."

"Sort of: 'Take us, lousy as we are?' "

"That's it."

Channing opened the door to his apartment and Arden went in. Channing followed, and then stopped cold.

"Great Jeepers!" he said in an awed tone. "If I didn't know—"

"Why, Don! What's so startling?"

"Have you noticed?" he asked. "It smells like the inside of a chicken coop in here!"

Arden sniffed. "It does sort of remind me of something that died and couldn't get out of its skin." She smiled. "I'll hold my breath. Any sacrifice for a drink."

"That isn't the point. This is purified air. It should be as sweet as a baby's breath."

"Some baby," whistled Arden. "What's baby been drinking?"

"It wasn't cow juice. What I've been trying to put over is that the air doesn't seem to have been changed in here for nine weeks."

Channing went to the ventilator and lit a match. The flame bent over, flickered, and went out.

"Air intake is O.K.," he said. "Maybe it is I. Bring on that bottle, Channing; don't keep the lady waiting."

He yawned again, deeply and jaw-stretchingly. Arden yawned, too, and the thought of both of them stretching their jaws to the breaking-off point made both of them laugh foolishly.

"Arden, I'm going to break one bottle of beer with you, after which I'm going to take you home, kiss you good night, and toss you into your own apartment. Then I'm coming back here and I'm going to hit the hay!"

Arden took a long, deep breath. "I'll buy that," she said. "And tonight, it wouldn't take much persuasion to induce me to snooze right here in this chair!"

"Oh, fine," Don cheered. "That would fix me up swell with the neighbors. I'm not going to get shot-gunned into anything like that!"

"Don't be silly," said Arden.

"From the look in your eye," said Channing, "I'd say that you were just about to do that very thing. I was merely trying to dissolve any ideas that you might have."

"Don't bother," she said pettishly. "I haven't any ideas. I'm as free as you are, and I intend to stay that way!"

Channing stood up. "The next thing we know, we'll be fighting," he observed. "Stand up, Arden. Shake."

Arden stood up, shook herself, and then looked at Channing with a strange light in her eyes. "I feel sort of dizzy," she admitted. "And everything irritates me."

She passed a hand over her eyes wearily. Then, with a visible effort, she straightened. She seemed to throw off her momentary ill feeling instantly, she smiled at Channing, and was her normal self in less than a minute.

"What is it?" she asked. "Do you feel funny, too?"

"I do!" he said. "I don't want that beer. I want to snooze."

"When Channing would prefer snoozing to boozing he is sick," she said. "Come on, fellow, take me home."

Slowly they walked down the long hallway. They said nothing. Arm in arm they went, and when they reached Arden's door, their good-night kiss lacked enthusiasm. "See you in the morning," said Don.

Arden looked at him. "That was a little flat. We'll try it again—tomorrow or next week."

Don Channing's sleep was broken by dreams. He was warm. His dreams depicted him in a humid, airless chamber, and he was forced to breathe that same stale air again and again. He awoke in a hot sweat, weak and feeling—lousy!

He dressed carelessly. He shaved hit-or-miss. His morning coffee tasted flat and sour. He left the apartment in a bad mood, and bumped into Arden at the corner of the hall.

"Hello," she said. "I feel rotten. But you have improved. Or is that passionate breathing just a lack of fresh air?"

"Hell! That's it!" he said.

He snapped up his wristwatch, which was equipped with a stop-watch hand. He looked about, and finding a man sitting on a bench, apparently taking it easy while waiting for someone, Channing clicked the sweep hand into gear. He started to count the man's respiration.

"What gives?" asked Arden. "What's 'It'? Why are you so excited? Did I say something?"

"You did," said Channing after fifteen seconds. "That bird's respiration is better than fifty! This whole place is filled to the gills with carbon dioxide. Come on, Arden, let's get going!"

Channing led the girl by several yards by the time that they were within sight of the elevator. He waited for her, and then sent the car upward at a full throttle. Minutes passed, and they could feel that stomach-rising sensation that comes when gravity is lessened. Arden clasped her hands over her middle and hugged. She squirmed and giggled.

"You've been up to the axis before," said Channing. "Take long, deep breaths."

The car came to a stop with a slowing effect. A normal braking stop would have catapulted them against the ceiling.

"Come on," he grinned at her, "here's where we make time!"

Channing looked up at the little flight of stairs that led to the innermost level. He winked at Arden and jumped. He passed up through the opening easily. "Jump," he commanded. "Don't use the stairs."

Arden jumped. She sailed upward, and as she passed through the opening, Channing caught her by one arm and stopped her flight. "At that speed you'd go right on across," he said.

She looked up, and there, about two hundred feet overhead, she could see the opposite wall.

Channing snapped on the lights. They were in a room two hundred feet in diameter and three hundred feet long. "We're at the center of the station," Channing informed her. "Beyond that bulkhead is the air lock. On the other side of the other bulkhead, we have the air plant, the storage spaces, and several rooms of machinery. Come on," he said.

He took her by the hand and with a kick he propelled himself along on a long, curving course to the opposite side of the inner cylinder. He gained the opposite bulkhead as well.

"Now, that's what I call traveling," said Arden. "But my tummy goes *whoosh, whoosh* every time we cross the center."

Channing operated a heavy door. They went in through rooms full of machinery and into rooms stacked to the center with boxes; stacked from the wall to the center and then packed with springs. Near the axis of the cylinder, things weighed so little that packing was necessary to keep them from floating around.

"I feel giddy," said Arden.

"High in oxygen," said he. "The CO_2 drops to the bottom, being heavier. Then, too, the air is thinner up here because centrifugal force swings the whole out to the rim. Out there we are so used to 'down' that here, a half-mile above—or to the center, rather—we have trouble in saying, technically, what we mean. Watch!"

He left Arden standing and walked rapidly around the inside of the cylinder. Soon he was standing on the steel plates directly over her head. She looked up, and shook her head.

"I know why," she called, "but it still makes me dizzy. Come down from up there or I'll be sick."

Channing made a neat dive from his position above her head. He did it merely by jumping upward from his place toward her place, apparently hanging head down from the ceiling. He turned a neat flip-flop in the air and landed easily beside her. Immediately, for both of them, things became right-side-up again.

Channing opened the door to the room marked AIR PLANT. He stepped in, snapped on the lights, and gasped in amazement.

"Hell!" he groaned.

The place was empty. Completely empty. Absolutely and irrevocably vacant. Oh, there was some dirt on the floor and some trash in the corners, and a trail of scratches on the floor to show that the life-giving air plant had been removed, hunk by hunk, out through another door at the far end of the room.

"Whoa, Tillie!" screamed Don. "We've been stabbed! Arden, get on the type and have— No wait a minute until we find out a few more things about this!"

They made record time back to the office level. They found Burbank in his office, leaning back, and talking to someone on the phone.

Channing tried to interrupt, but Burbank removed his nose from the telephone long enough to snarl, "Can't you see I'm busy? Have you no manners or respect?"

Channing, fuming inside, swore inwardly. He sat down with a show of being calm and folded his hands over his abdomen like the famed statue of Buddha. Arden looked at him, and for all the trouble they were in, she couldn't help giggling. Channing, tall, lanky, and strong, looked as little as possible like the popular, pudgy figure of the Sitting Buddha.

A minute passed.

Burbank hung up the phone.

"Where does Venus Equilateral get its air from?" snapped Burbank.

"That's what I want—"

"Answer me, please. I'm worried."

"So am I. Something—"

"Tell me first, from what source does Venus Equilateral get its fresh air?"

"From the air plant. And that is—"

"There must be more than one," said Burbank thoughtfully.

"There's only one."

"There *must* be more than one. We couldn't live if there weren't," said the Director.

"Wishing won't make it so. There is only one."

"I tell you, there must be another. Why, I went into the one up at the axis day before yesterday and found that instead of a bunch of machinery, running smoothly, purifying air, and sending it out to the various parts of the station, all there was was a veritable jungle of weeds. Those weeds, Mr. Channing, looked as though they must have been put in there years ago. Now, where did the air-purifying machinery go?"

Channing listened to the latter half of Burbank's speech with his chin at half-mast. He looked as though a feather would knock him clear across the office.

"I had some workmen clear the weeds out. I intend to replace the air machinery as soon as I can get some new material sent from Terra."

Channing managed to blink. It was an effort. "You had workmen toss the weeds out . . ." he repeated dully. "The weeds . . ."

There was silence for a minute. Burbank studied the man in the chair as though Channing were a piece of statuary. Channing was just as motionless.

"Channing, man, what ails you—" Burbank began. The sound of Burbank's voice aroused Channing from his shocked condition.

Channing leaped to his feet. He landed on his heels, spun, and snapped at Arden: "Get on the type. Have 'em slap as many oxy-drums on the fastest ship they've got! Get 'em here at full throttle. Tell 'em to load up the pilot and crew with gravanol and not to spare the horsepower! Scram!"

Arden gasped. She fled from the office.

"Burbank, what did you think an air plant was?" snapped Channing.

"Why, isn't it some sort of purifying machinery?" asked the wondering Director.

"What better purifying machine is there than a plot of grass?" shouted Channing. "Weeds, grass, flowers, trees, alfalfa, wheat, or anything that grows and uses chlorophyll. We breath oxygen, exhale CO_2. Plants inhale CO_2 and exude oxygen. An air plant means just that. It is a specialized type of Martian sawgrass that is chlorophyll. We breathe oxygen, exhale CO_2. Plants inhaling dead air and revitalizing it. And you've tossed the weeds out!" Channing snorted in anger. "We've spent years getting that plant so that it will grow just right. It got so good that the CO_2 detectors weren't even needed. The balance was so adjusted that they haven't even been turned on for three or four years. They were just another source of unnecessary expense. Why, save for a monthly inspection, that room isn't even opened, so efficient is the Martian sawgrass. We, Burbank, are losing oxygen!"

The Director grew white. "I didn't know," he said.

"Well, you know now. Get on your horse and do something. At least, Burbank, stay out of my way while I do something."

"You have a free hand," said Burbank. His voice sounded beaten.

Channing left the office of the Director and headed for the chem lab. "How much potassium chlorate, nitrate, sulphate, and other oxygen-bearing compounds have you?" he asked. "That includes mercuric oxide, spare water, or anything else that will give us oxygen if broken down."

A ten-minute wait followed until the members of the chem lab took a hurried inventory.

"Good," said Channing. "Start breaking it down. Collect all the oxygen you can in containers. This is the business! It has priority! Anything, no matter how valuable, must be scrapped if it can facilitate the gathering of oxygen. God knows, there isn't by half enough—not even a tenth. But try, anyway."

Channing headed out of the chemistry laboratory and into the electronics lab. "Jimmie," he shouted, "get a couple of stone jars and get an electrolysis outfit running. Fling the hydrogen out of a convenient outlet into space and collect the oxygen. Water, I mean. Use tap water, right out of the faucet."

"Yeah, but—"

"Jimmie, if we don't breathe, what chance have we to go on drinking? I'll tell you when to stop."

"O.K., Doc," said Jimmie.

"And look. As soon as you get that running, set up a CO_2 indicator and let me know the percentage at the end of each hour! Get me?"

"I take it that something has happened to the air plant?"

"It isn't functioning," said Channing shortly. He left the puzzled Jimmie and headed for the beam control room. Jimmie continued to wonder about the air plant. How in the devil could an air plant cease functioning unless it were—*dead!* Jimmie stopped wondering and began to operate on his electrolysis setup furiously.

Channing found the men in the beam control room worried and ill at ease. The fine coordination that made them expert in their line was ebbing. The nervous work demanded perfect motor control, excellent perception, and a fine power of reasoning. The perceptible lack of oxygen at this high level was taking its toll already.

"Look, fellows, we're in a mess. Until further notice, take five-minute shifts. We've got about thirty hours to go. If the going gets tough, drop it to three-minute shifts. But, fellows, keep those beams centered until you drop!"

"We'll keep 'em going if we have to call our wives up here to run 'em for us," said one man. "What's up?"

"Air plant's sour. Losing oxy. Got a shipload coming out from Terra, be here in thirty hours. But upon you fellows will rest the responsibility of keeping us in touch with the rest of the system. If you fail, we could call for help until hell freezes us all in—and no one would hear us!

"We'll keep 'em rolling," said a little fellow who had to sit on a tall stool to get even with the controls.

Channing looked out of the big, faceted plexiglass dome that covered one entire end of the Venus Equilateral Station. "Here messages go in and out," he mused. "The other end brings us things that take our breath away."

Channing was referring to the big air lock at the other end of the station, three miles away, right through the center.

At the center of the dome, there was a sighting 'scope. It kept Polaris on a marked circle, keeping the station exactly even with the Terrestrial North. About the periphery of the dome, looking out across space, the beam-control operators were sitting, each with a hundred-foot parabolic reflector below his position, outside the dome, and under the rim of the transparent bowl. These reflectors shot the interworld signals across space in tight beams, and the men, half the time anticipating the vagaries of space warp, kept them centered on the proper, shining speck in that field of stars.

Above his head the stars twinkled. Puny man, setting his will against the monstrous void. Puny man, dependent upon atmosphere. " 'Nature abhors a vacuum,' said Spinoza," groaned Channing. "Nuts! If nature abhorred a vacuum, why did she make so much of it?"

Arden Westland entered the apartment without knocking. "I'd give my right arm up to here for a cigarette," she said, marking above the elbow with the other hand.

"Na-hah," said Channing. "Can't burn oxygen."

"I know. I'm tired, I'm cold, and I'm ill. Anything you can do for a lady?"

"Not as much as I'd like to do," said Channing. "I can't help much. We've got most of the place stopped off with the airtight doors. We've been electrolyzing water, baking $KClO_3$ and everything else we can get oxy out of. I've a crew of men trying to absorb the CO_2 content and we are losing. Of course, I've known all along that we couldn't support the station on the meager supplies we have on hand. But we'll win in the end. Our microcosmic world is getting a shot in the arm in a few hours that will reset the balance."

"I don't see why we didn't prepare for this emergency," said Arden.

"This station is well balanced. There are enough people here and enough space to make a little world of our own. We can establish a balance that is pretty darned close to perfect. The imperfections are taken care of by influxes of supplies from the system. Until Burbank upset the balance, we could go on forever, utilizing natural purification of air and water. We grow a few vegetables and have some meat critters to give milk and steak. The energy to operate Venus Equilateral is supplied from the uranium pile. Atomic power, if you please. Why should we burden ourselves with a lot of cubic feet of supplies that would take up room necessary to maintain our balance? We are not in bad shape. We'll live, though we'll all be a bunch of tired, irritable people who yawn in one another's faces."

"And after it is over?"

"We'll establish the balance. Then we'll settle down again. We can take up where we left off," said Don.

"Not quite. Venus Equilateral has been seared by fire. We'll be tougher and less tolerant of outsiders. If we were a closed corporation before, we'll be tighter than a vacuum-packed coffee can afterwards. And the first bird that cracks us will get hissed at."

Three superliners hove into sight at the end of thirty-one hours. They circled the station, signaling by helio. They approached the air lock end of the station and made contact. The air lock was opened and space-suited figures swarmed over the South End Landing Stage. A stream of big oxygen tanks was brought into the air lock, admitted, and taken to the last bulwark of people huddled on the fourth level.

From one of the ships came a horde of men carrying huge square trays of dirt and green, growing sawgrass.

For six hours, Venus Equilateral was the scene of wild, furious activity. The dead air was blown out of bad areas, and the hissing of oxygen tanks was heard in every room. Gradually the people left the fourth level and returned to their rightful places. The station rang with laughter once more, and business, stopped short for want of breath, took a deep lungful of fresh air and went back to work.

The superliners left. But not without taking a souvenir. Francis Burbank went with them. His removal notice was on the first ship, and Don Channing's appointment as Director of Venus Equilateral was on the second.

Happily he entered the Director's office once more. He carried with him all the things he had removed just a few short weeks before. This time he was coming to stay.

Arden entered the office behind him. "Home again?" she asked.

"Yep," he grinned at her. "Open file B, will you, and break out a container of my favorite beverage?"

"Sure thing," she said.

There came a shout of glee. "Break out four glasses," she was told from behind. It was Walt Franks and Joe.

Arden proposed the toast. "Here's to a closed corporation," she said.

They drank on that.

She went over beside Don and took his arm. "You see?" she said, looking up into his eyes. "We aren't the same. Things have changed since Burbank came, and went. Haven't they?"

"They have," laughed Channing. "And now that you are my secretary, it is no longer proper for you to shine up to me like that. People will talk."

"What's he raving about?" asked Joe.

Channing answered, "It is considered highly improper for a secretary to make passes at her boss. Think of what people will say; think of his wife and kids."

"You have neither."

"People?" asked Channing innocently.

"No—you ape—the other."

"Maybe so," Don nodded, "but it is still in bad taste for a secretary—"

"No man can use that tone of voice on me!" stormed Arden with a glint in her eye. "I resign! You can't call me a secretary!"

"But Arden, darling—"

Arden relaxed in the crook of Channing's arm. She winked at Walt and Joe. "Me," she said, "I've been promoted!"

Interlude

Maintaining communications through the worst of interference is a type of problem in which dire necessity demands a solution. Often there are other problems of less demanding nature. These are sometimes called "projects" because they may be desirable but are not born of dire necessity.

Barring interference, the problem of keeping communication with another planet across a hundred million miles of interplanetary space is partially solved by the fact that you can see your target! Keeping the cross hairs in a telescope properly centered is a technical job more arduous than difficult.

But seeing a spacecraft is another problem. Consider the relative sizes of spacecraft and planet. Where Terra is eight thousand miles in diameter, the largest of spacecraft is eight hundred feet long. Reduced to a common denominator and a simple ratio, it reads that the earth is 50,000 times as large as the largest spacecraft. Now go outside and take a look at Venus. At normal distances, it is a mote in the sky. Yet Venus is only slightly smaller than the earth. Reduce Venus by fifty thousand times, and no astronomer would ever suspect its existence.

Then take the invisible mote and place it in a volume of *1,000,000,000,000,000,000* cubic miles and he who found the needle in a haystack is a piker by comparison.

It could have been lives at stake that drove the job out of the "project" class and into the "necessity" stage. The fact that it was ebb and flow of a mundane thing like money may lower the quality of glamour.

But there it was—a problem that cried out for a solution; a man who was willing to pay for the attempt; and a group of technicians more than happy to tackle the job.

CALLING THE EMPRESS

The chart in the terminal building at Canalopsis Spaceport, Mars, was a huge thing that was the focus of all eyes. It occupied a thirty-by-thirty-meter space in the center of one wall, and it had a far-flung iron railing about it to keep the people from crowding it too close, thus shutting off the view. It was a popular display, for it helped to drive home the fact that space travel was different from anything else. People were aware that their lives had been built upon going from one fixed place to another place, equally immobile. But on inter-planet travel, one left a moving planet for another planet, moving at a different velocity. You found that the shortest distance was not a straight line but a space curve involving higher mathematics.

The courses being traveled at the time were marked, and those that would be traversed in the very near future were drawn upon the chart, too, all appropriately labeled. At a glance, one could see that in fifty minutes and seventeen seconds the *Empress of Kolain* would take off from Mars, which was the red disk on the right, and she would travel along the curve so marked to Venus, which was almost one hundred and sixty degrees clockwise around the Sun. People were glad of the chance to go on this trip because the Venus Equilateral Relay Station would come within a telescope's sight on the way.

The *Empress of Kolain* would slide into Venus on the day side; and a few hours later she would lift again to head for Terra, a few degrees ahead of Venus and about thirty million miles away.

Precisely on the zero-zero, The *Empress of Kolain* lifted upward on four tenuous pillars of dull-red glow and drove a hole in the sky. The glow was almost lost in the bright sunshine, and soon it died. The ship became a little world in itself, and would so remain until it dropped onto the ground at Venus, almost two hundred million miles away.

Driving upward, the *Empress of Kolain* could not have been out of the thin Martian atmosphere when a warning bell rang in the telephone and telespace office at the terminal. The bell caught official ears, and all work was stopped as the personnel of the communications office ran to the machine to see what was so important that the "immediate attention" signal was rung.

Impatiently the operator waited for the tape to come clicking from the machine. It came, letter by letter, click by click, at fifty words per minute. The operator tore the strip from the machine and read aloud: "Hold *Empress of Kolain.* Reroute to Terra direct. Will be quarantined at Venus. Whole planet in epidemic of Venusian Fever."

"Snap answer," growled the clerk. "Tell 'em: 'Too little and too late. *Empress of Kolain* left thirty seconds before warning bell. What do we do now?' "

The operator's fingers clicked madly over the keyboard. Across space went the signal, across the void to the Relay Station. It ran through the station's mechanism and went darting to Terra. It clicked out, as sent, in the offices of Interplanetary Transport. A vice-president read the message and swore roundly. He swore in three Terran languages, in the language of the Venusians, and even managed to visualize a few choice remarks from the Martian Pictographs that were engraved on the temples of Canalopsis.

"Miss Deane," he yelled at the top of his voice. "Take a message! Shoot a line to Channing on Venus Equilateral. Tell him: '*Empress of Kolain* on way to Venus. Must be contacted and rerouted to Terra direct. Million dollars' worth of Martian line moss aboard; will perish under quarantine. Spare no expense.' Sign that 'Keg Johnson, Interplanet.' "

"Yes, Mr. Johnson," said the secretary. "Right away."

More minutes of light-fast communication. Out of Terra to Luna, across space to Venus Equilateral. The machines clicked and tape cleared away from the slot.

It was pasted neatly on a sheet of official paper, stamped *rush,* and put in a pneumatic tube.

As Don Channing began to read the message, Williams on Mars was chewing worriedly on his fourth fingernail, and Vice-President Keg Johnson was working on his second. But Williams had a head start and therefore would finish first. Both men knew that nothing more could be done. If Channing couldn't do it, nobody could.

Channing finished the 'gram and swore. It was a good-natured swear word, far from downright vilification, though it did consign certain items to the nether regions. He punched a button with some relish, and a rather good-looking woman entered. She smiled at him with more intimacy than a secretary should, and sat down.

"Arden, call Walt, will you?"

Arden Westland smiled. "You might have done that yourself," she told him. She reached for the call button with her left hand, and the diamond on her finger glinted like a pilot light.

"I know it," he answered, "but that wouldn't give me the chance to see you."

"Baloney," said Arden. "You just wait until next October. I'll be in your hair all the time then."

"By then I may be tired of you," said Channing with a smile. "But until then, take it or leave it." His face grew serious, and he tossed the message across the table to her. "What do you think of that?"

Arden read, and then remarked: "That's a huge order, Don. Think you can do it?"

"It'll cost plenty. I don't know whether we can contact a ship in space. It hasn't been done to date, you know, except for short distances."

The door opened without a knock and Walt Franks walked in. "Billing and cooing?" he asked. "Why do you two need an audience?"

"We don't," answered Don. "This was business."

"For want of evidence, I'll believe that. What's the dope?"

"Walt, what are the chances of hooking up with the

Empress of Kolain, which is en route from Mars to Venus?"

"About equal to a snowball—you know where," said Franks, looking slyly at Arden.

"Take off your coat, Walt. We've got a job."

"You mean— Hey! Remind me to quit, Saturday."

"This is dead in earnest, Walt." Don told the engineer all he knew.

"Boy, this is a job I wouldn't want my life to depend on. In the first place, we can't beam a transmitter at them if we can't see 'em. And in the second place, if we did, they couldn't receive us."

"We can get a good idea of where they are and how they're going," said Channing. "That is common knowledge."

"Astronomy is an exact science," chanted Franks. "But by the time we figure out just where the *Empress of Kolain* is with respect to us at any given instant we'll all be old men with gray beards. She's crossing toward us on a skew curve—and we'll have to beam it past Sol. It won't be easy, Don. And then if we do find them, what do we do about it?"

"Let's find them first and then work out a means of contacting them afterwards."

"Don," Arden interrupted, "what's so difficult?"

Franks fell backward into a chair. Don turned to the girl and asked: "Are you kidding?"

"No. I'm just ignorant. What is so hard about it? We shoot beams across a couple of hundred million miles of space like nothing, and maintain communications at any cost. What should be so hard about contacting a ship?"

"In the first place, we can see a planet, and they can see us, so they can hold their beams. A spaceship might be able to see us, but they couldn't hold a beam on us because of the side sway. We couldn't see them until they are right upon us and so we could not hope to hold a beam on them. Spaceships *might* broadcast, but you have no idea what the square law of radiated power will do to a broadcast signal when millions upon millions of miles are counted in. A half-million watts on any planet will not quite cover the planet as a service area on broadcast frequencies. But there's a lot of difference between covering a few stinking miles of planet and a volume the size of the Inner Solar System. So they don't try it. A spaceship may as well be on Rigel as far as contacting her in space goes.

"We might beam a wide-dispersion affair at them," continued Channing. "But it would be pretty thin by the time it got there. And, having no equipment, they couldn't hear us."

"May we amend that?" asked Franks. "They are equipped with radio. But the things are used only in landing operations, where the distance is measured in miles, not Astronomical Units."

"O.K." Channing smiled. "It's turned off during flight and we may consider the equipment as being non-existent."

"And, according to the chart, we've got to contact them before the turnabout," Arden offered. "They must have time to deflect their course to Terra."

"You think of the nicest complications," said Channing. "I was just about to hope that we could flash them, or grab at 'em with a skeeter. But we can't wait until they pass us."

"That will be the last hope," admitted Franks. "But say! Did any bright soul think of shooting a fast ship after them from Canalopsis?"

"Sure. The answer is the same as Simple Simon's answer to the Pieman: 'Alas, they haven't any!' "

"No use asking why," growled Franks. "O.K., Don, we'll after 'em. I'll have the crew set up a couple of mass detectors at either end of the station. We'll triangulate, and calculate, and hope to hit the right correction factor. We'll find them and keep them in line. You figure out a means of contacting them, huh?"

"I'll set up the detectors and *you* find the means," Don suggested.

"No go. You're the director of communications."

Don sighed a false sigh. "Arden, hand me my electronics text," he said.

"And shall I wipe your fevered brow?" she cooed.

"Leave him alone," Franks directed. "You distract him."

"It seems to me that you two are taking this rather lightly," said Arden.

"What do you want us to do?" Don asked. "Get

down on the floor and chew the rug? You know us better than that. If we can find the answer to contacting a spaceship in flight, we'll add another flower to our flag. But we can't do it by clawing through the first edition of Henney's *Handbook of Radio Engineering*. It will be done by the seat of our pants, if at all; a pair of sidecutters, and a spool of wire, a hunk of string and a lump of solder, a—"

"A rag, a bone, and a hank of hair?" asked Franks.

"Leave Kipling out of this. He didn't have to cover the entire Solar System. Let's get cooking."

Don and Walt left the office just a trifle on the fast side. Arden looked after them, out through the open door, shaking her head until she remembered something that she could do. She smiled and went to her typewriter, and pounded out a message back to Keg Johnson at Interplanet. It read:

> CHANNING AND FRANKS AT WORK ON CONTACTING THE EMPRESS OF KOLAIN.
> WILL DO OUR BEST.
>
> VENUS EQUILATERAL.

Unknowing of the storm, the *Empress of Kolain* sped silently through the void, accelerating constantly at one G. Hour after hour she was adding to her velocity, building it up to a speed that would make the trip in days, and not weeks. Her drivers flared dull red no more, for there was no atmosphere for the ionic stream to excite. Her few portholes sparkled with light, but they were nothing in comparison to the starry curtain of the background.

Her hull was of a neutral color, and though the sun glanced from her metal flanks, a reflection from a convex side is not productive of a beam of light. It spreads according to the degree of convexity and is lost.

What constitutes an apparent absence? The answer to that question is the example of a ship in space flight. The *Empress of Kolain* did not radiate anything detectable in the electromagnetic scale from ultra-long waves to ultra-high frequencies; nothing at all that could be detected at any distance beyond a few thousand miles. The sweep of her meteor-spotting equipment would pass a spot in micro-microseconds at a hundred miles; at the distance from Venus Equilateral the sweep of the beam would be so fleeting that the best equipment ever known or made would have no time to react, thus missing the signal.

Theorists claim a thing unexistent if it cannot be detected. The *Empress of Kolain* was invisible. It was undetectable to radio waves. It was in space, so no physical wave could be transmitted to be depicted as sound. Its mass was inconsiderable. Its size, as cosmic sizes go, was comparatively sub-microscopic, and therefore it would occult few, if any, stars. Therefore, to all intents and purposes, the *Empress of Kolain* was nonexistent, and would remain in that state of material non-being until it came to life again upon its landing at Venus.

Yet the *Empress of Kolain* existed in the minds of the men who were to find her. Like the shot unseen, fired from a distant cannon, the *Empress of Kolain* was coming at them with ever-mounting velocity, its unseen course a theoretical curve.

And the ship, like the projectile, would land if the men who knew of her failed in their purpose.

Don Channing and Walt Franks found their man in the combined dining room and bar. They surrounded him, ordered a sandwich and beer, and began to tell him their troubles.

Charles Thomas listened for about three minutes. "Boy," he grinned, "being up in that shiny, plush-lined office has sure done plenty to your think-tank, Don."

Channing stopped talking. "Proceed," he said. "In what way has my perspective been warped?"

"You talk like Burbank," said Thomas, mentioning a sore spot of some months past. "You think a mass detector would work at this distance? Nuts, fellow. It might, if there were nothing else in the place to interfere. But you want to shoot out near Mars. Mars is on the other side of the Sun—and Evening Star to anyone on Terra. You want us to shoot a slaphappy beam like a mass detector out past Sol; and then a hundred and forty million miles beyond, in the faint hope that you can triangulate upon a little mite of matter: a stinking six hundred-odd feet of aluminum hull mostly filled with air and some machinery and so on. Brother, what do you think all the rest of the planets will do to your piddling little beam? Retract, or perhaps abrogate the law of universal gravitation?"

"Crushed," said Franks with a sorry attempt at a smile.

"Phew!" agreed Channing. "Maybe I should know more about mass detectors."

"Forget it," said Thomas. "The only thing that mass detectors are any good for is to conjure up beautiful bubble dreams, which anyone who knows about 'em can break with the cold point of icy logic."

"What would you do?" asked Channing.

"Damned if I know. We might flash 'em with a big mirror—if we had a big mirror and they weren't heading into the Sun."

"Let's see," said Franks, making tabulations on the tablecloth. "They're a couple of hundred million miles away. In order that your mirror present a recognizable disk, it should be about twice the diameter of Venus as seen from Terra. That's eight thousand miles in—at the least visibility—say, eighty million, or a thousand-to-one ratio. The *Empress of Kolain* is heading at us from some two hundred million miles, so at a thousand-to-one ratio our mirror would have to be twenty thousand miles across. Some mirror!"

Don tipped Walt's beer over the edge of the table, and while the other man was busy mopping up and muttering unprintables, said to Thomas: "This is serious and it isn't. Nobody's going to lose their skin if we don't, but a problem has been put to us and we're going to crack it if we have to skin our teeth to do it."

"You can't calculate their position?"

"Sure. Within a couple of hundred thousand miles we can. That isn't close enough."

"No, it isn't," Chuck agreed.

Silence fell for a moment. It was broken by Arden, who came in waving a telegram. She sat down and appropriated Channing's glass, which had not been touched.

Don opened the sheet and read: "Have received information of your effort. I repeat, spare no expense!" It was signed: "Keg Johnson, Interplanet."

"Does that letter offer mean anything to you?" asked Arden.

"Sure," agreed Don. "But at the same time, we're stumped. Should we be doing anything?"

"Anything, I should think, would be better than what you're doing at present. Or does that dinner-and-beer come under 'expenses'?"

Arden stood up, tossed Channing's napkin at him, and started toward the door. Channing watched her go, his hand making motions on the tablecloth. His eyes fell to the table and he took Franks' pencil and drew a long curve from a spot of gravy on one side of the table to a touch of coffee stain on the other. The curve went through a bit of grape jelly near the first stain.

"Here goes the tablecloth strategist," said Franks. "What now, little man?"

"That spot of gravy," explained Don, "is Mars. The jelly is the *Empress of Kolain*. Coffee stain is Venus, and up here by this cigarette burn is Venus Equilateral. Get me?"

"Yep, that's clear enough."

"Now it would be the job for seventeen astronomers for nine weeks to predict the movements of this jelly spot with respect to the usual astral standards. But, fellows, we know the acceleration of the *Empress of Kolain*, and we know her position with respect to Mars at the instant of takeoff. We can correct for Mars' advance along her—or his—orbit. We can figure the position of the *Empress of Kolain* from her angular distance from Mars! That's the only thing we need know. We don't give a ten-dollar damn about her true position."

Channing began to write equations on the tablecloth. "You see, they aren't moving so fast in respect to us. The course is foreshortened as they are coming almost in line with Venus Equilateral, curving outward and away from the Sun. Her course, as we see it from the station here, will be a long radius-upward curve, slightly on the parabolic side. Like all long-range cruises, the *Empress of Kolain* will hoist herself slightly above the plane of the ecliptic to avoid the swarm of meteors that follow about the Sun in the same plane as the planets, lifting the highest at the point of greatest velocity."

"I get it," said Franks. "We get the best beam controller we have to keep the planet on the cross hairs. We apply a spiral cam to advance the beam along the orbit. Right?"

"Right." Don sketched a conical section on the tablecloth and added dimensions. He checked his dimensions against the long string of equations and nodded. "We'll drive this cockeyed-looking cam with an isochronic clock, and then squirt a beam out there. Thank the Lord for the way our beam transmitters work."

"You mean the effect of reflected waves?" asked Chuck.

"Sure," grinned Don. "There's plenty of radar operating at our transmitting frequencies or nearby. So far, no one has ever tried to radar anything as small as a spacecraft at that distance, though getting a radar signal from a planet is duck soup. Yet," he reflected cheerfully, "there are a couple of things we have handy out here, and one of them is a plethora of power output. We can soup up one of our beam transmitters and use it with a tightened beam to get a radar fix off of the *Empress of Kolain.*"

"And then?" asked Franks.

"Then we will have left the small end, which I'll give to you, Walt, so that you can have part of the credit."

Walt shook his head. "The easy part," he said uncheerfully. "By which you mean the manner in which we contact them and make them listen to us?"

"That's her," said Don with a cheerful smile.

"Fine," said Thomas. "Now what do we do?"

"Clear up this mess so we can make the cam. This drawing will do, just grab the tablecloth."

Joe, the operator of Venus Equilateral's one and only establishment for the benefit of the stomach, came up as the three men began to move their glasses and dishes over to an empty table.

"What makes with the tablecloth?" he asked. "Want a piece of carbon paper and another tablecloth?"

"No," said Don nonchalantly. "This single copy will do."

"We lose lots of tablecloths that way," said Joe. "It's tough, running a restaurant on Venus Equilateral. I tried using paper ones once, but that didn't work. I had 'em printed, but when the Solar System was on 'em, you fellows drew schematic diagrams for a new coupler circuit. I put all kinds of radio circuits on them, and the gang drew plans for antenna arrays. I gave up and put pads of paper on each table, and the boys used them to make folded paper airplanes and they shot them all over the place. Why don't you guys grow up?"

"Cheer up, Joe. But if this tablecloth won't run through the blueprint machine, we'll squawk!"

Joe looked downcast, and Franks hurried to explain: "It isn't that bad, Joe. We won't try it. We just want to have these figures so we won't have to run through the math again. We'll return the cloth."

"Yeah," said Joe at their retreating figures. "And for the rest of its usefulness it will be full of curves, drawings, and a complete set of astrogation equations." He shrugged his shoulders and went for a new tablecloth.

Don, Walt, and Chuck took their improvised drawing to the machine shop, where they put it in the hands of the master mechanic.

"This thing has a top requirement," Don told him. "Make it as quick as you can."

Master Mechanic Michael Warren took the cloth and said: "You forgot the note. You know, 'Work to dimensions shown, do not scale this drawing.' Lord, Don, this silly-looking cam will take a man about six hours to do. It'll have to be right on the button all over, no tolerance. I'll have to cut it to the 'T' and then lap it smooth with polishing compound. Then what'll you test it on?"

"Sodium light inferometer. Can you do it in four hours?"

"If nothing goes wrong. Brass all right?"

"Anything you say. It'll only be used once. Anything of sufficient hardness for a single usage will do."

"I'll use brass then. Or free-cutting steel may be better. If you make it soft you have the chance of cutting too much off with your lapping compound. We'll take care of it, Don. The rest of this stuff isn't too hard. Your framework and so on can be whittled out and pasted together from standard girders, right?"

"Sure. Plaster them together any way you can. And we don't want them painted. As long as she works, phooey to the looks."

"Fine," said Warren. "I'll have the whole business installed in the Beam Control Room in nine hours. Complete and ready to work."

"That nine hours is a minimum?"

"Absolutely. After we cut and polish that screwball cam, we'll have to check it, and then you'll have to check it. Then the silly thing will have to be installed and its concentricity must be checked to the last wave of cadmium light. That'll take us a couple of hours, I bet. The rest of the works will be ready, checked, and waiting for the goddam cam."

"Yeah," agreed Franks. "Then we'll have to get up there with our works and put the electricals on the mechanicals. My guess, Don, is a good, healthy twelve hours before we can begin to squirt our signal."

Twelve hours is not much in the life of a man; it is less in the life of a planet. The Terran standard of gravity is so small that it is expressed in feet per second. But when the two are coupled together as a measure of travel, and the standard Terran G is applied for twelve hours steady, it builds up to almost three hundred miles per second, and by the end of that twelve hours, six million miles have fled into the past.

Now take a look at Mars. It is a small, red mote in the sky, its diameter some four thousand miles. Sol is eight hundred thousand miles in diameter. Six million miles from Mars, then, can be crudely expressed by visualizing a point eight times the diameter of the Sun away from Mars, and you have the distance that the *Empress of Kolain* had come from Mars.

But the ship was heading in at an angle, and the six million miles did not subtend the above arc. From Venus Equilateral, the position of the *Empress of Kolain* was more like two diameters of the Sun away from Mars, slightly to the north, and on the side away from Sol.

It may sound like a problem for the distant future, this pointing a radio beam at a planet, but it is no different from Galileo's attempt to see Jupiter through his Optik Glass. Of course, it has had refinements that have enabled man to make several hundred hours of exposure of a star on a photographic plate. So if men maintain a telescope on a star, night after night, to build up a faint image, they can also maintain a beamed transmission wave on a planet.

All you need is a place to stand: a firm, immobile platform. The three-mile-long, one-mile-diameter mass of Venus Equilateral offered such a platform. It rotated smoothly, and upon its "business" end a hardened and highly polished set of rails maintained projectors that were pointed at the planets. These were parabolic reflectors that focused ultra-high-frequency waves into tight beams which were hurled at Mars, Terra, and Venus for communication.

And because the beams were acted upon by all of the trivia in the Solar System, highly trained technicians stood their tricks at the beam controls. In fifty million miles, even the bending of electromagnetic waves by the Sun's mass had to be considered. Sunspots made known their presence. And the vagaries of land transmission were present in a hundred ways due to the distance and the necessity of concentrating every milliwatt of available power on the target.

This problem of the *Empress of Kolain* was different. Spaceships were invisible, therefore the beam-control man must sight on Mars and the mechanical cam would keep the ship in sight of the beam.

The hours went past in a peculiar mixture of speed and slowness. On one hand the minutes sped by swiftly and fleetingly, each tick of the clock adding to the lost moments, never to be regained. Time, being precious, seemed to slip through their fingers like sifting sand.

On the other hand, the time that must be spent in preparation of the equipment went slowly. Always it was in the future, that time when their experiment must either prove a success or a failure. Always there was another hour of preparatory work before the parabolic reflector was mounted; and then another hour before it swung freely and perfectly in its new mounting. Then the minutes were spent in anticipation of the instant that the power stage of transmitter was tested and the megawatts of ultra-high-frequency energy poured into the single rod that acted as a radiator.

It was a singularly disappointing sight. The rod did not glow, and the reflector was the same as it was before the rod drew power. But the meters read and the generators moaned, and the pyrometers in the insulators mounted as the small quantity of energy lost was converted into heat. So the rod drew power, and the parabolic reflector beamed that power into a tight beam and hurled it out on a die-true line.

Invisible power that could be used in communications.

Then the cam was installed. The time went by even slower then, because the cam must be lapped and polished to absolute perfection, not only of its own surface but to absolute concentricity to the shaft on which it turned.

But eventually the job was finished, and the men stood back, their eyes expectantly upon Don Channing and Walt Franks.

Don spoke to the man chosen to control the beam. "You can start any time now. Keep her knifed clean, if you can."

The man grinned at Channing. "If the devils that roam the void are with us we'll have no trouble. We should all pray for a phrase used by some characters in a magazine I read once: 'Clear ether!' We could use some right now."

He applied his eyes to the telescope. He fiddled with the verniers for a brief time, made a major adjustment on a larger handwheel, and then said, without removing his eye from the 'scope, "That's it, Dr. Channing."

Don answered: "O.K., Jimmy, but you can use the screen now. We aren't going to make you squint through that pipe for the next few hours straight."

"That's all right. I'll use the screen as soon as you can prove we're right. Ready?"

"Ready," said Channing.

Franks closed a tiny switch. Below, in the transmitter room, relays clicked and heavy-duty contacts closed with blue fire. Meters began to climb upward across their scales, and the generators moaned in a descending whine. A shielded monitor began to glow, indicating that full power was vomiting from the mouth of the reflector.

And out from the projector there went, like a spearhead, a wavefront of circularly polarized microwaves. Die-true they sped, crossing the void like a line of sight to an invisible spot above Mars and to the left. Out past the Sun, where they bent inward just enough to make Jimmy's job tough. Out across the open sky they sped at the velocity of light, and taking sixteen minutes to get there.

A half-hour passed. "Now," said Channing, "are we . . . ?"

Ten minutes went by. The receiver was silent save for a constant crackle of cosmic static.

Fifteen minutes passed.

"Nuts," said Channing. "Could it be that we aren't quite hitting them?"

"Could be," admitted Franks. "Jimmy, waggle that beam a bit, and slowly. When we hit 'em, we'll know it because we'll hear 'em a half-hour later. Take it easy and slow. We've used up thirteen of our fifty-odd hours. We can use another thirty or so just in being sure."

Jimmy began to make the beam roam around the invisible spot in the sky. He swept the beam in microscopic scans, up and down, and advancing the beam by one-half of its apparent width at the receiver for each sweep.

Two more hours went by. The receiver was still silent of reflected signals.

It was a terrific strain, this necessary wait of approximately a half-hour between each minor adjustment and the subsequent knowledge of failure. Jimmy gave up the 'scope because of eyestrain, and though Don and Walt had confidence that the beam-control man was competent to use the cross-ruled screen to keep Mars on the beam, Jimmy had been none too sure of himself, and so he'd kept checking the screen against the 'scope.

At the end of the next hour of abject failure, Walt Franks began to scribble on a pad of paper. Don came over to peer over Franks' shoulder, and because he couldn't read Walt's mind, he was forced to ask what the engineer was calculating.

"I've been thinking," said Franks.

"Beginner's luck?" asked Don with a wry smile.

"I hope not. Look, Don, we're moving on the orbit of Venus, at Venus' orbital velocity. Oh, all right, say it scientifical: we are circling Sol at twenty-one point seven five miles per second. The reflected wave starts back right through the beam, remember?"

"I get it," shouted Channing in glee. "Thirty-two minutes' transmission time at twenty-one point seven five miles per second gives us—ah—"

Walt looked up from his slide rule. "Fifty-two thousand, two hundred and twenty-four miles," he said.

"Just what I was about to say," grinned Don.

"But why do you always get there second with your genius?" Walt complained with a pseudo-hurt whine. "So how to establish it?"

"Can't use space radar for range," grunted Channing. "That would louse up the receiver. We've got everything shut off tight, you know. How about some visual loran?"

"Yipe!" Walt exploded. "How?"

"I'd suggest an optical range finder excepting that the baseline of three miles—the length of Venus Equilateral—isn't long enough to triangulate for that fifty-two thousand—"

"Two hundred and twenty-four miles," Walt finished with a grin. "Proceed, genius, with caution."

"So we mount a couple of mirrors at either end of the station, and key a beam of light from the center, heading each way. When the pulses arrive at the space flitter at the same time, he's in position. We'll establish original range by radar, of course, but once the proper interval or range is established, the pilot can maintain his own position by watching the pulsed arrival of the twin flickers of light. Just like loran, excepting that we'll use light, and we can key it so it will run alternately, top and bottom. To maintain the proper angle, all the pilot will have to do is keep the light alternating—fluently. And overlapping will show him that he's drifted."

"Fine!" Walt glowed. "Now, how long will it take?"

"Ask the boys, Walt," suggested Don.

Walt made a canvass of the machine-shop gang, and came back saying: "Couple of hours, God willing."

The mounting of the mirrors at either end of the station took little time. It was the amount of detailed work that took time; the devising of the interrupting mechanism; and the truing-up of the mirrors.

Then it became evident that there was more. There were several hundred doorways centered on the axis of Venus Equilateral that must be opened, the space cleared of packing cases, supplies; and in a few cases machinery had to be partially dismantled to clear the way. A good portion of Venus Equilateral's personnel of three thousand were taken off their jobs, haled out of bed for the emergency, or made to work through their play period, depending upon which shift they worked.

The machinery could be replaced, the central storage places could be refilled, and the many doors closed again. But the central room containing the air plant was no small matter. Channing took a sad look at the lush growth of Martian sawgrass and sighed. It was growing nicely now, they had nurtured it into lusty growth from mere sprouts in trays, and it was as valuable—precisely—as the lives of the three thousand-odd that lived, loved, and pursued happiness on Venus Equilateral. It was a youthful plant, a replacement brought in a tearing hurry from Mars to replace the former plant that was heaved out by the well-meaning Burbank.

Channing closed his eyes and shuddered in mock horror. "Chop out the center," he said.

The "center" meant the topmost fronds of the long blades; their roots were embedded in the trays that filled the cylindrical floor. Some of the blades would die—Martian sawgrass is tender in spite of the wicked spines that line the edge—but this was an emergency with a capital "E."

Cleaning the centermost channel out of the station was no small job. The men who put up Venus Equilateral had no idea that someone would be using the station for a sighting tube some day. The many additions to the station through the years made the layout as regular and as well-planned as the Mammoth Cave in Kentucky.

So for hour upon hour, men swarmed in the central, weightless channel and wielded acetylene torches, cutting steel. Not in all cases, but there were many. In three miles of storage rooms, a lot of doors and bulkheads can be thrown up without crowding the size of the individual rooms.

Channing spoke into the microphone at the north end

of Venus Equilateral, and said: "Walt? We've got a sight. Can you see?"

"Yep," said Walt. "And say, what happens to me after that bum guess?"

"That was quite a stretch, Walt. That 'couple of hours, God willing,' worked itself into four hours, God help us."

"O.K., so I was optimistic. I thought that those doors were all on the center line."

"They are supposed to be, but they aren't huge, and a little misalignment can do a lot of light-stopping. Can we juggle mirrors now?"

"Sure as shooting. Freddie in the flitter?"

"Yep. He thinks he's at the right distance now. But he's got a light outfit, and this radar can be calibrated to the foot. Is the mirror-dingbat running?"

"We're cooking with glass right now."

"Brother," groaned Channing, "if I had one of those death rays that the boys were crowing about back in the days before space hopping became anything but a bit of fiction, I'd scorch your ears—or burn 'em off—or blow holes in you—or disintegrate you—depending on what stories you read. I haven't heard such a lousy pun in seventeen years! Hey, Freddie, you're a little close. Run out a couple of miles, huh? And Walt, I've heard some doozies."

There was a click in the phones and a cheerful voice chimed in with: "Good morning, fellows. What's with the Great Quest?"

Channing answered. "Hi, babe, been snoozing?"

"Sure, as any sensible person would. Have you been up all the time?"

"Yeah. We're still up against the main trouble with telephones—the big trouble, same as back in 1877—our friends have no telephone! You'd be surprised how elusive a spaceship can be in the deep. Sort of a nonexistent, microscopic speck, floating in absolutely nothing. We have a good idea of where they should be, and possibly why and what—but we're really playing with blindfolds, handcuffs, earplugs, mufflers, nose clamps, and tongue-ties. I am reminded—Hey, Freddie, about three more hundred yards—of the two blind men."

"Never mind the blind men," came back the pilot. "How'm I doing?"

"Fine. Slide out another hundred yards and hold her there."

"Who—me? Listen, Dr. Channing, you're the bird on the tape line. You have no idea just how insignificant you look from fifty-odd thousand miles away. Put a red-hot on the 'finders and have 'im tell me where the ship sits."

"O.K., Freddie, you're on the beam and I'll put a guy on here to give you the dope. Right?"

"Right!"

"Right," echoed Arden breaking in on the phone. "And I'm going to bring you a slug of coffee and a roll. Or did you remember to eat recently?"

"We didn't," chimed in Walt.

"You get your own girl," snorted Channing. "And besides, you are needed up here. We've got work to do."

Once again the signal lashed out. The invisible waves drove out and began their swift rush across the void. Time, as it always did during the waiting periods, hung like a Sword of Damocles. The half-hour finally ticked away, and Freddie called in: "No dice. She's as silent as the grave."

Minutes added together into an hour. The concentric wave left the reflector and just dropped out of sight.

"Too bad you can't widen her out," suggested Don.

"I'd like to tighten it down," Walt objected. "I think we're losing power and we can't increase the power—but we could tighten the beam."

"Too bad you can't wave it back and forth like a fireman squirting water on a lawn," said Arden.

"Firemen don't water lawns—" Walt Franks began, but he was interrupted by a wild yell from Channing.

"Something hurt?" asked Arden.

"No, Walt, we *can* wave the beam."

"Until we find 'em? We've been trying that. No worky."

Freddie called in excitedly: "Something went by just now and I don't think it was Christmas!"

"We might have hit 'em a dozen times in the last ten minutes and we'll never know it," said Channing. "But the spaceliner can be caught. Let's shoot at it like popping ducks. Shotgun effect. Look, Walt, we can electronically dance the beam at a high rate of speed, spraying the neighborhood. Freddie can hear us return, because we have to hit it all the time and the waver coming on the way back will pass through his position again and again. We'll set up director elements in the reflector, distorting the electrical surface of the parabolic reflector. That'll divert the beam. By making the phases swing right, we can scan the vicinity of the *Empress of Kolain* like a flying spot television camera."

Walt turned to one of the technicians and explained. The man nodded. He left Franks' laboratory and Walt turned back to his friends.

"Here shoots another couple of hours. I, for one, am going to grab forty winks."

Jimmy, the beam-control man, sat down and lighted a cigarette. Freddie let his flitter coast free. And the generators that fed the powerful transmitter came whining to a stop. But there was no sleep for Don and Walt. They kept awake to supervise the work, and to help in hooking up the phase-splitting circuit that would throw out-of-phase radio frequency into the director elements to swing the beam.

Then once again the circuits were set up. Freddie found the position again and began to hold it. The beam hurled out again, and as the phase shift passed from element to element, the beam swept through an infinitesimal arc that covered thousands of miles of space by the time the beam reached the position occupied by the *Empress of Kolain*.

Like a painter, the beam painted in a swipe a few hundred miles wide and swept back and forth, each sweep progressing ahead of the stripe before by less than its width. It reached the end of its arbitrary wall and swept back to the beginning again, covering space as before. Here was no slow, irregular swing of mechanical reflector; this was the electronically controlled wavering of a table antenna.

And this time the half-hour passed slowly but not uneventfully. Right on the tick of the instant, Freddie called back: "Got 'em!"

It was a weakling beam that came back in staccato

surges. A fading, wavering, spotty signal that threatened to lie down on the job and sleep. It came and it went, often gone for seconds and never strong for so much as a minute. It vied, and almost lost completely, with the constant crackle of cosmic static. It fought with the energies of the Sun's corona and was more than once the underdog. Had this returning beam carried intelligence of any sort, it would have been wasted. About all that could be carried on a beam as sorry as this was the knowledge that there was a transmitter—and that it was transmitting.

But its raucous note synchronized with the paintbrush swiping of the transmitter. There was no doubt.

Don Channing put an arm around Arden's waist and grinned at Walt Franks. "Go to work, genius. I've got the *Empress of Kolain* on the pipe. You're the bright-eyed lad that is going to wake them up! We've shot almost twenty hours of our allotted fifty. Make with the megacycles, Walter. Arden and I will take in a steak, a moom pitcher, and maybe a bit of woo. Like?" he asked the girl.

"I like," she answered.

Walt Franks smiled and stretched lazily. He made no move to the transmitter. "Don't go away," he cautioned them. "Better call up Joe and order beer and sandwiches for the boys in the back room. On you!"

"Make with the signals first," said Channing. "And lay off the potables until we finish this silly job."

"You've got it. Is there a common, garden-variety, transmitting key in the place?"

"Probably. We'll have to ask. Why?"

"Ask me."

Don removed his arm from Arden's waist. He picked up a spanner and advanced on Franks.

"Na!" Arden objected. "Poison him—I can't stand the sight of blood. Or better, bamboo splinters under the fingernails. He knows something simple, the big bum!"

"Beer and sandwiches?" asked Walt.

"Beer and sandwiches," Don agreed. "Now, Tom Swift, what gives?"

"I want to key the beam. Y'see, Don, we're using the

same frequency, by a half-dozen megacycles, as their meteor spotter. I'm going to retune the beam to their frequency and key it. Realize what'll happen?"

"Sure," agreed Don, "but you're still missing the boat. You can't transmit keyed intelligence with an intermittent contact."

"In words, what do you mean, Don?" asked Arden.

"International Code is a series of dots and dashes, you may know. Our wobbling beam is whipping through the area in which the *Empress of Kolain* is passing. Therefore, the contact is intermittent. And how could you tell a dot from a dash?"

"Easy," bragged Walt Franks. "We're not limited to the speed of deviation, are we?"

"Yes—limited by the speed of the selsyn motors that transfer the phase-shifting circuits to the director radiators. Yeah, I get it, Edison, and we can wind them up to a happy six or eight thousand r.p.m. Six would get us a hundred cycles per second—a nice, low growl."

"And how will they receive that kind of signal on the meteor spotter?" asked Arden.

"The officer of the day will be treated to the first meteor on record that has intermittent duration—it is there only when it spells in International Code!"

Prying the toy transmitting key from young James Burke was a job only surpassed in difficulty by the task of opening the vault of the Interplanetary Bank after working hours. But Burke, Junior, was plied with soda pop, ice cream, and candy. He was threatened, cajoled, and finally bribed. And what Venus Equilateral paid for the key finally would have made the toy manufacturer go out and look for another job. But Walt Franks carried the key to the scene of operations and set it on the bench to look at it critically.

"A puny gadget, at that," he said, clicking the key. "Might key a couple of hundred watts with it—but not too long. She'd go up like a skyrocket under our load!"

Walt opened up a cabinet and began to pull out parts. He piled several parts on a bread board, and in an hour had a very husky thyraton hooked into a circuit that was simplicity itself. He hooked the thyraton into the main power circuit and tapped the key gingerly. The transmitter followed the keyed thyraton and Don took a deep breath.

"Do you know code?" he asked.

"Used to. Forgot it when I came to Venus Equilateral. Used to hold a ham ticket on Terra. But there's no use hamming on the station here, where you can wake somebody by yelling at the top of your voice. The thing to ask is, 'Does anyone know code on board the *Empress of Kolain*?' "

They forgot their keying circuit and began to adjust the transmitter to the frequency used by the meteor spotter. It was a job. But it was done, all the way from the master oscillator stage through the several frequency-doubler stages and to the big power-driver stage. The output stage came next, and then a full three hours of tinkering with files and hacksaws were required to adjust the length of the main radiator and the director elements so that their length became right for the changed frequency.

Finally Walt took the key and said: "Here goes!"

He began to rattle the key. In the power room the generators screamed and the lights throughout the station flickered just a bit at the sudden surges.

Don Channing said to Arden: "If someone of the *Empress of Kolain* can understand code—"

The *Empress of Kolain* was zipping along in its silent passage through the void. It was an unseen, undetected, unaware bit of human manufacture marking man's will among the stars. In all the known universe it moved against the forces of celestial mechanics because some intelligent mote that infested the surface of a planet once had the longing to visit the stars. In all the Solar System, most of the cosmic stuff was larger than it—but it alone defied the natural laws of space.

Because it alone possessed the required *outside* force spoken of in Newton's *Universal Laws*.

And it was doing fine.

Dinner was being served in the dining room. A group of shapely girls added grace to the swimming pool on the promenade deck. The bar was filled with a merry crowd, which in turn were partly filled with liquor. A man in uniform, the Second Officer, was throwing darts with a few passengers in the playroom, and there were four oldish ladies on sabbatical leave who were stricken with *mal-de-void.*

The passage up to now had been uneventful. A meteor or two had come to make the ship swing a bit—but the swerve was less than the pitch of an ocean vessel in a moderate sea and it did not continue as did an ocean ship. Most of the time the *Empress of Kolain* seemed as steady as solid rock.

Only the First Officer, on the bridge, and the Chief Pilot, far below in the Control Room, knew just how erratic their course truly was. But they were not worried. They were not a shell, fired from a gun; they were a spaceship, capable of steering themselves into any port on Venus when they arrived, and the minute wobbulations in their course could be corrected when the time came. For nothing had ever prevented a ship of space from seeing where it was going.

Yes, it was uneventful.

Then the meteor screen flashed into life. A circle of light appeared in the celestial globe and the ship's automatic pilot swerved ever so little. The dot of light was gone.

Throughout the ship, people laughed nervously. A waiter replaced a glass of water that had been set too close to the edge of the table and a manly-looking fellow dived into the swimming pool to haul a good-looking blonde to the edge again. She'd been in the middle of a swan dive when the swerve came and the ship had swerved without her. The resounding smack of feminine stomach against the water was of greater importance than the meteor, now so many hundred miles behind.

The flash of light returned and the ship swerved again. Upon the third swerve, the First Officer was watching the celestial globe with suspicion. He went white. It was conceivable that the *Empress of Kolain* was about to encounter a meteor shower.

And that was bad.

He marked the place and set his observation telescope in synchronism with the celestial globe. He searched the sky. There was nothing but the ultimate starry curtain in the background. He snapped a switch and the voice of the pilot came out of a speaker in the wall.

"You called, Mr. Hendall?"

"Tony, take the levers, will you please? Something is rotten in the state of Denmark."

"O.K., sir. I'm riding personal."

"Kick out the meteor-spotting coupling circuits and forget the alarm."

"Right, Mr. Hendall, but will you confirm that in writing?"

Hendall scribbled on the telautograph and then abandoned the small 'scope. The flashing in the celestial globe continued, but the ship no longer danced in its path. Hendall went up into the big dome.

The big twenty-inch Cassegrain showed nothing at all, and Hendall returned to the bridge scratching his head. Nothing on the spotting 'scope and nothing on the big instrument.

That intermittent spot was large enough to mean a huge meteor. But wait. At the speed of the *Empress*, it should have retrogressed in the celestial globe unless it was so huge and so far away—but Sol didn't appear on the globe and it was big and far away, bigger by far. Nothing short of a planet at less-than-planetary distances would do this.

Not even a visible change in the position of the spot.

"Therefore," thought Hendall, "this is no astral body that makes this spot!"

Hendall went to a cabinet and withdrew a cable with a plug on either end. He plugged one end into the test plug on the meteor spotter and the opposite end into the speaker. A low humming emanated from the speaker in synchronism with the flashing of the celestial globe.

It hit a responsive chord.

Hendall went to the main communication microphone and spoke. His voice went all over the *Empress of Kolain* from pilot room and cargo spaces to swimming pool and infirmary.

"Attention!" he said in a formal voice. "Attention to official orders!"

Dancers stopped in midstep. Swimmers paused and then made their way to the edges of the pool and sat with their feet dangling in the warm water. Diners sat with their forks poised foolishly. "Official orders!" meant an emergency.

Hendall continued: "I believe that something never before tried is being attempted. I am forced against my better knowledge to believe that some agency is trying to make contact with us, a spaceship in flight! This is unknown in the annals of space flying and is, therefore, indicative of something important. It would not have been tried without preparations unless an emergency exists.

"However, the requirements of an officer of space do not include a knowledge of code, because of the lack of communication with the planets while in space. Therefore, I request that any person with a working knowledge of International Morse will please present himself to the nearest officer."

Minutes passed. Minutes during which the flashing lights continued.

Then the door of the bridge opened and Third Officer Jones entered with a thirteen-year-old youngster at his heels. The boy's eyes went wide at the sight of the instruments on the bridge, and he looked around in amazed interest.

"This is Timmy Harris," said Jones. "He knows code!"

"Go to it, Mr. Harris," said Hendall.

The boy swelled visibly. You could almost hear him thinking, "He called me 'mister'!"

Then he went to the table by the speaker and reached for pencil and paper. "It's code all right," he said. Then he winked at Jones. "He has a lousy fist!"

Timmy Harris began to write.

". . . *course and head for Terra direct*"—the beam faded for seconds—"*Venusian fever and you will be quarantined. Calling CQ, calling CQ, calling CQ. Calling Empress of Kolain . . . empowered us to contact you and convey . . . message: You are requested to correct your course and head . . . a plague of Venusian fever, and you . . . Johnson of Interplanet has empowered us . . . the following message: You are requested to correct your . . . head for Terra direct. Calling CQ . . .*"

"Does that hash make sense to you?" Jones asked of Hendall.

"Sure," smiled Hendall, "it is fairly plain. It tells us that Keg Johnson of Interplanet wants us to head for Terra direct because of a plague of Venusian fever that would cause us to stay in quarantine. That would ruin the line moss. Prepare to change course, Mr. Jones!"

"Who could it be?" Jones asked foolishly.

"There is only one outfit in the Solar System that could possibly think of a stunt like this. And that is Channing and Franks. This signal came from Venus Equilateral!"

"Wait a minute," said Timmy Harris. "Here's some more."

"As soon as this signal . . . intelligible . . . at right angles to your course for ten minutes. That will take . . . out of . . . beam and reflected . . . will indicate to us . . . left the area and know of our attempt."

"They're using a beam of some sort that indicates to them that we are on the other end but can't answer," Hendall said. "Mr. Jones, and Pilot Canton, ninety degrees north for ten minutes! Call the navigation officer to correct our course. I'll make the announcement to the passengers. Mr. Harris, you are given the freedom of the bridge for the remainder of the trip."

Mr. Harris was overwhelmed. He'd learn plenty—and that would help him when he applied for training as a space officer; unless he decided to take a position with Venus Equilateral when he grew up.

The signal faded from the little cruiser and silence prevailed.

Don spoke into the microphone and said, "Run her up a millisecond," to the beam controller. The beam wiped the space above the previous course for several minutes and Franks was sending furiously: *"You have answered our message. We'll be seeing you!"*

Channing told the man in the cruiser to return. He kicked the main switch and the generators whined down the scale and coasted to a stop. Tube filaments darkened and meters returned to zero.

"O.K., Warren. Let the spinach lay. Get the next

crew to clean up the mess and polish the setup into something presentable. I'll bet a cooky that we'll be chasing spaceships all the way to Pluto after this. We'll work it into a fine thing and perfect our technique. Right now I owe the gang a dinner."

Interlude

When necessity dictates a course of action and the course of action proves valuable, it is but a short step to the inclusion of the answer into the many facets of modern technical civilization. Thus it was that not many months after Venus Equilateral successfully established planet-to-planet communications with the *Empress of Kolain* that all course constants were delivered to the relay station and thereafter messages were transmitted as a part of the regular business of Interplanetary Communications.

This, of course, offered another problem. Ships in space were in the position of being able to catch messages but were not able to answer back. It would take, perhaps, another emergency to set up conditions which demanded the reverse of the problem of contacting a ship in space.

But there was a more immediate problem. Spacecraft were protected from meteors by means of radar that was coupled to the steering panels of the ships; when a meteor threatened, the ship merely turned aside by that fraction of a degree that gave it safety.

It took, however, but a few meteors, and the resulting few fractions of a degree to shut the swiftly moving ship out of the coverage area of the ship-seeking beams from Venus Equilateral. Then the power and ingenuity of Venus Equilateral was wasted on vacant space and the messages intended for the ship went undelivered.

Since the ship must avoid meteors, and the meteors could not be diverted from their courses, there was but one answer: swerve the ship and let the messages go hang, for a message is of no use to a riddled spacecraft!

But, thought several people, if the meteor cannot be steered, perhaps it might be removed . . .

RECOIL

Walter Franks sat in the Director's office, his feet on the Director's desk. He was smoking one of the Director's cigarettes. He was drinking the Director's liquor, filched shamelessly from the Director's private filing cabinet, where it reposed in the drawer marked "S." Drawer "B" would have given beer, but Walt preferred Scotch.

He leaned forward and dropped the Director's cigarette into the Director's wastebasket and then he pressed the button on the desk and looked up.

But it was not the Director's secretary who entered. It was his own, but that did not disturb Franks. He knew that the Director's ex-secretary was off on Mars enjoying a honeymoon with the Director.

Jeanne entered and smiled. "Must you call me in here to witness you wasting the company's time?" she asked in mock anger.

"Now look, Jeanne, this is what Channing does."

"No dice. You can't behave as Don Channing behaves. The reason is my husband."

"I didn't call to have you sit on my lap. I want to know if the mail is in."

"I thought so," she said. "And I brought it in with me. Anything more?"

"Not until you get a divorce," laughed Franks.

"You should live so long," she said with a smile. She stuck her tongue out at him.

Walt thumbed his way through the mail, making notations on some and setting others aside for closer reading. He came to one and tossed it across the desk to Jeanne.

She took the message and read:

DEAR ACTING DIRECTOR:
HAVING A WONDERFUL HONEYMOON; GLAD YOU AREN'T HERE.

DON AND ARDEN.

"Wonderful stuff, love." Franks smiled.

"It is," agreed Jeanne. A dreamy look came into her eyes.

"Scram, Jeanne. There are times when you can't work worth a damn. Mostly when you're thinking of that husband of yours. What's he got that I haven't?"

"Me," said Jeanne slyly. She arose and started for the door. "Oh," she said, "I almost forgot. Warren phoned and said that the turret is ready for a tryout."

"Fine," said Walt. "Swell." He unfolded himself from the chair with alacrity and almost beat the girl to the door.

"My," she laughed, "you *can* move, after all."

"Sure," he grinned. "Now that I have something for which to live."

"I hope it's worth it. You've sunk a lot of change into that bughouse."

"I know, but we can stand it. After all, since Don took over this affair, Venus Equilateral is an up-and-running business. We're out of the government subsidy class now, and are making money. If this works, we'll make more. It's worth a gamble."

"What are you trying to build?" asked Jeanne.

"Why, since this business of contacting ships-at-space has become so universally liked, we have a tough time keeping ships on the mobile beam. That's because they are always ducking out of the way of loose meteorites and stuff, and that screws up their course. We can't see 'em, and must take their position on the basis of their expected course. We never know whether we hit 'em until they land.

"Now, I've been trying to devise a space gun that will blast meteors directly instead of avoiding them by coupling the meteor detector to the autopilot."

"Gonna shoot 'em out of existence?"

"Not exactly. Popping at them with any kind of a rifle would be like trying to hit a flying bird with a spitball. Look, Jeanne, speed on the run from Mars to Terra at Major Opposition is up among the thousands of miles per second at the turnover. A meteor itself may be blatting along at fifty miles per second. Now a rifle, shooting a projectile at a few thousand feet per second, would be useless. You have the meteor in your lap and out of the other side while the projectile is making up its mind to move forward and relieve the pressure that is building up behind it due to the exploding powder.

"I've designed an electron gun. It is a superpowered, oversized edition of the kind they used to use in kinescope tubes, oscilloscope tubes, and electron microscopes. Since the dingbat is to be used in space, we can leave the works of the gun open and project a healthy stream of electrons at the offending object without the electrons' being slowed and dispersed by an impending atmosphere."

"But that sounds like shooting battleships with a toy gun."

"Not so fast on the objections, gal," said Franks. "I've seen a simple oscilloscope tube with a hole in the business end. It was burned right through a quarter-inch of glass because the fellows were taking pix and had the intensity turned up high. The sweep circuit blew a fuse and the beam stopped on one spot. That was enough to puncture the screen."

"I see. That was just a small affair."

"A nine-inch tube. The electron gun in a nine-inch kinescope tube is only about four inches long and three-quarters of an inch in diameter. Mine, out there in the turret, is six feet in diameter and thirty feet long. I can fire out quite a bundle of electrons from a tube of that size."

"It sounds as though you mean business."

"I do. This is the right place to do research of that kind. Out here on Venus Equilateral, we're in a natural medium for an electron gun, and we've the power requirements to run it. I can't think of any place in the system that offers better chances."

"When are you going to try it out?"

"As soon as a meteor comes over the pile, as long as Warren says we're ready."

Jeanne shook her head. "I wish Channing were here. Things are wild enough when you are both working on something screwball, but I could get scared something fierce at the thought of either one of you working without the other."

"Why?"

"You two sort of act as balance wheels to one another's craziness. Oh, don't take that word to heart. Everybody on the relay station thinks the world of you two, myself included. 'Craziness' in this case means a sort of friendly description of the way your brains work. Both of you dash off on tangents now and then, and when either one of you get off the beam, the other one seems to swing the weight required to bring the lost one back to the fold."

"That's a real mess of mixed metaphors, Jeanne. But I am going to surprise Don hairless when he gets back here and finds that I've done what people claimed couldn't be done. I'm going to be the bird whose bust sits in the Hall of Fame in between Edison, Einstein, Alexander Graham Bell, S. F. B. Morse, and—"

"Old Man River, Jack Frost, and Little Boy Blue," laughed Jeanne. "I hope it's not a bust, Walt."

"You mean I should have a whole statue?"

"I mean, I hope your dream is not a bust."

Jeanne left, with Walt right behind her. Franks made his way from the office level to the relay station by way of a not-often-used stairway that permitted him to drop to the outer skin. Above his head were the first levels of apartmental cubicles occupied by the personnel of Venus Equilateral. Out here, Walt had but a scant thickness of steel between him and the void of space.

Franks came to a room built from outer skin to inner skin and about fifty feet across. He unlocked the door with a key on his watch chain, and entered. Warren was waiting for him.

"Hi, ordnance expert. We're ready as soon as they are."

"How's she working?"

"I should know? We've been squirting ropes of electrons out to blank space for hours. She gets rid of them all right. But have we done any good? I dunno."

"Not a meteor in sight, I suppose."

"The detector hasn't blinked once. But when she does, your electron gun will pick it up a thousand miles before it gets here, and will follow the damned thing until it gets a half-thousand miles out of sight."

"That sounds fine. It's a good thing that we don't have to swivel that mess of tube around a whole arm in actual use. It would take too long. But we'll put one in each quadrant of a spaceship and devise it so that its working arc will be small enough to make it work. Time enough to find that out after we know if it works."

"That's something that I've been wondering about," said Warren. "Why didn't we build a small one out here and evacuate the inner skin for a few hundred feet? We could set up a few chunks of iron and squirt electrons at them."

"And have the folks upstairs screaming? Nope. I've a hunch that when this beam hits something hard, it will create quite a ruckus. It would be fine to have a hunk blown right off the skin, wouldn't it?"

"Guess you're right," admitted Warren.

The meteor alarm flashed, and a bell dinged once.

"Here's our chance," snapped Walt. "We've about fifteen seconds to work on this one."

He looked out of a tiny window, and saw that the big tube had lined up with the tiny model that was its monitor. He sighted through the model, which in itself was a high-powered telescope, and he saw the jagged meteor rushing forward at an angle to the station. It would miss by many miles, but it would offer a good target.

"Cathode's hot," said Warren.

Walt Franks grasped the power switch and thrust it down part way. Meters leaped up their scales, and from somewhere there came the protesting whine of tortured generators. Through the window, nothing very spectacular was happening. The cathode glowed slightly brighter due to the passage of current through its metal and out of the coated surface. But the electrostatic stresses that filled the gaps between the accelerator and focusing anodes was no more visible than the electricity that runs a toy motor. Its appearance had not changed a bit; but from the meters, Walt Franks knew that megawatts of electronic power, in the shape of high-velocity electrons, were being poured from the cathode, accelerated by the ring anodes, and focused to a narrow beam by the focusing anodes. And from the end of the framework that supported these anodes, a stream of high-velocity electrons poured forth, twelve inches in diameter.

Through the telescope, the meteor did not seem to be disturbed. It exploded not, neither did it melt. It came on inexorably, and if the inanimate nickel and iron of a meteor can be said to have such, it came on saucily and in utter disregard for the consequences.

Frantically, Walt cranked the power up higher and higher, and the lights all over the station dimmed as the cathode gun drained the resources of Venus Equilateral.

Still no effect.

Then, in desperation, Walt slammed the lower lever down to the bottom notch. The girders strained in the tube from the terrific electrostatic stresses, and for a second Walt was not certain that the meteor was not finally feeling the effects of the electron bombardment.

He was not to be sure, for the experiment came to a sudden stop.

An insulator arced where it led the high-voltage lines that fed the anodes through the wall. Immediately it flashed over, and the room filled to the brim with the pungent odor of burning insulation. A medium-voltage anode shorted to one of the high-voltage anodes, and the stress increased in the tube. They broke from the moorings, these anodes, and plunged backward, down the tube toward the cathode. They hit, and it was enough to jar the whole tube backward on the gimbals.

The shock warped the mounting of the tube, and it flexed slightly, but sufficiently to bring the farthermost and highest-voltage anode into the electron stream. It glowed redly, and the secondary emission rayed back through the series of electrodes, heating them and creating more warpage.

Then the pyrotechnics stopped. Great circuit breakers crashed open up in the power room hundreds of feet above them, high in the station.

Walt Franks looked out through the window at the tangled mess that had been a finely machined piece of equipment. He saw the men looking quizzically at him as he turned away from the window, and with a smile that cost him an effort, he said: "All right, so Marconi didn't WLW on his first try, either. Come on, fellows, and we'll clean up this mess."

With the utter disregard that inanimate objects show toward the inner feelings of the human being, the meteor alarm blinked again and the bell rang. The pilot tube swiveled quickly to one side, lining up with the spot in the celestial globe of the meteor detector. In the turret that housed the big tube, motors strived against welded commutators and the big tube tried to follow.

Walt looked at the pointing tube and said, "Bah! Go ahead and point!"

Don Channing smiled at Arden. "Mrs. Channing," he said, "must you persist in keeping me from my first love?"

Arden smiled winningly. "Naturally. That's what I'm here for. I intend to replace your first love entirely and completely."

"Yeah," drawled Don, "and what would we live on?"

"I'll permit you to attend to your so-called first love during eight hours every day, provided that you remember to think of me every half-hour."

"That's fine. But you really aren't fair about it. We were on Terra for two weeks. I was just getting interested in a program outlined by one of the boys that works for Interplanet, and what happened? You hauled me off to Mars. We stayed for a week at the Terraland Hotel at Canalopsis and the first time that Keg Johnson came to see us with an idea and a sheaf of papers, you rushed me off to Lincoln Head. Now I'm scared to death that some guy will try to open a blueprint here; at which, I'll be rushed off to Palanortis Country until someone finds us there. Then it'll be the Solar Observatory on Mercury or the Big Glass on Luna."

Arden soothed Don's ruffled feelings by sitting on his lap and snuggling. "Dear," she said in a voice that positively dripped, "we're on a honeymoon, remember?"

Don stood up, dumping her to the floor. "Yeah," he said, "but this is the highest-velocity honeymoon that I ever took!"

"And it's the first one I was ever on where the bridegroom took more time admiring beam installations than he took to whisper sweet nothings to his gal. What has a beam transmitter got that I haven't got?"

"One: its actions can be predicted. Two: it can be controlled. Three: it never says anything original, but only repeats what it has been told. Four: it can be turned off."

"Yeah?" drawled Arden, grinning wisely. "And how about this rumor?"

"Rumor?" Channing asked innocently.

"Yes, rumor!" Arden stormed with a chuckle. "Keep you from your first love, me eye. I'll play second fiddle to nothing, Donald. I'll just replace your original first love; but I'm too stinking bright to make you forget it entirely. That, my sweet, is why I've brought you here. You can go chase the rumor whilst I do a bit of shopping. May I borrow your checkbook?"

"Rumor?" repeated Channing with some puzzlement, "What rumor?"

"Rumor has it," said Arden in hyperbolic tones, "that two gentlemen, by name James Baler and Barney Carroll, who have spent years digging up and studying the ancient Martian artifacts, have recently uncovered a large and strange type of vacuum tube that seems to have been used by the Martians as a means of transmitting power. Since I felt that the time had come for the honeymooners to spend at least eight minutes apart, I insisted upon Lincoln Head for our next stop because Lincoln Head happens to have been the scene of some rare happenings, if rumor—"

"Oh, nuts." Channing grinned. "That's no rumor—"

"And you let me ramble on," cried Arden.

She caught Don on the point of the chin with a pillow and effectively smothered him. She followed her advantage with a frontal attack that carried him backward across the bed, where she landed on top viciously and proceeded to lambaste him with the other pillow.

It was proceeding according to plan, this private, good-natured war, until a knock on the door brought a break in operations. Channing struggled out from beneath Arden and went to the door, trying to comb his hair by running spread fingers through it. He went with a sense of failure caused by Arden's quiet laugh and the statement that he resembled a bantam rooster.

The man at the door apologized, and then said: "I'm Doug Ferris of the *Triworld News*."

"Come in," said Don, "and see if you can find a place to sit."

"Thanks."

"I didn't know that *Triworld News* was interested in the wedded life of the Channings. Why doesn't *Triworld* wait until we find out about it ourselves?"

"*Triworld* does not care to pry into the private life of the newlywed Channing family," Doug laughed. "We, and the rest of the system, do not give a damn whether Mrs. Channing calls you Bunny Bit or Sugar Pie—"

"Sweetums," Arden corrected with a gleam in her eye.

"—we've got something big to handle. I can't get a thing out of the gang at Canalopsis, they're all too busy worrying."

"And so you came here? What do you expect to get out of us? We're not connected in any way with Canalopsis."

"I know," said Doug, "but you do know space. Look, Channing, the *Solar Queen* has been missing since yesterday morning!"

Don whistled.

"See what I mean? What I want to know is this: what is your opinion on the matter? You've lived in space for years, on Venus Equilateral, and you've had experience beyond anybody I can reach."

"Missing since yesterday morning," mused Channing. "That means trouble."

"That's what I thought. Now if you were running the spaceport at Canalopsis, what would your own private opinion be?"

"I don't know whether I should speak for publication," said Don.

"It won't be official. I'll corroborate anything you say before it is printed, and so on. But I want an unofficial opinion, too. If you want this withheld, say so, but I still want a technical deduction to base my investigation on. I don't understand the ramifications and the implications of a missing ship. It is enough to make Keg

Johnson's hair turn gray overnight, though, and I'd like to know what is so bad before I start to turn stones."

"Well, keep it off the record until Canalopsis gives you the go-ahead. I can give you an opinion, but I don't want to sound official."

"O.K. Do you suppose she was hit by a meteor shower?"

"Doubt it like the devil. Meteor detectors are many and interconnected on a spaceship, as well as being alarmed and fused to the nth degree. Any trouble with them will bring a horde of ringing bells all through the ship which would bring the personnel a-running. They just don't go wrong for no reason at all."

"Suppose that so many meteors came from all directions that the factors presented to the autopilot—"

"No dice. The possibility of a concentration of meteors from all directions all about to pass through a certain spot in space is like betting on two Sundays in a row. Meteors don't just run in all directions, they have a general drift. And the meteor-detecting equipment would have been able to pick up the centroid of any group of meteors soon enough to lift the ship around it. Why, there hasn't been a ship hit by a meteor in ten years."

"But—"

"And if it had been," continued Channing, "the chances are more than likely that the ship wouldn't have been hit badly enough to make it impossible to steer, or for the crew to shoot out message tubes which would have landed on Canalopsis."

"Look, there's one thing I don't understand," said Doug. "Spacecraft are always dodging meteors, yet Venus Equilateral seems immune."

"It's the velocity," explained Don. "Venus Equilateral is traveling at the same speed as Venus, of course. A spacecraft hits it up in the hundreds of miles per second. Say two hundred and seventy miles per second, which is about ten times the orbital velocity of Venus Equilateral. Then with a given dispersion of meteors throughout space, any spacecraft has ten times the possible chances of encounter, because the ship covers ten times the volume in the same time. Besides, truly missing meteors is a hypothetical problem."

"How so?"

"To avoid only those whose courses will intersect yours would demand some sort of course-predicting gear that would read the course of the oncoming meteor and apply it in a space problem to the predicted course of the ship. That's just too much machinery, Doug. So spacecraft merely turn aside for anything that even *looks* close. They don't take any chances at all," said Channing. "They can't afford to."

"Suppose that the ship ducked a big shower and it went so far out of course that they missed Mars?"

"That's out, too," laughed Channing.

"Why?"

"A standard ship of space is capable of hitting it up at about four G all the way from Terra to Mars at Major Opposition and ending up with enough power and spare cathodes to continue to Venus in quadrature. Now, the velocity of the planets in their orbits is a stinking matter of miles per second, while the top speed of a ship in even the shortest passage runs up into four figures per second. You'd be surprised at what velocity you can attain at one G for ten hours."

"Yes?"

"It runs to slightly less than two hundred and fifty miles per second, during which you've covered only four million miles. In the shortest average run from Venus to Terra at conjunction, a skimpy twenty-five million miles, your time of travel is a matter of twenty-five hours odd running at the standard two G. Your velocity at turnover—or the halfway point where the ship stops going *up* from Terra and starts to go *down* to Venus—is a good cool five hundred miles per second. So under no condition would the ship miss its objective badly enough to cause its complete loss. Why, this business is run so quickly that were it not for the saving in time and money that amounts to a small percentage at the end of each flight, the pilot could head for his planet and approach the planet asymptotically."

"You know what you're doing, don't you?" asked the reporter.

"I think so."

"You're forcing my mind into accepting something

that has never happened before, and something that has no basis for its—"

"You mean piracy? I wonder. We've all read tales of the Jolly Roger being painted on the side of a sleek ship of space while the pirate, who is a fine fellow at heart, though uninhibited, hails down the cruiser carrying radium. He swipes the stuff and kisses all the women whilst menacing the men with a gun handful of searing, coruscating, violently lethal ray pistol. But that sounds fine in stories. The trick is tougher than it sounds, Douglas. You've got to catch your rabbit first."

"Meaning?"

"Meaning that finding a ship in space to prey upon is somewhat less difficult than juggling ten billiard balls whilst riding a horse blindfolded. Suppose you were to turn pirate. This is what would happen:

"You'd get the course of the treasure ship from the spaceport, fine and good, by resorting to spies and such. You'd lie in wait out there in the blackness of space, fixing your position by the stars and hoping that your error in fix was less than a couple of hundred thousand miles. The time comes. You look to your musket, sharpen your cutlass, and see to the priming of your derringers that are thrust into the red sash at your waist. You are right on the course, due to your brilliant though lawless navigator who was tossed out of astrogator's school for filching the teacher's whiskey. Then the treasure ship zoops past at a healthy hundred miles per second and you decide that since she is hitting it up at two G, you'd have had to start from scratch at a heck of a lot better to catch her within the next couple of light years."

"But suppose you took the course as laid and applied the same acceleration? Suppose you followed on the heels of your quarry until you were both in space? You could do it then, couldn't you?"

"Gosh," said Channing, "I never thought of that. That's the only way a guy could pirate a ship—unless he planted his men on board and they mutinied."

"Then it might be pirates?"

"It might be," Channing admitted. "It'd have to occur near beginning or end, of course, though. I can't think of anything being shot at out of a gun of any kind while both crates are hitting it up at a couple of hundred miles per second and at a distance of a few miles apart. It would be all right if you were both running free, but at two G acceleration, you'd have to do quite a bit of ballistic gymnastics to score a hit."

"Or run in front of your quarry and sow a bouquet of mines."

"Except that the meteor detector would show the position of the pirate craft in the celestial globe and the interconnecting circuits would cause the treasure ship to veer off at a sharp angle. Hell, Doug, this thing has got too many angles to it. I can't begin to run it off either way. No matter how difficult it may sound, there are still ways and means to do it. The thing that stands out like a sore thumb is the fact that the *Solar Queen* has turned up missing. Since no inanimate agency could cause failure, piracy is the answer."

"You're sure of that?"

"Not positive. There are things that might cause the ship to founder. But what they are depends on too many coincidences. It's like hitting a royal flush on the deal, or filling a full house from two pairs."

"Well, thanks, Channing. I'm heading back to Canalopsis right now. Want to come along?"

Channing looked at Arden, who was coming from the dressing room carrying her coat and he nodded. "The gal says yes," he grinned. "Annoy her until I find my shoes, will you?"

Arden wrinkled her nose at Don. "I'll like that," she said to Doug.

The trip from Lincoln Head to Canalopsis was a fast one. Doug drove the little flier through the thin air of Mars at a breakneck speed and covered the twelve hundred miles in just shy of an hour. At the spaceport, Channing found that he was not denied entrance as the reporter was. He was ushered into the office of Keg Johnson, who, with the manager of the Canalopsis Spaceport, greeted Don with a worried expression on his face.

"Still gone," said Johnson cryptically. "Like the job of locating her?"

Don shook his head with a sympathetic smile. "Like

trying to find a grain of sand on a beach—a specified grain, I mean. Wouldn't know how to go about it."

Keg nodded. "I thought as much. That leaves her out of the picture. Well, up to now space travel has been about as safe as spending the evening in your easy chair. Hello, Arden, how's married life?"

"Can't tell yet," she said with a twinkle. "I've got to find out whether I can break him of a dozen bad habits before I'll commit myself."

"I wish you luck, Arden, although from that statement, it's Don that needs the luck."

"We came to see if there was anything we could do about the *Solar Queen,*" offered Channing.

"What can anybody do?" asked Keg, with spread hands. "About all we can do is to put her down in our remembrances and turn to tomorrow. Life goes on, you know," said Keg in a resigned tone, "and either we keep up or we begin to live in the past. Are you going to stay here for a day or two?"

"Was thinking about it," said Don.

"Well, suppose you register at the Terraland and meet me back here for lunch. If anything occurs, I'll shoot you a quickie." Keg looked at his watch and whistled. "Lord," he said ruefully. "I didn't know how late it was. Look, kids, I'll run downtown myself, and we'll all have lunch at the Terraland. How's that?"

"That sounds better," Channing admitted. "My appetite, you know."

"I know," laughed Arden. "Come on, meat-eater, and we'll peel a calf."

It was during lunch that a messenger raced into the dining room and handed Keg a letter. Keg read, and then swore roundly. He tossed the letter across the table to Don and Arden.

TO THE OPERATORS OF ALL SPACELINES:

IT HAS COME TO MY ATTENTION THAT YOUR SHIPS NEED PROTECTION. THE ABSENCE OF THE SOLAR QUEEN IS PROOF ENOUGH THAT YOUR EFFORTS ARE INSUFFICIENT TO ENSURE THE ARRIVAL OF A SPACESHIP AT ITS DESTINATION.

I AM CAPABLE OF OFFERING PROTECTION AT

THE REASONABLE RATE OF ONE DOLLAR SOLARIAN FOR EVERY GROSS TON, WITH THE RETURN OF TEN DOLLARS SOLARIAN IF ANY SHIP FAILS TO COME THROUGH SAFELY. I THINK THAT YOU MAY FIND IT NECESSARY TO SUBSCRIBE TO MY INSURANCE, SINCE WITHOUT MY PROTECTION I CANNOT BE RESPONSIBLE FOR FAILURES.

ALLISON (HELLION) MURDOCH.

"Why, the dirty racketeer," stormed Arden. "Who is he, anyway?"

"Hellion Murdoch is a man of considerable ability as a surgeon and a theoretical physicist," Don explained. "He was sentenced to the gas chamber ten years ago for trying some of his theories out on human beings without their consent. He escaped with the aid of fifteen or twenty of his cohorts who had stolen the *Hippocrates* right out of the private spaceport of the Solarian Medical Research Institute."

"And they headed for the unknown," offered Keg. "Wonder where they've been for the last ten years?"

"I'll bet a hat that they've been in the Melapalan Jungle, using the machine shop of the *Hippocrates* to fashion guns. That machine shop was a dilly, if I remember correctly."

"It was. The whole ship was just made to be as self-sustaining as it could be. They used to run all over the System in it, you know, chasing bugs. But look, Don, if I were you, I'd begin worrying about Venus Equilateral. That's where he'll hit next."

"You're right. But what are you going to do?"

"Something that will drive him right out to the relay station," said Keg in a sorrowful tone. "Sorry, Don, but when I put an end to all space shipping for a period of six weeks, Hellion Murdoch will be sitting in your lap."

"He sure will," said Channing nervously. "Arden, are you willing to run a gauntlet?"

"Sure," she answered quickly. "Are you sure that there will be no danger?"

"Reasonably sure, or I wouldn't take you with me. Unless Murdoch has managed to build himself a couple of extra ships, we've got a chance in three that he'll be near one of the other two big spaceports. So we'll slide out of here unannounced and at a peculiar time of day. We'll load up with gravanol and take it all the way to the station at six G."

"He may have two or three ships," said Keg. "A man could cover all the standard space shipping in three, and he might not have too bad a time with two, especially if he were only out looking for those which weren't paid for. But, look, I wouldn't check out of the Terraland if I were you. Keep this under cover. Your heap is all ready to take sky from Canalopsis Spaceport and you can leave directly."

"Hold off on your announcement as long as possible," Don asked Keg.

Johnson smiled and nodded. "I'll give you time to get there, anyway. But I've no control over what will be done at Northern Landing or Mojave. They may kick over the traces."

"Arden, we're moving again," Don laughed. "Keg, ship us our duds as soon as this affair clears up." Channing scribbled a message on the back of Murdoch's letter. "Shoot this off to Walt Franks, will you? I won't wait for an answer, that'll take about fifty minutes, and by that time I'll have been in space for twenty."

They paused long enough to stop at the nurse's office at the spaceport for a heavy shot of gravanol and a thorough bracing with wide adhesive tape. Then they made their way to the storage space of the spaceport, where they entered their small ship. Channing was about to send the power lever home when the figure of Keg Johnson waved him to stop.

Keg ran up the space lock and handed in a paper.

"You're it," he said. "Good luck, Channings."

It was another message from Hellion Murdoch. It said, bluntly:

TO DONALD A. CHANNING, PH.D.,
DIRECTOR OF COMMUNICATIONS:

CONSIDERABLE DIFFICULTY HAS BEEN EXPERIENCED IN TRANSMITTING MESSAGES TO THE INTERESTED PARTIES. I DESIRE A FREE HAND IN TELLING ALL WHO CARE THE PARTICULARS OF MY INSURANCE.

SINCE YOUR RELAY STATION IS IN A POSITION TO CONTROL ALL COMMUNICATIONS BETWEEN THE WORLDS, I AM OFFERING YOU THE OPTION OF EITHER SURRENDERING THE STATION TO ME, OR OF FIGHTING ME FOR ITS POSSESSION. I AM CONFIDENT THAT YOU WILL SEE THE INTELLIGENT COURSE: AN UNARMED STATION IN SPACE IS NO MATCH FOR A FULLY ARMED AND EXCELLENTLY MANNED CRUISER.

YOUR ANSWER WILL BE EXPECTED IN FIVE DAYS.

ALLISON (HELLION) MURDOCH.

Channing snarled and thrust the power lever down to the last notch. The little ship leaped upward at five G, and was gone from sight in less than a minute.

Arden shook her head. "What was that message you sent to Franks?" she asked.

"I told him that there was a wild-eyed pirate on the loose, and that he might take a stab at the station. We are coming in as soon as we can get there and to be on the lookout for us on the landing-communications radio, and also for anything untoward in the nature of space vessels."

"Then this is not exactly a shock," said Arden, waving the message from Murdoch.

"Not exactly," said Channing dryly. "Now look, Arden, you've got to sleep. This'll take hours and hours, and gabbing about it will only lay you out cold."

"I feel fine," objected Arden.

"I know, but that's the gravanol, not you. The tape will keep you intact, and the gravanol will keep you awake without nausea. But you can't get something for nothing, Arden, and when that gravanol wears off, you'll spend ten times as long with one-tenth of the trouble you might have had. So take it easy for yourself now, and later you'll be glad that you aren't worse."

The sky blackened, and Channing knew that they were free in space. Give them another fifteen minutes and the devil himself couldn't find them. With no flight plan scheduled and no course posted, they might as well have been in the seventeenth dimension. As they emerged from the thin atmosphere, there was a fleeting flash of fire from several miles to the east, but Channing did not pay particular attention to it. Arden looked through a telescope and thought she saw a spaceship circling, but she could not be sure.

Whatever it was, nothing came of it.

The trip out to the station was a monotonous series of uneventful hours, proceeding along one after the other. They dozed and slept most of the time, eating sparingly and doing nothing that was not absolutely necessary.

Turnabout was accomplished and then the deceleration began, equally long and equally monotonous. It was equally inactive. Channing tried to plan, but failed because he could not plan without talking and discussing the affair with his men. Too much depended upon their cooperation. He fell into a morose, futile feeling that made itself evident in grousing; Arden tried to cheer him, but Don's usually bubbling spirit was doused too deep. Also, Arden herself was none too happy, which is necessary before one can cheer another.

Then they sighted the station and Channing's ill spirit left. A man of action, what he hated most was the no-action business of just sitting in a little capsule waiting for the relay station to come up out of the sky below. Once it was sighted, Channing foresaw action, and his grousing stopped.

They zipped past the station at a distance of ten miles, and Channing opened the radio.

"Walt Franks! Wake up, you slumberhead."

The answer came inside of half a minute. "Hello, Don. Who's asleep?"

"Where are you? In Joe's?"

"Joe has declared a drought for the duration," said Franks with a laugh. "He thinks we can't think on Scotch."

"We can't. Have you seen the boys?"

"Murdoch's crew? Sure, they're circling at about five miles, running around in the plane of the ecliptic. Keep running on the colure and the chances are that you won't even see 'em. But, Don, they can hear us!"

"How about the landing stage at the south end?"

"There are two of them running around the station at different heights from north to south. The third is running in a four-mile circle on a plane five miles south of the station. We've picked up a few HE shells, and I guess that, if you try to make a landing there, you'll be shot to bits. That devil is using the meteor detecter for a gun pointer."

"Walt, remember the visual loran?"

"Y'mean the one we used to find the *Empress*?"

"Uh-huh. Rig it without the mirrors? Get me? D'you know what I want to do?"

"Yep. All we have to do is clear away some of the sawgrass again. Not too much, though, because it hasn't been too long since we cut it before. I get you all right."

"Fine. How soon?"

"I'm in the beam control north. I've got a portable mike, and I walk over to the mirror and begin to tinker with the screws. *Ouch!* I've skun me a knuckle. Now look, Don, I'm going inside and crack the passage end. I've broadcast throughout the station that it is to be cracked, and the men are swarming all over the axis of the station doing just that. Come a-running!"

Channing circled the little ship high to the north and came down toward the axis of the station. He accelerated fiercely for a portion of the time, and then made a slam-bang turnabout. A pilot light on the instrument panel gleamed, indicating that some of the plates were strained and that the ship was leaking air. Another light lit, indicating that the automatic pressure control was functioning, and that the pressure was maintained, though it might not long be.

Then in deceleration, Channing fought the ship onto a die-straight line with the open door at the north end. He fixed the long, long passageway in the center of his sights, and prayed.

The ship hit the opening squarely, and only then did their terrific speed become apparent. Past bulkhead after bulkhead they drove, and a thin scream came to their ears as the atmosphere down in the bowels of the station was compressed by the tiny ship's passage.

Doors slammed behind the ship as it passed, and air locks were opened, permitting the station's center to fill to its normal pressure once more.

Then the rocketing ship slowed. Channing saw a flash of green and knew that the Martian sawgrass was halfway down the three-mile length of the station. He zipped past storerooms and rooms filled with machinery, and then the ship scraped lightly against one of the bulkheads.

It caromed from this bulkhead against the next, hitting it in a quartering slice. From side to side the ship bounced, crushing the bulkheads and tearing great slices from the flanks of the ship.

Then it slowed, and came to rest against a large room full of packing cases, and was immediately swarmed over by the men of Venus Equilateral.

They found Channing partly conscious. His nose was bleeding but otherwise he seemed all right. Arden was completely out, though a quick check by the station's medical staff assured Don that she would be all right as soon as they gave her a workout. He was leaving the center of the station when Franks came puffing up the stairway from the next lowest level.

"Gosh," he said. "It's a real job trying to guess where you stopped. I've been hitting every hundred feet and asking. Well, that was one for the book."

"Yeah," groaned Don. "Come along, Walt. I want a shower. You can give the resumé of the activities while I'm showering and trying to soak this adhesive off. Arden, lucky girl, will be unconscious when Doc rips it off; I never liked the way they remove tape."

"There isn't much to tell," said Franks. "But what there is, I'll tell you."

Channing was finishing the shower when Walt mentioned that it was too bad they hadn't started his electron gun a few weeks sooner.

Don shut off the water, fumbled for a towel, and said: "What?"

Franks repeated.

Again Channing said: "What? Are you nuts?"

"No. I've been tinkering with an idea of mine. If we had another month to work on it, I think we might be able to clip Murdoch's ears."

"Just what are you using in this superweapon, chum?"

Franks explained.

"Mind if I put in an oar?" asked Channing.

"Not at all. So far we might be able to fry a smelt at

twenty feet, or we could cook us a steak. But I haven't been able to do a thing yet. We had it working once, and I think we heated a meteor somewhat, but the whole thing went blooey before we finished the test. I've spent the last week and a half fixing the thing up again, and would have tried it out on the next meteor, but your message brought a halt to everything but cleaning up the mess and making ready, just in case we might think of something practical."

"I'll put in my first oar by seeing the gadget. Wait till I find my pants, and I'll go right along."

Don inspected the installation and whistled. "Not half bad, sonny, not half bad."

"Except that we haven't been able to make it work."

"Well, for one thing, you've been running on the wrong track. You need more power."

"Sure." Walt grinned. "More power, he says. I don't see how we can cram any more soup into this can. She'll melt."

"Walt, what happens in a big gun?"

"Powder burns; expanding products of combustion push—"

"Functionally, what are you trying to accomplish? Take it on the basis of a solid shot, like they used to use back in the sailing-ship days."

"Well," said Walt thoughtfully, "I'd say they were trying to heave something large enough to do damage."

"Precisely. Qualifying that statement a little, you might say that the projectile transmits the energy of the powder charge to its objective."

"Right," agreed Walt.

"And it is possible to transmit that energy mechanically. I think if we reason this idea out in analogy, we might be able to do it electrically. First, there is the method. There is nothing wrong with your idea, functionally. Electron guns are as old as radio. They—"

The door opened and Arden entered. "Hi, fellows," she said. "What's cooking?"

"Hi, Arden. Like marriage?" Walt asked.

"How long do people have to be married before people stop asking that damn fool question?" asked Arden.

"O.K., how about your question?"

"I meant that. I ran into Warren, who told me that the brains were down here tinkering on something that was either a brilliant idea or an equally brilliant flop—he didn't know which. What goes?"

"Walt has turned Buck Rogers and is now about to invent a ray gun."

"No!"

"Yes!"

"Here's where we open a psychopathic ward," said Arden sadly. "So far, Venus Equilateral is the only community that hasn't had a village idiot. But no longer are we unique. Seriously, Walt?"

"Sure enough," said Channing. "He's got an idea here that may work, with a little tinkering."

"Brother Edison, we salute you," said Arden. "How does it work?"

"Poorly. Punk. Lousy."

"Well, sound recording has come a long way from the tin-foil cylinder that scratched out: 'Mary had a little lamb!' And transportation has come along swell from the days of sliding sledges. You may have the nucleus of an idea, Walt. But I meant its operation instead of its efficiency."

"We have an electron gun of super size," Walt explained. "The cathode is a big affair six feet in diameter and capable of emitting a veritable storm of electrons. We accelerate them by means of properly spaced anodes of the proper voltage level, and we focus them into a nice bundle by means of electrostatic lenses—"

"Whoa, Tillie, you're talking like the venerable Buck Rogers himself. Say that in words of one cylinder, please," Arden chuckled.

"Well, any voltage gradient between electrodes of different voltage acts as a prism, sort of. When you have annular electrodes of the proper size, shape, and voltage difference, they act as a lens."

"In other words, the ring-shaped electrodes are electrostatic lenses?"

"Nope. It is the space between them. With light or electrons, a convex lens will converge the light no matter which direction the light is coming from."

"Uh-huh. I see in a sort of vague manner. Now, fellows, go on from there. What's necessary to make this dingbat tick?"

"I want to think out loud," said Channing.

"That's nothing unusual," said Arden. "Can't we go into Joe's? You can't think without a tablecloth, either."

"What I'm thinking is this, Walt. You've been trying to squirt electrons like a fireman runs a hose. Walt, how long do you suppose a sixteen-inch rifle would last if the explosives were constantly replaced and the fire burned constantly?"

"Not long," admitted Walt.

"A gun is an overloaded machine," said Don. "Even a little one. The life of a gun barrel is measured in seconds; totaling up the time of transit of all the rounds from new gun to worn barrel gives a figure expressed in seconds. Your electron gun, Walt, whether it be fish, flesh, or fowl, must be overloaded for an instant."

"Is overload a necessary requirement?" asked Arden. "It seems to me that you might be able to bore a sixteen-inch gun for a twenty-two. What now, little man?"

"By the time we get something big enough to do more than knock paint off, we'll have something bigger than a twenty-two," grinned Channing. "I was speaking in terms of available strength versus required punch. In the way that a girder will hold tremendous overloads for brief instants, a gun is overloaded for milliseconds. We'll have a problem—"

"O.K., aside from that, have you figured out why I haven't been able to do more than warm anything larger than a house brick?"

"Sure." Channing laughed. "What happens in a multi-grid radio tube when the suppressor grid is hanging free?"

"Charges negative and blocks the electron stream— Hey! That's it!"

"What?" Arden asked.

"Sure," said Walt. "We fire off a batch of electrons, and the first contingent that arrives charges the affair so that the rest of the beam sort of wriggles out of line."

"Your meteor is going to take on a charge of phenomenal negative value, and the rest of your beam is going to be deflected away, just as your electron lenses deflect the original beam," said Channing. "And now another thing, old turnip. You're squirting out a lot of electrons. That's much amperage. Your voltage—velocity—is nothing to rave about even though it sounds high. Watts is what you want, to corn a phrase."

"Phew," said Walt: "Corn, he says. Go on, prodigy, and make with the explanations. I agree, we should have more voltage and less quantity. But we're running the stuff at plenty of voltage now. Nothing short of a Van de Graaff generator would work—and while we've got one up on the forty-ninth level, we couldn't run a supply line down here without reaming a fifty-foot hole through the station, and then I don't know how we'd get that kind of voltage down here without— That kind of stuff staggers the imagination. You can't juggle a hundred million volts on a wire. She'd squirt off in all directions."

"Another thing, whilst I hold it in my mind," said Channing thoughtfully. "You go flinging electrons off the station in basketful after basketful, and the next bird that drops a ship on the landing stage is going to spot-weld himself right to the south end of Venus Equilateral. It wouldn't be long before the station would find itself being pulled into Sol because of the electrostatic stress—if we didn't run out of electrons first!"

"I hardly think that we'd run out—but we might have a tough time flinging them away after a bit. Could it be that we should blow out a fistful of protons at the same time?"

"Might make up a concentric beam and wave positive ions at the target," said Channing. "Might help."

"But this space-charge effect. How do we get around that?"

"Same way we make the electron gun work. Fire it off at a devilish voltage. Run your electron velocity up near the speed of light; the electrons at that speed will acquire considerable mass, in accordance with Lorenz's equation which shows that as the velocity of a mass reaches the speed of light, its mass becomes infinite. With a healthy mass built up by near–light velocities, the electrons will not be as easy to deflect. Then, too, we can do the damage we want before the charge can be built up that will deflect the stream. We ram 'em with a bundle of electrons moving so fast that the charging effect cannot work; before the space charge can build up to the level required for self-nullification of our beam, the damage is done."

"And all we need is a couple of trillion volts. Two times ten to the twelfth power. *Grrr.*"

"I can *see* that you'll need a tablecloth," said Arden. "You birds can think better over at Joe's. Come along and feed the missus, Don."

Channing surveyed the instrument again, and then said: "Might as well, Walt. The inner man must be fed, and we can wrangle at the same time. Argument assists the digestion—and vice versa."

"Now," said Channing as the dishes were pushed aside, clearing a space on the table. "What are we going to do?"

"That's what I've been worrying about," said Walt. "Let's list the things that make our gun ineffective."

"That's easy. It can't dish out enough. It's too dependent upon mobility. It's fundamentally inefficient because it runs out of ammunition too quick, by which I mean that it is a sort of gun with antiseptic bullets. It cures its own damage."

"Prevents," Arden corrected.

"All right, it acts as its own shield, electrostatically."

"About this mobility," said Walt. "I do not quite agree with that."

"You can't whirl a hunk of tube the size and weight of a good-sized telescope around fast enough to shoot holes in a racing spaceship," said Channing. "Especially one that is trying to dodge. We've got to rely upon something that can do the trick better. Your tube did all right following a meteor that runs in a course that can be predicted, because you can set up your meteor spotter to correct for the mechanical lag. But in a spaceship that is trying to duck your shot, you'll need something that works with the speed of light. And, since we're going to be forced into something heavy and hard-hitting, its inertia will be even more so."

"Heavy and hard-hitting means exactly what?"

"Cyclotron, betatron, or synchrotron. One of those

dinguses that whirls nucleons around like a stone on a string until the string breaks and sends the stone out at terrific speed. We need a velocity that sounds like a congressional figure."

"We've got a cyclotron."

"Yeah," drawled Channing. "A wheezy old heap that cries out in anguish every time the magnets are charged. I doubt that we could move the thing without it falling apart. The betatron is the ticket."

"But the cyclotron gives out with a lot more soup."

"If I had to increase the output of either one, I could do it a lot quicker with the betatron," said Channing. "In a cyclotron, the revolution of the ions in their acceleration period is controlled by an oscillator, the voltage output of which is impressed on the D chambers. In order to speed up the ion stream, you'd have to do two things. One: build a new oscillator that will dish out more power. Two: increase the strength of the magnets.

"But in the betatron, the thing is run differently. The magnet is built for A.C. and the electron gun runs off the same. As your current starts up from zero, the electron gun squirts a bouquet of electrons into a chamber built like a pair of angel-food-cake tins set rim to rim. The magnet's field begins to build up at the same time, and the resulting increase in field strength accelerates the electrons, and at the same time its increasing field keeps the little devils running in the same orbit. Shoot it with two-hundred-cycle current, and in the half-cycle your electrons are made to run around the center a few million times. That builds up a terrific velocity—measured in six figures, believe it or not. Then the current begins to level off at the top of the sine wave, and the magnet loses its increasing phase. The electrons, still in acceleration, begin to whirl outward. The current levels off for sure and begins to slide down—and the electrons roll off at a tangent to their course. This stream can be collected and used. In fact, we have a two-hundred-cycle beam of electrons at a couple of billion volts. That, brother, ain't hay!"

"Is that enough?"

"Nope."

"Then how do you hope to increase this velocity?"

Walt asked. "If it is easier to run this up than it would be the cyclotron, how do we go about it?"

Channing smiled and began to draw diagrams on the tablecloth. Joe looked over with a worried frown, and then shrugged his shoulders. Diagrams or not, this was an emergency—and besides, he thought, he needed another lesson in high-powered gadgetry.

"The nice thing about this betatron," said Channing, "is the fact that it can and does run both ends on the same supply. The current and voltage phases are correct so that we do not require two supplies which operate in a carefully balanced condition. The cyclotron is one of the other kinds; though the one supply is strictly D.C., the strength of the field must be controlled separately from the supply to the oscillator that runs the D plates. You're sitting on a fence, juggling knobs and stuff all the time you are bombarding with a cyc.

"Now let us inspect the supply of the betatron. It is sinusoidal. There is the catch. There is the thing that makes it possible. That single fact makes it easy to step the power up to terrific quantities. Since the thing is fixed by nature so that the output is proportional—electron gun initial velocity versus magnetic field strength—if we increase the input voltage, the output voltage goes up without having to resort to manipulistic gymnastics on the part of the operator."

"Go on, Professor Maxwell."

"Don't make fun of a great man's name," said Arden. "If it wasn't for Clerk Maxwell, we'd still be yelling out of the window at one another instead of squirting radio beams all over the Solar System."

"Then make him quit calling me Tom Swift."

"Go on, Don. Walt and I will finish this argument after we finish Hellion Murdoch."

"May I?" asked Channing with a smile. He did not mind the interruption; he was used to it in the first place and he had been busy with his pencil in the second place. "Now look, Walt, what happens when you smack a charged condenser across an inductance?"

"You generate a damped cycle of the amplitude of the charge on the condenser, and of frequency equal to the L, C constants of the condenser and inductance.

The amplitude decays according to the factor Q, following the equation for decrement—"

"Never mind, I've got it here on my whiteboard," smiled Channing, pointing to the tablecloth. "You are right. And the purity of the wave?"

"Sinusoidal— Hey! That's it!" Walt jumped to his feet and went to the telephone.

"What's 'it'?" asked Arden.

"The betatron we have runs off a five-hundred-volt supply," Channing chuckled. "We can crank that up ten to one without running into any difficulty at all. Five-hundred-volt insulation is peanuts, and the stuff they put on wires nowadays is always good for ten times that just because it wouldn't be economical to try to thin the installation down so that it only protects five hundred. I'll bet that he could crank the input up to fifty thousand volts without too much sputtering—though I wouldn't know where to lay my lunch hooks on a fifty-thousand-volt condenser of any appreciable capacity. Well, stepping up the rig ten to one will dish us out just shy of a couple of thousand million volts, which, as Brother Franks says, is not hay!"

Walt returned after a minute and said: "Warren's measuring the inductance of the betatron magnet. He will then calculate the value of C required to tune the thing to the right frequency and start to achieve that capacity by mazing up whatever high-voltage condensers we have on the station. Now, Don, let's calculate how we're going to make the thing mobile."

"That's a horse of a different color. We'll have to use electromagnetic deflection. From the constants of the electron stream out of our souped-up Suzy, we'll have to compute the necessary field to deflect such a beam. That'll be terrific, because the electrons are hitting it up at a velocity approaching that of light—maybe a hundred and seventy thousand miles per—and their mass will be something fierce. That again will help to murder Murdoch; increasing mass will help to keep the electrons from being deflected, since it takes more to turn a heavy mass—et cetera; see Newton's law of inertia for complete statement. Have 'em jerk the D plates out of the cyc and bring the magnet frame down here—to the turret, I mean—and set 'em up on the vertical. We'll use that to run the beam up and down; we can't possibly get one-hundred-and-eighty-degree deflection, of course, but we can run the deflection over considerable range. It should be enough to catch a spaceship that is circling the station. For the horizontal deflection, what have we got?"

"Nothing. But the cyc magnet is a double pole affair. We could break the frame at the D plates and set one winding sidewise to the other and use half on each direction."

"Sure. Have one of Warren's gang fit the busted pole pieces up with a return-magnetic frame so that the field will be complete. He can weld some girders on and around in an hour. That gives us complete deflection properties up and down; left and right. We should be able to cover a ninety-degree cone from your turret."

"That'll cover all of Murdoch's ships," said Walt.

"Too bad we haven't got some U-235 to use. I'd like to plate up one of his ships with some positive ions of U-235 and then change the beam to slow neutrons. That might deter him from his life of crime."

"Variations, he wants," said Arden. "You're going to impale one ship on a beam of electrons; one ship on a beam of U-235 ions; and what will you have on the third?"

"I'll think of something," said Channing. "A couple of hundred pounds of U-235 should make things hum, though."

"More like making them disappear," said Franks. "*Swoosh!* No ship. Just an incandescent mass falling into the Sun. I'm glad we haven't any purified U-235 or plutonium in any quantity out here. We catch a few slow neutrons now and then, and I wouldn't be able to sleep nights. The things just sort of wander right through the station as though it weren't here at all; they stop just long enough to register on the counter upstairs and then they're gone."

"Well, to work, people. We've got a job to do in the next three and a half days."

Those days were filled with activity. Hauling the heavy parts down to the turret was no small job, but it was accomplished after a lot of hard work and quite a bit of tinkering with a cutting torch. The parts were installed in the outer skin, and the crew with the torch went back over the trail and replaced the gaping holes they left in the walls and floors of Venus Equilateral. The engineering department went to work, and for some hours the place was silent save for the clash of pencil on paper and the scratching of scalps. The most popular book in the station became a volume on nuclear physics, and the second most popular book was a table of integrals. The stenographic force went to work combing the library for information pertaining to electronic velocities, and a junior engineer was placed in as buffer between the eager stenographers and the harried engineering department. This was necessary because the stenographers got to the point where they would send anything at all that said either "electrons" or "velocity," and one of the engineers read halfway through a text on atomic structure before he realized that he had been sold a bill of goods. Wire went by the mile down to the turret, and men proceeded to blow out half of the meters in the station with the high-powered beam. Luckily, the thing was completely nonspectacular, or Murdoch might have gained an inkling of their activities. The working crew manipulated constants and made haywire circuits, and finally announced that the beam would deflect—if the calculations were correct.

"They'd better be," said Channing. He was weary. His eyes were puffed from lack of sleep, and he hadn't had his clothing off in three days.

"They are," said Franks. He was in no better shape than Don.

"They'd better be right," said Channing ominously. "We're asking for a kick in the teeth. The first bundle of stuff that leaves our gun will energize Murdoch's meteor spotter by sheer electrostatic force. His gun mounts, which you tell me are coupled to the meteor detector for aiming, will swivel to cover the turret out here. Then he'll let us have it right in the betatron. If we don't get him first, he'll get us second."

"Don," said Walt in a worried voice, "how are we going to replace the charge on the station? Like the bird who was tossing baseballs out of the train—he quit when he ran out of them. Our gun will quit cold when we run out of electrons—or when the positive charge gets so high that the betatron can't overcome the electrostatic attraction."

"Venus Equilateral is a free grid," smiled Channing. "As soon as we shoot off electrons, Old Sol becomes a hot cathode and our station collects 'em until the charge is equalized again."

"And what is happening to the bird who is holding on to something when we make off with a million volts? Does he scrape himself off the opposite wall in a week or so—after he comes to—or can we use him for freezing ice cubes? Seems to me that it might be a little bit fatal."

"Didn't think of that," Channing said. "There's one thing: their personal charge doesn't add up to a large quantity of electricity. If we insulate 'em and put 'em in their spacesuits, they'll be all right as long as they don't try to grab anything. They'll be on the up and down for a bit, but the resistance of the spacesuit is high enough to keep 'em from draining out all their electrons at once. I recall the experiments with early Van de Graaff generators at a few million volts—the operator used to sit in the charged sphere because it was one place where he couldn't be hit by man-made lightning. It'll be rough, but it won't kill us. Spacesuits, and have 'em sit in plastic chairs, the feet of which are insulated from the floor by china dinner plates. This plastic wall covering that we have in the apartments is a blessing. If it were all bare steel, every room would be a miniature Hell. Issue general instructions to that effect. We've been having emergency drills for a long time; now's the time to use the grand collection of elastomer spacesuits. Tell 'em we give 'em an hour to get ready."

Hellion Murdoch's voice came over the radio at exactly the second of the expiration of his limit. He called Channing and said:

"What is your answer, Dr. Channing?"

Don squinted down the pilot tube of the meteor spotter and saw the *Hippocrates* passing. It was gone before he spoke, but the second ship came along, and the pilot tube leaped into line with it. Don checked meters on the crude panel before him, and then pressed the plastic handle of a long lever.

There was the crash of heavy-duty oil switch.

Crackles of electricity flashed back and forth through the station, and the smell of ozone arose. Electric-light filaments leaned over crazily, trying to touch the inner walls of the glass. Panes of glass ran blue for an instant, and the nap of the carpets throughout the station stood bolt upright. Hair stood on end, touched the plastic helmet dome, discharged, fell to the scalp, raised again and discharged, fell once more, and then repeated this raising and falling, again and again and again. Electric clocks ran crazily, and every bit of electronic equipment on the station began to act in an unpredictable manner.

Then things settled down again as the solar emission charged that station to equilibrium.

Aboard the ship, it was another story. The celestial globe of the meteor spotter blazed once in a blinding light and then went completely out of control. It danced with pinpoints of light, and the coupler that was used to direct the guns went crazy. Turrets tried to swivel, but the charge raised hob with the electronic controls, and the guns raised once, and then fell, inert. One of them belched flame, and the shell went wild. The carefully balanced potentials in the driver tubes were upset, and the ship lost headway. The heavy ion stream from the driving cathode bent and spread, touching the dynodes in the tubes. The resulting current brought them to a red heat, and they melted down and floated through the evacuated tube in round droplets. Instruments went wild, and gave every possible answer, and the ship became a bedlam of ringing bells and flashing danger lights.

But the crew was in no shape to appreciate this display. From metal parts in the ship there appeared coronas that reached for the unprotected men, and seared their flesh. And since their gravity-apparent was gone, they floated freely through the air, and came in contact with highly charged walls, ceilings, and floors; to say nothing of the standard metal furniture.

It was a sorry bunch of pirates that found themselves in a ship-without-motive-power that was beginning to leave their circular course on a tangent which would let them drop into the Sun.

"That's my answer, Murdoch!" snapped Channing. "Watch your second ship!"

"You young devil!" snarled Murdoch. "What did you do?"

"You never thought that it would be an electronics engineer that made the first energy gun, did you, Murdoch? I'm now going to take a shot at No. 3!"

No. 3's turret swiveled around and from the guns flashes of fire came streaming. Channing punched his lever savagely, and once again the station was tortured by the effects of its own offensive.

Ship No. 3 suffered the same fate as No. 2.

Then, seconds later, armor-piercing shells began to hit Venus Equilateral. They hit, and because of the terrific charge, they began to arc at the noses. The terrible current passed through the fuses, and the shells exploded on contact instead of boring in before detonation. Metal was bent and burned, but only a few tiny holes resulted. As the charge on the station approached equilibrium once more, men ran with torches to seal these holes.

"Murdoch," said Channing, "I want you!"

"Come and get me!"

"Land—or die!" Channing snapped in a vicious tone. "I'm no humanitarian, Murdoch. You'd be better off dead!"

"Never!" said Hellion Murdoch.

Channing pulled the lever for the third time, but as he did, Murdoch's ship leaped forward under several G. The magnets could not change in field soon enough to compensate for this change in direction, and the charge failed to connect as a bull's-eye. It did expend some of its energy on the tail of the ship. Not enough to cripple the *Hippocrates,* but the vessel took on a charge of enough value to make things hard on the crew.

Metal sparked, and instruments went mad. Meters wound their needles around the end pegs. The celestial globe glinted in a riot of color and then went completely dead. Gun servers dropped their projectiles as they became too heavily charged to handle, and they rolled across the turret floors, creating panic in the gun crews. The pilot fought the controls, but the charge on his driver tubes was sufficient to make his helm completely unpredictable. The panel sparked at him and seared his hands, spoiling his nervous control and making him heavy-handed.

"Murdoch," cried Channing in a hearty voice, "that was a miss! Want a hit?"

Murdoch's radio was completely dead. His ship was yawing from side to side as the static charges raced through the driver tubes. The pilot gained control after a fashion, and decided that he had taken enough. He circled the station warily and began to make a shaky landing at the south end.

Channing saw him coming, and with a glint in his eye, he pressed the lever for the fourth and last time.

Murdoch's ship touched the landing stage just after the charge had been driven out into space. The heavy negative charge on the *Hippocrates* met the heavy positive charge on Venus Equilateral. The ship touched, and from that contact, there arose a cloud of incandescent gas. The entire charge left the ship at once, and through that single contact.

When the cloud dissipated, the contact was a crude but efficient welded joint that was gleaming white-hot.

Channing said to Walt: "That's going to be messy."

Inside the *Hippocrates,* men were frozen to their handholds. It was messy, and cleaning up the *Hippocrates* was a job not relished by those who did it.

But cleaning up Venus Equilateral was no small matter, either.

A week went by before the snarled-up instruments were repaired. A week in which the captured *Hippocrates* was repaired, too, and used to transport prisoners to and material and special supplies from Terra, and Venus, and Mars. A week in which the service from planet to planet was erratic.

Then service was restored, and life settled down to a reasonable level. It was after this that Walt and Don found time to spend an idle hour together.

Walt raised his glass and said: "Here's to electrons!"

"Yeah," grinned Channing, "here's to electrons. Y'know, Walt, I was a little afraid that space might become a sort of Wild West show, with the ships bristling with space guns and betatrons and stuff like that. In which case you'd have been a stinking benefactor. But if the recoil is as bad as the output—and Newton said that it must be—I can't see ships cluttering up their insides with stuff that'll screw up their instruments and driver tubes. But the thing that amuses me about the whole thing is the total failure you produced."

"Failure?" asked Walt. "What failed?"

"Don't you know? Have you forgotten? Do you realize that spaceships are still ducking around meteors instead of blasting them out of the way with the Franks Electron Gun? Or did you lose sight of the fact that this dingbat started out in life as a meteor-sweeper?"

Walt glared over the rim of his glass, but he had nothing to say.

Interlude

Once the threat of piracy was over, Don Channing returned to his major problem: how to devise two-way communication between ship and planet, or better, from ship to ship. It was not to come easily.

But it is not hard to come to the mistaken conclusion that nothing much was taking place outside of Venus Equilateral, and that all of the science of communication was centered there. The truth is different. For, uncounted centuries earlier, on the now-arid plains of Mars, a highly civilized culture developed sophisticated equipment and then died away, leaving some of its gear to be puzzled over, not by engineers, but by archaeologists . . .

LOST ART

Sargon of Akkad was holding court in all of his splendor in Mesopotamia, which he thought to be the center of the universe. The stars to him were but holes in a black bowl which he called the sky. They were beautiful then, as they are now, but he thought that they were put there for his edification only; for was he not the ruler of Akkadia?

After Sargon of Akkad, there would come forty-odd centuries of climbing before men reached the stars and found not only that there had been men upon them, but that a civilization on Mars had reached its peak four thousand years before Christ and was now but a memory and a wealth of pictographs that adorned the semi-preserved temples of Canalopsis.

And forty-odd centuries after, the men of Terra wondered about the ideographs and solved them sufficiently to piece together the wonders of the long-dead Martian civilization.

Sargon of Akkad did not know that the stars that he beheld carried on them wonders his mind would not, could not, accept.

Altas, the Martian, smiled tolerantly at his son. The young man boasted on until Altas said: "So you have memorized the contents of my manual? Good, Than, for I am growing old and I would be pleased to have my son fill my shoes. Come into the workshop that I may pass upon your proficiency."

Altas led Than to the laboratory that stood at the foot of the great tower of steel; Altas removed from a cabinet a replacement element from the great beam above their heads, and said: "Than, show me how to hook this up!"

Than's eyes glowed. From other cabinets he took small auxiliary parts. From hooks upon the wall, he took lengths of wire. Working with a brilliant deftness that was his heritage as a Martian, Than spent an hour attaching the complicated circuits. After he was finished, Than stepped back and said: "There—and believe it or not, this is the first time you have permitted me to work with one of the beam elements."

"You have done well," said Altas with that same cryptic smile. "But now we shall see. The main question is: does it work?"

"Naturally," answered Than in youthful pride. "Is it not hooked up exactly as your manual says? It will work."

"We shall see," repeated Altas. "We shall see."

Barney Carroll and James Baler cut through the thin air of Mars in a driver-wing flier at a terrific rate of speed. It was the only kind of flier that would work on Mars with any degree of safety, since it depended upon the support of its drivers rather than the wing surface. They were hitting it up at almost a thousand miles per hour on their way from Canalopsis to Lincoln Head; their trip would take an hour and a half.

As they passed over the red sand of Mars, endlessly it seemed, a glint of metal caught Barney's eye, and he shouted.

"What's the matter, Barney?" asked Jim.

"Roll her over and run back a mile or so," said Barney. "I saw something down there that didn't belong in this desert."

Jim snapped the plane around in a sharp loop that nearly took their heads off, and they ran back along their course.

"Yep," Barney called, "there she is!"

"What?"

"See that glint of shiny metal? That doesn't belong in this mess of erosion. Might be a crash."

"Hold tight." Jim laughed. "We're going down."

They did. Jim's piloting had all the aspects of a daredevil racing pilot's, and Barney was used to it. Jim snapped the nose of the little flier down and they power-dived to within a few yards of the sand before he set the plane on its tail and skidded flatwise to kill speed. He leveled off, and the flier came screaming in for a perfect landing not many feet from the glinting object.

"This is no crash," said Baler. "This looks like the remains of an air-lane beacon of some sort."

"Does it? Not like any I've seen. It reminds me more of some of the gadgets they find here and there—the remnants of the Ancients. They used to build junk like this."

"Hook up the sand-blower," Baler suggested. "We'll clear some of this rubble away and see what she really looks like. Can't see much more than what looks like a high-powered searchlight."

Barney hauled equipment out of the flier and hitched it to a small motor in the plane. The blower created a small storm for an hour or so, its blast directed by the suitclad archaeologist. Working with experience gained in uncovering the remains of a dozen dead and buried cities, Barney cleared the shifting sand from the remains of the tower.

The head was there, preserved by the dry sand. Thirty feet below the platform, the slender tower was broken off. No delving could find the lower portion.

"This is quite a find," said Jim. "Looks like some of the carvings on the Temple of Science at Canalopsis—that little house on the top of the spire with the three-foot runway around it; then this dingbat perched on top of the roof. Never did figure out what it was for."

"We don't know whether the Martians' eyes responded as ours do," suggested Barney. "This might be a searchlight that puts out with Martian-visible spectrum. If they saw with infrared, they wouldn't be using Terran fluorescent lighting. If they saw with long heat frequencies, they wouldn't waste power with even a tungsten filament light, but would have invented something that cooked with most of its energy in the visible spectrum, just as we have in the last couple of hundred years."

"That's just a guess, of course."

"Naturally," said Barney. "Here, I've got the door cracked. Let's be the first people in this place for six thousand years Terran. Take it easy, this floor is at an angle of thirty degrees."

"I won't slide. G'wan in. I'm your shadow."

They entered the thirty-foot circular room and snapped on their torches. There was a bench that ran almost around the entire room. It was empty save for a few scraps of metal and a Martian book of several hundred metal pages.

"Nuts," said Jim, "we would have to find a thing like this but empty. That's our luck. What's the book, Barney?"

"Some sort of text, I'd say. Full of diagrams and what seems to be mathematics. Hard to tell, of course, but we've established the fact that mathematics is universal, though the characters cannot possibly be."

"Any chance of deciphering it?" asked Jim.

"Let's get back in the flier and try. I'm in no particular hurry."

"Nor am I. I don't care whether we get to Lincoln Head tonight or the middle of next week."

"Now let's see that volume of diagrams," Barney said as soon as they were established in the flier.

Jim passed the book over, and Barney opened the book to the first page. "If we never find anything else," he said, "this will make us famous. I am now holding the first complete volume of Martian literature that anyone has ever seen. The damned thing is absolutely complete, from cover to cover!"

"That's a find," Jim agreed. "Now go ahead and transliterate it—you're the expert on Martian pictographs."

For an hour, Barney scanned the pages of the volume. He made copious notes on sheets of paper which he inserted between the metal leaves of the book. At the end of that time, during which Jim Baler had been inspecting the searchlight thing on top of the little house, Barney called to his friend, and Jim entered the flier lugging the thing on his shoulders.

"What'cha got?" he grinned. "I brought this along. Nothing else in that shack, so we're complete except for the remnants of some very badly corroded cable that ran from this thing to the flapping end down where the tower was broken."

Barney smiled and blinked.

It was strange to see this big man working studiously over a book; Barney Carroll should have been leading a horde of Venusian engineers through the Palanortis Country instead of delving into the artifacts of a dead civilization.

"I think that this thing is a sort of engineer's handbook," he said. "In the front there is a section devoted to mathematical tables. You know, a table of logs to the base twelve, which is because the Martians had six fingers on each hand. There is what seems to be a table of definite integrals—at least, if I were writing a handbook I'd place the table of integrals at the last part of the math section. The geometry and trig is absolutely recognizable because of the designs. So is the solid geom and the analyt for the same reason. The next section seems to be devoted to chemistry; the Martians used a hexagonal figure for a benzene ring, too, and so that's established. From that we find the key to the Periodic Chart of the Atoms, which is run vertically instead of horizontally, but still unique. These guys were sharp, though; they seem to have hit upon the fact that isotopes are separate elements, though so close in grouping to one another that they exhibit the same properties. Finding this will uncover a lot of mystery."

"Yeah," agreed Baler, "from a book of this kind we can decipher most anything. The keying on a volume of physical constants is perfect and almost infinite in number. What do they use for Pi?"

"Circle with a double dot inside."

"And Planck's Constant?"

"Haven't hit that one yet. But we will. But to get back to the meat of this thing, the third section deals with something strange. It seems to have a bearing on this gadget from the top of the tower. I'd say that the volume was a technical volume on the construction, maintenance, and repair of the tower and its functions—whatever they are."

Barney spread the volume out for Jim to see. "That dingbat is some sort of electronic device. Or, perhaps subelectronic. Peel away that rusted side and we'll look inside."

Jim peeled a six-inch section from the side of the big metal tube, and they inspected the insides. Barney looked thoughtful for a minute and then flipped the pages of the book until he came to a diagram.

"Sure," he said exultantly, "this is she. Look, Jim, they draw a cathode like this, and the grids are made with a series of fine parallel lines. Different, but more like the real grid than our symbol of a zigzag line. The plate is a round circle instead of a square, but that's so clearly defined that it comes out automatically. Here's your annular electrodes, and the—call 'em deflection plates. I think we can hook this do-boodle up as soon as we get to our place in Lincoln Head."

"Let's go, then. Not only would I like to see this thing work, but I'd give anything to know what it's for!"

"You run the crate," said Barney, "and I'll try to decipher this mess into voltages for the electrode-supply and so on. Then we'll be in shape to go ahead and hook her up."

The trip to Lincoln Head took almost an hour. Barney and Jim landed in their landing yards and took the book and the searchlight thing inside. They went to their laboratory, and called for sandwiches and tea. Jim's sister brought in the food a little later and found them tinkering with the big beam tube.

"What have you got this time?" she groaned.

"Name it and it's yours," Barney laughed.

"A sort of gadget that we found on the Red Desert."

"What does it do?" asked Christine Baler.

"Well," said Jim, "it's a sort of a kind of dingbat that does things."

"Uh-huh," said Christine. "A do-lolly that plings the inghams."

"Right!"

"You're well met, you two. Have your fun. But for Pete's sake, don't forget to eat. Not that you will—I know you—but a girl has got to make some sort of attempt at admonishment. I'm going to the moom pitcher. I'll see you when I return."

"I'd say stick around," said Barney. "But I don't think we'll have anything to show you for hours and hours. We'll have something by the time you return."

Christine left, and the men applied themselves to their problem. Barney had done wonders in unraveling the unknown. Inductances, he found, were spirals; resistances were dotted lines; capacitances were parallel squares.

"What kind of stuff do we use for voltages?" asked Jim.

"That's a long, hard trail," laughed Barney. "Basing my calculations on the fact that their standard voltage cell was the same as ours, we apply the voltage as listed on my schematic here."

"Can you assume that their standard is the same as ours?"

"Better," said Barney. "The Terran standard cell—the well-known Weston Cell—dishes out what we call 1.0183 volts at twenty degrees C. Since the Martian description of their standard cell is essentially the same as the Terran, they are using the same thing. Only they use sense and say that a volt is the unit of a standard cell, period. Calculating their figures on the numerical base of twelve is tricky, but I've done it."

"You're doing fine. How do you assume their standard is the same?"

"Simple," said Barney in a cheerful tone. "Thank God for their habit of drawing pictures. Here we have the well-known H tube. The electrodes are signified by the symbols for the elements used. Their Periodic Chart came in handy here. But look, mastermind, this dinky should be evacuated don't you think?"

"If it's electronic or subelectronic, it should be. We can solder up this breach here and apply the hyvac pump. Rig us up a power supply whilst I repair the blowout."

"Where's the BFO?"

"What do you want with that?" asked Jim.

"The second anode takes about two hundred volts worth of eighty-four cycles," Barney explained. "Has a sign that seems to signify 'In Phase,' but I'll be darned if I know with what. Y'know, Jim, this dingbat looks an awful lot like one of the drivers we use in our spaceships and driver-wing fliers."

"Yeah," drawled Jim. "About the same recognition as the difference between Edison's first electric light and a twelve-element, electron-multiplier, power-output tube. Similarly: they both have cathodes."

"Edison didn't have a cathode—"

"Sure he did. Just because he didn't hang a plate inside of the bottle doesn't stop the filament from being a cathode."

Barney snorted. "A monode, hey?"

"Precisely. After which come diodes, triodes, tetrodes, pentodes, hexodes, heptodes—"

"—and the men in the white coats. How's your patching job?"

"Fine. How's your power-supply job?"

"Good enough," said Barney. "This eighty-four cycles is not going to be a sine wave at two hundred volts; the power stage of the BFO overloads just enough to bring in a bit of second harmonic."

"A beat-frequency oscillator was never made to run at that level," complained Jim Baler. "At least, not this one. She'll tick on a bit of second, I think."

"Are we ready for the great experiment?"

"Yep, and I still wish I knew what the thing was for. Go ahead, Barney. Crack the big switch!"

Altas held up a restraining hand as Than grasped the main power switch. "Wait," he said. "Does one stand in his sky flier and leave the ground at full velocity? Or does one start an internal combustion engine at full speed?"

"No," said the youngster. "We usually take it slowly."

"And like the others, we must tune our tube. And that we cannot do under full power. Advance your power lever one-tenth step and we'll adjust the deflection anodes."

"I'll get the equipment," said Than. "I forgot that part."

"Never mind the equipment," smiled Altas. "Observe."

Altas picked up a long screwdriver-like tool and inserted it into the maze of wiring that surrounded the tube. Squinting in one end of the big tube, he turned the tool until the cathode surface brightened slightly. He adjusted the instrument until the cathode was at its brightest, and then withdrew the tool.

"That will do for your experimental setup." Altas smiled. "The operation in service is far more critical and requires equipment. As an experiment, conducted singly, the accumulative effect cannot be dangerous, though if the deflection plates are not properly served with their supply voltages, the experiment is a failure. The operation of the tube depends upon the perfection of the deflection-plate voltages."

"No equipment is required, then?"

"It should have been employed," said Altas modestly. "But in my years as a beam-tower attendant, I have learned the art of aligning the plates by eye. Now, Son, we may proceed from there."

Barney Carroll took a deep breath and let the power switch fall home. Current meters swung across their scales for an instant, and then the lights went out in the house!

"Fuse blew," said Barney shortly. He grumbled his way through the dark house and replaced the fuse. He returned smiling. "Fixed that one," he told Jim. "Put a washer behind it."

"O.K. Hit the switch again."

Barney cranked the power over, and once more the meters climbed up across the scales. There was a groaning sound from the tube, and the smell of burning insulation filled the room. One meter blew with an audible sound as the needle hit the end stop, and immediately afterward the lights in the entire block went out.

"Fix that one by hanging a penny behind it," said Jim with a grin.

"That's a job for Martian Electric to do," laughed Barney.

Several blocks from there, an attendant in the substation found the open circuit-breaker and shoved it in with a grim smile. He looked up at the power-demand meter and grunted. High for this district, but not dangerous. Duration, approximately fifteen seconds. Intensity, higher than usual but not high enough to diagnose any failure of the wiring in the district. "Ah, well," he thought, "we can crank up the blow point on this breaker if it happens again."

He turned to leave and the crashing of the breaker scared him out of a week's growth. He snarled and said a few choice words not fit for publication. He closed the breaker and screwed the blow-point control up by two to one. "That'll hold 'em," he thought, and then the ringing of the telephone called him to his office, and he knew that he was in for an explanatory session with some people who wanted to know why their lights were going on and off. He composed a plausible tale on his way to the phone. Meanwhile, he wondered about the unreasonable demand and concluded that one of the folks had just purchased a new power saw or something for their home workshop.

"Crack the juice about a half," suggested Barney. "That'll keep us on the air until we find out what kind of stuff this thing takes. The book claims about one-tenth of the current drain for this unit. Something we've missed, no doubt."

"Let's see that circuit," said Jim. After a minute, he asked: "Look, guy, what are these screws for?"

"They change the side plate voltages from about three hundred to about three hundred and fifty. I've got 'em set in the middle of the range."

"Turn us on half voltage and diddle one of 'em."

"That much of a change shouldn't make the difference," Barney objected.

"Brother, we don't know what this thing is even for," Jim reminded him. "Much less do we know the effect of anything on it. Diddle, I say."

"O.K., we diddle." Barney turned on half-power and reached into the maze of wiring and began to tinker with one of the screws. "Hm-m-m," he said after a minute. "Does things, all right. She goes through some kind of reasonance point or something. There is a spot of minimum current here. There! I've hit it. Now for the other one."

For an hour, Barney tinkered with first one screw and then the other one. He found a point where the minimum current was really low; the two screws were interdependent and only by adjusting them alternately was he able to reach the proper point on each. Then he smiled and thrust the power on full. The current remained at a sane value.

"Now what?" asked Barney.

"I don't know. Anything coming out of the business end?"

"Heat."

"Yeah, and it's about as lethal as a sun lamp. D'ye suppose the Martians used to artificially assist their crops by synthetic sunshine?"

Barney applied his eye to a spectroscope. It was one of the newer designs that encompassed everything from short ultraviolet to long infrared by means of fluorescent screens at the invisible wavelengths. He turned the instrument across the spectrum and shook his head.

"Might be good for a chest cold," he said, "but you wouldn't get a sunburn off of it. It's all in the infra. Drops off like a cliff just below the deep red. Nothing at all in the visible or above. Gee," he said with a queer smile, "you don't suppose that they died off because of a pernicious epidemic of colds and they tried chest-cooking *en masse*?"

"I'd believe anything if this darned gadget were found in a populated district," said Jim. "But we know that the desert was here when the Martians were here, and that it was just as arid as it is now. They wouldn't try farming in a place where iron oxide abounds."

"Spinach?"

"You don't know a lot about farming, do you?" asked Jim.

"I saw a cow once."

"That does not qualify you as an expert on farming."

"I know one about the farmer's daughter, and—"

"Not even an expert on dirt farming," continued Jim. "Nope, Barney, we aren't even close."

Barney checked the book once more and scratched his nose.

"How about that eighty-four cycle supply," asked Jim.

"It's eighty-four, all right. From the Martian habit of using twelve as a base, I've calculated the number to be eighty-four."

"Diddle that, too," suggested Jim.

"O.K.," said Barney. "It doesn't take a lot to crank that one around from zero to about fifteen thousand c.p.s. Here she goes!"

Barney took the main dial of the beat-frequency oscillator and began to crank it around the scale. He went up from eighty-four to the top of the dial and then returned. No effect. Then he passed through eighty-four and started down toward zero.

He hit sixty cycles and the jackpot at the same time!

At exactly sixty cycles, a light near the wall dimmed visibly. The wallpaper scorched and burst into a smoldering flame on a wall opposite the dimmed light.

Barney removed the BFO from the vicinity of sixty cycles and Jim extinguished the burning wallpaper.

"Now we're getting somewhere," said Barney.

"This is definitely some sort of weapon. She's not very efficient right now, but we can find out why and then we'll have something hot."

"What for?" Barney asked. "Nobody hates anybody anymore."

"Unless the birds who made this thing necessary return," said Jim soberly. His voice was ominous. "We know that only one race of Martians existed, and they were all amicable. I suspect an inimical race from outer space—"

"Could be. Some of the boys are talking about an expedition to Centauri right now. We could have had a visitor from somewhere during the past."

"If you define eternity as the time required for everything to happen once, I agree. In the past or in the future, we have or will be visited by a super race. It may have happened six thousand years ago."

"Did you notice that the electric light is not quite in line with the axis of the tube?" asked Barney.

"Don't turn it any closer," said Jim. "In fact, I'd turn it away before we hook it up again."

"There she is. Completely out of line with the light. Now shall we try it again?"

"Go ahead."

Barney turned the BFO gingerly, and at sixty cycles the thing seemed quite sane. Nothing happened. "Shall I swing it around?"

"I don't care for fires as a general rule," said Jim. "Especially in my own home. Turn it gently, and take care that you don't focus the tube full on that electric light."

Barney moved the tube slightly, and then with a cessation of noise, the clock on the wall stopped abruptly. The accustomed ticking had not been noticed by either man, but the unaccustomed lack-of-ticking became evident at once. Barney shut off the BFO immediately and the two men sat down to a head-scratching session.

"She's good for burning wallpaper, dimming electric lights, and stopping clocks," said Barney. "Any of which you could do without a warehouse full of cockeyed electrical equipment. Wonder if she'd stop anything more powerful than a clock."

"I've got a quarter-horse motor here. Let's wind that up and try it."

The motor was installed on a bench nearby, and the experiment was tried again. At sixty cycles the motor groaned to a stop, and the windings began to smolder. But at the same time the big tube began to exhibit the signs of strain. Meters raced up their scales once more, reached the stops and bent. Barney shut off the motor, but the strains did not stop in the tube. The apparent overload increased linearly and finally the lights went out all over the neighborhood once more.

"Wonderful," said Barney through the darkness. "As a weapon, this thing is surpassed by everything above a fly swatter."

"We might be able to cook a steak with it—if it would take the terrific overload," said Jim. "Or we could use it as an insect exterminator."

"We'd do better by putting the insect on an anvil and hitting it firmly with a five-pound hammer," said Barney. "Then we'd only have the anvil and hammer to haul around. This thing is like hauling a fifty-thousand-watt radio transmitter around. Power supplies, BFO, tube, meters, tools, and a huge truck full of spare fuses for the times when we miss the insect. Might be good for a central heating system."

"Except that a standard electric unit is more reliable and considerably less complicated. You'd have to hire a corps of engineers to run the thing."

The lights went on again, and the attendant in the substation screwed the blow-point control tighter. He didn't know it, but his level was now above the rating for his station. But had he known it he might not have cared. At least, his station was once more in operation.

"Well," said Barney, getting up from the table, "what have we missed?"

Altas said: "Now your unit is operating at its correct level. But, Son, you've missed one thing. It is far from efficient. Those two leads must be isolated from one another. Coupling from one to the other will lead to losses."

"Gosh," said Than, "I didn't know that."

"No, for some reason the books assume that the tower engineer has had considerable experience in the art. Take it from me, Son, there are a lot of things that are not in the books. Now isolate those leads from one another and we'll go on."

"While you're thinking," said Jim, "I'm going to lockstitch these cables together. It'll make this thing less messy."

Jim got a roll of twelve-cord from the cabinet and began to bind the many supply leads into a neat cable.

Barney watched until the job was finished, and then said: "Look, chum, let's try that electric-light trick again."

They swung the tube around until it was in the original position, and turned the juice on. Nothing happened.

Barney looked at Jim, and then reached out and pointed the big tube right at the electric light.

Nothing happened.

"Check your anode voltages again."

"All O.K."

"How about the aligning job?"

Barney fiddled with the alignment screws for minutes, but his original setting seemed to be valid.

"Back to normal," said Barney. "Rip out your cabling."

"Huh?"

"Sure. You did something. I don't know what. But

rip it out and fan out the leads. There is something screwy in the supply lines. I've been tied up on that one before; this thing looks like electronics, as we agree, and I've had occasion to remember coupling troubles."

"All right," said Jim, and he reluctantly ripped out his lockstitching. He fanned the leads and they tried it again.

Obediently, the light dimmed and the wallpaper burned.

"Here we go again," said Jim, killing the circuits and reaching for a small rug to smother the fire. "No wonder the Martians had this thing out in the middle of the desert. D'ye suppose that *they* were trying to find out how it works, too?"

"Take it easier this time and we'll fan the various leads," said Barney. "There's something tricky about the lead placement."

"Half-power," announced Barney. "Now, let's get that sixty cycles."

The light dimmed slightly and a sheet of metal placed in front of the tube became slightly warm to the touch. The plate stopped the output of the tube, for the wallpaper did not scorch. Jim began to take supply line after supply line from the bundle of wiring. About halfway through the mess, he hit the critical lead, and immediately the light went out completely and the plate grew quite hot.

"Stop her!" yelled Barney.

"Why?"

"How do we know what we're overloading this time?"

"Do we care?"

"Sure. Let's point this thing away from that light. Then we can hop it up again and try it at full power."

"What do you want to try?"

"This energy-absorption thing."

"Wanna burn out my motor?" Jim asked.

"Not completely. This dingbat will stop a completely mechanical gadget, like a clock. It seems to draw power from electric lights. It stops electromechanical power. I wonder just how far it will go toward absorbing power. And also I want to know where the power goes."

The tube was made to stop the clock again. The motor groaned under the load put upon it by the tube. Apparently the action of the tube was similar to a heavy load being placed on whatever its end happened to point to. Barney picked up a small metal block and dropped it over the table.

"Want to see if it absorbs the energy of a falling object— Look at that!"

The block fell until it came inside of the influence of the tube. Then it slowed in its fall and approached the table slowly. It did not hit the table, it touched and came to rest.

"What happens if we wind up a spring and tie it?" asked Jim.

They tried it. Nothing happened.

"Works on kinetic energy, not potential energy," said Barney.

He picked up a heavy hammer and tried to hit the table. "Like swinging a club through a tub of water," he said.

"Be a useful gadget for saving the lives of people who are falling," said Jim thoughtfully.

"Oh, sure. Put it on a truck and rush it out to the scene of the suicide."

"No. How about people jumping out of windows on account of fires? How about having one of the things around during a flier-training course? Think of letting a safe down on one of those beams, or taking a piano from the fifth floor of an apartment building."

"The whole apartment full of furniture could be pitched out of a window," said Barney.

"Mine looks that way now," said Jim, "and we've only moved a couple of times. No, Barney, don't give 'em any ideas."

Jim picked up the hammer and tried to hit the table. Then, idly, he swung the hammer in the direction of the tube's end.

Barney gasped. In this direction there was no resistance. Jim's swing continued, and the look on Jim's face indicated that he was trying to brake the swing in time to keep from hitting the end of the tube. But it seemed as though he were trying to stop an avalanche. The swing continued on and on and finally ended when the hammer head contacted the end of the tube.

There was a burst of fire. Jim swung right on through, whirling around off-balance and coming to a stop only when he fell to the floor. He landed in darkness again. The burst of fire emanated from the insulation as it flamed under the heat of extreme overload.

This time the lights were out all over Lincoln Head. The whole city was in complete blackout!

Candles were found, and they inspected the tube anxiously. It seemed whole. But the hammer head was missing. The handle was cut cleanly, on an optically perfect surface.

Where the hammer head went, they couldn't say. But on the opposite wall there was a fracture in the plaster that Jim swore hadn't been there before. It extended over quite an area, and after some thought, Barney calculated that if the force of Jim's hammer blow had been evenly distributed over that area on the wall, the fracturing would have been just about that bad.

"A weapon, all right," said Barney.

"Sure. All you have to do is to shoot your gun right in this end and the force is dissipated over quite an area out of that end. In the meantime you blow out all of the powerhouses on the planet. If a hammer blow can raise such merry hell, what do you think the output of a sixteen-inch rifle would do? Probably stop the planet in its tracks. D'ye know what I think?"

"No, do you?"

"Barney, I think that we aren't even close as to the operation and use of this device."

"For that decision, Jim, you should be awarded the Interplanetary Award for Discovery and Invention—posthumously!"

"So what do we do now?"

"Dunno. How soon does this lighting situation get itself fixed?"

"You ask me . . . I don't know either."

"Well, let's see what we've found so far."

"That's easy," said Jim. "It might be a weapon, but it don't weap. We might use it for letting elevators down easy, except that it would be a shame to tie up a room full of equipment when the three-phase electric motor is so simple. We could toast a bit of bread, but the electric toaster has been refined to a beautiful piece of breakfast furniture that doesn't spray off and scorch the wallpaper. We could use it to transmit hammer blows, or to turn out electric lights, but both of those things have been done very simply; one by means of sending the hammerer to the spot, and the other by means of turning the switch. And then in the last couple of cases, there is little sense in turning out a light by short-circuiting the socket and blowing all the fuses."

"That is the hard way," smiled Barney. "Like hitting a telephone pole to stop the car, or cutting the wings off a plane to return it to the ground."

"So we have a fairly lucid book that describes the entire hookup of the thing except what it's for. It gives not only the use of this device, but also variations and replacements. Could we figure it out by sheer deduction?"

"I don't see how. The tower is in the midst of the Red Desert. There is nothing but sand that assays high in iron oxide between Canalopsis, at the junction of the Grand Canal, and Lincoln Head. Might be hid, of course, just as this one was, and we'll send out a crew of expert sub-sand explorers with under-surface detectors to cover the ground for a few hundred miles in any direction from the place where we found this. Somehow, I doubt that we'll find much."

"And how do you—ah, there's the lights again—deduce that?" asked Jim.

"This gadget is or was of importance to the Martians. Yet in the Temple of Science and Industry at Canalopsis, there is scant mention of the towers."

"Not very much, hey?"

"Very little, in fact. Of course the pictographs on the temple at Canalopsis show one tower between what appear two cities. Wavy lines run from one city to the tower and to the other city. Say! I'll bet a cooky that this is some sort of signaling device!"

"A beam transmitter?" asked Jim skeptically. "Seems like a lot of junk for just signaling. Especially when such a swell job can be done with standard radio equipment. A good civilization—such as the Martians must have had—wouldn't piddle around with relay stations between two cities less than a couple of thousand miles apart. With all the juice this thing can suck, they'd be more than able to hang a straight broadcast station and cover halfway around the planet as ground-wave area. What price relay station?"

"Nevertheless, I'm going to tinker up another one of these and see if it is some sort of signaling equipment."

The door opened and Christine Baler entered. She waved a newspaper before her brother's eyes and said, "Boy, have you been missing it!"

"What?" Barney asked.

"Pixies or gremlins loose in Lincoln Head."

"Huh-huh. Read it," said Jim.

"Just a bunch of flash headlines. Fire on Manley Avenue. Three planes had to make dead-tube landings in the center of the city; power went dead for no good reason for about ten minutes. Façade of the City Hall caved in. Power plants running wild all over the place. Ten thousand dollars' worth of electrical equipment blown out. Automobiles stalled in rows for blocks."

Jim looked at Barney. "Got a bear by the tail," he said.

"Could be," admitted Barney.

"Are you two blithering geniuses going to work all night?" asked Christine.

"Nope. We're about out of ideas. Except the one that Barney had about the gadget being some sort of signaling system."

"Why don't you fellows call Don Channing? He's the signaling wizard of the Solar System."

"Sure, call Channing. Every time someone gets an idea, everyone says, 'Call Channing!' He gets called for everything from Boy Scout wigwag ideas to supercyclotronic-electron-stream beams to contact the outer planets. Based upon the supposition that people will eventually get there, of course."

"Well?"

"Well, I—we, I mean—found this thing and we're jolly well going to tinker it out. In spite of the fact that it seems to bollix up everything from electric lights to moving gears. I think we're guilty of sabotage. Façade of the City Hall, et cetera. Barney, how long do you think it will take to tinker up another one of these?"

"Few hours. They're damned simple things in spite of the fact that we can't understand them. In fact, I'm of the opinion that the real idea would be to make two: one with only the front end for reception, one for the rear end for transmission, and the one we found for relaying. That's the natural bent, I believe."

"Could be. Where are you going to cut them?"

"The transmitter will start just before the cathode, and the receiver will end just after the . . . uh, cathode."

"Huh?"

"Obviously the cathode is the baby that makes with the end product. She seems to be a total intake from the intake end and a complete output from the opposite end. Right?"

"Right, but it certainly sounds like heresy."

"I know," said Barney thoughtfully, "but the thing is obviously different from anything that we know today. Who knows how she works?"

"I give up."

Christine, who had been listening in an interested manner, said: "You fellers are the guys responsible for the ruckus that's been going on all over Lincoln Head?"

"I'm afraid so."

"Well, brother warlocks, unless you keep your activities under cover until they're worth mentioning, you'll both be due for burning at the stake."

"O.K., Chris," said Jim. "We'll not let it out."

"But how are you going to tinker up that transmitter-relay-receiver system?"

"We'll take it from here to Barney's place across the avenue and into his garage. That should do it."

"O.K., but now I'm going to bed."

"Shall we knock off, too?" asked Jim.

"Yep. Maybe we'll dream a good thought."

"So long, then. We'll leave the mess as it is. No use cleaning up now, we'll only have to mess it up again tomorrow with the same junk."

"And I'll have that—or those—other systems tinkered together by tomorrow noon. That's a promise," said Barney. "And you," he said to Christine, "will operate the relay station."

Altas said to Than: "Now that your system is balanced properly, and we have proved the worth of this tube as a replacement, we shall take it to the roof and install it. The present tube is about due for retirement."

"I've done well, then?" asked Than.

"Considering all, you've done admirably. But balancing the device in the tower, and hooking into the circuit as an integral part is another thing. Come, Than. We shall close the line for an hour whilst replacing the tube."

"Is that permissible?"

"At this time of the night the requirements are small. No damage will be done; they can get along without us for an hour. In fact, at this time of night, only the people who are running the city will know that we are out of service. And it is necessary that the tube be maintained at full capability. We can not chance a weakened tube; it might fail when it is needed the most."

Than carried the tube to the top of the tower, and Altas remained to contact the necessary parties concerning the shutoff for replacement purposes. He followed Than to the top, after a time, and said: "Now disconnect the old tube and put it on the floor. We shall replace the tube immediately, but it will be an hour before it is properly balanced again."

It was not long before Than had the tube connected properly.

"Now," said Altas, "turn it on one-tenth power and we shall align it."

"Shall I use the meters?"

"I think it best. This requires perfect alignment. We've much power and considerable distance, and any losses will create great amounts of heat."

"All right," said Than.

He left the tower top to get the meters.

Barney Carroll spoke into a conveniently placed microphone. "Are you ready?" he asked.

"Go ahead," said Christine.

"We're waiting," said Jim.

"You're the bird on the transmitter," said Barney to Jim. "*You* make with the juice."

Power rheostats were turned up gingerly, until Barney shouted to stop. His shout was blotted out by cries from the other two. They met in Barney's place to confer.

"What's cooking?" asked Jim.

"The meters are all going crazy in my end," said Barney. "I seem to be sucking power out of everything in line with my tube."

"The so-called relay station is firing away at full power and doing nothing but draining plenty of power from the line," complained Christine.

"And on my end, I was beginning to scorch the wallpaper again. I don't understand it. With no receiver end, how can I scorch wallpaper?"

"Ask the Martians. They know."

"You ask 'em. What shall we do, invent a time machine and go back sixty centuries?"

"Wish we could," said Barney. "I'd like to ask the bird that left this textbook why they didn't clarify it more."

"Speaking of Don Channing again," said Jim, "I'll bet a hat that one of his tube-replacement manuals for the big transmitters out on Venus Equilateral do not even mention that the transmitter requires a receiver before it is any good. We think we're modern. We are, and we never think that someday some poor bird will try to decipher our technical works. Why, if Volta himself came back and saw the most perfect machine ever invented—the transformer—he'd shudder. No connection between input and output, several kinds of shorted loops of wire; and instead of making a nice simple electromagnet, we short the lines of force and on top of that we use a lot of laminations piled on top of one another instead of a nice, soft iron core. We completely short the input, et cetera, but how do we make with a gadget like that?"

"I know. We go on expecting to advance. We forget the simple past. Remember the lines of that story: 'How does one chip the flint to make the best arrowhead?' I don't know who wrote it anymore than I know how to skin a boar, but we do get on without making arrowheads or skinning boars or trimming birchbark canoes."

"All right, but there's still this problem."

"Remember how we managed to align this thing? I

wonder if it might not take another alignment to make it work as a relay."

"Could be," said Jim. "I'll try it. Christine, you work these screws at the same time we do, and make the current come out as low as we can."

They returned to their stations and began to work on the alignment screws. Jim came out first on the receiver. Christine was second on the transmitter, while Barney fumbled for a long time with the relay tube.

Then Christine called: "Fellows, my meter readings are climbing up again. Shall I diddle?"

"Wait a minute," said Barney. "That means I'm probably taking power out of that gadget you have in there. Leave 'em alone."

He fiddled a bit more, and then Jim called: "Whoa, Nellie. Someone just lost me a milliammeter. She wound up on the far end."

"Hm-m-m," said Barney, "so we're relaying."

"Go ahead," said Jim. "I've got a ten-ampere meter on here now."

Barney adjusted his screws some more.

"Wait a minute," said Jim. "I'm going to shunt this meter up to a hundred amps."

"What?" yelled Barney.

"Must you yell?" asked Christine ruefully. "These phones are plenty uncomfortable without some loud-mouthed bird screaming."

"Sorry, but a hundred amps . . . *Whoosh!* What have we got here, anyway?"

"Yeah," said Christine. "I was about to say that my input meter is running wild again."

"Gone?"

"Completely. You shouldn't have hidden it behind that big box. I didn't notice it until just now, but she's completely gone."

"I'll be over. I think we've got something here."

An hour passed, during which nothing of any great importance happened. By keying the transmitter tube, meters in the receiver tube were made to read in accordance. Then they had another conclave.

"Nothing brilliant," said Jim. "We could use super-output voice amplifiers and yell halfway across the planet if we didn't have radio. We can radio far better than this cockeyed system of signaling."

"We might cut the power."

"Or spread out quite a bit. I still say, however, that this is no signaling system."

"It works like one."

"So can a clothesline be made to serve as a transmitter of intelligence. But its prime function is completely different."

"S'pose we have a super-clothesline here?" asked Christine.

"The way that hammer felt last night, I'm not too sure that this might not be some sort of tractor beam," said Jim.

"Tractor beams are mathematically impossible."

"Yeah, and they proved conclusively that a bird cannot fly," said Jim. "That was before they found the right kind of math. Up until Clerk Maxwell's time, radio was mathematically impossible. Then he discovered the electromagnetic equations, and we're squirting signals across the Inner System every day. And when math and fact do not agree, which changes?"

"The math. Galileo proved that. Aristotle said that a heavy stone will fall faster. Then Galileo changed the math of that by heaving a couple of boulders off the Leaning Tower. But what have we here?"

"Has anyone toyed with the transmission of power?"

"Sure," Barney answered. "A lot of science-fiction writers have their imaginary planets crisscrossed with transmitted power. Some broadcast it, some have it beamed to the consumer. When they use planes, they have the beam coupled to an object finder so as to control the direction of the beam. I prefer the broadcasting, myself. It uncomplicates the structure of the tale."

"I mean actually?"

"Oh, yes. But the losses are terrific. Useful power transmission is a minute percentage of the total output of the gadget. Absolutely impractical, especially when copper and silver are so plentiful to string along the scenery on steel towers. No good."

"But look at this cockeyed thing. Christine puts in a couple of hundred amps; I take them off my end. Believe it or not, the output meter at my end was getting a lot more soup than I was pouring in."

"And my gadget was not taking anything to speak of," said Barney.

"Supposing it was a means of transmitting power. How on Mars did they use a single tower there in the middle of the Red Desert? We know there was a Martian city at Canalopsis, and another one not many miles from Lincoln Head. Scribbled on the outer cover of this book is the legend: 'Tower Station, Red Desert,' and though the Martians didn't call this the 'Red Desert,' the terminology will suffice for nomenclature."

"Well?" asked Jim.

"You notice they did not say: 'Station No. 1,' or '3' or '7.' That means to me that there was but one."

"Holy Smoke! Fifteen hundred miles with only one station? On Mars the curvature of ground would put such a station below the electrical horizon—" Jim thought that one over for a minute and then said: "Don't tell me they bent the beam?"

"Either they did that or they heated up the sand between," said Barney cryptically. "It doesn't mind going through nonconducting walls, but a nice, fat ground—*Blooey*, or I miss my guess. That'd be like grounding a high line."

"You're saying that they did bend—*Whoosh*, again!"

"What was that alignment problem? Didn't we align the defecting anodes somehow?"

"Yeah, but you can't bend the output of a cathode ray tube externally of the deflection plates."

"But this is not electron-beam stuff," Barney objected. "This is as far ahead of cathode ray tubes as they are ahead of the Indian signal drum or the guy who used to run for twenty-four miles from Ghent to Aix."

"That one was from Athens to Sparta," explained Christine, "the Ghent-to-Aix journey was a-horseback, and some thousand-odd years after."

"Simile's still good," said Barney. "There's still a lot about this I do not understand."

"A masterpiece of understatement, if I ever heard one," laughed Jim. "Well, let's work on it from that angle. Come on, gang, to horse!"

"Now," said Altas, "you will find that the best possible efficiency is obtained when the currents in these two resistances are equal and opposite in direction. That floats the whole tube on the system, and makes it possible to run the tube without any external power source. It requires a starter source for aligning and for standby service, and for the initial surge; then it is self-sustaining. Also the in-phase voltage cannot be better obtained than by exciting the phasing anode with some of the main-line power. That must always be correctly phased. We now need the frequency generator no longer, and by increasing the power rheostat to full, the tube will take up the load. Watch the meters, and when they read full power you may throw the cutover switch and make the tube self-sustaining. Our tower will then be in perfect service, and you and I may return to our home below."

Than performed the operations, and then they left, taking the old tube with them.

And on Terra, Sargon of Akkad watched ten thousand slaves carry stone for one of his public buildings. He did not know that on one of the stars placed in the black bowl of the evening sky for his personal benefit, men were flinging more power through the air than the total output of all his slaves combined. Had he been told, he would have had the teller beheaded for lying, because Sargon of Akkad couldn't possibly have understood it—

"You know, we're missing a bet," said Jim. "This in-phase business here. Why shouldn't we hang a bit of the old wall-socket juice in here?"

"That might be the trick," said Barney.

Jim made the connections, and they watched the meters read up and up and up—and from the street below them a rumbling was heard. Smoke issued from a crevasse in the pavement, and then with a roar, the street erupted and a furrow three feet wide and all the way across the street from Jim Baler's residence to Barney Carroll's garage lifted out of the ground. It blew straight up and fell back, and from the bottom of the furrow the smoldering of burned and tortured wiring cast a foul smell.

"*Wham!*" said Barney, looking at the smoking trench. "What was that?"

"I think we'll find that it was the closest connection between our places made by the Electric Co.," said Jim.

"But what have we done?"

"I enumerate," said Christine, counting off on her fingers. "We've blasted in the façade of the City Hall. We've caused a couple of emergency flier landings within the city limits. We've blown fuses and circuit-breakers all the way from here to the main powerhouse downtown. We've stalled a few dozen automobiles. We've torn or burned or cut the end off one hammer and have fractured the wall with it— Where did that go, anyway, the hammerhead? We've burned wallpaper. We've run our electric bill up to about three hundred dollars, I'll bet. We've bunged up a dozen meters. And now we've ripped up a trench in the middle of the street."

"Somewhere in this setup, there is a return circuit," said Jim thoughtfully. "We've been taking power out of the line, and I've been oblivious of the fact that a couple of hundred amperes is too high to get out of our power line without trouble. What we've been doing is taking enough soup out of the public utility lines to supply the losses only. The power we've been seeing on our meters is the buildup, recirculated!"

"Huh?"

"Sure. Say we bring an amp in from the outside and shoot it across the street. It goes to the wires and comes back because of some electrical urge in our gadgets here, and then goes across the street in-phase with the original. That makes two amps total crossing our beam. The two come back and we have two plus two. Four come back, and we double again and again until the capability of our device is at saturation. All we have to do is to find the ground return and hang a load in there. We find the transmitter-load input, and supply that with a generator. Brother, we can beam power all the way from here to Canalopsis on one relay tower!"

Barney looked at his friend. "Could be."

"Damned right. What other item can you think of that fits this tower any better? We've run down a dozen ideas, but this works. We may be arrested for wrecking

Lincoln Head, but we'll get out as soon as this dingbat hits the market. Brother, what a find!"

"Fellows, I think you can make your announcement now," smiled Christine. "They won't burn you at the stake if you can bring electric power on a beam of pure nothing. This time you've hit the jackpot!"

It is approximately forty-five hundred Terran years since Sargon of Akkad held court, lighted by torch. It is the same number of years, Terran, since Than and Altas replaced the link in a power system that tied their cities together.

It is about the same number of years since the beam tower fell into the Red Desert and the mighty system of beamed power became lost as an art. But once again the towers dot the plains, not only of Mars, but of Venus and Terra, too.

And though they are of a language understood by the peoples of three worlds, the manuals of instruction would be as cryptic to Than as his manual was to Barney Carroll and Jim Baler.

People will never learn.

Interlude

Don Channing's initial problem was to develop ship-to-planet communication, if not ship-to-ship. And since, as a general rule, anything that could be used to transmit power could also be used to transmit information, Channing went to Mars to seek out Messrs. Baler and Carroll.

Strangely enough, the problem of communicating from planet to ship was not solved—nor would it be complete until some means of returning messages was devised, for the cams that kept the beams pointed to the place where the invisible spacecraft was supposed to be had no way of knowing when the ship might swerve to miss a meteor. Many were the messages that went into space—undelivered

—because a ship dodged a meteor that might have been dangerous. Postulating the rather low possibility of danger made little difference: misdirected messages were of less importance than even the remote danger of death in the skies.

But Don Channing's luck was running low. On arrival at Lincoln Head, he discovered that Baler and Carroll had packed up their tube and left for Terra. Keg Johnson knew about it; he informed Channing that the foremost manufacturer of electrical apparatus had offered a lucrative bid for the thing as it stood and that Big Jim Baler had grinned, saying that the money which the Terran Electric Company was tossing around would permit the two of them, Carroll and himself, to spend the rest of their lives digging around the artifacts of Mars in style.

So Channing sent word to Venus Equilateral and told them to get in touch with either the Baler-Carroll combine or Terran Electric and make dicker.

Then he started to make the journey back to Venus Equilateral on the regular spacelanes . . .

OFF THE BEAM

Thirty hours out of Mars for Terra, the *Ariadne* sped along her silent, invisible course. No longer was she completely severed from all connection with the planets of the inner system; the trick cams that controlled the beams at Venus Equilateral kept the ship centered by sheer mathematics in spite of her thirty hours at two G, which brought her velocity to eleven hundred miles per second.

What made this trip ironic was the fact that Don Channing was aboard. The beams had been bombarding the *Ariadne* continually ever since she left Mars with messages for the Director of Communications. In one sense, it seemed funny that Channing was for once on the end of a communications line where people could talk to him but from which he could not talk back. On the other hand, it was a blessing in disguise, for the Director was beginning to papertalk himself into some means of contacting Venus Equilateral from a spaceship.

A steward found Channing in the salon and handed him a 'gram. Channing smiled, and the steward returned the smile, adding: "You'll fix these ships to talk back one day. Wait till you read that one—you'll burn from here to Terra!"

"Reading my mail?" asked Channing cheerfully.

The average spacegram was about as secret as a postcard, so Channing didn't mind. He turned the page over and read:

> HOPE YOU'RE WELL FILLED WITH GRAVANOL AND ADHESIVE TAPE FOR YOUR JUMP FROM TERRA TO STATION. SHALL TAKE GREAT DELIGHT IN RIPPING ADHESIVE TAPE OFF YOUR MEASLY BODY.
>
> LOVE,
>
> ARDEN.

"She will, too," Don grinned. "Well, I'd like to toss her one back, but she's got me there. I'll just fortify myself at the bar and think up a few choice ones for when we hit Mojave."

"Some day you'll be able to answer those," the steward promised. "Mind telling me why it's so tough?"

"Not at all," smiled Channing. "The problem is about the same as encountered by the old-time cowboy. It's a lot easier to hit a man on a moving horse from a nice, solid rock than it is to hit a man on a nice, solid rock from a moving horse. Venus Equilateral is quite solid as things go. But a spaceship's course is fierce. We're wobbling a few milliseconds here and a few there, and by the time you use that arc to swing a line of a hundred million miles, you're squirting quite a bit of sky. We're tinkering with it right now, but so far we have come up with nothing. Ah, well, the human race got along without electric lights for a few million years, so we can afford to tinker with an idea for a few months. Nobody is losing lives or sleep because we can't talk with the boys back home."

"We've been hopping from planet to planet for quite a number of years, too," said the steward. "Quite a lot of them went by before it was even possible to contact a ship in space."

"And that was done because of an emergency. Probably this other thing will go on until we hit an emergency; then we shall prove that old statement about a loaf of bread being the maternal parent of a locomotive." Channing lit a cigarette and puffed deeply. "Where do we stand?"

"Thirty hours out," answered the steward. "About ready for turnover. I imagine that the power engineer's gang is changing cathodes about now."

"It's a long drag," said Channing. He addressed himself to his glass and began to think of a suitable answer for his wife's latest thrust.

Bill Hadley, of the power engineer's gang, spoke to the pilot's greenhouse below the ship. "Hadley to the pilot room; cathodes 1 and 3 ready."

"Pilot Greenland to Engineer Hadley: Power fade-over from even to odd now under way. Tubes 2 and 4 now dead; load on 1 and 3. You may enter 2 and 4."

"Check!"

Hadley cracked an air valve beside a circular air door. The hiss of entering air crescendoed and died, and then Hadley cracked the door that opened in upon the huge driver tube. With casual disregard for the annular electrodes that would fill the tube with sudden death if the pilot sent the driving power surging into them, Hadley climbed to the top of the tube and used a spanner to remove four huge bolts. A handy differential pulley permitted him to lower the near-exhausted cathode from the girders to the air door, where it was hauled to the deck. A fresh cathode was slung to the pulley and hoisted to place. Hadley bolted it tight and clambered back into the ship. He closed the air door and the valve, and then opened the valve that led from the tube to outer space. The tube evacuated and Hadley spoke once more to the pilot room.

"Hadley to Greenland: Tube 4 ready."

"Check."

The operation was repeated on tube 2, and then Pilot

Greenland said: "Fadeback beginning. Power diminishing on 1 and 3, increasing on 2 and 4. Power equalized, acceleration two G as before. Deviation from norm: two-tenths G."

Hadley grinned at the crew. "You'd think Greenland did all that himself, the way he talks. If it weren't for autopilots, we'd have been all over the sky."

Tom Bennington laughed. He was an old-timer, and he said in a reminiscent tone: "I remember when we did that on manual. There were as many cases of *mal-de-void* during cathode change as during turnover. Autopilots are the nuts— Look! We're about to swing right now, and I'll bet a fiver that the folks below won't know a thing about it."

A coincidence of mammoth proportions occurred at precisely that instant. It was a probability that made the chance of drawing a royal flush look like the chances of tomorrow coming on time. It was, in fact, one of those things that they said couldn't possibly happen, which went to prove only how wrong they were. It hadn't happened yet and probably wouldn't happen again for a million million years, but it did happen once.

Turnover was about to start. A relay circuit that coupled the meteor-spotter to the autopilot froze for a bare instant, and the coincidence happened between the freezing of the relay contacts and the closing of another relay whose purpose it was to shunt the coupler circuits through another line in case of relay failure. In the conceivably short time between the failure and the device that corrected failure, the *Ariadne* hit a meteor head-on.

It is of such coincidence that great tragedies and great victories are born.

The meteor, a small one as cosmic objects go, passed in through the broad observation dome at the top of the ship. Unhampered, it zipped through the central well of the *Ariadne* and passed out through the pilot's greenhouse at the bottom of the ship. Its speed was nothing worth noting: a scant twenty miles per second almost sunward. But the eleven hundred miles per second of the *Ariadne* made the passage of the meteor through the six hundred feet of the ship's length of less duration than the fastest camera shutter.

In those microseconds, the meteor did much damage. It passed through the main pilot-room cable and scrambled those circuits which it did not break entirely. It tore the elevator system from its moorings. It entered as a small hole in the observation dome and left, taking the entire pilot's greenhouse and all of the complex paraphernalia with it.

The lines to the driver tubes were scrambled, and the ship shuddered and drove forward at 10 gravities. An inertia switch tried to function, but the resetting solenoid had become shorted across the main battery and the weight could not drop.

Air doors clanged shut, closing the central well from the rest of the ship and effectively sealing the well from the crew.

The lights in the ship flickered and died. The cable's shorted lines grew hot and fire crept along its length and threatened the continuity. The heat opened fire-quenching vents and a cloud of CO_2 emerged together with some of the liquid gas itself. The gas quenched the fire and the cold liquid cooled the cable. Fuses blew in the sorted circuits—

And the *Ariadne* continued to plunge on and on at 10 gravities: the maximum speed possible out of her driving system.

The only man who remained aware of himself aboard the *Ariadne* was the man who was filled with gravanol and covered with adhesive tape. No other person expected to be hammered down by high acceleration. Only Channing, intending to leave Terra in his own little scooter, was prepared to withstand high G. He, with his characteristic hate of doing anything slowly, was ready to make the Terra-to-Venus Equilateral passage at 5 or 6 gravities.

It might as well have caught him, too. With all of the rest unconscious, hurt, or dead, he was alone and firmly fastened to the floor of the salon under eighteen hundred pounds of his own, helpless weight.

And as the hours passed, the *Ariadne* was driving farther and farther from the imaginary spot that was the focus of the communicator beams from Venus Equilateral.

The newly replaced cathodes in the driving tubes were capable of driving the ship for about two hundred G-hours at one G, before exhaustion to the point of necessary replacement for safety purposes. The proportion is not linear, nor is it a square law, but roughly it lies in the region just above linear, so that the *Ariadne* drove on and on through space for ten hours at 10 G before the cathodes died for want of emitting surface. They died, not at once, but in irregular succession so that when the last erg of power was gone from the drivers it was zooming on a straight line tangent from its point of collision but rolling in a wild gyration through the void.

And twenty-five hundred miles per second, added to her initial velocity of eleven hundred miles per second, summed up to thirty-six hundred miles per second. She should have had about seventy-five million miles to go at minus 2 G to reach Terra in thirty hours from the halfway point, where she turned ends to go into deceleration. Instead, the *Ariadne* after ten hours of misdirected ten-G acceleration was thirty million miles on her way, or about halfway to Terra. Three hours later, driving free, the *Ariadne* was passing Terra, having missed the planet by several million miles.

Back in space, at a no-longer-existent junction between the beams from Venus Equilateral and the *Ariadne,* Arden Channing's latest message was indicating all sorts of minor punishment for her husband when she got him home.

By the time that the *Ariadne* should have been dropping out of the sky at Mojave Spaceport, the ship would be one hundred and ninety million miles beyond Terra and flirting with the imaginary line that marked the orbit of Mars.

That would be in seventeen hours.

Weightless, Channing pursued a crazy course in the salon of the spinning ship. He ached all over from the pressure, but the gravanol had kept his head clear and the adhesive tape had kept his body intact. He squirmed around in the dimness and could see the inert figures of the rest of the people who had occupied the salon at the time of the mishap. He became sick. Violence was not a part of Channing's nature—at least he confined his violence to those against whom he required defense. But he knew that many of those people who pursued aimless orbits in the midair of the salon with him would never set foot on solidness again.

He wondered how many broken bones there were among those who had lived through the ordeal. He wondered if the medical staff of one doctor and two nurses could cope with it.

Then he wondered what difference it made, if they were to go on and on? Channing had a rough idea of what had happened. He knew something about the conditions under which they had been traveling, how long, and in what direction. It staggered him, the figures he calculated in his mind. It behooved him to do something.

He bumped an inert figure and grabbed. One hand took the back of the head and came away wet and sticky. Channing retched, and then threw the inert man from him. He coasted back against a wall, and caught a handrail. Hand-over-hand, he went to the door and into the hall. Down the hall he went to the passengers' elevator shaft, and with no thought of what his action would have been on any planet, Channing opened the door and dove down the shaft for several decks. He emerged and headed for the sick ward.

He found the doctor clinging to his operating table with his knees and applying a bandage to one of his nurses' head.

"Hello, Doc," said Channing. "Help?"

"Grab Jen's feet and hold her down," the doctor snapped.

"Bad?" asked Don as he caught the flailing feet.

"Seven stitches, no fracture," said the doctor.

"How's the other one?"

"Unconscious, but unharmed. Both asleep in bed, thank God. So was I. Where were—? You're Channing; all doped up with gravanol and adhesive. Thank yourself a god for that one, too. I'm going to need both of my nurses, and we'll all need you."

"Hope I can do some good," said Don.

"You'd better. Or any good I can do will be wasted. Better start right now. Here," the doctor produced a set of keys, "these will unlock anything on the ship but the purser's safe. You'll need 'em. Now get along and do something and leave the body-mending to me. Scram!"

"Can you make out all right?"

"As best I can. But you're needed to get us help. If you can't, no man in the Solar System can. You're in the position of a man who cannot afford to help in succoring the wounded and dying. It'll be tough, but there it is. Get cutting. And for Heaven's sake, get us two things: light and a floor. I couldn't do more than slap on tape whilst floating in air. See you later, Channing, and good luck."

The nurse squirmed, groaned, and opened her eyes. "What happened?" she asked, blinking into the doctor's flashlight.

"Tell you later, Jen. Get Fern out of her coma in the ward and then we'll map out a plan. Channing, get out of here!"

Channing got, after borrowing a spare flashlight from the doctor.

He found Hadley up in the instrument room with a half-dozen of his men. They were a mass of minor and major cuts and injuries, and were working under a single incandescent lamp that had been wired to the battery direct by means of spare cable. The wire went snaking through the air in a foolish, crooked line, suspended on nothing. Hadley's gang were applying first aid to one another and cursing the lack of gravity.

"Help?" asked Channing.

"Need it or offer it?" Hadley asked with a smile.

"Offer it. You'll need it."

"You can say that again—and then pitch in. You're Channing, of Communications, aren't you? We're going to have a mad scramble on the main circuits of this tub before we can unwind it. I don't think there's an instrument working in the whole ship."

"You can't unravel the whole works, can you?"

"Won't try. About all we can do is replace the lighting system and hang the dead cathodes in again. They'll be all right to take us out of this cockeyed skew curve and probably will last long enough to keep a half-G floor under us for tinkering, for maybe forty or fifty hours. Assistant Pilot Darlange will have to learn how to run a ship by the seat of his pants—as far as I can guess there isn't even a splinter of glass left in the pilot room. So he'll have to correct this flight by feel and by using a haywire panel."

"Darlange is a school pilot," one of Hadley's men objected.

"I know, Jimmy, but I've seen him work on a bum autopilot, and he can handle haywire all right. It'll be tough without Greenland, but Greenland—" Hadley let the sentence fall; there was no need to mention the fact that Greenland was probably back there with the rest of the wreckage torn from the *Ariadne*.

Jimmy nodded, and the action shook him from his position. He floated. He grabbed at a roll of tape that was floating near him and let it go with a laugh as he realized it was too light to do him any good.

"Too bad that this gyration is not enough to make a decent gravity at the ends, at least," snorted Hadley. He hooked Jimmy by an arm and hauled the man back to a place beside him. "Now look," he said. "I can't guess how many people are still in working condition after this. Aside from our taped and doped friend here, the only ones I have are we who were snoozing in our beds when the crush came. I'll bet a cookie that the rest of the crowd are all nursing busted ribs, and worse. Lucky that full ten G died slowly as the cathodes went out; otherwise we'd all have been tossed against the ceiling with bad effects.

"Jimmy, you're a committee of one to roam the crate and make a list of everyone who is still in the running and those who can be given minor repairs to make them fit for limited work. Doc has a pretty good supply of Stader splints; inform him that these are to be used only on men who can be useful with them. The rest will have to take to plaster casts and the old-fashioned kind of fracture support.

"Pete, you get to the executive desk and tell Captain Johannson that we're on the job and about to make with repairs. As power engineer, I've control of the maintenance gang, too, and we'll collect the whole, hale, and hearty of Michaels' crew on our merry way.

"Tom, take three of your men and begin to unravel the mess with an eye toward getting us lights.

"Tony, you can do this alone since we have no weight. You get the stale cathodes from the supply hold and hang 'em back in the tubes.

"Channing, until we get a stable place, you couldn't do a thing about trying to get help, so I suggest you pitch in with Bennington, there, and help unscramble the wiring. You're a circuit man, and though power-line stuff is not your forte, you'll find that running a lighting circuit is a lot easier than neutralizing a microwave transmitter. Once we get light, you can help us haywire a control panel. Right?"

"Right," said Channing. "And as far as contacting the folks back home goes, we couldn't do a darned thing until the time comes when we should be dropping in on Mojave. They won't be looking for anything from us until we're reported missing; then I imagine that Walt Franks will have everything from a spinthariscope to a gold-foil electroscope set up. Right now I'm stumped, but we have seventeen hours before we can start hoping to be detected. Tom, where do we begin?"

Bennington smiled inwardly. To have Don Channing asking him for orders was like having Captain Johannson request the batteryman's permission to change course. "If you can find and remove the place where the shorted line is, and then splice the lighting circuit again, we'll have a big hunk of our work done. The rest of us will begin to take lines off of the pilot's circuits right here in the instrument room, so that our jury controls can be hooked in. You'll need a suit, I think, because I'll bet a hat that the shorted circuit is in the well."

For the next five hours, the instrument room became a beehive of activity. Men began coming in driblets, and were put to work as they came. The weightlessness gave quite a bit of trouble; had the instrument panels been electrically hot, it would have been downright dangerous, since it was impossible to do any kind of work without periodically coming into contact with bare connections. Tools floated around the room in profusion, and finally Hadley appointed one man to do nothing but roam the place to retrieve "dropped" tools. The soldering operations were particularly vicious, since the instinctive act of flinging excess solder from the tip of an iron made droplets of hot solder go zipping around the room to splash against something, after which the splashes would continue to float.

Men who came in seeking to give aid were handed tools and told to do this or that, and the problem of explaining how to free a frozen relay to unskilled help was terrific.

Then, at the end of five hours, Channing came floating into the instrument room. He flipped off his helmet and said to Hadley: "Make with the main switch. I think I've got it."

Throughout the ship the lights blinked on.

With the coming of light, there came hope also. Men took a figurative hitch in their belts and went to work with renewed vigor. It seemed as though everything came to a head at about this time, too. Hadley informed Darlange that his jury control was rigged and ready for action, and about the same time, the galley crew came in with slender-necked bottles of coffee and rolls.

"It was a job, making coffee," grinned the steward. "The darned stuff wanted to get out of the can and go roaming all over the place. There isn't a one of us that hasn't got a hot-coffee scar on us somewhere. Now if he"—nodding at Darlange—"can get this thing straightened out, we'll have a real dinner."

"Hear that, Al? All that stands between us and a dinner is you. Make with the ship-straightening. Then we'll all sit around and wait for Channing to think."

"Is the ship's communicator in working order?" asked Darlange.

"Sure. That went on with the lights."

Darlange called for everyone in the ship to hold himself down, and then he tied his belt to the frame in front of the haywired panel. He opened the power on drivers 1 and 2, and the ship's floor surged ever so little.

"How're you going to know?" Hadley asked.

"I've got one eye on the gyrocompass," said Darlange. "When it stops turning, we're going straight. Then all we have to do is to set our bottom end along the line of flight and pack on the decel. Might as well do it that way, since every MPS we can lose is to our advantage."

He snapped switches that added power to driver 3. Gradually the gyrocompass changed from a complex rotation progress to a simpler pattern, and eventually the simple pattern died, leaving but one freedom of rotation. "I'm sort of stumped." Darlange grinned. "We're now hopping along, but rotating on our long axis. How we stop axial rotation with drivers set parallel to that axis I'll never guess."

"Is there a lifeship in working order?" asked Hadley.

"Sure."

"Tom, turn it against the rotation and apply the drivers on that until we tell you to stop."

An hour later the ship had ceased to turn. Then Darlange jockeyed the big ship around so that the bottom was along the line of flight. Next, he set the power for a half-G, and everyone relaxed.

Ten minutes later Captain Johannson came in.

"You've done a fine job," he told Hadley. "And now I declare an hour off for dinner. Dr. MacLain has got a working medical center with the aid of a few people who understand how such things work, and the percentage of broken bones, though terrific in number, is being taken care of. The passengers were pretty restive at first, but the coming of light seemed to work wonders. This first glimmer of power is another. About nine or ten who were able to do so were having severe cases of skysickness." He smiled ruefully. "I'm not too sure that I like no-weight myself."

"Have you been in the observation dome?" Channing asked.

"Yes. It's pierced, you know."

"Did the meteor hit the telescope?"

"No, why?"

"Because I'm going to have to get a sight on Venus Equilateral before we can do anything. We'll have to beam them something, but I don't know what right now."

"Can we discuss that over a dinner?" asked the captain. "I'm starved, and I think that the rest of this gang is also."

"You're a man after my own heart," laughed Channing. "The bunch out at the station wouldn't believe me if I claimed to have done anything without drawing it up on a tablecloth."

"Now," said Channing over his coffee, "what have we in the way of electronic equipment?"

"One X-ray machine, a standard set of communicating equipment, one beam receiver with 'type machine for collecting stuff from your station, and so on."

"You wouldn't have a betatron in the place somewhere?" asked Don hopefully.

"Nope. Could we make one?"

"Sure. Have you got about a hundred pounds of number 18 wire?"

"No."

"Then we can't."

"Couldn't you use a driver? Isn't that some kind of a beam?"

"Some kind," Channing admitted. "But it emits something that we've never been able to detect except in an atmosphere where it ionizes the air into a dull red glow."

"You should have been wrecked on the *Sorcerer's Apprentice*," laughed Hadley. "They're the guys who have all that kind of stuff."

"Have they?" asked Johannson.

"The last time I heard, they were using a large hunk of their upper hull for a Van de Graaff generator."

"That would do it," said Channing thoughtfully. "But I don't think I'd know how to modulate a Van de Graaff. A betatron would be the thing. You can modulate that, sort of, by keying the input. She'd give out with hundred-and-fifty-cycle stuff. How much of a trick is it to clear the observation dome from the top?"

"What do you intend to do?"

"Well, we've got a long, hollow tube in this ship. Knock out the faceted dome above, and we can rig us up a huge electron gun. We'll turn the ship to point at the station and beam 'em with a bouquet of electrons."

"How're you going to do that?"

"Not too tough, I don't think. Down here," and Channing began to trace on the tablecloth, "we'll put in a hot cathode. About this level we'll hang the first anode, and at this level we'll put the second anode. Here'll be an acceleration electrode and up near the top we'll put a series of focusing anodes. We'll tap in to the driver-tube supply and take off voltage to suit us. Might use a tube at that, but the conversion to make an honest electron gun out of it would disrupt our power, and then it would be impossible to remake a driver out of it without recourse to a machine shop."

"How are you going to make electrodes?"

"We'll use the annular gratings that run around the central well at each level," said Channing. "We'll have a crew of men cut 'em free and insulate the resulting rings with something. Got anything?"

"There is a shipment of methyl-methacrylate rods for the Venus Power Company in hold 17," said the cargo master.

"Fine," said Channing. "What size?"

"Three inches by six feet."

"It'll be tricky work, and you'll have to wait until your cut edge has cooled before you hook on the rods," Don mused. "But that's the ticket."

"Which floors do you want?"

"Have you got a scale drawing of the *Ariadne*?"

"Sure."

"Then this is where my tablecloth artistry falls flat. The focusing of an electron beam depends upon the electrode spacing and the voltage. Since our voltage is fixed if we take it from the drivers' electrodes, we'll have to do some mighty fine figuring. I'll need that scale drawing."

Channing's tablecloth engineering was not completely wasted. By the time the scale drawing was placed before him, Channing had half of the table filled with equations. He studied the drawing, and selected the levels which were to serve as electrodes. He handed the drawings to Hadley, and the power engineer began to issue instructions to his gang.

Then the central well began to swarm with space-suited men who bore cutting torches. Hot sparks danced from the cut girders that held the floorings and, at the same time, a crew of men were running cables from the various levels to the instrumented room. More hours passed while the circular sections were insulated with the plastic rods.

The big dome above was cut in sections and removed, and then the sky could be seen all the way from the bottom of the ship where the pilot's greenhouse should have been.

Channing looked it over and then remarked: "All we need now is an electron collector."

"I thought you wanted to shoot 'em off," Hadley objected.

"I do. But we've got to have a source of supply. You can't toss baseballs off of the Transplanet Building in Northern Landing all afternoon, you know, without having a few brought to you now and then. Where do you think they come from?"

"Hadn't thought of it that way. What'd happen?"

"We'd get along for the first upmty-gillion electrons, and then all the soup we could pack on would be equalized by the positive charge on the ship and we couldn't shoot out any more until we got bombarded by the sun—and that bombardment is nothing to write home about as regards quantity. We're presenting too small a target. What we need is a selective solar intake plate of goodly proportions."

"We could use a mental telepathy expert, too. Or one of those new beam tubes that Baler and Carroll dug up out of the Martian desert. I've heard that those things will actually suck power out of any source, and bend beams so as to enter the intake vent, or end."

"We haven't one of those, either. Fact of the matter is," grinned Channing, ruefully, "we haven't much of anything but our wits."

"Unarmed, practically." Hadley laughed.

"Half armed, at least. Ah, for something to soak up electrons. I'm now wondering if this electron gun is such a good idea."

"Might squirt some protons out the other direction," offered Hadley.

"That would leave us without either," said Don. "We'd be like the man who tossed baseballs off one side and himself off the other— Hey! Of course, we have some to spare. We can cram electrons out of the business end, thus stripping the planetary rings from the atoms in our cathode. From the far side we'll shoot the canal rays, which in effect will be squirting protons, or the nuclei. Since the planetaries have left for the front, it wouldn't be hard to take the protons away, leaving nothing. At our present voltages, we might be able to do it."

Channing began to figure again, and came up with another set of anodes to be placed beyond the cathode. "We'll ventilate the cathode and hang these negative electrodes on the far side. They will attract the protons, impelled also by the positive charge on the front end. We'll maintain a balance that way, effectively throwing away the whole atomic structure of the cathode. The latter will fade, just as the cathodes do in the driving tubes, only we'll be using electronic power instead of sub-electronic. Y'know, Hadley, someday someone is going to find a way to detect the—we'll call it radiation for want of anything better—of the driver. And then there will be opened an entirely new field of energy. I don't think that anybody has done more about the so-called sub-electronic field than to make a nice, efficient driving device out of it.

"Well, let's get our canal-ray electrodes in place. We've got about two hours before they realize that we aren't going to come in at Mojave. Then another two hours of wild messages between Venus Equilateral and Mojave. Then we can expect someone to be on the lookout. I hope to be there when they begin to look for us. At our present velocity, we'll be flirting with the Asteroid Belt in less than nothing flat. That isn't too bad—normally—but we're running without any meteor detector and autopilot coupler. We couldn't duck anything from a robin's egg on up."

"We'll get your anodes set," said Hadley.

Walt Franks grinned at Arden Channing. "That'll burn him," he assured her.

"It's been on the way for about twenty minutes," laughed Arden. "I timed it to arrive at Terra at the same time the *Ariadne* does. They'll send out a special messenger with it, just as Don is getting aboard his little scooter. It'll be the last word, for we're not following him from Terra to here."

"You know what you've started?" Franks asked.

"Nothing more than a little feud between husband and self."

"That's just the start. Before he gets done, Don will have every ship capable of answering back. I've found that you can catch him off base just once. He's a genius—one of those men who never make the same mistake twice. He'll never again be in a position to be on the listening end only."

"Don's answer should be on the way back by now," said Arden. "Could be you're right. Something should be done."

"Sure I'm right. Look at all the time that's wasted in waiting for a landing to answer 'grams. In this day and age, time is money—squared. The latter is to differentiate between this time and the first glimmering of speedy living."

"Was there a first glimmering?" asked Arden sagely. "I've often thought that the speedup was a stable acceleration from the dawn of time to the present."

"All right, go technical on me." Walt laughed. "Things do move. That is, all except the message from your loving husband."

"You don't suppose he's squelched?"

"I doubt it. Squelching Donald Channing is a job for a superbeing. And I'm not too sure that a superbeing could squelch Don and make him stay squelched. Better check on Mojave."

"Gosh, if Don missed the *Ariadne* and I've been shooting him all kinds of screwy 'types every hour on the hour, Walt, that'll keep him quiet for a long, long time."

"He'd have let you know."

"That wouldn't have been so bad. But if the big bum missed, and was ashamed of it—that'll be the payoff. Whoa, there goes the 'type!"

Arden drew the tape from the machine:

MESSAGE BEING HELD FOR ARRIVAL OF ARIADNE.

Walt looked at his watch and checked the course constants of the *Ariadne*. He called the beam-control dome and asked for the man on the ship's beam.

"Benny," he said, "has the *Ariadne* arrived yet?"

"Sure," answered Benny. "According to the mechanical mind here, they've been on Mojave for twenty minutes."

"Thanks." To Arden he said: "Something's strictly fishy."

Arden sat at the machine and pounded the keys:

ARIADNE DUE TO ARRIVE AT 19:06:41. IT IS NOW 19:27:00. BEAM CONTROL SAYS TRANSMISSIONS ENDED BECAUSE OF COINCIDENCE BETWEEN TERRA BEAM AND STATION-TO-SHIP BEAM. PLEASE CHECK.

Arden fretted and Walt stamped up and down the room during the long minutes necessary for the message to reach Terra and the answer to return. It came right on the tick of the clock:

HAVE CHECKED COURSE CONSTANTS. SHIP OVERDUE NOW FIFTY MINUTES. OBVIOUSLY SOMETHING WRONG. CAN YOU HELP?

Walt smiled in a grim fashion. "Help!" he said. "We go on and on for years with no trouble—and now we've lost the third ship in a row."

"They claim that those things always run in threes," said Arden. "What are we going to do?"

"I don't know. We'll have to do something. Funny, but the one reason we must do something is the same reason why something can be done."

"I don't get that."

"With Channing on the *Ariadne,* something can be done. I don't know what. But I'll bet you a new hat that Don will make it possible for us to detect the ship. There is not a doubt in my mind that if the ship is still spaceworthy, we can narrow the possibilities down to a thin cone of space."

"How?"

"Well," said Franks, taking the fountain pen out the holder on the desk and beginning to sketch on the blotter, "the course of the *Ariadne* is not a very crooked one, as courses go. It's a very shallow skew curve. Admitting the worst, collision, we can assume only one thing: if the meteor were small enough to leave the ship in a floating but undirigible condition, it would also be small enough to do nothing to the general direction of the ship. Anything else would make it useless to hunt, follow?"

"Yes, go on."

"Therefore, we may assume that the present position of the ship is within the volume of a cone made by the tangents of the outermost elements of the space curve that is the ship's course. We can take an eight-thousand-mile cylinder out of one place—for the origin of their trouble is between Mars and Terra and the 'shadow' of Terra in the cone will not contain the *Ariadne*."

"Might have passed close enough to Terra to throw her right into the 'shadow' of Terra by attraction," Arden objected.

"Yeah, you're right. O.K., so we can't take out that cylinder of space. And we add a sort of sidewise cone onto our original cone, a volume through which the ship might have passed after flying close enough to Terra to be deflected. I'll have the slipstick experts give a guess as to the probability of the *Ariadne*'s course, and at the same time we'll suspend all incoming operations. I'm going to set up every kind of detector I can think of, and I don't want anything upsetting them."

"What kind of stuff do you expect?" asked Arden.

"I dunno. They might have a betatron aboard. In that case we'll eventually get a blast of electrons that'll knock our front teeth out. Don may succeed in tinkering up some sort of electrostatic field. We can check the solar electrostatic field to about seven decimal places right here, and any deviation in the field to the tune of a couple of million electron volts at a distance of a hundred million miles will cause a distortion in the field that we can measure. We'll ply oscillating beams through the area of expectation and hope for an answering reflection, though I do not bank on that. We'll have men on the lookout for everything from smoke signals to helio. Don't worry too much, Arden, your husband is capable of doing something big enough to be heard. He's just the guy to do it."

"I know," Arden said soberly. "But I can't help worrying."

"Me, too. Well, I'm off to set up detectors. We'll collect something."

"Have we got anything like a piece of gold leaf?" asked Channing.

"I think so. Why?"

"I want to make an electroscope. That's about the only way I'll know whether we are getting out with this cockeyed electron gun."

"How so?" Hadley asked.

"We can tell from the meter that reads the beam current whether anything is going up the pipe," Channing explained. "But if we just build us a nice heavy-duty charge—as shown by the electroscope—we'll be sure that the electrons are not going far. This is one case where no sign is good news."

"I'll have one of the boys set up an electroscope in the instrument room."

"Good. And now have the bird on the telescope find Venus Equilateral. Have him set the 'scope angles to the figures here and then have him contact Darlange to get the ship slued around so that Venus Equilateral is on the cross hairs. That'll put us on a line with the station. A bundle of electrons of this magnitude will make a reading on any detectors that Walt can set up."

Hadley called the observation dome. "Tim," he said, giving a string of figures, "set your 'scope for these and then get Darlange to slue the crate around so that your cross hairs are on Venus Equilateral."

"O.K.," answered Tim. "That's going to be a job. This business of looking through a 'scope while dressed in a spacesuit is no fun. Here goes."

He called Darlange, and the communicator system permitted the men in the instrument room to hear his voice. "Dar," he said, "loop us around about forty-one degrees from driver 3."

Darlange said, "Right!" and busied himself at his buttons.

"Three degrees on driver 4."

"Right!"

"Too far, back her up a degree on 4."

Darlange laughed. "What do you think these things

are, blocks and tackles? You mean: 'Compensate a degree on 2.' "

"You're the pilot. That's the ticket—and I don't care if you lift it on one hand. Can you nudge her just a red hair on 3?"

"Best I can do is a hair and a half," said Darlange.

He gave driver 3 just a tiny, instantaneous surge.

"Then take it up two and back one and a half," laughed Tim. "Whoa, Nellie, you're on the beam."

"Fine."

"Okay, Dar, but you'll have to play monkey on a stick. I'll prime you for any moving so that you can correct immediately."

"Right. Don, we're on the constants you gave us. What now?"

"At this point I think a short prayer would be of assistance," said Channing soberly. "We're shooting our whole wad right now."

"I hope we make our point."

"Well, it's all or nothing," Don agreed as he grasped the switch.

He closed the switch, and the power-demand meters jumped up across their scales. The gold-leaf electroscope jumped once; the ultra-thin leaves jerked apart by an inch, and then oscillated stiffly until they came to a balance. Channing, who had been looking at them, breathed deeply and smiled.

"We're getting out," he said.

"Can you key this?" asked Hadley.

"No need," said Channing. "They know we're in the grease. We know that if they can collect us, they'll be on their way. I'm going to send out for a half-hour, and then resort to a five-minute transmission every fifteen minutes. They'll get a ship after us with just about everything we're liable to need, and they can use the five-minute transmission for direction finding. The initial shot will serve to give them an idea as to our direction. All we can do now is to wait."

"And hope," added Captain Johannson.

Electrically, Venus Equilateral was more silent than it had ever been. Not an electrical appliance was running on the whole station. People were cautioned about walking on deep-pile rugs, or combing their hair with plastic combs, or doing anything that would set up any kind of electronic charge. Only the highly filtered generators in the power rooms were running, and these had been shielded and filtered long years before; nothing would emerge from them to interrupt the ether. All incoming signals were stopped.

And the men who listened with straining ears claimed that the sky was absolutely clear, save for a faint crackle of cosmic static which they knew came from the corona of the Sun.

One group of men sat about a static-field indicator and cursed the minute wiggling of the meter, caused by the ever-moving celestial bodies and their electronic discharges. A sunspot emission passed through the station once, and though it was but a brief passage, it sent the electrostatic field crazy and made the men jump.

The men who were straining their ears to hear became nervous and were jumping at every loud crackle.

And though the man at the telescope knew that his probability of picking up a sight of the *Ariadne* was as slender as a spider's web, he continued to search the starry sky. He swept the narrow cone of the heavens wherein the *Ariadne* was lost, according to the mathematical experts, and he looked at every bit of brightness in the field of his telescope as though it might be the missing ship.

The beam scanners watched their return plates closely. It was difficult because the receiver gains were set to maximum and every tick of static caused brief flashes of light upon their plates. They would jump at such a flash and hope for it to reappear on the next swipe, for a continuous spot of light would indicate the ship they sought. Then, as the spot did not reappear, they would go on with their beams to cover another infinitesimal portion of the sky. Moving forward across the cone of expectancy bit by bit, they crossed and recrossed until they were growing restive.

Surely the ship must be there!

At the south-end landing stage, a group of men were busy stocking a ship. Supplies and necessities were carried aboard, while another group of men tinkered with the electrical equipment. They cleared a big space in the observation dome, and began to install a replica of the equipment used on the station for detection. No matter what kind of output Channing sent back, they would be able to follow it to the bitter end.

They made their installations in duplicate, with one piece of each equipment on opposite sides of the blunt dome. Balancing the inputs of each kind by turning the entire ship would give them an indication of direction.

Franks did not hope that the entire installation could be completed before the signal came, but he was trying to outguess himself by putting some of everything aboard. When and if it came, he would be either completely ready with everything, or he at least would have a good start on any one of the number of detectors. If need be, the detecting equipment in the station itself could be removed and used to complete the mobile installation.

Everything was in a complete state of nervous expectancy. Watchers watched, meter readers squinted for the barest wiggle, audio observers listened, trying to filter any kind of man-made note out of the irregular crackle that came in.

And the station announcing equipment was dead quiet, to be used only in case of emergency or to announce the first glimmer of radiation, whether it be material, electrical, kinetic, potential, or wave-front.

Long they listened—and then it came.

The station announcing equipment broke forth in a multitude of voices.

"Sound input on radio!"

"Visual indication on scanner plates!"

"Distortion on electrostatic field indicator!"

"Super-electroscopes indicate negative charge!"

"Nothing on the telescope!"

There were mingled cheers and laughter as the speaker system broke away from babel, and each group spoke its piece with no interference. Walt Franks left the ship at the south end and raced to the beam control dome, just as fast as the runway car would take him. He ran into the dome in spacesuit and flipped the helmet back over his shoulder.

"What kind of indication?" he yelled.

Men crowded around him, offering him papers and showing figures.

"Gosh," he said, "Don can't have everything going up there."

"He's hit just about everything but the guy squinting through the 'scope."

"What's he doing?" asked Franks of nobody in particular.

Charles Thomas, who had been busy with the electrostatic field indicator said: "I think maybe he's using some sort of electron gun—like the one you tried first-off on the meteor destroyer job, remember?"

"Yeah, but that one wouldn't work—unless Don has succeeded in doing something *we* couldn't do. Look, Chuck, we haven't had time to set up a complete field indicator on the ship. Grab yours and give the boys a lift installing it, hey?"

"Sure thing," said Thomas.

"And look, fellows, any indication of direction, velocity, or distance?"

"Look for yourself," said the man on the beam scanner. "The whole plate is shining. We can't get a fix on them this way—they're radiating, themselves, and that means our scanner-system finder is worthless."

"We can, but it's rough," offered one of the radio men. "It came from an area out beyond Terra—and as for our readings, it might have covered a quarter of the sky."

"The field indicator is a short-base finder," explained Thomas. "And no less rough than the radio boys. I'd say it was out beyond Terra by fifty million miles at least."

"Close enough. We'll have to track 'em down like a radio-equipped bloodhound. Chuck, come along and run that mechanico-electro-monstrosity of yours. Gene, you can come along and run the radio finder. Oh, yes, you, Jimmy, may continue to squint through that eyepiece of yours—but on the *Relay Girl*. We need a good, first-class squinter, and you should have an opportunity to help."

Jimmy laughed shortly. "The only guy on the station that didn't get an indication was me. Not even a glimmer."

"Channing didn't know we'd be *looking* for him, or he'd probably light a flare, too. Cheer up, Jimmy, after all this crude, electrical rigmarole is finished—and we gotta get right down to the last millimeter—it's the guy with the eye that polishes up the job. You'll have your turn."

Twenty minutes after the first glimmer of intelligent signal, the *Relay Girl* lifted from the south end and darted off at an angle, setting her nose roughly in the direction of the signal.

Her holds were filled with spare batteries and a whole dozen replacement cathodes, as well as her own replacements. Her crew was filled to the eyebrows with gravanol, and there must have been a mile of adhesive tape and cotton on their abdomens. At six G she left, and at six G she ran, her crew immobilized but awake because of the gravanol. And though the acceleration was terrific, the tape kept the bodies from folding of their own weight. When they returned, they would all be in the hospital for a week, but their friends would be with them.

Ten minutes after takeoff, the signals ceased.

Walt said: "Keep her running. Don's saving electricity. Tell me when we pick him up again."

Franklen, the pilot, nodded. "We haven't got a good start yet. It'll be touch and go. According to the slip-stick boys, they must be clapping it up at between twenty-five hundred and five thousand miles per second to get that far—and coasting free or nearly so. Otherwise they'd have come in. Any suggestions as to course?"

"Sure. Whoop it up at six until we hit about six thousand. Then decelerate to four thousand by using one G. We'll vacillate in velocity between four and five until we get close."

Forty-one hours later, the *Relay Girl* made turnover and began to decelerate.

Channing said to Captain Johannson: "Better cut the decel to about a quarter G. That'll be enough to keep our heads from bumping the ceiling, and it will last longer. This is going to be a long chase, and cutting down a few MPS at a half G isn't going to make much never-mind. I'll hazard a guess that the boys are on their way right now."

"If you say so," said Johannson. "You're the boss from now on. You know that wild bunch on the station better than I do. For myself, I've always felt that an answer was desirable before we do anything."

"I know Franks and my wife pretty well—about as well as they know me. I've put myself in Walt's place—and I know what Walt would do. So, if Walt didn't think of it, Arden would. I can assume that they are aware of us, have received our signals, and are, therefore, coming along as fast as they can. They'll come zipping out here from five to seven G to what they think is halfway and then decelerate again to a sane velocity. We won't catch sight of them for sixty or seventy hours, and when we do, they'll be going so fast that it will take another twenty hours' worth of manipulation to match their speed with ours. Meanwhile, I've got the gun timed to shoot our signal. When the going gets critical, I'll cut the power and make it continuous."

"You're pretty sure of your timing?"

"Well, the best they can do as for direction and velocity and distance is a crude guess. They'll place us out here beyond Terra somewhere. They'll calculate the course requirements to get us this far in the time allotted, and come to a crude figure. I'd like to try keying this thing, but I know that keying it won't work worth a hoot at this distance. Each bundle of keyed electrons would act as a separate negative charge that would spread out and close up at this distance. It's tough enough to hope that the electron beam will hold together that far, let alone trying to key intelligence with it. We'll leave well enough alone—and especially if they're trying to get a fix on us; there's nothing worse than trying to fix an intermittent station. Where are we now?"

"We're on the inner fringe of the Asteroid Belt, about thirty million miles north, and heading on a secant course at thirty-four hundred MPS."

"Too bad Jupiter isn't in the neighborhood," said Channing. "We'll be flirting with his orbit by the time they catch us."

"Easily," Johannson said. "In sixty hours, we'll have

covered about six hundred and fifty million miles. We'll be nearer the orbit of Saturn, in spite of the secant course."

"Your secant approaches a radius as you get farther out," said Don, absently. "As far as distances go, Titan, here we come!"

Johannson spoke to the doctor. "How're we doing?"

"Pretty well," Doc answered. "There's as pretty an assortment of fractured limbs, broken ribs, cracked clavicles, and scars, mars, and abrasions as you ever saw. There are a number dead, worse luck, but we can't do a thing about them. We can hold on for a week as far as food and water goes. Everyone is now interested in the manner of our rescue rather than worrying about it." He turned to Channing. "The words Channing and Venus Equilateral have wonderful healing powers," he said. "They all think your gang are part magician and part sorcerer."

"Why, for goodness' sake?"

"I didn't ask. Once I told 'em you had a scheme to contact the relay station, they were all satisfied that things would happen for the better."

"Anything we can do to help you out?"

"I think not," answered Doc. "What I said before still goes. Your job is to bring aid—and that's the sum total of your job. Every effort must be expended on that and that alone. You've got too many whole people depending on you to spend one second on the hurt. That's my job."

"O.K.," said Channing. "But it's going to be a long wait."

"We can afford it."

"I hope we're not complicating the job of finding us by this quartering deceleration," said Captain Johannson.

"We're not. We're making a sort of vector from our course, but the deviation is very small. As long as the fellows follow our radiation, we'll be found," Channing said with a smile. "The thing that is tough is the fact that all the floors seem to lean over."

"Not much, though."

"They wouldn't lean at all if we were running with the whole set of equipment," said Darlange. "We run a complete turnover without spilling a drop from the swimming pool."

"Or even making the passengers aware of it unless they're looking at the sky."

"Stop worrying about it," said Doc. "I'm the only guy who has to worry about it and as long as the floor is still a floor, I can stand sliding into the corner once in a while."

"We might tinker with the turnover drivers," Don offered. "We can bring 'em down to a place where the velocity-deceleration vectors are perpendicular to the floor upon which we stand while our ship is sluing. We've got a lot of time on our hands, and I, for one, feel a lot happier when I'm doing something."

"It's a thought," said Hadley. "Wanna try it?"

"Let's go."

Thirty hours after the *Relay Girl* left the station, Walt and Franklen held a council of war, in which Chuck Thomas was the prime factor.

"We've come about two hundred million miles, and our present velocity is something like four thousand miles per second," said Walt. "We're going toward Mars on a slightly-off radial course, to the north of the ecliptic. That means we're a little over a quarter of a billion miles from Sol, or about to hit the Asteroid Belt. Thinking it over a little, I think we should continue our acceleration for another thirty hours. What say?"

"The field has shown no change in intensity that I can detect," said Thomas. "If they haven't dropped their radiated intensity, that means that we are no closer to them than we were before. Of course, we'd probably have to cut the distance by at least half before any measurable decrement made itself evident."

"They must be on the upper limit of that four thousand MPS," observed Walt. "There's one thing certain, we'll never catch them by matching their speed."

"Where will another thirty hours at six G put us, and how fast?" asked Franklen.

Silence ensued while they scribbled long figures on scratch paper.

"About eight hundred million miles from Sol," Walt announced.

"And about eight thousand MPS," added Chuck.

"That's a little extreme, don't you think?" Franklen asked.

"By about thirty percent," said Walt, scratching his chin. "If we hold to our original idea of hitting it for six thousand, where will we be?"

"That would make it about forty-five hours from takeoff, and we'd be about four hundred and sixty million miles from Sol." Chuck grinned widely and said: "By Jove!"

"What?"

"By Jove!"

" 'By Jove!' What?"

"That's where we'd be—by Jove!"

"Phew!"

"I agree with you," said Franklen to Walt. "Better ignore him."

"Sure will after that. So then we'll be 'by Jove' at six thousand. That would be a swell place to make turnover, I think. At one G decel to about four thousand MPS, that'll put us about—um, that'd take us about ninety hours! We'll make that three G at twenty hours, which will put us about three hundred and fifty million miles along, which plus the original four hundred and sixty million adds up to eight hundred and ten million—"

"When an astronaut begins to talk like that," Arden interrupted, "we of the skyways say that he is talking in congressional figures. The shoe is on the other foot. What on earth are you fellows figuring?"

"Where we'll be and how fast we'll be going at a given instant of particular importance," offered Walt. "When did *you* wake up?"

"About the third hundred million. All of those ciphers going by made a hollow sound, like a bullet whistling in the wind."

"Well, we're trying to make the theories of probability match with figures. We'll know in about forty-five hours whether we were right or not."

"It's a good thing we have all space to go around in. Are you sure that we have all eternity?"

"Don't get anxious, Arden. They're still coming in like a ton of bricks four times per hour, which means that they're riding easy. I don't want to overrun them at about three thousand MPS and have to spend a week decelerating, returning, more decelerating, and then matching velocities."

"I see. You know best. And where is this Asteroid Belt that I've heard so much about?"

"To the south of us by a few million miles. Those bright specks that you can't tell from stars are asteroids. The common conception of the Asteroid Belt being filled to overflowing with a collection of cosmic rubble like the rings of Saturn is a lot of hooey. We'll be past in a little while and we haven't even come close to one. Space is large enough for all of us, I think."

"But not when all of us want the same space."

"I don't care for their area," said Walt with a smile. "Let 'em have it, I don't care. I'll stay up here and let them run as they will."

"You mean the ones that are moving downward?" asked Arden, indicating the sky.

"Those are asteroids, yes. We're up to the north, as you may check by going around the ship to the opposite side. You'll see Polaris almost directly opposite, there. Sol is almost directly below us, and that bright one that you can see if you squint almost straight up is Saturn."

"I won't bother crossing the ship to see Polaris. I prefer the Southern Cross, anyway. The thing I'm most interested in is: are we accomplishing anything?"

"I think that we've spent the last thirty hours just catching up," Walt explained. "Up to right now, we are going backward, so to speak; we're on even terms now, and will be doing better from here on in."

"It's the waiting that gets me down," said Arden. "Oh, for something to do."

"Let's eat," suggested Walt. "I'm hungry, and now that I think of it, I haven't eaten since we left the station. Arden, you are hereby elected to the post of galley chief. Get Jimmy from the dome if you need help."

"Help? What for?"

"He can help you lift it out of the oven. Don must have a cast-iron stomach."

"That's hearsay. *I'll* show you! As soon as I find the can opener, breakfast will be served."

"Make mine dinner," said Chuck. "We've been awake all the time."

"O.K., we will have a combined meal, from grapefruit to ice cream. Those who want any or all parts may choose at will. And fellows, please let me know as soon as you get something tangible."

"That's a promise," said Walt. "Take it easy, and don't worry. We'll be catching up with them one of these days."

"Hadley, how much coating have we got on those cathodes?" asked Don Channing.

"Not too much. We had about twenty G hours to begin with. We went to a half G for twenty hours, and now we're running on a quarter G, which would let us go for forty hours more."

"Well, look. If it should come to a choice between floor and signal gun, we'll choose the gun. We've about eight hours left in the cathodes, and since everybody is now used to quarter G we might even slide it down to an eighth G, which would give us about sixteen hours."

"Your gun is still putting out?"

"So far as I can tell. Six hours from now, we should know, I think, predicating my guess on whatever meager information they must have."

"We could save some juice by killing most of the lights in the ship."

"That's a thought. Johannson, have one of your men run around and remove all lights that aren't absolutely necessary. He can kill about three-quarters of them, I'm certain. That'll save us a few kilowatt hours," said Channing. "And another thing. I'm about to drop the power of our electron gun and run it continuously. If the boys are anywhere in the neighborhood, they'll be needing continuous disturbance for direction finding. I'd say in another five hours that we should start continuous radiation."

"You know, Channing, if this thing works out all right, it will be a definite vote for pure, deductive reasoning," Johannson replied.

"I know. But the deductive reasoning is not too pure. It isn't guesswork. There are two factors of known quality. One is that I know Walt Franks and the other is that he knows me. The rest is a simple matter of the boys on the station knowing space to the last inch, and applying the theory of probabilities to it. We'll hear from them soon, or I'll miss my guess. Just you wait."

"Yeah," drawled Captain Johannson, "we'll wait!"

Chuck Thomas made another computation and said: "Well, Walt, we've been narrowing them down for quite a long time now. We're getting closer and closer to them, according to the field intensity. I've just got a good idea of direction on that last five-minute shot. Have Franklen swivel us around on this course; pretty soon we'll be right in the middle of their shots."

"We're approaching them asymptotically," Walt observed. "I wish I knew what our velocity was with respect to theirs. Something tells me that it would be much simpler if I knew."

"Walt," asked Arden, "how close can you see a spaceship?"

"You mean how far? Well, I don't know that it has ever been tried and recorded. But we can figure it out easy enough by analogy. A period is about thirty thousandths of an inch in diameter, and visible from a distance of thirty inches. I mean visible with no doubt about its being there. That's a thousand to one. Now, the *Ariadne* is about six hundred feet tall and about four hundred feet in its major diameter, so we can assume a little more than the four hundred feet—say five hundred feet average of circular area—follow me?"

"Go on, you're vague, but normal."

"Then at a thousand to one, that becomes five hundred thousand feet, and dividing by five thousand—round figures because it isn't important enough to use that two hundred and eighty feet over the five thousand—gives us one thousand miles. We should be able to see the *Ariadne* from a distance of a thousand miles."

"Then at four thousand miles per second we'll be in and through and out of visual range in a half-second?"

"Oh, no. They're rambling on a quite similar course at an unknown but high velocity. Our velocity with respect to theirs is what will determine how long they're within visual range."

"Hey, Walt," came the voice of Chuck Thomas. "The intensity of Don's beam has been cut to about one-quarter and is now continuous. Does that mean anything?"

"Might mean trouble for them. Either they're running out of soup and mean for us to hurry up, or they assume we're close enough to obviate the need for high power. We'd better assume they want haste, and act accordingly. How're the boys on the radio detectors coming along?"

"Fine. They've taken over the direction finding and claim that we are right on their tail."

"Anything in the sights, Jimmy?"

"Not yet. But the electroscope boys claim that quarter power or not, the input is terrific."

"Take a rest, Jimmy. We won't be there for a while yet. No use burning your eyes out trying to see 'em. There'll be time enough for you to do your share after we get 'em close enough to see with the naked eye. What do the beam scanners say?"

"Shucks," answered the man on the scanners, "they're still radiating. How are we going to fix 'em on a reflected wave when they're more powerful on their own hook? The whole plate is glaring white. And, incidentally, so is the celestial globe in the meteor spotter. I've had to cut that or we'd never be able to hold this course. Anything like a meteor that comes in our way now will not register, and—"

The *Relay Girl* lurched sickeningly. All over the ship, things rattled and fell to the floors. Men grabbed at the closest solid object, and then the *Relay Girl* straightened out once more.

"*Whoosh!*" said Franks. "That was a big one!"

"Big one?" called Jimmy. "That, my friend, was none other than the *Ariadne*!"

"Can you prove that?"

"Sure," Jimmy chuckled. "I saw 'em. I can still see 'em!"

"Franklen, hang on at about seven G and follow Jimmy's orders. Chuck, see if you can get anything cogent out of your gadget. Holy green fire, with a cubic million million million megaparsecs in which to run, we have to be so good that we run right into our quarry. Who says that radio direction finding is not a precise science? Who says that we couldn't catch—"

"Walt, they're losing fast."

"O.K., Jimmy, can you give me any idea as to their velocity with respect to ours?"

"How long is she?"

"Six hundred feet."

Jimmy was silent for some seconds. "They're out of sight again, but I make it about four to seven hundred miles per second."

"At seven G we should match that seven hundred in about four hours."

"And then go on decelerating so that they'll catch up?"

"No," said Walt. "I used the max figures and we can assume they aren't going that fast, quite. At the end of four hours, we'll turnover and wait until they heave in sight again, and then we'll do some more oscillating. We can match their velocity inside of ten hours, or Franklen will get fired."

"If I don't," promised Franklen, "I'll quit. You can't fire me!"

"We should be able to contact them by radio," Walt said.

"We are!" called the radio man. "It's Channing. He says: 'Fancy meeting you here.' Any answer?"

"Just say, 'Dr. Channing, I presume?' "

Channing's voice came out of the ship's announcer system as the radio man made the necessary connections. It said: "Right—but what kept you so long?"

"Our boss was away," replied Walt. "And we can't do a thing without him."

"Some boss. Some crew of wild men. Can't go off on a fishing trip without having my bunch chasing all over the Solar System."

"What's wrong with a little sight-seeing tour? We didn't mean any harm. And speaking of harm, how are you and the rest of that bunch getting along?"

"We're O.K. What do you plan after we finally get close enough together to throw stones across?"

"We've got a whole hold full of spare batteries and a double set of replacement cathodes. There is a shipload of gravanol aboard, too. You'll need that and so will we. By the time we finish this jaunt, we'll have been about as far out as anybody ever gets."

"Yeah? Got any precise figures? We've been running on a guess and a hope. I make it about seven hundred million."

"Make it eight and a half. At six G you'll cover another hundred and fifty million miles before you stop. Take it twenty-two hours at six G—and then another twenty-two at six. That should put you right back here but going the other way at the same velocity. But wait, you've been coasting. Mark off that last twenty-two hours and make it like this: you'll be one thousand million miles from Sol when you come to a stop at the end of the first twenty-two hours at six G. That hangs you out beyond the orbit of Saturn by a couple of hundred million. Make it back forty-four hours at six G, turnover and continue. By that time we'll all be in so close that we can make any planet at will—preferably you to Terra and we'll head for Venus Equilateral. You'll come aboard us? No need for you to land with the rest."

"I can have the scooter sent out from Terra," said Channing. "How's Arden?"

"I'm fine, you big runabout. Wait until I get you!"

"Why, Arden, I thought you might be glad to see me."

"Glad to see you?"

"But Arden—"

"Don't you 'But Arden' me, you big gadabout. Glad to see you! Boy, any man that makes me chase him all over the Solar System! You just wait. As soon as I get ahold of you, Don Channing, I'm going to—to bust out and bawl like a kid! Hurry up, willya?"

"I'll be right over," said Don soberly.

And, strangely enough, Don did not deviate.

Interlude

Four and a half thousand years ago, Sargon of Akkad held court on the plains of Assyria by torchlight. Above his head there shone the myriad of stars, placed there to increase his power and glory.

But on one of the stars above, called Mars, were people who knew a mighty civilization and a vast world of science. They flew above the thin air of Mars and they hurled power by energy beam across the face of the planet.

Then they—died. They died, and they left but broken fragments of their once-mighty civilization buried in the shifting, dusty sands of Mars. Long centuries afterward, man crossed space to find these fragments and wonder.

How or why they died is a matter of conjecture. It is known that iron is the most stable of all known atomic structures besides helium. It is also known that the surface of Mars has its characteristic reddish hue because of the preponderance of iron compounds there. From the few remaining artifacts, it is known that Mars exceeded the present Terran science, which includes atomic power. The inference is that Mars died completely in the horror of atomic war.

This is but reasoning. The facts that are of interest include the finding of a gigantic vacuum tube fastened to a shattered steel tower in the sands between Canalopsis and Lincoln Head, Mars.

The original finders, Martian archaeologists Baler and Carroll, were versed enough in electronics to make tests. They discovered many interesting facts about this tube before they sold it to Terran Electric for a monumental sum of money. Their reasons for selling the thing were simple. They preferred digging in the sands of Mars to plunging into the depths of a highly technical manufacturing business, and the money was more than adequate.

Don Channing's main objection was that Carroll and Baler did not consult Venus Equilateral before they disposed of their find.

That made it necessary for Venus Equilateral to acquire a tube for their research by dealing with Terran Electric, which in this case was similar to obtaining a ton of uranium ore from Oak Ridge back in the year 1945. Often, of course, the shortest distance home is . . .

THE LONG WAY

Don Channing stood back and admired his latest acquisition with all of the fervency of a high school girl inspecting her first party dress. It was so apparent, this affection between man and gadget, that the workmen who were now carrying off the remnants of the packing case did so from the far side of the bench so that they would not come between the Director of Communications and the object of his affection.

So intent was Channing to the adoration of the object that he did not hear the door open, nor the click of high heels against the plastic flooring. He was completely unaware of his surroundings until Arden said:

"Don, what on earth is that?"

"Ain't she a beaut," breathed Channing.

"Jilted for a jimcrack," Arden groaned. "Tell me, my quondam husband, what is it?"

"Huh?" asked Don, coming to life once more.

"In plain, unvarnished words of one cylinder, what is that . . . that *that?*"

"Oh, you mean the transmission tube?"

"How do you do?" said Arden to the big tube. "Funny looking thing, not like any transmitting tube I've ever seen before."

"Not a transmitting tube," exclaimed Channing. "It is one of those power transmission tubes that Baler and Carroll found on the Martian desert."

"I presume that is why the etch says: MADE BY TERRAN ELECTRIC, CHICAGO?"

Channing laughed. "Not the one found—there was only *one* found. This is a carbon copy. They are going to revolutionize the transmission of power with them."

"Funny-looking gadget."

"Not so funny. Just alien."

"Know anything about it?"

"Not too much. I've got Barney Carroll coming out here and a couple of guys from Terran Electric. I'm going to strain myself to keep from tinkering with the thing until they get here."

"Can't you go ahead? It's not like you to wait."

"I know," said Channing. "But the Terran Electric boys have sewed up the rights of this dingus so tight that it's squeaking. Seems to be some objection to working on them in the absence of their men."

"Why?"

"Probably because Terran Electric knows a good thing when they see it. Barney's latest 'gram said that they were very reluctant to lend this tube to us. Legally they couldn't refuse, but they know darned well that we're not going to run power in here from Terra—or anywhere else. They know we want it for experimentation, and they feel that it is their tube and that if any experimentation is going to take place, they're going to do it."

The workmen returned with two smaller cases; one each they placed on benches to either side of the big tube. They knocked the boxes apart and there emerged two smaller editions of the center tube—and even Arden could see that these two were quite like the forward half and the latter half, respectively, of the larger tube.

"Did you buy 'em out?" she asked.

"No," said Don simply. "This merely makes a complete circuit."

"Explain that one, please."

"Sure. This one on the left is the input-terminal tube which they call the power end. The good old DC goes in across these big terminals. It emerges from the big end, here, and bats across in a beam of intangible something-or-other until it gets to the relay tube, where it is once more tossed across to the load-end tube. The power is taken from these terminals on the back end of the load-end tube and is then suitable for running motors, refrigerators, and so on. The total line loss is slightly more than the old-fashioned transmission line. The cathode-dynode requires replacement about once a year. The advantages over high-tension wires are many; in spite of the slightly higher line losses, they are replacing long-lines everywhere.

"When they're properly aligned, they will arch right over a mountain of solid iron without attenuation. It takes one tower every hundred and seventy miles, and the only restriction on tower height is that the tube must be above ground by ten to one the distance that could be flashed over under high-intensity ultraviolet light."

"That isn't clear to me."

"Well, high-tension juice will flash over better under ultraviolet illumination. The tube must be high enough to exceed this distance by ten to one at the operating voltage of the stuff down the line. The boys in the Palanortis jungles say they're a godsend, since there are a lot of places where the high-tension towers would be impossible since the Palanortis whitewood grows about a thousand feet tall."

"You'd cut a lot of wood to ream a path through from Northern Landing to the power station on the Boiling River," said Arden.

"Yeah," Don drawled, "and towers a couple of hundred miles apart are better than two thousand feet. Yeah, these things are the nuts for getting power shipped across country."

"Couldn't we squirt it out from Terra?" asked Arden. "That would take the curse off of our operating expenses."

"It sure would," agreed Channing heartily. "But think of the trouble in aligning a beam of that distance. I don't know—there's this two-hundred-miles' restriction, you know. They don't transmit worth a hoot over that distance, and it would be utterly impossible to maintain stations in space a couple of hundred miles apart, even from Venus, from which we maintain a fairly close tolerance. We might try a hooting big one, but the trouble is that misalignment of the things result in terrible effects."

The door opened and Chuck Thomas and Walt Franks entered.

"How're our playthings?" asked Walt.

"Cockeyed-looking gadgets," Chuck commented.

"Take a good look at 'em," said Channing. "Might make some working X-ray plates, too. It was a lucky day that these got here before the boys from Terran Electric. I doubt that they'd permit that."

"O.K.," said Chuck. "I'll bring the X-ray up here and make some pix. We'll want working prints; Warren will have to take 'em and hang dimensions on to fit."

"And we," said Channing to Walt Franks, "will go to our respective offices and wait until the Terran Electric representatives get here."

The ship that came with the tubes took off from the landing stage, and as it passed their observation dome, it caught Don's eye. "There goes our project for the week," he said.

"Huh?" asked Walt.

"He's been like that ever since we tracked him down on the *Ariadne*," said Arden.

"I mean the detection of driver radiation," said Channing.

"Project for the week?" Walt asked. "Brother, we've been tinkering with that idea for months now."

"Well," said Don, "there go four drivers, all batting out umpty-ump begawatts of something. They can hang a couple of G on a six-hundred-foot hull for hours and hours. The radiation they emit must be detectable; don't tell me that such power is not."

"The interplanetary companies have been tinkering with drivers for years and years," said Walt. "They've never detected it?"

"Could be, but there are a couple of facts that I'd like to point out. One is that they're not interested in detection. They only want the best in driver efficiency. Another thing is that the radiation from the drivers is sufficient to ionize atmosphere into a dull red glow that persists for several minutes. Next item is the fact that we on Venus Equilateral should be able to invent a detector; we've been tinkering with detectors long enough. Oh, I'll admit that it is secondary electronics—"

"Huh? That's a new one on me."

"It isn't electronics," said Channing. "It's sub-etheric or something like that. We'll call it sub-electronics for lack of anything else. But we should be able to detect it somehow."

"Suppose there is nothing to detect?"

"That smacks of one hundred percent efficiency," laughed Don. "Impossible."

"How about an electric heater?" Arden asked.

"Oh, Lord, Arden, an electric heater is the most ineffic—"

"Is it?" interrupted Arden with a smile. "What happens to radiation when intercepted?"

"Turns to heat, of course."

"That takes care of the radiation output," said Arden. "Now, how about electrical losses?"

"Also heat."

"Then everything that goes into an electric heater emerges as heat," said Arden.

"I get it." Walt laughed. "Efficiency depends on what you hope to get. If what you want is losses, anything that is a total loss is one hundred percent efficient. Set your machine up to waste power and it becomes one hundred percent efficient as long as there is nothing coming from the machine that doesn't count as waste."

"Fine point for arguing," smiled Channing. "But anything that will make atmosphere glow dull red after the passage of a ship will have enough waste to detect. Don't tell me that the red glow enhances the drive."

The door opened again and Chuck Thomas came in with a crew of men. They ignored the three, and started to hang heavy cloth around the walls and ceiling. Chuck watched the installation of the barrier cloth, and then said: "Beat it—if you want any young Channings!"

Arden, at least, had the grace to blush.

The tall, slender man handed Don an envelope full of credentials. "I'm Wesley Farrell," he said. "Glad to have a chance to work out here with you fellows."

"Glad to have you," said Don. He looked at the other man.

"This is Mark Kingman."

"How do you do?" said Channing.

Kingman did not impress Channing as being a person whose presence in a gathering would be demanded with gracious shouts of glee.

"Mr. Kingman is an attorney for Terran Electric," Wesley explained.

Kingman's pedestal was lowered by Channing.

"My purpose," said Kingman, "is to represent my company's interest in the transmission tube."

"In what way?" asked Don.

"Messrs. Baler and Carroll sold their discovery to Terran Electric outright. We have an iron-bound patent on the device and/or any developments of the device. We hold absolute control over the transmission tube, and therefore may dictate all terms on which it is to be used."

"I understand. You know, of course, that our interest in the transmission tube is purely academic."

"I have been told that. We're not too certain that we approve. Our laboratories are capable of any investigation you may desire, and we prefer that such investigations be conducted under our supervision."

"We are not going to encroach on your power rights," explained Channing.

"Naturally," said Kingman in a parsimonious manner. "But should you develop a new use for the device, we shall have to demand that we have complete rights."

"Isn't that a bit high-handed?" asked Don.

"We think not. It is our right."

"You're trained technically?"

"Not at all. I am a lawyer, not an engineer. Dr. Farrell will take care of the technical aspects of the device."

"And in looking out for your interests, what will you require?"

"Daily reports from your group. Daily conferences with your legal department. These reports should be prepared prior to the day's work, so that I may discuss with the legal department the right of Terran Electric to permit or disapprove the acts."

"You understand that there may be a lot of times

when something discovered at ten o'clock may change the entire program by ten oh six?"

"That may be," said Kingman, "but my original statements must be adhered to, otherwise I am authorized to remove the devices from your possession. I will go this far however: if you discover something that will change your program for the day, I will then call an immediate conference which should hurry your program instead of waiting until the following morning for the decision."

"Thanks," said Channing dryly. "First, may we take X-ray prints of the devices?"

"No. Terran Electric will furnish you with blueprints which we consider suitable." Kingman paused for a moment. "I shall expect the complete program of tomorrow's experiments by five o'clock this evening."

Kingman left, and Wes Farrell smiled uncertainly. "Shall we begin making the list?"

"Might as well," said Channing. "But, how do you lay out a complete experimental program for twelve hours ahead?"

"It's a new one on me, too," said Farrell.

"Well, come on. I'll get Walt Franks, and we'll begin."

"I wonder if it might not be desirable for Kingman to sit in on these program-settings?" Channing said, after a moment of staring at the page before him.

"I suggested that to him. He said 'No.' He prefers his information in writing."

Walt came in on the last words. Channing brought Franks up-to-date and Walt said: "But why should he want a written program if he's going to disallow certain ideas?"

"Sounds to me like he's perfectly willing to let us suggest certain lines of endeavor; he may decide that they look good enough to have the Terran Electric labs try, themselves," said Channing.

Wes Farrell looked uncomfortable.

"I have half a notion to toss him out," Channing told Farrell. "I also have half a notion to make miniatures of this tube and go ahead and work regardless of Kingman *or* Terran Electric. O.K., Wes, we won't do anything illegal. We'll begin by making our list."

"What is your intention?" Wes asked.

"We hope that these tubes will enable us to detect driver radiation, which will ultimately permit us to open ship-to-ship two-way communications."

"May I ask how you hope to do this?"

"Sure. We're going to cut and try. No one knows a thing about the level of driver energy; we've selected a name for it: subelectronics. The driver tube is akin to this transmission tube, if what I've been able to collect on the subject is authentic. By using the transmission tube—"

"Your belief is interesting. I've failed to see any connection between our tube and the driver tube."

"Oh, sure," said Channing expansively. "I'll admit that the similarity is of the same order as the similarity between an incandescent lamp and a ten-dynode electron multiplier such as we use in our final beam stages. But recall this business of the cathode-dynode. In both, the emitting surface is bombarded by electrons from electron guns. They both require changing."

"I know that, but the driver cathode disintegrates at a rate of loss that is terrific compared to the loss of emitting surface in the transmission tube."

"The driver cathode is worth about two hundred G-hours. But remember, there is no input to the driver such as you have in the transmission tube. The power from the driver comes from the disintegration of the cathode surface—there isn't a ten thousandth of an inch of plating on the inside of the tube to show where it went. But the transmission tube has an input, and the tube itself merely transduces this power to some level of radiation for transmission. It is re-transduced again for use. But the thing is this: your tube is the only thing that we know of that will accept sub-electronic energy and use it. If the driver and the transmission tubes are similar in operational spectrum, we may be able to detect driver radiation by some modification."

"That sounds interesting," said Wes. "I'll be darned glad to give you a lift."

"Isn't that beyond your job?" asked Channing.

"Yeah," drawled Farrell, "but could you stand by and watch me work on a beam transmitter?"

"No—"

"Then don't expect me to watch without getting my fingers dirty," said Farrell cheerfully. "Sitting around in a place like this would drive me nuts without something to do."

"O.K., then." Don smiled. "We'll start off by building about a dozen miniatures. We'll make 'em about six inches long—we're not going to handle much power, you know. That's first."

Kingman viewed the list with distaste. "There are a number of items here which I may not allow," he said.

"For instance?" asked Channing with lifted eyebrows.

"One, the manufacture or fabrication of power transmission tubes by anyone except Terran Electric is forbidden. Two, your purpose in wanting to make tubes is not clearly set forth. Three, the circuit in which you intend to use these tubes is unorthodox, and must be clearly and fully drawn and listed."

"Oh, spinach! How can we list and draw a circuit that is still in the embryonic stage?"

"Then clarify it. Until then I shall withhold permission."

"But look, Mr. Kingman, we're going to develop this circuit as we go along."

"You mean that you're going to fumble your way through this investigation?"

"We do not consider a cut-and-try program as fumbling," said Walt Franks.

"I am beginning to believe that your research department has not the ability to reduce your problems to a precise science," said Kingman coldly.

"Name me a precise science," snapped Channing, "or even a precise art!"

"The legal trade is as precise as any. Everything we do is done according to legal precedent."

"I see. And when there is no precedent?"

"Then we all decide upon the proper course, and establish a precedent."

"But I've got to show you a complete circuit before you'll permit me to go ahead?"

"That's not all. Your program must not include reproducing these tubes either in miniature or in full size—or larger. Give me your requirements and I shall request Terran Electric to perform the fabrication."

"Look, Kingman, Venus Equilateral has facilities to build as good a tube as Terran Electric. I might even say better, since our business includes the use, maintenance, and development of radio tubes; your tubes are not too different from ours. Plus the fact that we can whack out six in one day, while it will take seventy-three hours to get 'em here after they're built on Terra."

"I'm sorry, but the legal meaning of the patent is clear. Where is your legal department?"

"We have three. One on each of the Inner Planets."

"I'll request you to have a legal representative come to the station so that I may confer with him. One with power of attorney to act for you."

"Sorry," said Channing coldly. "I wouldn't permit any attorney to act without my supervision."

"That's rather a backward attitude," said Kingman. "I shall still insist on conducting my business with one of the legal mind."

"O.K. We'll have Peterman come out from Terra. But he'll still be under my supervision."

"As you wish. I may still exert my prerogative and remove the tubes from your possession."

"You may find that hard to do," said Channing.

"That's illegal!"

"Oh, no, it won't be. You may enter the laboratory at any time and remove the tubes. Of course, if you are without technical training you may find it most difficult to disconnect the tubes without getting across a few thousand volts. That might be uncomfortable."

"Are you threatening me?" said Kingman, bristling. His stocky frame didn't take to bristling very well, and he lost considerable prestige in the act.

"Not at all. I'm just issuing a fair warning that the signs that say DANGER! HIGH VOLTAGE! are not there for appearance."

"Sounds like a threat to me."

"Have I threatened you? It sounds to me as though I were more than anxious for your welfare. Any threat of which you speak is utterly without grounds, and is a figment of your imagination; based upon distrust of Venus Equilateral, and the personnel of Venus Equilateral Relay Station."

Kingman shut up. He went down the list, marking off items here and there. While he was marking, Channing scribbled a circuit and listed the parts. He handed it over as Kingman finished.

"This is your circuit?" asked the lawyer skeptically.

"Yes."

"I shall have to ask for an explanation of the symbols involved."

"I shall be happy to present you with a book on essential radio technique," offered Channing. "A perusal of which will place you in possession of considerable knowledge. Will that suffice?"

"I believe so. I cannot understand how, being uncertain of your steps a few minutes ago, you are now presenting me with a circuit of your intended experiment."

"The circuit is, of course, merely symbolic. We shall change many of the constants before the day is over—in fact, we may even change the circuit."

"I shall require a notice before each change so that I may pass upon the legal aspects."

"Walt," said Don, "will you accompany me to a transparency experiment on the ninth level?"

"Be more than glad to," said Walt. "Let's go!"

They left the office quickly, and started for Joe's. They had not reached the combined liquor vending and restaurant establishment when the communicator called for Channing. It was announcing the arrival of Barney Carroll, so instead of heading for Joe's they went to the landing stage at the south end of the station to greet the visitor.

"Barney," said Don, "of all the companies, why did you pick on Terran Electric?'

"Gave us the best deal," said the huge, grinning man.

"Yeah, and they're getting the best of my goat right now."

"Well, Jim and I couldn't handle anything as big as the power transmission setup. They paid out a large slice of jack for the complete rights. All of us are well paid now. After all, I'm primarily interested in Martian artifacts, you know."

"I wonder if *they* had lawyers," smiled Walt dryly.

"Probably. And, no doubt, the legals had a lot to do with the fall of the Martian civilization."

"As it will probably get this one so wound up with red tape that progress will be impossible—or impractical."

"Well, Barney, let's take a run up to the lab," said Channing. "We can make paper talk even if Brother Kingman won't let us set it to soldering iron. There are a lot of things I want to ask you about the tube."

They sat around a drawing table and Channing began to sketch. "What I'd hoped to do is this," he said, drawing a schematic design. "We're not interested in power transmission, but your gadget will do a bit of voltage amplification because of its utter indifference to the power-line problem of impedance matching. We can take a relay tube and put in ten watts, say, across ten thousand ohms. That means the input will be somewhat above three hundred volts. Now, if our output is across a hundred thousand ohms, ten watts will give us one thousand volts. So we can get voltage amplification at the expense of current—which we will not need. Unfortunately, the relay tube as well as the rest of the system will give out with the same kind of power that it is impressed with—so we'll have amplification of driver radiation. Then we'll need a detector. We haven't been able to get one either yet, but this is a start, providing that Terran Electric will permit us to take a deep breath without wanting to pass on it."

"I think you may be able to get amplification," said Barney. "But to do it, you'll have to detect it first."

"Huh?"

"Sure. Before these darned things will work, this in-phase anode must be right on the beam. That means that you'll require a feedback circuit from the final stage to feed the in-phase anodes. Could be done without detection, I suppose."

"Well, for one thing, we're going to get some amplification if we change the primary anode—so. That won't permit the thing to handle any power, but it will isolate the output from the input and permit more amplifications. Follow?"

"Can we try it?"

"As soon as I get Terran Electric's permission."

"Here we go again!" groaned Walt.

"Yeah," said Don to Barney, "now you'll see the kind of birds you sold your gadget to."

They found Kingman and Farrell in conference. Channing offered his suggestion immediately, and Kingman looked it over, shaking his head.

"It is not permitted to alter, change, rework, or repair tubes owned by Terran Electric," he said.

"What are we permitted to do?" asked Channing.

"Give me your recommendation and I shall have the shop at Terran Electric perform the operation."

"At cost?"

"Cost plus a slight profit. Terran Electric, just as Venus Equilateral, is not in business from an altruistic standpoint."

"I see."

"Also," said Kingman severely, "I noticed one of your men changing the circuit slightly without permission. Why?"

"Who was it?"

"The man known as Thomas."

"Charles Thomas is in charge of development work," said Channing. "He probably noted some slight effect that he wanted to check."

"He should have notified me first—I don't care how minute the change. I must pass on changes first."

"But you wouldn't know their worth," Barney objected.

"No, but Mr. Farrell does, and will so advise me."

Wes looked at Channing. "Have you been to the ninth level yet?"

"Nope," said Channing.

"May I accompany you?"

Channing looked at Farrell critically. The Terran Electric engineer seemed sincere, and the pained expression on his face looked like frustrated sympathy to Don.

"Come along," he said.

Barney smiled cheerfully at the sign on Joe's door.

"That's a good one, 'Best Bar in Twenty-seven Million Miles, Minimum!' What's the qualification for?"

"That's as close as Terra ever gets. Most of the time the nearest bar is at Northern Landing, Venus; sixty-seven million miles from here. Come on in and we'll get plastered."

Farrell said, "Look, fellows, I know how you feel. They didn't tell me that you weren't going to be given permission to work. I understood that I was to sort of walk along, offer suggestions, and sort of prepare myself to take over some research myself. This is sickening."

"I think you mean that."

"May I use your telephone? I want to resign."

"Wait a minute. If you're that sincere, why don't we outguess 'em?"

"Could do," said Wes. "But how?"

"Is there any reason why we couldn't take a poke to Sol himself?"

"You mean haul power out of the sun?"

"That's the general idea. Barney, what do you think?"

"Could do—but it would take a redesign."

"Fine. And may we pray that the redesign is good enough to make a difference to the Interplanetary Patent Office." Channing called Joe. "The same. Three Moons all around. Scotch," he explained to the others, "synthesized in the Palanortis Country."

"Our favorite import," said Walt.

Joe grinned. "Another tablecloth session in progress?"

"Could be. As soon as we oil the think tank, we'll know for sure."

"What does he mean?" asked Barney.

Joe smiled. "They all have laboratories and draftsmen and textbooks," he said. "But for real engineering, they use my tablecloths. Three more problems and I'll have a complete tablecloth course in astrophysics, with a sideline in cartooning and a minor degree in mechanical engineering."

"Oh?"

"Sure. Give 'em a free hand, and a couple of your tubes and a tablecloth, and they'll have 'em frying eggs by morning. When I came out here, they demanded a commercial bond and I thought they were nuts. Who ever heard of making a restaurateur post a bond? I discovered that all of their inventions are initially tinkered out right here in the dining room—I could steal 'em blind if I were dishonest!" Joe smiled hugely. "This is the only place in the System where the tablecloths have been through blueprint machines. That," he said confidentially to Barney, "is why some of the stuff is slightly garbled. Scotch mixed with the drawings. They have the cloths inspected by the engineering department before they're laundered; I lose a lot of tablecloths that way."

Joe left cheerfully amid laughter.

The Three Moons came next, and then Don began to sketch. "Suppose we make a driver tube like this," he said. "And we couple the top end, where the cathode is, to the input side of the relay tube. Only the input side will require a variable-impedance anode, coupled back from the cathode to limit the input to the required value. Then the coupling anodes must be served with an automatic-coupling circuit so that the limiting power is passed without wastage."

Barney pulled out a pencil. "If you make that automatic-coupling circuit dependent upon the output from the terminal ends," he said, "it will accept only the amount of input that is required by the power being used from the output. Overcooling these two anodes will inhibit the power intake."

"Right," said Wes. "And I am of the opinion that the power available from Sol is of a magnitude that will permit operation over and above the limit."

"Four million tons of energy per second!" Walt exploded. "That's playing with fire!"

"You bet. We'll fix 'em with that!"

"Our experience with relay tubes," said Farrell slowly, "indicates that some increase in range is possible with additional anode focusing. Build your tube top with an extra set of anodes, and that'll give us better control of the beam."

"We're getting farther and farther from the subject of communications," said Channing with a smile. "But I think that we'll get more of this."

"How so?"

"Until we get a chance to tinker with those tubes, we

won't get ship-to-ship two ways. So we'll gadgeteer up something that will make Terran Electric foam at the mouth, and swap a hunk of it for full freedom in our investigations. Or should we bust Terran Electric wholeheartedly?"

"Let's slug 'em," said Walt.

"Go ahead," said Wes. "I'm utterly disgusted, though I think our trouble is due to the management of Terran Electric. They like legal tangles too much."

"We'll give 'em a legal tangle," said Barney. He was adding circuits to the tablecloth sketch.

Channing, on his side, was sketching in some equations, and Walt was working out some mechanical details. Joe came over, looked at the tablecloth, and forthright went to the telephone and called Warren.

The mechanical designer came, and Channing looked up in surprise. "Hi," he said, "I was just about to call you."

"Joe did."

"O.K. Look, Warren, can you fake up a gadget like this?"

Warren looked the thing over. "Give me about ten hours," he said. "We've got a spare turnover drive from the *Relay Girl* that we can hand-carve. There are a couple of water boilers that we can strip, cut open, and make to serve as the top end. How're you hoping to maintain the vacuum?"

"Yes," said Wes Farrell, "that's going to be the problem. If there's any adjusting of electrodes to do, this'll take months."

"That's why we, on Venus Equilateral, are ahead of the whole dingbusted Solar System in tube development," said Don. "We'll run the thing out in the open—and I *do* mean open! Instead of the tube having the insides exhausted, the operators will have their envelopes served with fresh, canned air."

"Like a cartoon I saw somewhere," grinned Walt. "Had a bird in full armor tinkering with a radio set. The caption was: 'Why shield the set?' "

"Phooey," said Warren. "Look, Tom Swift, is this another of Franks' brainchildren?"

"Tom Swift?" asked Wes.

"Yeah. That's the nom de plume he invents under. The other guy we call Captain Lightning."

"Oh?" asked Farrell. "Do you read him, too?"

"Sure," Warren grinned. "And say, speaking of comics, I came upon an old, old volume of *Webster's International Dictionary* in a rare-edition library in Chicago a couple of months ago, and they define "comic" as amusing, funny, and ludicrous; not imaginative fiction. How things change."

"They do."

"But to get back to this Goldberg, what is it?"

"Warren," said Channing soberly, "sit down!" Warren did. "Now," said Channing, "this screwball gadget is an idea whereby we hope to draw power out of the sun."

Warren swallowed once, and then waved for Joe. "Double," he told the restaurateur. Then to the others he said, "Thanks for seating me. I'm ill, I think. Hearing things. I could swear I heard someone say that this thing is to take power from Sol."

"That's it."

"Um-m-m. Remind me to quit Saturday. This is no job for a man beset by hallucinations."

"You grinning idiot, we're not fooling!"

"Then *you'd* better quit," Warren told Don. "This is no job for a bird with delusions of grandeur, either. Look, Don, you'll want this in the experimental blister at south end? On a coupler to the beam turret, so that it'll maintain direction at Sol?"

"Right. Couple it to the rotating stage if you can. Remember, that's three miles from south end."

"We've still got a few high-power selsyns," said Warren, making some notations of his own on the tablecloth. "And thanks to the guys who laid out this station some years ago, we've plenty of unused circuits from one end to the other. We'll couple it, all right. Oh, Mother. Seems to me like you got a long way off of your intended subject. Didn't you start out to make a detector for driver radiation?"

"Yep."

"And you end up tapping the sun. D'ye think it'll ever replace the horse?"

"Could be. Might even replace the coal mine. That's to be seen. Have you any idea of how long you'll be?"

"Make it ten hours. I'll get the whole crew on it at once."

"Fine."

"But look. What's the reason for this change in program?"

"That's easy," said Don. "First, we had a jam session. Second, we've come to the conclusion that the longest way 'round is the shortest way home. We're now in the throes of building something with which to dazzle the bright-minded management of Terran Electric and thus make them susceptible to our charm. We want a free hand at the transmission tubes, and this looks like a fair bit of bait."

"I get it. Quote: 'Why buy power from Terran Electric? Hang a Channing Power Beam on your chimney pot and tap the sun!' Whoa, Mazie. Bring on the needle, Watson. Hang out the flags, fire the cannon, ring the bells; for Venus Equilateral is about to hang a pipeline right into four million tons of energy per second! Don, that's a right smart bit of power to doodle with. Can you handle it?"

"Sure," said Channing with a wave of his hand, "we'll hang a fuse in the line!"

"O.K.," said Warren sweeping the tablecloth off the table like Mysto, the Magician, right out from under the glasses. "I'll be back—wearing my asbestos pants!"

Wes Farrell looked dreamily at the ceiling. "This *is* a screwy joint," he said idly. "What do we do for the next ten hours?"

"Red herring stuff," said Channing with what he hoped was a Machiavellian leer.

"Such as?"

"Making wise moves with the transmission tubes. Glomming the barrister's desk with proposed ideas for his approval; as many as we can think of, so that he'll be kept busy. We might even think of something that may work, meanwhile. Come, fellow conspirators, to horse!" Channing picked up his glass and drained it, making a wry face. "Rotten stuff—I wish I had a barrel of it!"

Channing surveyed the setup in the blister. He inspected it carefully, as did the others. When he spoke, his voice came through the helmet receivers with a slightly tinny sound: "Anything wrong? Looks O.K. to me."

"O.K. by me, too," said Farrell.

"Working in suit is not the best," said Don. "Barney, you're the bright-eyed lad. Can you align the plates?"

"I think so," came the muffled booming of Barney's powerful voice. "Gimme a screwdriver!"

Barney fiddled with the plate controls for several minutes. "She's running on dead-center alignment, now," he announced.

"Question," put in Wes, "do we get power immediately, or must we wait while the beam gets there and returns?"

"You must run your power line before you get power," said Walt. "My money is on the wait."

"Don't crack your anode-coupling circuit till then," warned Wes. "We don't know a thing about this; I'd prefer to let it in easy-like, instead of opening the gate and letting the whole four million tons per second come tearing in through this ammeter!"

"Might be a little warm having Sol in here with us," laughed Channing. "This is once in my life when we don't need a milliammeter, but a million-ammeter!"

"Shall we assign a pseudonym for it?" chuckled Walt.

"Let's wait until we see how it works."

The minutes passed slowly, and then Wes announced: "She should be here. Check your anode coupler, Barney."

Barney advanced the dial gingerly. The air that could have grown tense was, of course, not present in the blister. But the term is just a figure of speech, and therefore it may be proper to say that the air grew tense. Fact is, it was the nerves of the men that grew tense. Higher and higher went the dial, and still the meter stayed inert against the zero-end pin.

"Not a wiggle," said Barney in disgust. He twisted the dial all the way around and snorted. The meter left the zero pin ever so slightly.

Channing turned the switch that increased the sensitivity of the meter until the needle stood halfway up the scale.

"Solar power, here we come," he said in a dry voice. "One-half ampere at seven volts! Three and one-half watts. Bring on your atom smashers. Bring on your power-consuming factory districts. Hang the whole load of Central United States on the wires, for we have three and one-half watts! Just enough to run an electric clock!"

"But would it keep time?" asked Barney. "Is the frequency right?"

"Nope—but we'd run it. Look, fellows, when anyone tells you about this, insist that we got thirty-five hundred milliwatts on our first try. It sounds bigger."

"O.K., so we're getting from Sol just about three-tenths of the soup we need to make the setup self sustaining," said Walt. "Wes, this in-phase anode of yours—what can we do with it?"

"If this thing worked, I was going to suggest that there is enough power out there to spare. We could possibly modulate the in-phase anode with anything we wanted, and there would be enough junk floating round in the photosphere to slam on through."

"Maybe it is that lack of selectivity that licks us now," said Don. "Run the voltage up and down a bit. There should be DC running around in Sol, too."

"Whatever this power level is running at," said Barney, "we may get in-phase voltage—or in-phase power by running a line from the power terminal back. Moreover, boys, I'm going to hang a test clip in here."

Barney's gloved hands fumbled a bit, but the clip was attached. He opened the anode counter once again, and the meter slammed against the full-scale peg.

"See?" he said triumphantly.

"Yep," said Channing cryptically. "You, Bernard, have doubled our input."

"Mind if I take a whack at aligning it?" Wes asked.

"Go ahead. What we need is a guy with eyes in his fingertips. Have you?"

"No, but I'd like to try."

Farrell worked with the deflection plate alignment, and then said, ruefully: "No dice. Barney had it right on the beam."

"Is she aligned with Sol?" asked Channing.

Walt squinted down the tube. "Couldn't be better," he said, blinking.

"Could it be that we're actually missing Sol?" Don asked. "I mean, could it be that line-of-sight and line-of-power aren't one and the same thing?"

"Could be," Wes acknowledged.

Walt stepped to the verniers and swung the big intake tube over a minute arc. The meter jumped once more, and Channing stepped the sensitivity down again. Walt fiddled until the meter read maximum and then he left the tube that way.

"Coming up," said Channing. "We've now four times our original try. We now have enough juice to run an electric train—toy size! Someone think of something else, please. I've had my idea for the day."

"Let's juggle electrode spacing," suggested Wes.

"Can do," said Walt, brandishing a huge spanner wrench in one gloved hand.

Four solid, futile hours later, the power output of the solar beam was still standing at a terrifying fourteen watts. Channing was scratching furiously on a pad of paper with a large pencil; Walt was trying voltage variations on the supply anodes in a desultory manner; Barney was measuring the electrode spacing with a huge vernier rule; and Wes was staring at the sun, dimmed to seeable brightness by a set of dark glasses.

Wes was muttering to himself. "Electrode voltages, O.K. . . . alignment perfect . . . solar power output . . . not like power-line electricity . . . solar composition . . . Russell's Mixture—"

"Whoooo said that!" roared Channing.

"Who said what?" asked Barney.

"Why bust our eardrums?" Walt objected.

"What do you mean?" asked Wes, coming to life for the moment.

"Something about Russell's Mixture. Who said that?"

"I did. Why?"

"Look, Wes, what are your cathodes made of?"

"Thorium, CP metal. That's why they're shipped in metal containers in a vacuum."

"What happens if you try to use something else?"

"Don't work very well. In fact, if the output cathode

and the input dynode are not the same metal, they won't pass power at all."

"You're on the trail right now!" shouted Channing. "Russell's Mixture!"

"Sounds like a brand of smoking tobacco to me. Mind making a noise like an encyclopedia and telling me what is Russell's Mixture?"

"Russell's Mixture is a conglomeration of elements which go into the making of Sol—and all the other stars," Don explained. "Hydrogen, oxygen, sodium, and magnesium, iron, silicon, potassium, and calcium. They, when mixed according to the formula for Russell's Mixture, which can be found in any book on the composition of the stars, become the most probable mixture of metals. They—Russell's Mixture—go into the composition of all stars. What isn't mentioned in the mix isn't important."

"And what has this Russell got that we haven't got?" asked Walt.

"H, O, Na, Mg, Fe, Si, K, and Ca. And we, dear people, have Th, which Russell has not. Walt, call up the metallurgical lab and have 'em whip up a batch."

"Cook to a fine edge and serve with a spray of parsley? Or do we cut it into cubes—"

"Go ahead," said Channing. "Be funny. You just heard the man say that dissimilar dyno-cathodes do not work. What we need for our solar beam is a dynode of Russell's Mixture so that it will be similar to our cathode—which in this case is Sol. Follow me?"

"Yeah," said Walt, "I follow, but, brother, I'm a long way behind. But I'll catch up," he promised as he made connection between his suit-radio and the station communicator system. "Riley," he said, "here we go again. Can you whip us up a batch of Russell's Mixture?"

Riley's laugh was audible to the others, since it was broadcast by Walt's set. "Yeah, man, we can—if it's got metal in it. What, pray tell, is Russell's Mixture?"

Walt explained the relation between Russell's Mixture and the composition of Sol.

"Sun makers, hey?" asked Riley. "Is the chief screwball up there?"

"Yep," said Walt, grinning at Don.

"Sounds like him. Yeah, we can make you an alloy

consisting of Russell's Mixture. Tony's got it here, now, and it doesn't look hard. How big a dynode do you want?"

Walt gave him the dimensions of the dynode in the solar tube.

"Cinch," said Riley. "You can have it in two hours."

"Swell."

"But it'll be hotter than hell. Better make that six or seven hours. We may run into trouble making it jell."

"I'll have Arden slip you some pectin," said Walt. "Tomorrow morning, then?"

"Better. That's a promise."

Walt turned to the rest. "If any of us can sleep," he said, "I suggest it. Something tells me that tomorrow is going to be one of those days that mother told me about. I'll buy a drink."

Walt opened the anode-coupler circuit, and the needle of the output ammeter slammed across the scale and wound the needle halfway around the stop pin. The shunt, which was an external, high-dissipation job, turned red, burned the paint off its radiator fins, and then proceeded to melt. It sputtered in flying droplets of molten metal. Smoke spewed from the case of the ammeter, dissipating in the vacuum of the blister.

Walt closed the coupler circuit.

"Whammo!" he said. "Mind blowing a hundred-amp meter?"

"No," Don grinned. "I have a thousand-amp job that I'll sacrifice in the same happy-hearted fashion. Get an idea of the power?"

"Voltmeter was hanging up around ten thousand volts just before the ammeter went by."

"Um-m-m. Ten thousand volts at a hundred amps. That is one million watts, my friends, and no small potatoes. To run the station's communicating equipment we need seven times that much. Can we do it?"

"We can. I'll have Warren start running the main power bus down here and we'll try it. Meanwhile, we've got a healthy cable from the generator room; we can run the non-communicating drain of the station from our plaything here. That should give us an idea. We can use a couple of million watts right there. If this gadget will handle it, we can make one that will take the whole load without groaning. I'm calling Warren right now. He can start taking the load over from the generators as we increase our intake. We'll fade, but not without a flicker."

Walt hooked the output terminals of the tube to the huge cable blocks, using sections of the same heavy cable.

Warren called: "Are you ready?"

"Fade her in," said Walt. He kept one eye on the line voltmeter and opened the anode coupler slightly.

The meter dipped as Warren shunted the station load over to the tube circuit. Walt brought the line voltage up to above normal, and it immediately dropped as Warren took more load from the solar intake.

This jockeying went on for several minutes until Warren called: "You've got it all. Now what?"

"Start running the bus down here to take the communications load," said Don. "We're running off of an eight-hundred-thousand-mile cathode now, and his power output is terrific. Or better, run us a high-tension line down here and we'll save silver. We can ram ten thousand volts up there for transformation. Get me?"

"What frequency?"

"Yeah," drawled Channing, "have Chuck Thomas run us a control line from the primary frequency standard. We'll control our frequency with that. O.K.?"

"Right-o."

Channing looked at the setup once more. It was singularly unprepossessing, this conglomeration of iron and steel and plastic. There was absolutely nothing to indicate that two and one-third million watts of power coursed from Sol, through its maze of anodes, and into the electric lines of Venus Equilateral. The cathodes and dynode glowed with their usual dull red glow, but there was no coruscating aura of power around the elements of the system. The gimbals that held the big tube slid easily, permitting the tube to rotate freely as the selsyn motor kept the tube pointing at Sol. The supply cables remained cool and operative, and to all appearances the setup was inert.

"O.K., fellows," said Channing, "this is it—"

He was interrupted by the frantic waving of Kingman, from the other side of the air lock.

"I feel slightly conscience-stricken," Don said with a smile that showed that he didn't mean it at all. "But let us go and prepare the goat for shearing."

Kingman's trouble was terrific, according to him. "Mr. Channing," he complained, "you are not following our wishes. And you, Mr. Farrell, have been decidedly amiss in your hobnobbing with the engineers here. You were sent out as my consultant, not to assist them in their endeavors."

"What's your grief?" asked Channing.

"I find that your laboratory has been changing the circuits without having previously informed me of the proposed change," Kingman complained. "I feel that I am within my rights in removing the tubes here. Your investigations have not been sanctioned—" He looked out through the air lock. "What are you doing out there?"

"We have just succeeded in taking power from the sun," said Don. He tried to keep his voice even, but the exultation was too high in him, and his voice sounded like sheer joy.

"You have been—" Kingman did a double take. "You *what?"* he yelled.

"Have succeeded in tapping Sol for power."

"Why, that's wonderful!"

"Thank you," said Don. "You will no doubt be glad to hear that Wes Farrell was instrumental in this program."

"Then a certain part of the idea is rightfully the property of Terran Electric," said Kingman.

"I'm afraid not," said Don. "Dr. Farrell's assistance was not requested. Though his contribution was of great value, it was given freely. He was not solicited. Therefore, since Terran Electric was not consulted formally, Dr. Farrell's contribution to our solar power beam can not be considered as offering a hold on our discovery."

"This is true, Dr. Farrell?"

"I'm afraid so. You see, I saw what was going on and became interested, academically. I naturally offered a few minor suggestions in somewhat the same manner as a motorist will stop and offer another motorist assistance in changing a tire. The problem was interesting to me, and as a problem it did not seem to me—"

"Your actions in discussing this with members of the Venus Equilateral technical staff without authorization will cost us plenty," snapped Kingman. "However, we shall deal with you later."

"You know," said Farrell with a cheerfully malicious grin, "if you had been less stuffy about our tubes, they might be less stuffy about my contribution."

"Ah, these non-legal agreements are never satisfactory. But that is to be discussed later. What do you intend to do with your invention, Dr. Channing?"

Channing smiled in a superior manner. "As you see, the device is small. Yet it handles a couple of million watts. An even smaller unit might be made that would suffice to supply a home, or even a community. As for the other end, I see no reason why the size might not be increased to a point where it may obsolete all existing power-generating stations."

Kingman's complexion turned slightly green. He swallowed hard. "You, of course, would not attempt to put this on the market yourself."

"No?" asked Channing. "I think you'll find that Venus Equilateral is as large, if not larger, than Terran Electric, and we have an enviable reputation for delivering the goods. We could sell refrigerators to the Titan colony, if we had the VE label on them and claimed they were indispensable. Our escutcheon is not without its adherents."

"I see," said Kingman. His present volubility would not have jogged a jury into freeing the armless wonder from a pickpocketing charge. "Is your invention patentable?"

"I think so. While certain phases of it are like the driver tube—which, of course, is public domain—the applications are quite patentable. I must admit that certain parts are of the power transmission tube, but not enough for you to claim a hold. At any rate, I shall be busy for the next hour, transmitting the details to Washington, so that the Interplanetary Patent Office may rule on it. Our Terran legal department has a direct line there, you know, and they have been directed to maintain that contact at all costs."

"May I use your lines?"

"Certainly. They are public carriers. You will not be restricted any more than any other man. I am certain that our right to transmit company business without waiting for the usual turn will not be contested."

"That sounds like a veiled threat."

"That sounds like slander!"

"Oh, no. Believe me. But wait, Dr. Channing. Is there no way in which we can meet on a common ground?"

"I think so. We want a free hand in this tube proposition."

"For which rights you will turn over a nominal interest in solar power?"

"Forty percent," said Channing.

"But we—"

"I know, you want control."

"We'd like it."

"Sorry. Those are our terms. Take 'em or leave 'em."

"Supposing that we offer you full and unrestricted rights to any or all developments you or we make on the Martian transmission tubes?"

"That might be better to our liking."

"We might buck you," said Kingman, but there was doubt in his voice.

"Yes? You know, Kingman, I'm not too sure that Venus Equilateral wants to play around with power except as a maintenance angle. What if we toss the solar beam to the public domain? That is within our right, too."

Kingman's green color returned, this time accompanied with beads of sweat. He turned to Farrell. "Is there nothing we can do? Is this patentable?"

"No— Yes," grinned Farrell.

Kingman excused himself. He went to the office provided for him and began to send messages to the Terran Electric Company offices at Chicago. The forty-minute wait between message and answer was torture to him, but it was explained to him that light and radio crossed space at one hundred and eighty-six thousand miles per second and that even an Act of Congress could do nothing to help him hurry it. Meanwhile, Channing's description tied up the Terran beam for almost an hour at the standard rate of twelve hundred words per minute. Their answers came within a few minutes of one another.

Channing tossed the 'gram before Kingman. "Idea definitely patentable," said the wire.

Kingman stood up. Apparently the lawyer believed that his pronouncement would carry more weight by looming over the smiling, easygoing faces of his parties-of-the-second-part. "I am prepared to negotiate with your legal department; offering them, and you, the full rights to the transmission tube. This will include full access to any and all discoveries, improvements, and/or changes made at any time from its discovery to the termination of this contract, which shall be terminated only by absolute mutual agreement between Terran Electric and Venus Equilateral. In return for this, Venus Equilateral will permit Terran Electric to exploit the solar beam tube fully and freely, and exclusively—"

"Make that slightly different," said Channing. "Terran Electric's rights shall prevail exclusively—*except* within the realm of space, upon man-made celestial objects, and upon the satellites and minor natural celestial bodies where sub-relay stations of the Interplanetary Communications Company are established."

Kingman thought that one over. "In other words, if the transport companies desire to use the solar beam, you will hold domain from the time they leave an atmosphere until they again touch—"

"Let's not complicate things," Don smiled cheerfully. "I like uncomplicated things."

Kingman smiled wryly. "I'm sure," he agreed with fine sarcasm. "But I see your point. You intend to power the communications system with the solar beam. That is natural. Also, you feel that a certain amount of revenue should be coming your way. Yes, I believe that our legal departments can agree."

"So let's not make the transport companies change masters in midspace."

"You are taking a lot on your shoulders," said Kingman. "We wouldn't permit our technicians to dictate the terms of an agreement."

"You are not going to like Venus Equilateral at all," laughed Don. "We wouldn't permit our legal department to dabble in things of which they know nothing. Years ago, when the first concentric beam was invented, which we now use to punch a hole in the Heaviside Layer, communications was built about a group of engineers. We held the three inner planets together by the seat of our pants, so to speak, and nurtured communications from a slipshod, hope-to-God-it-gets-through proposition to a sure thing. Funny thing, but when people were taking their messages catch-as-catch-can, there was no reason for legal lights. Now that we can and do insure messages against their loss, we find that we are often tied up with legal red tape.

"Otherwise, we wouldn't have a lawyer on the premises. They serve their purpose, no doubt, but in this gang the engineers tell the attorneys how to run things. We shall continue to do so. Therefore you are speaking with the proper parties, and once the contract is prepared by you, we shall have an attorney run through the whereases, wherefores, and parties-of-the-first, -second, and -third parts to see that there is no sleight of hand in the microscopic type."

"You're taking a chance," Kingman warned. "All men are not as fundamentally honest as Terran Electric."

"Kingman," Channing smiled, "I hate to remind you of this, but who got what just now? We wanted the transmission tube."

"I see your point. But we have a means of getting power out of the sun."

"We have a hunk of that, too. It would probably have been a mere matter of time before some bright bird at Terran found the thing, as it was."

"I shall see that the contract gives you domain over man-made objects in space—including those that occasionally touch upon the natural celestial objects. Also the necessary equipment operating under the charter of Venus Equilateral, wherever or whenever it may be, including any future installations."

"Fine. You may have trouble understanding our feelings. We are essentially a space-born company, and as such we can have no one at the helm who is not equipped to handle the technical details of operations in space." Channing smiled reminiscently. "We had a so-called efficiency expert running Venus Equilateral a couple of years ago, and the fool nearly wrecked us because he didn't know that the airplant was not a mass of highly complicated, chemical-reaction machinery instead of what it really is. Kingman, do you know what an airplant is?"

"Frankly, no. I should imagine it is some sort of air-purifying device."

"You'll sit down hard when I tell you that the airplant is just what it is. Martian sawgrass! Brother Burbank tossed it out because he thought it was just weeds, cluttering up the place. He was allergic to good engineering, anyway."

"That may be good enough in space," said Kingman, "but on Terra, we feel that our engineers are not equipped to dabble in the legal tangles that follow when they force us to establish precedent by inventing something that has never been covered by a previous decision."

"O.K.," said Don. "Every man to his own scope. Write up your contract, Kingman, and we'll all climb on the band wagon with our illiterate X's."

In Evanston, north of Chicago, the leaves changed from their riotous green to a somber brown, and fell to lay a blanket over the earth. Snow covered the dead leaves, and Christmas, with its holly, went into the past, followed closely by New Year's Eve with its hangover.

And on a roof by the shore of Lake Michigan, a group of men stood in overcoats beside a huge machine that towered above the great letters of the Terran Electric Company sign that could be seen all the way from Gary, Indiana.

It was a beautiful thing, this tube; a far cry from the haywire thing that had brought solar power to Venus Equilateral. It was mounted on gimbals, and the metal was bright-plated and perfectly machined. Purring motors caused the tube to rotate to follow the sun.

"Is she aligned?" asked the project engineer.

"Right on the button."

"Good. We can't miss with this one. There may have been something sour with the rest, but this one ran Venus Equilateral—the whole relay station—for ten days without interruption."

He faced the anxious men in overcoats. "Here we go," he said, and his hand closed upon the switch that transferred the big tube from test power to operating power.

The engineer closed the switch, and stepped over to the great, vaned, air-cooled ammeter shunt. On a panel just beyond the shunt the meter hung—

At Zero!

"Um," said the project engineer. "Something wrong, no doubt."

They checked every connection, every possible item in the circuit. "Nothing wrong!"

"Oh, now look," said the engineer. "This isn't Hell, where the equipment is always perfect except that it doesn't work."

"This *is* Hell," announced his assistant. "The thing is perfect—except that it doesn't work."

"It worked on Venus Equilateral."

"We've changed nothing, and we handled that gadget like it was made of cello-gel. We're running the same kind of voltage, checked on standard voltmeters. We're within one-tenth of one percent of the original operating conditions. But—no power."

"Call Channing."

The beams between Terra and Venus Equilateral carried furious messages for several hours. Channing's answer said:

I'M CURIOUS. AM BRINGING THE EXPERIMENTAL SHIP TO TERRA TO INVESTIGATE.

The assistant asked: "Isn't that the job they hooked up to use the solar power for their drive?"

The project engineer: "That's it. And it worked."

"I know. I took a run on it!"

Channing was taking a chance, running the *Relay Girl* to Terra, but he knew his ship, and he was no man to be overcautious. He drove it to Terra at three G and by dead reckoning, started down into Terra's blanket of air, heading for the Terran Electric plant which was situated on the lake shore.

Then down out of the cloudless sky came the *Relay*

Girl in a free fall. It screamed with the whistle of tortured air as it fell, and it caught the attention of every man who was working at Terran Electric.

Only those on the roof saw the egg-shaped hull fall out of the sky unchecked, landing fifteen hundred yards offshore in Lake Michigan.

The splash was terrific.

"Channing—!" said the project engineer, aghast.

"No, look there—a lifeship!"

Cautiously gliding down, a minute lifeship less than the size of a freight car came to a landing in the Terran Electric construction yard. Channing emerged, his face white. He bent down and kissed the steel grille of the construction yard fervently.

Someone ran out and gave Channing a brown bottle. Don nodded, and took a draw of monstrous proportions. He gagged, made a face, and smiled in a very wan manner.

"Thanks," he said shakily. He took another drink, of more gentlemanly size.

"What happened?"

"Dunno. Was coming in at three G. About four hundred miles up, the deceleration just quit. Like that! I made it to the skeeter, here, in just about enough time to get her away with about two miles to go. *Whoosh!*"

Don dug into his pocket and found cigarettes. He lit up and drew deeply. "Something cockeyed, here. That stoppage might make me think that my tube failed; but—"

"You suspect that our tube isn't working for the same reason?" finished the project engineer.

"Yes. I'm thinking of the trick, ultra-high powered, concentric beams we have to use to ram a hole through the Heaviside Layer. We start out with three million watts of sheer radio frequency and end up with just enough to make our receivers worth listening to. Suppose this had some sort of Heaviside Layer?"

"In which case, Terran Electric hasn't got solar power," said the project engineer. "Tim, load this bottle into the *Electric Lady*, and we'll see if we can find this barrier." To Channing, he said: "You look as though you could stand a rest. Check into a hotel in Chicago and we'll call you when we're ready to try it out."

Channing agreed.

A shave, a bath, and a good night's sleep did wonders for his nerves, as did a large amount of Scotch. He was at Terran Electric in the morning, once more in command of himself.

Up into the sky went the ship that carried the solar tube. It remained inert until the ship passed above three hundred and forty miles. Then the ammeter needle swung over, and the huge shunt grew warm. The tenuous atmosphere outside of the ship was unchanged, yet the beam drew power of gigantic proportions.

They dropped again. The power ceased.

They spent hours rising and falling, charting this unknown barrier that stopped the unknown radiation from bringing solar power right down to earth. It was there, all right, and impervious. Above, megawatts raced through the giant shunt. Below, not even a microammeter could detect a trace of current.

"O.K., Don," said the project engineer. "We'll have to do some more work on it. It's nothing of your doing."

Mark Kingman's face was green again, but he nodded in agreement. "We seem to have a useless job here, but we'll think of something."

They studied the barrier and established its height as a constant three hundred and thirty-nine point seven six miles above Terra's mythical sea level. It was almost a perfect sphere, that did not change with the night and day, as did the Heaviside Layer. There was no way to find out how thick it was, but thickness was of no importance, since it effectively stopped the beam.

Then as Don Channing stepped aboard the *Princess of the Sky* to get home again, the project engineer said: "If you don't mind, I think we'll call that one the Channing Layer!"

"Yeah," grinned Don, pleased at the thought, "and forever afterward it will stand as a cinder in the eye of Terran Electric."

"Oh," said the project engineer, "we'll beat the Channing Layer."

But the project engineer was a bum prophet.

Interlude

Baffled and beaten, Mark Kingman returned to Terran Electric empty-handed. He hated science and the men who reveled in it, though he was not above using science—and the men who reveled in it—to further his own unscientific existence. The poetic justice that piled blow upon blow on his unprotected head was lost on Mark Kingman and he swore eternal vengeance.

With a say in the operations at Terran Electric, Kingman directed that the engineers and scientists work furiously to discover something about this strange radiation that made the energy beam possible, that drove spacecraft across the void, and which was now drawing power out of the sun to feed the requirements of men who owed allegiance to Venus Equilateral.

Kingman was losing his sense of values. He accused Venus Equilateral of trickery—quietly, of course, for people had faith in the operations of the relay station personnel and would stand for no criticism. Because people found Venus Equilateral and all that went with it both good and upstanding in the face of what Mark Kingman believed, it infuriated him to the point of illegality.

And the evil fate that makes evil men appear to flourish smiled upon Mark Kingman, while all that Channing had to fight back with was his faith in the unchanging physical laws of science.

But Kingman thought he was smart enough to beat Venus Equilateral at its own business!

BEAM PIRATE

Mark Kingman was in a fine state of nerves. He looked upon life and the people in it as one views the dark-brown taste of a hangover. It seemed to him at the present time that the Lord had forsaken him, for the entire and complete success of the solar beam had been left to Venus Equilateral by a sheer fluke of nature.

Neither he, nor anyone else, could have foreseen the Channing Layer, that effectively blocked any attempt to pierce it with the strange, sub-level energy spectrum over which the driver tube and the power-transmission tube worked, representing the so-called extremes of the spectrum.

But Venus Equilateral, for their part, was well set. Ships plied the spaceways, using their self-contained power only during atmospheric passage, and paid Venus Equilateral well for the privilege. The relay station itself was powered on the solar beam. There were other relay stations that belonged to the Interplanetary Communications Company: Luna, Deimos, and Phobos, and the six that circled Venus in lieu of a satellite—all were powered by the solar beam. The solar observatory became the sole income for Terran Electric's planetary rights of the solar beam, since Mercury owned no air of its own.

Kingman was beginning to feel the brunt of Channing's statement to the effect that legal-minded men were of little importance when it came to the technical life in space, where men's lives and livelihood depended more on technical skill than upon the legal pattern set for their protection in the complex society of planetary civilization.

He swore vengeance.

So, like the man who doggedly makes the same mistake twice in a row, Kingman was going to move Heaven, Hell, and three planets in an effort to take a swing at the same jaw that had caught his fist between its teeth before.

Out through the window of his office, he saw men toiling with the big tube on the far roof; the self-same tube that had carried the terrific load of Venus Equilateral for ten days without interruption and with no apparent overload. Here on Terra, its output meter, operating through a dummy load, showed not the slightest inclination to leave the bottom peg and seek a home among the higher brackets.

So Kingman cursed and hated himself for having backed himself into trouble. But Kingman was not a complete fool. He was a brilliant attorney, and his record has placed him in the position of Chief Attorney for Terran Electric, which was a place of no mean importance. He had been licked on the other fellow's ground, with the other fellow's tools.

He picked up papers that carried, side by side, the relative assets of Venus Equilateral and Terran Electric. He studied them and thought deeply.

To his scrutiny, the figures seemed about equal, though perhaps Venus Equilateral was a bit ahead.

But, he had been licked on the other fellow's ground with the other fellow's weapons. He thought that if he fought on his own ground with his own tools he might be able to swing the deal.

Terran Electric was not without a modicum of experience in the tools of the other fellow. Terran Electric's engineering department was brilliant and efficient, too; at least the equal of Channing and Franks and their gang of laughing gadgeteers. That not only gave him the edge of having his own tools and his own ground, but a bit of the other fellow's instruments, too. Certainly his engineering department should be able to think of something good.

William Cartwright, business manager for Venus Equilateral, interrupted Don and Walt in a discussion. He carried a page of stock market quotations and a few hundred feet of ticker tape.

Channing put down his pencil and leaned back in his

chair. Walt did likewise, and said: "What's brewing?"

"Something I do not like."

"So?"

"The stock has been cutting didoes. We've been up and down so much it looks like a scenic railway."

"How do we come out?"

"Even, mostly; but from my experience, I would say that some bird is playing hooky with Venus Equilateral, Preferred. The common is even worse."

"Look bad?"

"Not too good. It is more than possible that some guy with money and the desire might be able to hook a large slice of VE, Preferred. I don't think they could get control, but they could garner a plurality from stock outstanding on the planets. Most of the preferred stock is in the possession of the folks out here, you know, but aside from yourself, Walt, and a couple dozen of the executive personnel, the stock is spread pretty thin. The common stock has a lot of itself running around loose outside. Look!"

Cartwright began to run off the many yards of ticker tape. "Here some guy dumped a boatload at Canalopsis, and some other guy glommed on to a large hunk at New York. The Northern Landing Exchange showed a bit of irregularity during the couple of hours of tinkering, and the irregularity was increased because some bright guy took advantage of it and sold short." He reeled off a few yards and then said: "Next, we have the opposite tale. Stuff was dumped at Northern Landing, and there was a wild flurry of bulling at Canalopsis. The Terran Exchange was just flopping up and down in a general upheaval, with the boys selling at the top and buying at the bottom. That makes money, you know, and if you can make the market tick your way—I mean control enough stuff—your purchases at the bottom send the market up a few points, and then you dump it and it drops again. It wouldn't take more than a point or two to make a guy rich, if you had enough stock and could continue to make the market vacillate."

"That's so," agreed Don. "Look, Bill, why don't we get some of our Terran agents to tinkering, too? Get one of our best men to try to outguess the market. As long as it is being done systematically, he should be able to follow the other guy's thinking. That's the best we can do unless we go Gestapo and start listening in on all the stuff that goes through the station here."

"Would that help?"

"Yeah, but we'd all land in the hoosegow for breaking the secrecy legislation. You know. 'No one shall . . . intercept . . . transmit . . . eavesdrop upon . . . any message not intended for the listener, and . . . shall not . . . be party to the use of any information gained . . . et cetera.' That's us. The trouble is this lag between the worlds. They can prearrange their bulling and bearing ahead of time and play smart. With a little trick, they can get the three markets working just so—going up at Northern Landing, down at Terra, and up again at Canalopsis—just like waves in a rope. By playing fast and loose on paper, they can really run things hell, west, and crooked. Illegal, probably, since they each no doubt will claim to have all the stock in their possession, and yet will be able to sell and buy the same stock at the same time in three places."

"Sounds slightly precarious to me," Cartwright objected.

"Not at all, if you figure things just right. At a given instant, Pete may be buying at sixty-five on Venus; Joe might be selling like furious at seventy-one on Mars; and Jim may be bucking him up again by buying at sixty-five on Terra. Then the picture and the tickers catch up with one another, and Joe will start buying again at sixty-five, while Pete and Jim are selling at seventy-one. Once they get their periodicity running, they're able to tinker the market for quite a time. That's where your man comes in, Bill. Have him study the market and step in at the right time and grab us all a few cheap ones. Get me?"

"Sure," said Cartwright. "I get it. In that way, we'll tend to stabilize the market, as well as getting the other guy's shares."

"Right. I'll leave it up to you. Handle this thing for the best interest of all of us."

Cartwright smiled once again, and left with a thoughtful expression on his face. Channing picked up the miniature of the power-transmission tube and studied it as though the interruption had not occurred.

"We'll have to use about four of these per stage," he said. "We'll have to use an input terminal tube to accept the stuff from the previous stage, drop it across the low-resistance load, resistance-couple the stage to another output terminal tube where we can make use of the coupling circuits without feedback. From there into the next tube, with the high-resistance load, and out of the power-putter-outer tube across the desk and to the next four-bottle stage."

"That's getting complicated," said Walt. "Four tubes per stage of amplification."

"Sure. As the arts and sciences get more advanced, things tend to get more complicated."

"That's essentially correct," Walt agreed with a smile. "But you're foreguessing. We haven't even got a detector that will detect driver radiation."

"I know, and perhaps this thing will not work. But after all, we've got the tubes and we might just as well try them out, just in case. We'll detect driver radiation soon enough, and then we might as well have a few odd thoughts on how to amplify it for public use. Nothing could tickle me more than to increase those three circles on our letterhead to four. 'Planet to Planet, and Ship to Ship' is our hope. This one-way business is not to my liking. How much easier it would have been if I'd been able to squirt a call in to the station when I was floating out there beyond Jupiter in that wrecked ship. That gave me to think, Walt. Driver radiation detection is the answer."

"How so?"

"We'll use the detector to direct our radio beam, and the ship can have a similar gadget coupled to its beam, detecting a pair of drivers set at one hundred and eighty degrees from one another so the thrust won't upset the station's celestial alignment. We can point one of them at the ship's course, even, making it easier for them."

"Speaking of direction," said Walt thoughtfully, "have you figured why the solar beam is always pointing behind Sol?"

"I haven't given that much thought. I've always thought that it was due to the alignment plates not being in linear perfection, so that the power beam bends.

They can make the thing turn a perfect right angle, you know."

"Well, I've been toying with the resurrected heap you dropped into Lake Michigan a couple of months ago, and I've got a good one for you. You know how the beam seems to lock into place when we've got it turned to Sol—not enough to make it certain, but more than detectably directive?"

"Yep. We could toss out the motor control that keeps her face turned to the sun."

"That's what I was hoping to gain—" Walt started, but he stopped as the door opened and Arden entered, followed by a man and woman.

"Hello," said Walt in a tone of admiration.

"This is Jim Baler and his sister Christine," said Arden. "Baler, the guy with the worried look on his face is my legally wedded souse—no, spouse. And the guy with the boudoir-gorilla gleam in his vulpine eyes is that old vulture, Walt Franks."

Walt took the introduction in his stride and offered Christine his chair. Arden stuck her tongue out at him, but Walt shrugged it off. Channing shook hands with Jim Baler and then sought the "S" drawer of his file cabinet. He found the Scotch and soda, and then grinned.

"Should have the ice under 'I' but it's sort of perishable, and so we keep it in the refrigerator. Arden, breach the 'G' drawer, please, and haul out the glasses. I suppose we could refrigerate the whole cabinet, but it wouldn't sound right if people heard that we kept their mail on ice. Well—"

"Here's how, if we don't already know," said Walt, clinking glasses with Christine.

"Walt earned that 'wolf' title honestly," laughed Arden, "he likes to think. Frankly, he's a sheep in wolf's clothing!"

"What are his other attributes?" asked Christine.

"He invents. He scribbles a bit. He cuts doodles on tablecloths, and he manages to get in the way all the time," said Don. "We keep him around the place for his entertainment value."

"Why—"

"Quiet, Walter, or I shall explain the sordid details of the Walter Franks Electron Gun."

"What was that one?" asked Christine.

"You really wouldn't want to know," Walt told her.

"Oh, but I would."

"Yeah," growled Franks, "you would!"

"Would you rather hear it from him or me?" Arden asked.

"He'll tell me," said Christine. Her voice was positive and assured.

"And that'll take care of that," said Arden. "But I think we interrupted something. What were you saying about gaining, Walt?"

"Oh, I was saying that I was tinkering around with the *Anopheles*. We hooked it up with the solar beam for power, and I got to wondering about that discrepancy. The faster you go, the greater is the angular displacement, and then with some measurements, I came up with a bugger factor—"

"Whoa, goodness," laughed Christine. "What is a bugger factor?"

"You'll learn," said Arden, "that the boys out here have a language all their own, I've heard them use that one before. The bugger factor is a sort of multiplying, or dividing, or additive, or subtractive quantity. You perform the mathematical operation with the bugger factor, and your original wrong answer turns into the right answer."

"Is it accepted?"

"Oh, sure," Arden answered. "People don't realize it, but that string of 4's in the derivation of Bode's Law is a bugger factor."

"You," Christine said to Walt, "will also tell me what Bode's Law is—but later."

"O.K.," grinned Walt. "At any rate, I came up with a bugger factor that gave me to think. The darned solar beam points to where Sol actually is!"

"Whoosh!" exclaimed Channing. "You don't suppose we're tinkering with the medium that propagates the law of gravity?"

"I don't know. I wouldn't know. Has anyone ever tried to measure the velocity of propagation of the attraction of gravity?"

"No, and no one will until we find some way of modulating it."

Jim Baler smiled. "No wonder Barney was a little wacky when he got home. I come out here to take a look around and maybe give a lift to your gang on the transmission tube—and bump right into a discussion on the possibility of modulating the law of gravity!"

"Not the law, Jim, just the force."

"Now he gets technical about it. You started out a couple of months ago to detect driver radiation, and ended up by inventing a beam that draws power out of the sun. Think you'll ever find the driver radiation?"

"Probably."

"Yeah," drawled Arden. "And I'll bet my hat that when they do, they won't have any use for it. I've seen 'em work before."

"Incidentally," said Christine, "you mentioned the *Anopheles*, and I think that is the first ship I've ever heard of that hasn't a feminine name. How come?"

"The mosquito that does the damage is the female." Jim grinned. "The Mojave spaceyards owns a sort of tender craft. It has a couple of big cranes on the top and a whole assortment of girders near the bottom. It looks like, and is also called the *Praying Mantis*. Those are also female; at least the ones that aren't afraid of their own shadow are."

Channing said suddenly: "Walt, have you tried the propagation time of the solar beam on the *Anopheles*?"

"No. How would we go about doing that?"

"By leaving the controls set for one G, and then starting the ship by swapping the tube energizing voltages from test power to operating power."

"Should that tell us?"

"Sure. As we know, the amount of energy radiated from the sun upon a spot the size of our solar tube is a matter of peanuts compared to the stuff we must get out of it. Ergo, our beam must go to Sol and collect the power and draw it back down the beam. Measure the transit time, and we'll know."

"That's an idea. I've got a micro clock in the lab. We can measure it to a hundredth millionth of a second. Anyone like to get shook up?"

"How?" asked Jim.

"Snapping from zero to one G all at once-like isn't too gentle. She'll knock your eyes out."

"Sounds like fun. I'm elected."

"So am I," insisted Christine.

"No," said Jim. "I know what he's talking about."

"So do I," said Arden. "Don't do it."

"Well, what better have you to offer?" asked Christine unhappily.

"You and I are going down to the Mall."

Channing groaned in mock anguish. "Here comes another closetful of female haberdashery. I'm going to close that corridor someday, or put a ceiling on the quantity of sales, or make it illegal to sell a woman anything unless she can prove that 'she has nothing to wear'!"

"That, I'd like to see," said Walt.

"You would," Arden snorted. "Come on, Chris. Better than the best of three worlds is available."

"That sort of leaves me all alone," said Don. "I'm going to look up Wes Farrell and see if he's been able to make anything worth looking at for a driving detector."

Don found Wes in the laboratory, poring over a complicated circuit. Farrell was muttering under his breath, and probing deep into the maze of haywire on the bench.

"Wes, when you get to talking to yourself, it's time to take a jaunt to Joe's."

"Not right now," Wes objected. "I haven't got that hollow leg that your gang seemed to have developed. Besides, I'm on the trail of something."

"Yes?" Channing forgot about Joe's, and was all interest.

"I got a wiggle out of the meter there a few minutes ago. I'm trying to get another one."

"What was it like?"

"Wavered up and down like fierce for about a minute after I turned it on. Then it died quick, and has been dead ever since."

"Could it have been anything cockeyed with the instruments?"

"Nope. I've checked every part in this circuit, and

everything is as good as it ever will be. No, something external caused that response."

"You've tried the solar tube with a dynode of the same alloy as the driver cathodes?"

"Uh-huh. Nothing at all. Oh, I'll take that back. I got a scratch. With a pre-meter gain of about four hundred decibels, I read three micro-microamperes. That was detected from a driver tube forty feet across the room, running at full blast. I wondered for a minute whether the opposing driver was doing any cancellation, and so I took a chance and killed it for about a half-second, but that wasn't it."

"Nuts. Does the stuff attenuate with distance?"

"As best as I could measure, it was something to the tune of inversely proportional to the cube of the distance. That's not normal for beams, since it shows that the stuff isn't globularly radiated. But the amplifier gain was hanging right on the limit of possible amplification, and the meter was as sensitive as a meter can be made, I think. You couldn't talk from one end of Venus Equilateral to the other with a set like that."

"No, I guess you're right. Hey! Look!"

The meter took a sudden upswing, danced for a minute, and died once more.

"What have you got in there? What did you change?"

"Oh, I got foolish and tried a tuned circuit across the output of one of the miniature transmission tubes. It's far enough away from the big beams and stuff at the north end, so that none of the leakage can cause trouble. Besides, I'm not getting anything like our beam transmissions."

Channing laughed. "Uh-huh, looks to me like you're not getting much of anything at all."

Farrell smiled wryly. "Yeah, that's so," he agreed. "But look, Don, Hertz himself didn't collect a transcontinental shortwave broadcast on his first attempt."

"If Hertz had been forced to rely upon vacuum tubes, his theories couldn't have been formulated, I think," said Channing. "At least, not by him. The easier frequencies and wavelengths are too long; a five-hundred-meter dipole can't be set up in a small room for laboratory tinkering. The kind of frequencies that come of dipoles a couple of feet long, such as Hertz used, are pretty hard to work with unless you have special tubes."

"Hertz had rotten detectors, too. But he made his experiments with spark gap generators, which gave sufficient high-peak transcients to induce spark-magnitude voltages in his receiving dipole."

"I'm not too sure of that tuned-circuit idea of yours, Wes. Go ahead and tinker to your heart's content, but remember that I'm skeptical of the standard resonance idea."

"Why?"

"Because we've been tinkering with driver tubes for years and years—and we have also been gadgeting up detectors, radio hootnannies, and stuff of the electronic spectrum all the way from direct current to hard X-rays, and we have yet to have anything react to driver radiation. Ergo, I'm skeptical."

The call bell rang for Channing, and he answered. It was Walt Franks.

"Don," he said with a laugh in his voice, though it was apparent that he felt slightly guilty about laughing, "got a 'gram from Addison, the project engineer on the solar beam from Terran Electric. Says:

> FINALLY GOT THROUGH CHANNING LAYER. POWER BY THE MEGAWATT HOUR IN GREAT SHAPE. BUT THE ATMOSPHERE FROM THE CHANNING LAYER RIGHT DOWN TO THE SNOUT OF THE TUBE IS A DULL RED SCINTILLATION. LIKE THE DRIVER TUBE TRAIL—IT IONIZES THE ATMOSPHERE INTO OZONE. POWER BY THE MEGAWATT, AND OZONE BY THE MAGATON.

"Ozone, hey? Lots of it?"

"Plenty, according to the rest of this. It looks to me like a sort of 'denatured' power system. There it is, all nice and potent, cheap, and unlicensed. But the second swallow going down meets the first one on the way back. Power they got—but the ozone they can't take. It's poisonous like a nice dose of chlorine. Poor Terran Electric!"

Mark Kingman sat in the control room of a ship of space and worried. Below the dome, Venus covered three-quarters of the sky, and it circled slowly as the Terran Electric ship oscillated gently up and down.

Before Kingman, on the desk, were pages of stock market reports. On a blackboard, a jagged line denoted the vacillation of Venus Equilateral, Preferred. This phase of his plan was working to perfection. Gradually, he was buying share after share out of uninterested hands by his depredations. Soon he would have enough stock to stage a grand show, and then he could swing the thing his way.

His worry was not with this affair.

He gloated over that. His belief that he could beat this Venus Equilateral crowd if he fought them on *his* ground with *his* weapon was being corroborated. That, plus the fact that he was using some of Venus Equilateral's own thunder to do the job, was giving him to think that it was but a matter of time.

And the poor fools were not aware of their peril. Oh, some bird was trying to buck him, but he was not prepared as Kingman was, nor had he the source of information that Kingman had.

No, the thing that worried him was—

And there it came again. A wild, cacophonous wailing, like a whole orchestra of instruments playing at random, in random keys. It shook the very roots of the body, that terrible caterwauling, and not only did it shake the body, and the mind, but it actually caused loose plates to rattle in the bulkhead, and the cabinet doors followed in unison. The diapason stop was out for noon, and the racket filled the small control room and bounced back and forth, dinning at the ears of Kingman as it went by. It penetrated to the upper reaches of the ship, and the crew gritted their teeth and cursed the necessity of being able to hear orders, for cotton plugs would have been a godsend and a curse simultaneously. Anything that would blot that racket out would also deafen them to the vital orders necessary to the operation of the ship in this precarious poising maneuver.

Two hundred sheer watts of undistorted audio power boomed forth in that tiny room—two hundred watts of pure, undistorted power to racket forth something that probably started out as sheer distortion.

And yet—

Faintly striving against that fearful racket there came a piping, flat-sounding human voice that said: "Kingman! VE Preferred, just hit eighty-nine!"

Kingman scowled and punched on the intership teletype machine. Using the communicator set with that racket would have been impossible.

The radio man read the note that appeared on his 'type, and smiled grimly. He saw to his helio-mirror and sighted through a fine telescope at a spot on Venus, three thousand miles below. The helio began to send its flashing signal to this isolated spot near the Boiling River, and it was read, acknowledged, and repeated for safety's sake. The radio man flashed "O.K." and went back to his forty-seventh game of chess with the assistant pilot.

The helio man on the Boiling River read the message, grinned, and stepped to the telephone. He called a number at Northern Landing, and a tight beam sped across the northern quarter of Venus to a man connected with the Venus Stock Market. The man nodded, and said to another: "Buy fifteen hundred—use the name of Ralph Gantry this time."

The stock purchased under the name of Ralph Gantry was signed, sealed, and delivered exactly fifteen minutes before the ticker projection on the grand wall of the exchange showed the VE, Preferred, stock turn the bottom curve and start upward by hitting eighty-nine!

Back in the Terran Electric spaceship Kingman's ears were still beset by the roaring, alien music.

He was sitting in his chair with his head between his hands, and did not see the man approaching the instrument panel with a pair of side cutters in one hand. The man reached the panel, lifted it slightly, and reached forward. Then Kingman, hearing a slight imperfection in the wail of the speaker, looked up, jumped from his chair, and tackled the engineer.

"You blasted fool!" blazed Kingman. "You idiot!"

The music stopped at his third word, and the scream

of his voice in the silence of the room almost scared Kingman himself.

"Mark, I'm going nuts. I can't stand that racket."

"You're going to stand it. Unless you can get something to cut it out."

"I can't. I'm not brilliant enough to devise a circuit that will cut that noise and still permit the entry of your fellow on Luna."

"Then you'll live with it."

"Mark, why can't we take that relay apart and work on it?"

"Ben, as far as I know, that relay is what Channing and his gang would give their whole station for—and will, soon enough. I don't care how it works—or why!"

"That's no way to make progress," Ben objected.

"Yeah, but we've got the only detector for driver radiation in this part of the universe! I'm not going to have it wrecked by a screwball engineer who doesn't give a care what's going on as long as he can tinker with something new and different. What do we know about it? Nothing. Therefore how can you learn anything about it? What would you look for? What would you expect to find?"

"But where is that music coming from?"

"I don't know. As best as we can calculate, driver radiation propagates at the square of the speed of light, and that gives us a twenty-four minute edge on Venus Equilateral at the present time. For all I know, that music may be coming from the other end of the galaxy. At the square of the speed of light, you could talk to Centauri and get an answer in not too long."

"But if we had a chance to tinker with that relay," Ben said, "we might be able to find out what tunes it, and then we can tune in the Lunar station and tune out that cat-melody."

"I'm running this show—and this relay is going to stay right where it is. I don't care a hoot about the control circuit it breaks; these controls are set, somehow, so that we can detect driver radiations, and I'm not taking any chances of having it ruined."

"Can't you turn the gain down, at least?"

"Nope. We'd miss the gang at Luna."

The speaker spoke in that faint, flat-toned human

voice again. It was easy to see that all that gain was necessary to back up the obviously faint response of Kingman's detector. The speaker said: "Kingman! Addison got power through the Channing Layer!"

That was all for about an hour. Meanwhile, the mewling tones burst forth again and again, assaulting the ears with intent to do damage. The messages were terse and for the most part uninteresting. They gave the market reports; they intercepted the beam transmissions through the Terran Heaviside Layer before they got through the Lunar Relay Station, inspected the swiftly moving tape, and transmitted the juicy morsels to Kingman via the big driver tube that stood poised outside of the landed spaceship.

Kingman enjoyed an hour of celebration at Addison's success, and then the joy turned to bitter hate as the message came through telling of the ozone that resulted in the passage of the solar beam through the atmosphere. The success of the beam, and the utter impossibility of using it, were far worse than the original fact of the beam's failure to pass the Channing Layer.

So Kingman went back to his stock market machinations and applied himself diligently. And as the days wore on, Kingman's group manipulated their watered stock and ran the price up and down at will, and after each cycle Kingman's outfit owned just one more bit of Venus Equilateral.

Terran Electric would emerge from this battle with Venus Equilateral as a subsidiary—with Kingman at the helm!

Walt Franks, entered Channing's office with a wild-eyed look on his face. "Don! C^2!"

"Huh! What are you driving about?"

"C^2. The speed of light, squared!"

"Fast—but what is it?"

"The solar beam! It propagates at C^2!"

"Oh, now look. Nothing can travel that fast!"

"Maybe this isn't *something!*"

"It has energy, energy has mass, mass cannot travel faster than the limiting speed of light."

"O.K. It can't do it. But unless my measurements are

all haywire, the beam gets to Sol and back at C^2. I can prove it."

"Yeah? How? You couldn't possibly measure an interval so small as two times sixty-seven million miles—the radius of Venus' orbit—traversed at the speed of light, squared."

"No. I admit that. But, Don, I got power out of Sirius!"

"You WHAT?" yelled Channing.

"Got power out of Sirius. And unless I've forgotten how to use a microclock, it figured out from here to Sirius and back with the bacon in just about ninety-three percent of the speed of light, squared. Seven percent is well within the experimental error, I think, since we think of Sirius as being eight and one-half light-years away. That's probably not too accurate as a matter of fact, but it's the figure I used. But here we are. Power from Sirius at C^2. Thirty-five billion miles per second! This stuff doesn't care how many laws it breaks!"

"Hm-m-m. C^2, hey? Oh, lovely. Look, Walt, let's run up and take a whirl at Wes Farrell's detector. I'm beginning to envision person-to-person, ship-to-ship service, and possibly the first Interplanet Network. Imagine hearing a play-by-play account of the Solar Series!"

"Wool-gathering," Walt snorted. "We've gotta catch our detector first!"

"Wes has something. First glimmer we've had. I think this is the time to rush it with all eight feet and start pushing!"

"O.K. Who do we want?"

"Same gang as usual. Chuck and Freddie Thomas, Warren, Wes Farrell, of course, and you can get Jim Baler into it, too. No, Walt, Christine Baler is not the kind of people you haul into a screwdriver meeting."

"I was merely thinking."

"I know. But you're needed, and if she were around, you'd be a total loss as far as cerebration."

"I like her."

"So does Barney Carroll."

"Um! But he isn't here. O.K., no Christine in our conference. I'll have Jeanne call the screwballs on the communicator."

They dribbled into Farrell's laboratory one by one, and then Don said: "We have a detector. It is about as efficient as a slab of marble; only more so. We can get a tinkle of about ten micro-microamps at twenty feet distance from a driver tube using eight KVA input, which if we rate this in the usual spaceship efficiency, comes to about one-half G. That's about standard, for driver tubes, since they run four to a ship at two G total.

"Now, that is peanuts. We should be able to wind a megammeter around the peg at twenty feet. Why, the red ionization comes out of the tube and hits our so-called detector, and the amount of ozone it creates is terrific. Yet we can't get a good reading out of it."

Walt asked: "Wes, what worked, finally?"

"A four-turn coil on a ceramic form, in series with a twenty micro-microfarad tuning condenser. I've been using a circular plate as a collector."

"Does it tune?"

"Nope. Funny thing, though, it won't work without a condenser in the circuit. I can use anything at all there without tuning it. But, damn it, the coil is the only one that works."

"That's slightly ridiculous. Have you reconstructed all factors?"

"Inductance, distributed capacity, and factor 'Q' are all right on the button with two more I made. Nothing dioding."

"Hm-m-m. This takes the cake. Nothing works, you say?"

"Nothing in my mind. I've tried about three hundred similar coils, and not a wiggle since. That's the only one."

Chuck Thomas said: "Wes, have you tried your tube-amplifier system ahead of it?"

"Yes, and nothing at all happens then. I don't understand that one, because we know that any kind of input power will be re-beamed as similar power. I should think that the thing will amplify the same kind of stuff. I've used a solar beam miniature with a driver-alloy dynode in it, but that doesn't work either."

"Shucks," said Thomas.

Don stood up and picked up the coil. "Fellows, I'm going to make a grand old college try."

"Yes?" asked Walt.

"I've got a grand idea, here. One, I'm still remembering that business of making the receptor dynode of the same alloy as the transmitter cathode. I've a hunch that this thing is not so much an inductor, but something sour in the way of alloy selectivity. If I'm right, I may cut this in half, and make two detectors, each of similar characteristics. Shall I?"

"Go ahead. We've established the fact that it is not the physico-electrical characteristics of that coil," said Wes. "I, too, took my chances and rewound that same wire on a couple of other forms. So it doesn't count as far as inductance goes. So we can't ruin anything but the total makeup of the wire. I think we may be able to re-establish the wire by self-welding if your idea doesn't work. Now, unless we want to search the three planets for another hunk of wire to work like this one did, without knowing what to look for and therefore trying every foot of wire on three planets—"

"I'll cut it," said Channing with a smile.

His cutters snipped, and then fastened one end of the wire to the coil, stripping the other portion off and handing it to Chuck Thomas, who rewound it on another form.

"Now," Don said, "crank up your outfit and we'll try this hunk."

The beam tubes were fired up, and the smell of ozone began to make itself prominent. Channing cranked up the air-vent capacity to remove the ozone more swiftly. The men applied themselves to the detector circuits, and Wes, who recognized the results, said: "This hunk works. About as good as the whole coil."

Channing replaced the first coil with the second. Wes inspected the results and said: "Not quite as good, but it does work."

Walt nodded, and said: "Maybe it should be incandescent."

"That's a thought. Our solar beam uses an incandescent dynode." Channing removed the second coil and handed it to Freddie. "Take this thing down to the metallurgical lab and tell 'em to analyze it right down to the trace of sodium that seems to be in everything. I want quantitative figures on every element in it. Also, cut off a hunk and see if the crystallographic expert can detect anything peculiar that would make this hunk of copper wire different from any other hunk. Follow?"

"Yep," said Freddie. "We'll also start making similar alloys with a few percent variation on the composition metals. Right?"

"That's the ticket. Wes, can we evacuate a tube with this wire in it and make it incandescent?"

"Let's evacuate the room. I like that stunt."

"You're the engineer on this trick. Do it your way."

"Thanks. I get the program, all right. Why not have Chuck build us a modulator for the driver tube? Then when we get this thing perfected, we'll have some way to test it."

"Can do, Chuck?"

"I think so. It's easy. We'll just modulate the cathode current of the electron guns that bombard the big cathode. That is the way we adjust for drive; it should work as a means of amplitude modulation."

"O.K.," said Channing. "We're on the rails for this one. We'll get together as soon as our various laboratories have their answers and have something further to work with."

Above Venus, Mark Kingman was listening to the wailing roar of alien symphony and cursing because he could hardly hear the voice of his Lunar accomplice saying: "VE, Preferred, just hit one hundred and two!"

Fifteen minutes before the peak hit Northern Landing, share after share was being dumped, and in addition, a message was on its way back to Terra. It went on the regular beam transmission through Venus Equilateral, carefully coded. It said:

HAVE SUFFICIENT STOCK AND ADDITIONAL COLLATERAL TO APPLY THE FIRST PRESSURE. APPLY PHASE TWO OF PLAN.

KINGMAN.

In the ten hours that followed, Venus Equilateral stock went down and down, passed through a deep valley, and started up again. Kingman's crowd was offering twice the market for the preferred stock, and there was little to have. It took a short-time dip at three hundred, and the few minutes of decline smoked a lot of stock out of the hands of people who looked upon this chance as the right time to make their money and get out.

Then the stock began to climb again, and those people who thought that the price had been at its peak and passed were angrily trying to buy in again. That accelerated the climb, but Kingman's crowd, operating on Venus and on Mars and on Terra, were *buying* only, and selling not one share of Venus Equilateral.

Terran Electric stock took a gradual slide, for Kingman's crowd needed additional money. But the slide was slow, and controlled, and manipulated only for the purpose of selling short. Terran Electric stock eventually remained in the hands of Kingman's crowd, though its value was lessened.

Venus Equilateral, Preferred, hit four hundred and sixty-eight, and hovered. It vacillated around that point for another hour, and the market closed at four hundred and sixty-nine and three-eighths.

Kingman looked at his watch and smiled. He reached forth and cut the dinning sound of the cacophony with a vicious twist of the gain knob. Silence reigned in the spaceship; grand, peaceful silence. Kingman, his nerves frayed by the mental activity and the brain-addling music-from-nowhere, took a hot shower and went to bed.

He locked the panel of the control room first, however. He wanted no engineer tinkering with his pet relay.

Cartwright came into Channing's living room with a long face. "It's bad," he said. "Bad."

"What's bad?"

"Oh, I, like the rest of the fools, got caught in his trap."

"Whose trap?"

"The wild man who is trying to rock Venus Equilateral on its axis."

"Well, how?"

"They started to buy like mad, and I held out. Then

the thing dropped a few points, and I tried to make a bit of profit, so that we could go on bolstering the market. They grabbed off my stock, and then, just like *that!* the market was on the way up again and I couldn't find more than a few odd shares to buy back."

"Don't worry," said Channing, "I don't think anyone is big enough to really damage us. Someone is playing fast and loose, making a killing. When this is over, we'll still be in business."

"I know, Don, but whose business will it be? Ours, or theirs?"

"Is it that bad?"

"I'm afraid so. One more flurry like today, and they'll be able to tow Venus Equilateral out and make Mars Equilateral out of it, and we won't be able to say a word."

"Hm-m-m. You aren't beaten?"

"Not until the last drop. I'm not bragging when I say that I'm as good an operator as the next. My trouble today was not being a mind reader. I'd been doing all right, so far. I've been letting them ride it up and down with little opposition, and taking off a few here and there as I rode along. Guessing their purpose, I could count on their next move. But this banging the market sky-high has me stumped, or had me stumped for just long enough for me to throw our shirt into the ring. They took that quick—our shirt, I mean."

"That's too bad. What are you leading up to?"

"There are a lot of unstable stocks that a guy could really play hob with; therefore their only reason to pick on us is to gain control!"

"Pirates?"

"Something like that."

"Well," Channing said in a resigned voice, "about all we can do is do our best and hope we are smart enough to outguess 'em. That's your job, Cartwright. A long time ago Venus Equilateral made their decision concerning the executive branch of this company, and they elected to run the joint with technical men. The business aspects and all are under the control of men who know what they are fighting. We hire businessmen, just like businessmen hire engineers, and for the opposite purpose. You're the best we could get, you know that.

If those guys get Venus Equilateral, they'll get you, too. But if you do your best and fail, we can't shoot you in the back for it. We'll all go down together. So keep pitching, and remember that we're behind you all the way!"

"Can we float a bit of a loan?"

"Sure, if it's needed. I'd prefer Interplanetary Transport. Keg Johnson will do business with us. We've been in the way of helping them out of a couple of million-dollar losses; they might be anxious to reciprocate."

"O.K. I have your power of attorney, anyway. If I get in a real crack, I'll scream for IT to help. Right?"

"Right!"

Cartwright left, and as he closed the door, Channing's face took on a deep, long look. He was worried. He put his head between his hands and thought himself into a tight circle from which he could not escape. He did not hear Walt Franks enter behind Arden and Christine.

"Hey!" said Walt. "Why the gloom? I bear glad tidings!"

Channing looked up. "Spill," he said with a glum smile. "I could use some glad tidings right now."

"The lab just reported that the hunk of copper wire was impure. Got a couple of traces of other metals in it. They've been concocting other samples with more and less of the impurities, and Wes has been trying them as they were ready. We've got the detector working to the point where Freddie has taken the *Relay Girl* out for a run around the station at about five hundred miles and Wes is still getting responses!"

"Is he? How can he know?"

"Chuck rigged the *Relay Girl*'s drivers with a voice modulator, and Freddie is jerking his head off because the acceleration is directly proportional to the amplitude of his voice, saying: 'One, two, three, four, test.' Don, have you ever figured out why an engineer can't count above four?"

"Walt, does it take a lot of soup to modulate a driver?" Arden asked.

"Peanuts," grinned Franks. "This stuff is not like the good old radio; the power for driving the spaceship is derived mostly from the total disintegration of the cathode, and the voltage applied to the various electrodes is merely for the purpose of setting up the proper field conditions. They draw quite a bit of current, but nothing like that which would be required to lift a spaceship at two G for a hundred hours flat." He turned to Channing. "What's the gloom?"

Don smiled in a thoughtful fashion. "It doesn't look so good right now. Some gang of stock market cutthroats have been playing football with Venus Equilateral, and Cartwright says he is sure they want control. It's bad; he's been clipped a couple of hard licks, but we're still pitching. The thing I'm wondering right now is this: shall we toss this possibility of person-to-person and ship-to-ship communication just at the right turn of the market to bollix up their machinations, or shall we keep it to ourselves and start up another company with this as our basis?"

"Can we screw 'em up by announcing it?"

"Sure. If we drop this idea just at the time they're trying to run the stock down, it'll cross over and take a run up, which will set 'em on their ear."

"I don't know. Better keep it to ourselves for a bit. Something may turn up. But come on down to Wes' lab and give a look at our new setup."

Channing stood up and stretched. "I'm on the way," he said.

Farrell was working furiously on the detector device, and as they entered he indicated the meter that was jumping up and down. Out of a speaker was coming the full, rich tones of Freddie Thomas' voice, announcing solemnly: "One, two, three, four, test."

Wes said, "I'm getting better. Chuck has been bettering his modulator now, and the detector is three notches closer to whatever this level of energy uses for resonance. Evacuation and the subsequent incandescence was the answer. Another thing I've found is this—" Farrell held up a flat disk about six inches in diameter with one saw cut from edge to center. "As you see, the color of this disk changes from this end of the cut, varying all the way around the disk to the other side of the cut. The darned disk is a varying alloy—I've discovered how to tune the driver radiation through a limited range. We hit resonance of the *Relay Girl*'s driver system just off the end of this disk. But watch while I turn the one in the set."

Farrell took a large knob and turned it. Freddie's voice faded, and became toneless. Farrell returned the knob to its original position and the reception cleared again.

"Inside of that tube there," said Farrell, "I have a selsyn turning the disk, and a small induction loop that heats the whole disk to incandescence. A brush makes contact with the edge of the disk and the axle makes the center connection. Apparently this stuff passes on a direct line right through the metal, for it works."

"Have you tried any kind of tube amplification?" asked Don.

"Not yet. Shall we?"

"Why not? I can still think that the relay tube will amplify if we hook up the input and output loads correctly."

"I've got a tube already hooked up," said Walt. "It's mounted in a panel with the proper voltage supplies and so on. If your resistance calculation is correct, we should get about three thousand times' amplification out of it."

He left, and returned in a few minutes with the tube. They busied themselves with the connections, and then Don applied the power.

Nothing happened.

"Run a line from the output back through a voltage-dividing circuit to the in-phase anode," suggested Walt.

"How much?"

"Put a potentiometer in it so we can vary the amount of voltage. After all, Barney Carroll said that the application of voltage in phase with the transmitted power is necessary to the operation of the relay tube. In transmission of DC, it is necessary to jack up the in-phase anode with a bit of DC. That's in-phase with a vengeance!"

"What you're thinking is that whatever this sub-level energy is, some of it should be applied to the in-phase anode?"

"Nothing but."

The cabinet provided a standard potentiometer, and as Don advanced the amount of fed-back voltage, Freddie's voice came booming in louder and louder. It overloaded the audio amplifier, and they turned the gain down as Channing increased the in-phase voltage more and more. It passed through a peak, and then Don left the potentiometer set for maximum.

"Wes," he said, "call Freddie and tell him to take off for Terra, at about four G. Have the gang upstairs hang a ship beam on him so we can follow him with suggestions. Too bad we can't get there immediately."

"What I'm worrying about is the available gain," said Wes. "That thing may have given us a gain of a couple of thousand, but that isn't going to be enough. Not for planet-to-planet service."

"Later on we may be able to hang a couple of those things in cascade," Walt suggested.

"Or if not, I know a trick that will work—one that will enable us to get a gain of several million," said Don.

"Yeah? Mirrors, or adding machines? You can't make an audio amplifier of a three-million gain."

"I know it—at least not a practical one. But we can probably use our audio modulator to modulate a radio frequency, and then modulate the driver with the RF. Then we hang a receiver onto the detector gadget here, and collect RF, modulated, just like a standard radio transmission, and amplify it at RF, convert it to IF, and detect it to AF. Catch?"

"Sure. And that gives me another thought. It might just be possible, if your idea is possible, that we can insert several frequencies of RF into the tube and hang a number of receivers on the detector, here."

Arden laughed. "From crystal detection to multiplex transmission in ten easy lessons!"

"Call Chuck and have him begin to concoct an RF stage for tube modulation," said Don. "It'll have to be fairly low—not higher than a couple of megacycles, so that he can handle it with the stuff he has available. But as long as we can hear his dulcet voice chirping that 'one, two, three, four, test,' of his, we can also have ship-to-station two-way. We squirt out on the ship beam, and he talks back on the driver transmitter."

"That'll be a help," observed Wes. "I'd been thinking by habit that we had no way to get word back from the *Relay Girl*."

"So had I," Walt confessed. "But we'll get over that."

"Meanwhile, I'm going to get this alloy selectivity investigated right down to the last nub," said Don. "Chuck's gang can take it from all angles and record their findings. We'll ultimately be able to devise a system of mathematics for it from their analysis. You won't mind being bothered every fifteen minutes for the first week, will you, Wes? They'll be running to you in your sleep with questions until they catch up with your present level of ability in this job. Eventually they'll pass you up, and then you'll have to study their results in order to keep up."

"Suits me. That sounds like my job, anyway."

"It is. O.K. Arden, I'm coming now."

"It's about time." Arden smiled. "I wouldn't haul you away from your first love excepting that I know you haven't eaten in eight or nine hours. I've got roast knolla."

"S'long, fellows," grinned Channing. "I'm one of the few guys in the inner system who can forget that the knolla is the North Venus brother to a pussycat."

"I could feed you pussycat and you'd eat it if I called it knolla," said Arden. "But you wouldn't eat knolla if I called it pussycat."

"You can't tell the difference," said Walt.

"Tell me," asked Wes, "what does pussycat taste like?"

"I mean by visual inspection. Unfortunately, there can be no comparison drawn. The Venusians will eat pussycat, but they look upon the knolla as a household pet, not fit for Venusian consumption. So unless we revive one of the ancient Martians, who may have the intestinal fortitude—better known as guts—to eat both and describe the difference, we may never know," Walt offered.

"Stop it," said Arden, "or you'll have my dinner spoiled for me."

"All the more for me," said Don. "Now, when I was in college, we cooked the dean's cat and offered it to some pledges under the name of knolla. They said—"

"We'll have macaroni for dinner," said Arden firmly. "I'll never be able to look a fried knolla in the pan again without wondering whether it caterwauled on some back fence in Chicago, or a Palanortis whitewood on Venus."

She left, and Channing went with her, arguing with her to the effect that she should develop a disregard for things like their discussion. As a matter of interest, Channing had his roast knolla that evening, so he must have convinced Arden.

Walt said: "And then there were three. Christine, has our little pre-dinner talk disturbed your appetite?"

"Not in the least," said the girl stoutly. "I wouldn't care whether it was knolla or pussycat. I've been on Mars so long that either one of the little felines is alien to me. What have you to offer?"

"We'll hit Joe's for dinner, which is the best bar in sixty million miles today. Later we may take in the latest celluloid epic, then there will be a bit of mixed wrestling in the ballroom."

"Mixed wres— Oh, you mean dancing. Sounds interesting now. Now?"

"Now. Wes, what are you heading for?"

"Oh, I've got on a cockeyed schedule," said Wes. "I've been catching my sleep at more and more out-of-phase hours until this is not too long after breakfast for me. You birds all speak of 'Tomorrow,' 'Today,' and 'Yesterday' out here, but this business of having no sun to come up in the morning, and the electric lights running all the time has me all bollixed up."

"That daily nomenclature is purely from habit," said Walt. "As you know, we run three equal shifts of eight hours each, and therefore what may be 'Morning' to Bill is 'Noon' to James and 'Night' to Harry. It is meaningless, but habitual, to speak of 'Morning' when you mean 'Just after I get up'! Follow me?"

"Yep. This, then, is morning to me. Run along and have fun."

"We'll try," said Walt.

"We will," said Christine.

Farrell grinned as they left. He looked at Walt and said: "You will!"

Walt wondered whether he should have questioned Wes about that remark, but he did not. Several hours later, he wondered how Wes could have been so right.

Venus Equilateral, Preferred, started in its long climb as soon as the markets opened on the following day. Cartwright, following his orders and his experience, held on to whatever stock he had, and bought whatever stock was tossed his way. Several times he was on the verge of asking Interplanetary Transport for monetary assistance, but the real need never materialized.

Kingman alternately cursed the whining music and cheered the pyramiding stock. About the only thing that kept Kingman from going completely mad was the fact that the alien music was not continuous, but it came and went in stretches of anything from five to fifty minutes, with varied periods for silence in between selections.

Up and up it went, and Kingman was seeing the final, victorious coup in the offing. A week more, and Venus Equilateral would belong to Terran Electric. The beam from Terra was silent, save for a few items of interest not connected with the market. Kingman's men were given the latest news, baseball scores, and so forth, among which items was another message to Channing from the solar beam project engineer, Addison. They had about given up. Nothing they could do would prevent the formation of ozone by the ton as they drew power by the kilowatt from Sol.

On Venus Equilateral, Channing said: "Ask Freddie what his radio frequency is."

Ten minutes later, at the speed of light, the ship beam reached the *Relay Girl* and the message clicked out. Freddie read it and spoke into the microphone. The *Relay Girl* bucked unmercifully, as the voice amplitude made the acceleration change. Then at the speed of light, squared, the answer came back in less than a twinkle.

"Seventeen hundred kilocycles."

Channing began to turn the tuner of the radio receiver. The band was dead, and he laughed. "This is going to be tricky, what with the necessity of aligning both the driver-alloy disk and the radio receiver. Takes time."

He changed the alloy disk in minute increments, and waved the tuner across the portion of the band that would most likely cover the experimental error of Freddie Thomas' frequency measurement. A burst of sound caught his ear, was lost for a moment, and then swelled into perfect tune as Don worked over the double tuning system.

"Whoa, Tillie," said Walt. "That sounds like—"

"Like hell."

"Right. Just what I was going to say. Is it music?"

"Could be. I've got a slightly tin ear, you know."

"Mine is fair," said Walt, "but it might as well be solid brass as far as this mess is concerned. It's music of some kind, you can tell it by the rhythm. But the scale isn't like anything I've ever heard before."

"Might be a phonograph record played backward," suggested Wes.

"I doubt it," said Channing seriously. "The swell of that orchestra indicates a number of instruments—of some cockeyed kind or other. The point I'm making is that anything of a classical or semiclassical nature played backwards on a phonograph actually sounds passable. I can't say the same for jamstead music, but it holds for most of the classics, believe it or not. This sounds strictly from hunger."

"Or hatred. Maybe the musicians do not like one another."

"Then they should lambaste one another with their instruments, not paste the sub-ether with them."

Channing lit a cigarette. "Mark the dial," he said. "Both of 'em. I've got to get in touch with the Thomas boys."

Walt marked the dials and tuned for the *Relay Girl.* He found it coming in not far from the other setting. Chuck was speaking, and they tuned in near the middle of his speech.

". . . this thing so that it will not buck like a scenic railway finding the fourth derivative of space with respect to time. For my non-technical listeners, that is none other than the better-known term: jerkiness. We applied the modulation to the first driver anode—the little circular one right above the cathode. I don't know whether this is getting out as it should, so I'm going to talk along for the next fifteen minutes straight until I hear from you. Then we're switching over and repeating. Can you hear me?"

Channing cut the gain down to a whisper and put a message on the beam, confirming his reception.

Ten minutes later, Chuck changed his set speech, and said: "Good! Too bad we haven't got one of those receivers here, or we could make this a two-way with some action. Now listen, Don. My idiot brother says that he can make the beam transmit without the drive. Unfortunately, I am not a drive expert like he is and so I can not remonstrate with the half-wit. So, and right now, we're cutting the supply voltage to the final focusing anode. *Whoops!* I just floated off the floor and the mike cable is all tangled up in my feet. This free stuff is not as simple as the old fiction writers claimed it was. Things are floating all over the place like mad. The accelerometer says exactly zero, and so you tell me if we are getting out. We're going back on one G so that we can sit down again. That's better! Though the idiot—it's a shame to be forced to admit that one of your family is half-witted—didn't wait until we were in position to fall. I almost landed on my head—which is where he was dropped as an infant. How was it? Did you hear my manly voice while we were going free? Say 'No' so that my idiot brother will not have anything to say about his brilliant mind. I'm out of breath, and we're going back home on that home recording of Freddie saying—and I will let him quote, via acetate . . ."

The sound of a phonograph pickup being dropped on a record preceded Freddie's voice, saying: "One, two, three, four, test, one—"

Channing cut the gain again. "That's red-hot. I thought he was talking all this time."

"Not the Thomas boys. That comes under the classification of 'Work,' which they shun unless they cannot get any kind of machine to do it for them," Walt laughed.

Walt turned the dials back to the unearthly symphony. "At C^2, that might come from Sirius," he said, listening carefully. "Sounds like Chinese."

"Oh, now look," Don objected. "What on earth would a Chinese symphony be doing with a driver modulator system?"

"Broadcasting—"

"Nope. The idea of detecting driver radiation is as old as the hills. If any culture had uncovered driver-beam transmission we'd all have been aware of it. So far as I know, we and the Terran Electric crowd are the only ones who have had any kind of an opportunity of working with this sub-etheric energy. Wes, have you another miniature of the relay tube handy?"

"Sure. Why?"

"I'm going to see if this stuff can be made directional. You're bringing whatever it is into the place on a collector plate and slamming it into an input-terminal power transmission tube. It goes across the table to the relay tube, and is amplified, and then is tossed across more table to the load-terminal tube, where the output is impressed across your alloy disk. Right?"

"Right."

"I want another relay tube. I'm going to use it for a directional input beam, aligning it in the same way that Jim Baler and Barney Carroll did their first find. The one that sucked power out of the electric light, turned off the city hall, and so on. Follow?"

"Perfectly. Yes, I've got a couple of them. But they're not connected like Walt's setup was."

"Well, that three-tube system was built on sheer guesswork some time ago. We can tap in the relay tube and haul out a set of cables that will energize the first relay tube. Hang her on gimbals, and we'll be going hunting."

"Shall I have Freddie return?"

"Yes. We'll have Warren's gang build us up about six of these things just as we have here."

"That won't take long," said Walt. "They're working on the tuning disks now, and we should have 'em by the time that Freddie gets back here."

"But this wild and wooly music. It's alien."

Wes turned from the teletype and dug in the cabinet for the extra relay tube. He up-ended the chassis containing Walt's setup and began to attach leads to the voltage supply, cabling them neatly and in accordance with the restrictions on lead capacities that some of the anodes needed.

"It's alien," said Wes in agreement. "I'm going to shut it off now while I tinker with the tube."

"Wait a minute," said Don. "Here comes Jim. Maybe he'd like to hear it."

"Hear what," asked Jim Baler, entering the door.

"We've a Syrian symphony," explained Don, giving Jim the background all the way to the present time.

Jim listened, and then said:

"As an engineer, I've never heard anything like that in my life before. But, as a student of ancient languages and arts and sciences, I have. That's Chinese."

"Oh, no!"

"Oh, yes, but definitely."

"Ye gods!"

"I agree."

"But how—where?"

"And/or when?"

Channing sat down hard. He stared at the wall for minutes. "Chinese. Oh, great, slippery, green, howling catfish!" He picked up the phone and called the decoupler room, where the messages were sorted as to destination upon their entry into the station.

"Ben? Look, have we a ship beam on anything of Chinese registry?"

Ben said wait a minute while he checked. He returned and said: "Four. the *Lady of Cathay,* the *Mandarin's Daughter*, the *Dragoness,* and the *Mongol Maid.* Why?"

"Put a message on each of 'em, asking whether they have any Chinese music on board."

"And then what? They can't answer."

"Make this an experimental request. If any of them are using any recordings of Chinese music, tell them to have their electronics chief replace the phonograph pickup with a microphone—disturbing absolutely nothing—and to reply as if we could hear them. Get me?"

"Can you? Hear 'em I mean."

"We hear something, and Jim says it's Chinese."

"It's worth a try, then. See you later."

"Will they?" asked Jim, interested in the workings of this idea.

"Sure. Ever since we steered the *Empress of Kolain* out of the grease with the first station-to-ship beam, all three of the interplanetary companies have been more than willing to cooperate with any of our requests as long as we precede the message with the explanation that it's experimental. They'll do anything we ask 'em to, short of scuttling the ship."

"Nice hookup. Hope it works."

"So do I," said Wes. "This, I mean. I've got our directional gadget hooked up."

"Turn it on."

The wailing of the music came in strong and clear. Wes turned the input tube on its support, and the music passed through a loud peak and died off on the far side to almost zero. He adjusted the mobile tube for maximum response and tightened a small set screw.

"It's a shame we haven't got a nice set of protractors and gimbals," he said. "I had to tear into the desk lamp to get that flexible pipe."

"Small loss. She's directional, all right. We'll get the gimbals later. Right now I don't want this turned off, because we may hear something interesting— *Whoops!* It went off by itself!"

"Could we dare to hope?" asked Walt.

"Let's wait. They'll have to hitch the microphone on."

"Give 'em a half-hour at least."

Twenty minutes later, a strange voice came through the speaker. "Dr. Channing, of Venus Equilateral? We have been contacted by your organization with respect to the possibility of your being able to hear the intership communicator system. This seems impossible, but we are not ones to question. The fact that you are in possession of the facts concerning our love of the music of our ancestors is proof enough that you must have heard something. I presume that further information is desired, and I shall wait for your return. This is Ling Kai Chang, Captain of the *Lady of Cathay.*"

"We got it!" chortled Don.

He did a war dance in the lab, and the rest followed suit. Bits of wire and oddments of one sort or another filled the air as the big, grown-up men did a spring dance and strewed the floor with daintily thrown junk. At the height of the racket, Arden and Christine entered—no, they were literally hauled in, completely surrounded, and almost smothered.

Arden fought herself free and said: "What's going on?"

"We've just contacted a ship in space!"

"So what? Haven't we been doing that for months?"

"They've just contacted us, too!"

"Huh?" Arden asked, her eyes widening.

"None other. Wait, I'll get an answer." Don contacted Ben, in the decoupler room, and said: "Ben, hang this line on the *Lady of Cathay* beam, will you?"

"Is that her?"

"None other."

"Go ahead. She's coupled."

Don pecked out a message. "Please describe the intercommunication system used by your ship in detail. We have heard you, and you are, therefore, the first ship to contact Venus Equilateral from space flight. Congratulations."

Eight minutes later, the voice of Captain Chang returned.

"Dr. Channing, I am handing the microphone over to Ling Wei, our electronics engineer, who knows the system in and out. He'll work with you on this problem."

Ling Wei said: "Hello. This is great. But I'm not certain how it's done. The output of the phono system is very small, and certainly not capable of putting out the power necessary to reach Venus Equilateral from here. However, we are using a wired-radio system at seventeen hundred and ninety kilocycles in lieu of the usual cable system. The crew all like music, and, therefore, we play the recordings of our ancestral musicians almost incessantly."

He paused for breath, and Channing said: "Walt, tap out a message concerning the lead length of the cables that supply the driver anodes. Have him check them for radio frequency pickup."

"I get it."

The 'type began to click.

The communication was carried on for hour after hour. Don's guess was right: the lead that connected the first driver anode was tuned in wavelength to almost perfect resonance with the frequency of the wired-radio communicator system. Channing thanked them profusely, and they rang off. Soon afterward, the wailing, moaning music returned to the air.

"Wonder if we could get that without the radio?" said Don.

"Don't know. We can pack the juice on in the amplifier and see, now that we have it tuned on the button," Walt said.

"It won't," said Wes. "I've been all across the dial of the alloy disk. Nothing at all."

"O.K. Well, so what if it doesn't? We've still got us a ship-to-ship communications system. Hey! What was that?"

That was a pale, flat-sounding human voice saying: "Kingman! VE Pfd. has been at six hundred and nine for two days, now. What's our next move?"

"Kingman!" Channing exploded. "Why, the . . . the—"

"Careful," warned Arden. "There's a lady present."

"Huh?"

"Her," said Arden pointing at Christine.

"Wait," Walt said. "Maybe he'll answer."

Don fiddled with the dials for a full fifteen minutes, keeping them very close to the spot marked, hoping that Kingman's answer might not be too far out of tune. He gave up as the answer was not to be found, and returned to the original setting.

Ten minutes later the voice said: "Kingman, where in the devil is my answer. I want to know what our next move is. There isn't a bit of VE stock available. Why don't you answer?"

Then, dimly in the background, a voice spoke to the operator of the instrument. "Kingman's probably asleep. That terrible moaning stuff he's been complaining about makes him turn the thing off as soon as the day's market is off. He—and the rest of that crew—can't stand it. You'll have to wait until tomorrow's market opens before he'll be listening."

"O.K.," said the operator, and then went silent.

"Kingman!" said Don Channing. "So he's the bright guy behind this. I get it now. Somehow he discovered a detector, and he's been playing the market by getting the quotations by sub-etheric transmission at C^2 and beating the Northern Landing market. And did you get the latest bit of luck? Kingman still is unaware of the fact that we are onto him—and have perfected this C^2 transmission. Here's where he gets caught in his own trap!"

"How?"

"We're not in too bad shape for making good, honest two-ways out of this sub-ether stuff. Kingman is still behind because he hasn't got a return line back to Terra—he must be using our beams, which gives us a return edge."

"Why not get him tossed into the clink?" asked Walt.

"That's practical. Besides, we're sitting in a great big pile of gravy right now. We can prove Kingman has been violating the law to embezzle, mulct, steal, commit grand larceny, and so on. We're going to take a swing at Mr. Kingman and Terran Electric that they won't forget. We can't lose, because I'm not a good sportsman when I find that I've been tricked. We're going after Kingman in our own fashion—and if we lose, we're going to tinhorn and cry for the gendarmes. I'm not proud."

"What do you plan?"

"We'll put a horde of folks on the decoupler files with the code of Terran Electric filed with the government offices. We can get the code, and I'm of the opinion that Kingman wouldn't take time to figure out a new code, so he'll be using the old one. As soon as we find a message in that code that is either addressed 'Terran Electric' or pertains to VE, Preferred, stock, we'll start to intercept all such messages and use them for our own good."

"That's illegal."

"Yep. But who's gonna holler? Kingman can't."

"But suppose we lose—"

"Kingman will not know we've been tricking him. Besides, we can't lose with two ways to get ahead of this one. Come on, fellows, we've got to help get the extra receivers together."

"How are we going to cut through the Channing Layer?"

"Easy. That's where we'll use the relay stations at Luna, Deimos, and the six portables that circle Venus."

"I get it. O.K., Don, let's get to work."

"Right. And we'd better leave a guy here to collect any more interesting messages from Kingman's crowd. We can tune it right onto Kingman's alloy, and that'll make that music take a back seat. We need narrower selectivity."

"Chuck's gang will find that, if it is to be found," Walt smiled. "We're really on the track this time."

A dead-black spaceship drifted across the face of Luna slowly, and its course, though apparently aimless, was the course of a ship or a man hunting something. It darted swiftly, poised, and then zigzagged forward, each straightside of the jagged course shorter than the one before. It passed over a small crater and stopped short.

Below, there was a spaceship parked beside a driver tube anchored in the pumice.

The black ship hovered above the parked ship, and then dropped sharply, ramming the observation dome on top with its harder, smaller bottom. The two ships tilted and fell, crushing the ground near the poised driver tube. Space-suited men assaulted the damaged ship, broke into the bent and battered plates, and emerged with three men who were still struggling to get their suits adjusted properly.

Channing's men took over the poised driver tube, and in their own ship Walt spoke over a sub-ether radio of a different type.

"Don, we got him."

Don answered from Venus Equilateral, and his voice had no more delay than if he had been within a hundred yards of the crater on Luna.

"Good. Stay where you are; you can contact the Lunar Relay Station from there. Wes is all ready on Station 3 above Northern Landing with his set, and Jim Baler is at the Deimos station."

"Hi, Walt," came Wes' voice.

"Hi," said Jim Baler.

"Hello, fellows," said Walt. "Well, what cooks?"

"Kingman!" said Channing, with a tone of finality. "You've got your orders, Walt. When Kingman expects the market to go down, tell him it's still going up. We'll figure this out as we go along, but he won't like it at all."

There was silence for a few minutes, and then Don said: "Walt, Kingman's sent a message through to Northern Landing station now. He says: 'Dump a block to shake the suckers loose. This is pyramided so high that they should all climb on the sell wagon; running the market down of their own weight. When it hits a new low, we'll buy, and this time end up by having control.' When he starts to run the market down, you buy at Terra."

Minutes later, the message hit the Terra market, and Kingman's agents started to unload. The stock started off at six hundred and nine, and it soon dropped to five-forty. It hovered there, and then took another gradual slide to four-seventy.

Then a message came through the regular beam station, which Walt intercepted, decoded with Terran Electric's own code book, and read as follows: "VE, Preferred, coming in fast. Shall we wait?" He chuckled and spoke into the driver modulator. "Kingman," he said, "some wiseacre is still buying. VE, Preferred, is running at seven-ninety! What now?" In the Venus Equilateral radio, he said: "Don, I just fixed him."

From Venus, Wes said: "You sure did. He's giving orders to drop more stock. This is too dirty to be funny, but Kingman asked for it. I know him. He's got this set up so that no one can do a thing on this market program without orders from him. Too bad we can't withhold the Northern Landing quotations from him."

The Luna beam brought forth another message intended for Kingman's interceptor at Luna. "VE, Preferred, is dropping like a plummet. When can we buy?"

Walt smiled and said into Kingman's setup, "Kingman! VE, Preferred, is now at eight hundred and seventy!"

Not many minutes later, Wes said: "That was foul, Walt. He's just given orders to run the market down at any cost."

"O.K.," said Walt. "But he's going to go nuts when the Northern Landing Exchange starts down without ever getting to that mythical nine hundred."

"Let him wonder. Meanwhile, fellows, let's run ourselves a slide on Terran Electric. Sell the works!"

Terran Electric started down as VE, Preferred, took its third drop. It passed three hundred, and started down the two hundred numbers.

Walt shook his head and said to Kingman: "Kingman, we're getting results now. She's dropped back again—to six hundred and three." Then he said: "Kingman, someone is playing hob with TE, Preferred. She's up to two hundred and fifty-one." To Don, Walt said: "Good thing that Kingman has that Chinese symphony for a bit of good music, or he'd recognize my voice."

"Which way will he jump?" laughed Don. "That was a slick bit of Kingman-baiting, Walt, in spite of your voice."

"Kingman's taking it hard," said Wes. "He says to drop some of his own stock so that they can use the money to manipulate the VE stuff."

"O.K.," said Jim Baler. "This looks like a good time to think about buying some of Kingman's stuff. Right?"

"Wait until the sales hit bottom," Don said. "Walt, tip us off."

"O.K. What now?"

"Wait a bit and see."

Terran Electric went down some more, and then Jim said: "Now?"

"Now," answered Don. "You, too, Wes."

"Me, too?" Walt asked.

"You continue to sell!"

"Oh-oh," said Wes. "Kingman is wild. He wants to know what's the matter with the market."

"Tell him that your end is all right, and that VE, Preferred, is still going down, but steady."

"O.K.," said Walt.

The hours went by, and Kingman became more and more frantic. VE, Preferred, would be reported at five hundred, but the Northern Landing Exchange said two-ten. Meanwhile, Terran Electric—

"Oh, lovely!" said Don. "Beautiful. We've got us a reciprocating market now, better than Kingman's. When she's up at Terra, they're down at Canalopsis and Northern Landing—and vice versa. Keep it pumping boys, and we'll get enough money to buy Kingman out."

The vacillating market went on, and Don's gang continued to rock the Terran Electric stock. Then, as the market was about to close for the day, Don said: "Sell 'em short!"

Terran Electric stock appeared on the market in great quantities. Its value dropped down and down and down, and Kingman—apprised of the fall by Walt, who magnified it by not less than two to one—apparently got frantic again, for he said: "We're running short. Drop your Terran stock to bolster the VE job!"

"Oh, lovely!" said Don.

"You said that."

"I repeat it. Look, fellows, gather all the TE, Preferred, and VE, Preferred, you can. Wait, tell them that Terran Electric is dropping fast, so he'll scuttle more of his stuff, and we'll pick it up slowly enough so that we won't raise the market. How're we fixed for VE, Preferred?"

"Not too bad. Can we hit him once more?"

"Go ahead," said Don.

"Kingman," Walt announced. "Kingman! Hell's loose! The Interplanetary Bureau of Criminal Investigations has just decided to look into the matter of this stock juggling. They want to know who's trying to grab control of a public carrier!"

Minutes later, Wes said: "Oh, Brother Myrtle! That did it. He just gave orders to drop the whole thing short!"

"Wait until VE, Preferred, hits a new low and then we'll buy," said Don.

The flurry dropped VE, Preferred, to forty-seven, and then the agents of Venus Equilateral stepped forth and offered to buy, at the market, all offered stock.

They did.

Then, as no more stock was offered, Venus Equilateral, Preferred, rose sharply to ninety-four and stabilized at that figure. Terran Electric stock went through a valley, made by Kingman's sales, and then headed up, made by purchases on Terra, on Mars, and on Venus.

Don said: "Look, fellows, this has gone far enough. We have control again, and a goodly hunk of Terran Electric as well. Enough, I think, to force them to behave like a good little company and stay out of other people's hair. Let's all get together and celebrate."

"Right," the men echoed.

A month later, Joe's was the scene of a big banquet.

Barney Carroll got up and said: "Ladies and gentlemen, we all know why we're here and what we're celebrating. So I won't have to recount the whole affair. We all think Don Channing is a great guy, and Walt Franks isn't far behind, if any. I'm pretty likable myself, and my lifelong sparring partner, Jim Baler, is no smelt either. And so on, ad nauseam. But, ladies and gentlemen, Don Channing has a deep, dark, dire, desperate phase of his life, one that will be remembered and cursed; one that will weigh about his neck like a milestone—or is it millstone?—for all of his life. Benefactor though he is, this much you shall know: I still say there is no place in the Inner System for a man who has made this possible. Listen!"

Barney raised his hand, and an attendant turned on a standard, living-room model radio receiver. It burst into sound immediately.

". . . Ladies and gentlemen, the Interplanetary Network now brings to you the Whitewood Nutsies Program. Karven and Norwhal, the Venusian Songbirds; Thalla; and Lillas, in person, coming to you from the jungles of Palanortis, on Venus, by courtesy of the Interplanet Food Company of Battle Creek, Michigan! Ladies and gentlemen, Whitewood Nutsies are GOOD for you—"

Walt Franks said to Christine: "Let's get out of here."

Christine inspected Walt carefully, then nodded. "Yep," she grinned. "Even *you* sound better than the Interplanetary Network!"

For once, Walt did not argue, having gained his point.

Interlude

When the final problem of communicating with a ship in space was solved, the laboratories on Venus Equilateral returned to their original trends. These lines of research and study were wide and varied. Men dabbled brilliantly with insane, complex gadgets that measured the work functions of metals in electron emission and they made conclusive measurements on electrical conductivity under extremes of heat and cold. From the uranium pile that powered Venus Equilateral there came metals that had been under neutron bombardment long enough to have their crystal structure altered in unfathomable ways. These were investigated by men who toyed with them to ascertain whether or not they possessed any new properties that might make them useful. Many were the fields studied, too, because it is often that a chemist may be baffled by a problem that could be solved by a thorough education in electronics, for instance.

And from the diversified studies and researches often came strange byproducts. The quick leap of the physicist from a harebrained theory to a foregone conclusion has been the subject of laughter, but it is no less related than the chain of events that led from an exposed photographic plate to Hiroshima.

Or the chain of events that led Wes Farrell from his observation of a technician cleaning up a current-sputtered knife switch to a minor space war . . .

FIRING LINE

Mark Kingman was surprised by the tapping on his windowpane. He thought that the window was unreachable from the outside—and then he realized that it was probably someone throwing bits of dirt or small stones. But who would do that when the doorway was free for any bell ringer?

He shrugged, and went to the window to look out—and became cross-eyed as his eyes tried to cope with a single circle not more than ten inches distant. He could see the circle—and the lands on the inside spiraling into the depths of the barrel—and a cold shiver ran up his spine from there to here. Behind the heavy automatic, a dark-complected man with a hawklike face grinned mirthlessly.

Kingman stepped back and the stranger swung in and sat upon the windowsill.

"Well?" asked the lawyer.

"Is it well?" asked the stranger. "You know me?"

"No. Never saw you before in my life. Is this a burglary?"

"Nope. If it were, I'd have drilled you first so you couldn't describe me."

Kingman shuddered. The stranger looked as though he meant it.

"In case you require an introduction," said the hard-faced man. "I'm Allison Murdoch."

"Hellion?"

"None other."

"You were in jail—"

"I know. I've been there before."

"But how did you escape?"

"I'm a doctor of some repute," said Hellion. "Or was, until my darker reputation exceeded my reputation for neural surgery. It was simple. I slit my arm and deposited therein the contents of a cigarette. It swelled up like gangrene and they removed me to the hospital. I removed a few guards and lit out in the ambulance. And I am here."

"Why?" Kingman then became thoughtful. "You're not telling me this for mutual friendship, Murdoch. What's on your mind?"

"You were in the clink, too. How did you get out?"

"The court proceedings were under question for procedure. It was further ruled that—"

"I see. You bought your way out."

"I did not—"

"Kingman, you're a lawyer. A smart one, too."

"Thank you—"

"But you're capable of buying your freedom, which you did. Fundamentally, it makes no difference whether you bribe a guard to look the other way or bribe a jury to vote the other way. It's bribery in either case."

Kingman smiled in a superior way. "With the very important difference that the latter means results in absolute freedom. Bribing a guard is freedom only so long as the law may be avoided."

"So you did bribe the jury?"

"I did nothing of the sort. It was a ruling over a technicality that did me the favor."

"You created the technicality."

"Look," said Kingman sharply. "You didn't come here to steal, by your own admission and your excellent logic. You never saw me before, and I do not know of you save what I've heard. Revenge for something real or fancied is obviously no reason for this visit. I was charged with several kinds of larceny, which charges fell through and I was acquitted of them—which means I did not commit them. I, therefore, am no criminal. On the other hand, you have a record. You were in jail, convicted, and you escaped by some means that may have included first-degree murder. You came here for some reason, Murdoch. But let me tell you this: I am in no way required to explain the workings of my mind. If you expect me to reveal some legal machination by which I gained my freedom, you are mistaken. As far as the Solar System is concerned, everything was legal and above board."

"I get it," smiled Murdoch. "You're untouchable."

"Precisely. And rightfully so."

"You're the man I want, then."

"It isn't mutual. I have no desire to be identified with a criminal of your caliber."

"What's wrong with it?" Murdoch asked.

"It is fundamentally futile. You are not a brilliant criminal. You've been caught."

"I didn't have the proper assistance. I shall not be caught again. Look," he said suddenly, "how is your relationship with Venus Equilateral?"

Kingman gritted his teeth and made an animal noise.

"I thought so. I have a score of my own to settle. But I need your help. Do I get it?"

"I don't see how one of your caliber is capable—"

"Will I or won't I? Your answer may decide the duration of your life."

"You needn't threaten. I'm willing to go to any lengths to get even with Channing and his crowd. But it must be good."

"I was beaten by a technical error," Murdoch explained. "The coating on my ship did it."

"How?"

"They fired at me with a super-electron gun. A betatron. It hit me and disrupted the ship's apparatus. The thing couldn't have happened if the standard space finish hadn't been applied to the *Hippocrates*."

"I'm not a technical man," said Kingman. "Explain, please."

"The average ship is coated with a complex metallic oxide, which among other things inhibits secondary emission. Had we been running a ship without this coating, the secondary emission would have left the *Hippocrates* in fair condition electrically, but Venus Equilateral would have received several times the electronic charge. But the coating accepted the terrific charge and prevented the normal urge of electrons to leave by secondary emission—"

"What is secondary emission?"

"When an electron hits at any velocity, it drives from one to as high as fifty electrons from the substance it hits. The quantity depends upon the velocity of the original electron, the charges on cathode and anode, the material from which the target is made, and so on. We soaked 'em in like a sponge and took it bad. But the next time, we'll coat the ship with the opposite stuff. We'll take a bit of Venus Equilateral for ourselves."

"I like the idea. But how?"

"We'll try no frontal attack. Storming a citadel like Venus Equilateral is no child's play, Kingman. As you know, they're prepared for anything either legal or technical. I have a great respect for the combined abilities of Channing and Franks. I made my first mistake by giving them three days to make up their minds. In that time, they devised, tested, and approved an electron weapon of some power. Their use of it was as dangerous to them as it was to me—or would have been, if I'd been prepared with a metallic-oxide coating of the proper type."

"Just what are you proposing?" asked Kingman. "I do not understand what you are getting at."

"You are still one of the officials of Terran Electric?"

"Naturally."

"You will be surprised to know I handle considerable stock in that company."

"How, may I ask?"

"The last time you bucked them, you did it on the market. You lost," grinned Murdoch. "Proving that you haven't a hundred percent record, either. Well, while Terran Electric was dragging its par value down around the twos and threes, I took a few shares."

"How do you stand?"

"I rather imagine that I hold fifteen or twenty percent."

"That took money."

"I have money," Murdoch said modestly. "Plenty of it. I should have grabbed more stock, but I figured that between us we have enough to do as we please. What's your holding?"

"I once held forty-one percent. They bilked me out of some of that. I have less than thirty percent."

"So we'll run the market crazy again, and between

us we'll take control. Then, Kingman, we'll use Terran Electric to ruin Venus Equilateral."

"Terran Electric isn't too good a company now," Kingman admitted. "The public stays away in huge droves since we bucked Venus Equilateral. That bunch of electronic screwballs has the public acclaim. They're now in solid since they opened person-to-person service on the driver frequencies. You can talk to some one in the Palanortis Country of Venus with the same quality and speakability that you get in making a call from here to the house across the street."

"Terran Electric is about finished," said Murdoch flatly. "They shot their wad and lost. You'll be bankrupt in a year and you know it."

"That includes you, doesn't it?"

"Terran Electric is not the mainstay of my holdings," smiled Murdoch. "Under assumed names, I have picked up quite a few bits. Look, Kingman, I'm advocating piracy!"

"Piracy?" asked Kingman, aghast.

"Illegal piracy. But I'm intelligent. I realize that a pirate hasn't a chance against civilization unless he is as smart as they are. We need a research and construction organization, and that's where Terran Electric comes in. It's an old company, well established. It's now on the rocks. We can build it up again. We'll use it for a base, and set the research boys to figuring out the answers we need. Eventually we'll control Venus Equilateral, and half of the enterprises throughout the System."

"And your main plan?"

"You run Terran Electric, and I'll run the space piracy. Between us we'll have the System over a barrel. Spacecraft are still run without weapons because no weapons are suited for space fighting. But the new field opened up by the driver-radiation energy may exhibit something new in weapons. That's what I want Terran Electric to work on."

"We'll have to plan a bit more," said Kingman thoughtfully. "I'll cover you up, and eventually we'll buy you out. Meanwhile, we'll go to work on the market and get control of Terran Electric. And plan, too. It'll have to be foolproof."

"It will be," said Murdoch. "We'll plan it that way."

"We'll drink on it," said Kingman.

"*You'll* drink on it," Murdoch answered. "I never touch the stuff. I still pride myself on my skill with a scalpel, and I do not care to lose it. Frankly, I hope to keep it long enough to uncover the metatarsal bones of one Donald A. Channing, Director of Communications."

Kingman shuddered. At times, murder had passed through his mind when thinking of Channing. But this cruel idea of vivisecting an enemy indicated a sadism that was far beyond Kingman's idea of revenge. Of course, Kingman never considered that ruining a man financially, reducing him to absolute dependency upon friends or government, when the man had spent his life in freedom and plenty—the latter gained by his ability under freedom—was cruel and inhuman.

And yet it would take a completely dispassionate observer to tell which was worse: to ruin a man's body or to ruin a man's life.

The man in question was oblivious to these plans on his future. He was standing before a complicated maze of laboratory glassware and a haywire tangle of electronic origin. He looked it over in puzzlement, and his lack of enthusiasm bothered the other man. Wesley Farrell thought that his boss would have been volubly glad to see the fruits of his labor.

"No doubt it's wonderful," smiled Channing. "But what is it, Wes?"

"Why, I've been working on an alloy that will not sustain an arc."

"Go on. I'm interested, even though I do not climb the chandelier and scream, beating my manly chest."

"Oil switches are cumbersome. Any other means of breaking contact is equally cumbersome if it is to handle much power. My alloy is non-arcing. It will not sustain an arc, even though the highest current and voltage are broken."

"Now I'm really interested," Channing admitted. "Oil switches in a spaceship are a definite drawback."

"I know. So—here we are."

"What's the rest of this stuff?" asked Channing, laying a hand on the glassware.

"Be careful!" said Farrell in concern. "That's hot stuff."

"Oh?"

"In order to get some real voltages and currents to break without running the main station bus through here, I cooked this stuff up. The plate grilleworks in the large tubes exhibit a capacity between them of one microfarad. Empty, that is—or I should say, precisely, point nine eight microfarads in vacuum. The fluid is of my own devising, concocted for the occasion, and has a dielectric constant of thirteen times ten to the sixth power. It—"

"Great howling rockets!" exploded Channing. "That makes the overall capacity equal to thirteen *farads*!"

"Just about. Well, I have the condenser charged to three kilovolts, and then I discharge it through this switch made of the non-arcing alloy. Watch! No, Don, from back there, please, behind this safety glass."

Channing made some discomforting calculations about thirteen farads at three thousand volts and decided that there was definitely something unlucky about the number thirteen.

"The switch, now," continued Farrell, as though thirteen farads was just a mere drop in the bucket, "is opened four milliseconds after it is closed. The time constant of the discharging resistance is such that the voltage is zero point eight three of its peak three thousand volts, giving a good check of the alloy."

"I should think so," groused Channing. "Eighty-three percent of three thousand volts is just shy of twenty-five hundred volts. The current of discharge passing through a circuit that will drop the charge in a thirteen-farad condenser eighty-three percent in four milliseconds will be something fierce, believe me."

"That's why I use the heavy busbars from the condenser bank through the switch."

"I get it. Go ahead, Wes. I want to see this non-arcing switch of yours perform."

Farrell checked the meters, and then said: "Now!" and punched the switch at his side.

Across the room a solenoid drove the special alloy bar between two clamps of similar metal. Almost immediately, four thousandths of a second later, to be exact, the solenoid reacted automatically and the no-arc alloy was withdrawn. A minute spark flashed briefly between the contacts.

"And that is that," said Channing, dazed by the magnitude of it all, and the utter simplicity of the effects. "But, look, Wes, may I ask you a favor? Please discharge that infernal machine and drain that electrolyte out. Then make the thing up in a tool-steel case and seal it. Also hang on busbars right at the plates themselves, and slap a peak-voltage fuse across the terminals. One that will open at anything above three thousand volts. Follow me?"

"I think so. But that is not the main point of interest—"

"I know," Channing grinned, mopping his forehead. "The non-arc is. But that fragile glassware makes me as jittery as a Mexican jumping bean."

"But why?"

"Wes, if that glassware fractures somewhere, and that electrolyte drools out, you'll have a condenser of one microfad—charged to thirteen million times three thousand volts. Or, in nice, hollow, round numbers, forty billion volts! Of course, it won't get that far. It'll arc across the contacts before it gets that high, but it might raise particular hell on the way out. Take it easy, Wes. We're seventy million-odd miles from the nearest large body of dirt, all collected in a little steel bottle about three miles long and a mile in diameter. I'd hate to stop all interplanetary communications while we scraped ourselves off the various walls and treated ourselves for electric shock. It would—the discharge itself, I mean—raise hell with the equipment, anyway. So play it easy, Wes. We do not permit certain experiments out here because of the slow neutrons that sort of wander through here at fair density. Likewise, we cannot permit dangerous experiments. And anything that includes a dangerous experiment must be out, too."

"Oh," said Wes. His voice and attitude were altogether crestfallen.

"Don't take it so hard, fella," grinned Channing. "Any time we have to indulge in dangerous experiments, we always do it with an assistant—and in one of the blister laboratories. But take that fragile glassware out of the picture, and I'll buy it," he finished.

Walt Franks entered and asked what was going on.

"Wes was just demonstrating the latest equipment in concentrated deviltry," Channing smiled.

"That's my department," said Walt.

"Oh, it's not so bad as your stuff," said Channing. "What he's got here is an alloy that will break several million watts without an arc. Great stuff, Walt."

"Sounds swell," said Walt. "Better scribble it up and we'll get a patent. It sounds useful."

"I think it may bring us a bit of change," said Channing. "It's great stuff, Wes."

"Thanks. It annoyed me to see those terrific oil-breakers we have here. All I wanted to do was replace 'em with something smaller and more efficient."

"You did, Wes. And that isn't all. How did you dream up that high-dielectric?"

"Applied several of the physical phenomena."

"That's a good bet, too. We can use several fluids of various dielectric constants. Can you make solids as well?"

"Not as easily. But I can try?"

"Go ahead and note anything you find above the present listed compounds and their values."

"I'll list everything, as I always do."

"Good. And the first thing to do is to can that stuff in a steel case."

"It'll have to be a plastalloy."

"That's as strong as steel and non-conducting. Go ahead."

Channing led Franks from the laboratory, and once outside the Director gave way to a session of the shakes. "Wait," he said plaintively, "take me by the hand and lead me to Joe's. I need some vitamins."

"Bad?"

"Did you see that glassblower's nightmare?"

"You mean that collection of cut glass?" grinned Walt. "Uh-huh. It looked as though it were about to collapse of its own dead weight!"

"That held an electrolyte of dielectric constant thirteen times ten to the sixth. He had it charged to a mere three thousand volts. Ye gods, Walt. Thirteen farads at three KV. *Whew!* And when he discharged it, the confounded leads that went through the glass side walls to the condenser plates positively glowed in the cherry red. I swear it!"

"He's like that," said Walt. "You shouldn't worry about him. He'll have built that condenser out of good stuff—the leads will be alloys like those we use in the bigger tubes. They wouldn't fracture the glass seals no matter what the temperature difference between them and the glass was. Having that alloy around the place—up in the tube maintenance department they have a half-ton of quarter-inch rod—he'd use it naturally."

"Could be, Walt. Maybe I'm a worrywart."

"You're not used to working with his kind."

"I quote: 'Requiring a high-voltage source of considerable current capacity, I hit upon the scheme of making a super-high-capacity condenser and discharging it through my no-arc alloy. To do this it was necessary that I invent a dielectric material of K equals thirteen times ten to the sixth. Unquote.' "

"Wes is a pure scientist," Walt reminded him. "If he were investigating the electrical properties of zinc, and required a solar power magnitude to complete his investigation, he'd invent it and then include it as an incidental to the investigation on zinc. He's never really understood our recent divergence in purpose over the power tube. That we should make it soak up power from Sol was purely incidental, and useful only as a lever or means to make Terran Electric give us our way. He'd have forgotten it, I'll bet, since it was not the ultimate goal of the investigation."

"He knows his stuff, though."

"Granted. Wes is brilliant. He is a physicist, though, and neither engineer nor inventor. I doubt that he is really interested in the physical aspects of anything that is not directly concerned with his eating and sleeping."

"What are we going to do about him?"

"Absolutely nothing. You aren't like *him*—"

"I hope not!"

"And conversely, why should we try to make him like *you?*"

"That I'm against," chimed in a new voice. Arden Channing took each man by the arm and looked up on either side of her, into one face and then the other. "No matter how, why, when, who, or what, one like him is all that the Solar System can stand."

"Walt and I are pretty much alike."

"Uh-huh. You are. That's as it should be. You balance one another nicely. You couldn't use another like you. You're speaking of Wes Farrell?"

"Right."

"Leave him alone," Arden said sagely. "He's good as he is. To make him similar to you would be to spoil a good man. He'd then be neither fish, flesh, nor fowl. He doesn't think as you do, but instead proceeds in a straight line from remote possibility to foregone conclusion. Anything that gets needed en route is used, or gadgeteered, and forgotten. That's where you come in, fellows. Inspect his byproducts. They may be darned useful."

"O.K. Anybody care for a drink?"

"Yep. All of us," said Arden.

"Don, how did you rate such a good-looking wife?"

"I hired her," grinned Channing. "She used to make all of my stenographic mistakes, remember?"

"And gave up numerous small errors for one large one? Uh-huh, I recall. Some luck."

"It was my charm."

"Baloney. Arden, tell the truth. Didn't he threaten you with something terrible if you didn't marry him?"

"You tell him," Channing smiled. "I've got work to do."

Channing left the establishment known as Joe's advertised as the "Best Bar in Twenty-Seven Million Miles, Minimum," and made his way to his office, slowly. He didn't reach it. Not right away. He was intercepted by Chuck Thomas, who invited him to view a small experiment. Channing smiled and said that he'd prefer to see an experiment of any kind to going to his office, and followed Chuck.

"You recall the gadget we used in order to get perfect tuning with the alloy-selectivity transmitter?"

"You mean that variable-alloy disk all bottled up and

rotated with a selsyn?" Don asked, wondering what came next. "Naturally I remember it. Why?"

"Well, we've found that certain submicroscopic effects occur with inert objects. What I mean is this: given a chunk of cold steel of goodly mass and tune your alloy disk to pure steel, and you can get a few micro-microamperes output if the tube is pointed at the object."

"Sounds interesting. How much amplification do you need to get this reading and how do you make it tick?"

"We run the amplifier up to the limit and then sweep the tube across the object sought, and the output meter leaps skyward by just enough to make us certain of our results. Watch!"

Chuck set the tube in operation and checked it briefly. Then he took Don's hand and put it on the handle that swung the tube on its gimbals. "Sort of paint the wall with it," he said. "You'll see the deflection as you pass the slab of tool steel that's standing there."

Channing did, and watched the minute flicker of the ultra-sensitive meter. "Wonderful," he grinned, as the door opened and Walt Franks entered.

"Hi, Don. Is it true that you bombarded her with flowers?"

"Nope. She's just building up some other woman's chances. Have you seen this effect?"

"Yeah. It's wonderful, isn't it?"

"That's what I like about this place," said Chuck with a huge smile. "That's approximately seven micro-microamperes output after amplification on the order of two hundred million times. We're either working on something so small we can't see it, or something so big we can't count it. It's either fifteen decimal places to the left or to the right. Every night when I go home I say a little prayer. I say: 'Dear God, please let me find something today that is based upon unity, or at least no more than two decimal places,' but it is no good. If He hears me at all He's too busy to bother with things that the human race classifies as 'One.' "

"How do you classify resistance, current, and voltage?" asked Channing, manipulating the tube on its gimbals and watching the effect.

"One million volts across ten megohms equals one

hundred thousand microamperes. That's according to Ohm's Law."

"He's got the zero madness, too," Walt chuckled. "It obtains from thinking in astronomical distances, with interplanetary coverages in watts, and celestial input, and stuff like that. Don, this thing may be handy some day. I'd like to develop it."

"I suggest that a couple of stages of tube amplification might help. Amplify it before transduction into electronic propagation."

"We can get four or five stages of sub-electronic amplification, I think. It'll take some working."

"O.K., Chuck. Cook ahead. We do not know whither we are heading, but it looks damned interesting."

"Yeah," added Walt, "it's a damn rare scientific fact that can't be used for something, somewhere. Well, Don, now what?"

"I guess we now progress to the office and run through a few reams of paper work. Then we may relax."

"O.K. Sounds good to me. Let's go."

Hellion Murdoch pointed to the luminous speck in the celestial globe. His finger stabbed at the market button, and a series of faint concentric spheres marked the distance from the center of the globe to the object, which he read and mentioned: "Twelve thousand miles."

"Asteroid?" asked Kingman.

"What else?" asked Murdoch. "We're lying next to the Asteroid Belt."

"What are you going to do?"

"Burn it," said Murdoch.

His fingers danced upon the keyboard, and high above him, in the dome of the *Black Widow,* a power-intake tube swiveled and pointed at Sol. Coupled to the output of the power-intake tube, a power-output tube turned to point at the asteroid. And Murdoch's poised finger came down on the last switch, closing the final circuit.

Meters leaped up across their scales as the intangible beam of solar energy came silently in and went as silently out. It passed across the intervening miles with the velocity of light, squared, and hit the asteroid. A second later the asteroid glowed and melted under the terrific bombardment of solar energy directed in a tight beam.

"It's O.K.," said Hellion. "But have the gang build us three larger tubes to be mounted turretwise. Then we can cope with society."

"What do you hope to gain by that? Surely piracy and grand larceny are not profitable in the light of what we have and know."

"I intend to institute a 'reign of terror.' "

"You mean to go through with your plan?"

"I am a man of my word. I shall levy a tax against any and every ship leaving any spaceport. We shall demand one dollar solarian for every gross ton that lifts from any planet and reaches the planetary limit."

"How do you establish that limit?" asked Kingman interestedly.

"Ironically, we'll use the Channing Layer," said Murdoch with dark humor. "Since the Channing Layer describes the boundary below which our solar beam will not work. Our reign of terror will be identified with Channing because of that; it will take some of the praise out of people's minds when they think of Channing and Venus Equilateral."

"That's pretty deep psychology," said Kingman.

"You should recognize it." Murdoch smiled. "That's the kind of stuff you legal lights pull. Mention the accused in the same sentence with one of the honored people; mention the defendant in the same breath with one of the hated people—it's the same stunt. Build them up or tear them down by reference."

"You're pretty shrewd."

"I am," agreed Murdoch placidly.

"Mind telling me how you found yourself in the fix you're in?"

"Not at all. I've been interested for years in neurosurgery. My researches passed beyond the realm of rabbits and monkeys, and I found it necessary to investigate the more delicate, more organized, the higher-strung. That means human beings—though some of them are less sensitive than a rabbit and less delicate than a monkey." Murdoch's eyes took on a cynical expression at this. Then it passed, and he continued: "I became famous, as you know. Or do you?"

Kingman shook his head.

"I suppose not. I became famous in my own circle. Lesser neurosurgeons sent their complex cases to me; unless you were complex, you would never hear of Allison Murdoch. Well, anyway, some of them offered exciting opportunities. I—frankly—experimented. Some of them died. It was quite a bit of cut-and-try because not too much has been written on the finer points of the nervous system. But there were too few people who were complex enough to require my services, and I turned to clinical work and experimented freely."

"And there you made your mistake?"

"Do you know how?"

"No. I imagine that with many patients you exceeded your rights once too often."

"Wrong. It's a funny factor in human relationship. Something that makes no sense. When people were paying me three thousand dollars an hour for operations, I could experiment without fear. Some died, some regained their health under my ministrations. But when I experimented on charity patients, I could not experiment because of the 'protection' given the poor. The masses were not to be guinea pigs. Ha!" laughed Murdoch. "Only the rich are permitted to be subjects of an experiment. Touch not the poor, who offer nothing. Experiment upon those of intellect, wealth, fame, or anything that sets them above the mob. Yes, even genius came under my knife. But I couldn't give a poor man a fifty-fifty chance at his life, when the chances of his life were less than one in ten. From a brilliant man, operating under fifty-fifty chances for life, I became an inhuman monster that cut without fear. I was imprisoned, and later escaped with some friends."

"And that's when you stole the *Hippocrates* and decided that the Solar System should pay you revenge money?"

"I would have done better if I'd not made that one mistake. I forgot that in the years of imprisonment I fell behind in scientific knowledge. I know now that no one can establish anything at all without technical minds behind him."

Kingman's lips curled. "I wouldn't agree to that."

"You should. Your last defeat at the hands of the technicians you scorn should have taught you a lesson. If you had been sharp, you would have outguessed them; out-engineered them. They, Kingman, were not afraid to rip into their detector to see what made it tick."

"But I had only the one—"

"They know one simple thing about the universe. That rule is that if anything works once, it may be made to work again." He held up his hand as Kingman started to speak. "You'll bring all sorts of cases to hand and try to disprove me. You can't. Oh, you couldn't cause a quick return of the diplodocus, or re-enact the founding of the solar government, or even re-burn a ton of coal. But there is other carbon, there will be other governmental introductions and reforms, and there may be some day the rebirth of the dinosaur—on some planet there may be carboniferous ages now. Any phenomena that are true phenomena—and your detector was definite, not a misinterpretation of effect—can be repeated. But, Kingman, we'll not be out-engineered again."

"That I do believe."

"And so we will have our revenge on Venus Equilateral and upon the System itself."

"We're heading home now?"

"Right. We want this ship fitted with the triple turret I mentioned before. Also I want the interconnecting links between the solar intake and the power projectors beefed up. When you're passing several hundred megawatts through any system, losses of the nature of .000,000,1% cause heating to a dangerous degree. We've got to cut the I^2R losses. I gave orders that the turret be started, by the way. It'll be almost ready when we return."

"*You* gave orders?" said Kingman.

"Oh, yes," said Hellion Murdoch with a laugh. "Remember our *last* bout with the stock market? I seem to have accumulated about forty-seven percent. That's sufficient to give me control of our company."

"But—but—" Kingman spluttered. "That took money—"

"I still have enough left," said Murdoch quietly. "After all, I spent years in the Melanortis Country of Venus. I was working on the *Hippocrates* when I wasn't doing a bit of mining. There's a large vein of platiniridium there. You may answer the rest."

"I still do not get this piracy."

Murdoch's eyes blazed.

"That's my interest. That's my revenge! I intend to ruin Don Channing and Venus Equilateral. With the super-turret they'll never be able to catch us, and we'll run the entire System."

Kingman considered. As a lawyer, he was finished. His last try at the ruination of the Venus Equilateral crowd by means of pirating the interplanetary communications beam was strictly a violation of the Communications Code. The latter absolutely prevented any man or group of men from diverting communications not intended for them and using these communications for their own purpose. His defense that Venus Equilateral had also broken the law went unheard. It was pointed out to him that Venus Equilateral tapped his own line, and the tapping of an illegal line was the act of a communications agent in the interest of the government. He was no longer a lawyer, and, in fact, he had escaped a long jail term by sheer bribery.

He was barred from legal practice, and he was barred from any business transactions. The stock market could be manipulated, but only through a blind—which was neither profitable nor safe.

His holdings in Terran Electric were all that stood between him and ruin. He was no better off than Murdoch, save that he was not wanted.

But—

"I'm going to remain on Terra and run Terran Electric like a model company," he said. "That'll be our base."

"Right. Except for a bit of research along specified lines, you'll do nothing. Your job will be to act apologetic for your misdeeds. You will grovel on the floor before any authority, and beseech the legal profession to accept you once more. I will need your help, there. You are to establish yourself in the good graces of the Interplanetary Patent Office, and report to me any applications that may be of interest. The research that Terran Electric will conduct will be along innocuous lines. The real research will be in a secret laboratory. The one in the Melanortis Country. Selected men will work there, and the Terran Electric fleet of cargo carriers will carry the material needed. My main failure was not to have provided a means of knowing what the worlds were doing. I'll have that now, and I shall not be defeated again."

"We'll say that one together!" said Kingman.

He flipped open a large book and set the autopilot from a set of figures. The *Black Widow* turned gently and started to run for Terra at two G.

Walt Franks frowned at the memorandum in his hand.

"Look, Don, are we ever going to get to work on that deal with Keg Johnson?"

"Uh-huh," Don answered, without looking up.

"He's serious. Transplanet is getting the edge, and he doesn't like it."

"Frankly, I don't like dabbling in stuff like that either. But Keg's an old friend, and I suppose that's how a guy gets all glommed up on projects, big business deals, and so forth. We'll be going in directly. Why the rush?"

"A bit of personal business on Mars which can best be done at the same time, thus saving an additional trip."

"O.K.," said Don idly. "Might as well get it over with. Date with Christine Baler?"

"Sure," grinned Franks.

Actually, it was less than an hour before the *Relay Girl* went out of the south end landing stage, turned, and headed for Mars. Packing, to the Channings, was a matter of persuading Arden not to take everything but the drapes in the apartment along with her, while for Walt Franks it was a matter of grabbing a trunkful of instruments and spare parts. Space travel is a matter of waiting for days in the confines of a small bubble of steel. Just waiting. For the scenery is unchanging all the way from Sol to Pluto—and is the same scenery that can be seen from the viewports of Venus Equilateral.

Walt enjoyed his waiting time by tinkering; having nothing to do would have bored him, and so he took with him enough to keep him busy during the trip.

At two Terran gravities, the velocity of the *Relay Girl* built up bit by bit and mile by mile, until they were going just shy of one thousand miles per second. This occurred an hour before turnover, which would take place at the twenty-third hour of flight.

And at that time there occurred a rarity. Not an impossibility like the chances of collision with a meteor—those things happen only once in a lifetime, and Channing had had his collision. Nor was it as remote as getting a royal flush on the deal. It happened, not often, but it did happen to ships occasionally.

Another ship passed within detector range.

The celestial globe shimmered faintly and showed a minute point at extreme range. Automatic marker spheres appeared concentrically within the celestial globe, and colures and diameters marked the globe off into octants.

Bells rang briefly, and the automatic meteor circuits decided that the object was not approaching the *Relay Girl.* Then they relaxed. Their work was done until another object came within range for them to inspect. They were no longer interested, and they forgot about the object with the same powers of complete oblivion that they would have exerted on a meteor of nickel and iron.

They were mechanically incapable of original thought. So the object, to them, was harmless.

Channing looked up at the luminescent spot, sought the calibration spheres, made a casual observation, and forgot about it. To him it was a harmless meteor.

Even the fact that his own velocity was a thousand miles per second, and the object's velocity was the same, coming to them on a one-hundred-and-seventy-degree course and due to pass within five thousand miles, did not register. Their total velocity of two thousand miles did not register just because of that rarity with which ships pass within detector range, while meteors are encountered often.

Had Channing been thinking about the subject in earnest, he would have known—for it is only man, with all too little time, who uses such velocities. The universe, with eternity in which to work her miracle, seldom moves in velocities greater than forty or fifty miles per second.

Channing forgot it, and as the marker spheres switched to accommodate the object, he turned to more important things.

In the other ship, Hellion Murdoch frowned. He brightened, then, and depressed the plunger that energized his solar beam and projector. He did not recognize the oncoming object for anything but a meteor, either; and *his* desire was to find out how his invention worked at top speeds.

Kingman asked: "Another one?"

"Uh-huh," said Murdoch idly. "I want to check my finders."

"But they can't miss."

"No? Look, lawyer, you're not running a job that may be given a stay or reprieve. The finders run on light velocities. The solar beam runs on the speed of light, squared. We'll pass that thing at five thousand miles' distance and at two thousand miles per second velocity. A microsecond of misalignment, and we're missing, see? I think we're going to be forced to put correction circuits in, so that the vector sums and velocities and distances will all come out with a true hit. It will not be like sighting down a searchlight beam at high velocity."

"I see. You'll need compensation?"

"Plenty, at this velocity and distance. This is the first time I've had a chance to try it out."

The latter fact saved the *Relay Girl*. By a mere matter of feet and inches; by the difference between the speed of light and the speed of light, squared, at a distance of five thousand miles, plus a slight miscompensation. The intolerably hot umbra of Murdoch's beam followed below the pilot's greenhouse of the *Relay Girl* all the way past, a matter of several seconds. The spillover was tangible enough to warm the *Relay Girl* to uncomfortable temperatures.

Then with no real damage done, the contact with ships in space was over, but not without a certain minimum of recognition.

"Hell!" said Kingman. "That was a spacecraft!"

"Who?"

"I don't know. You missed."

"I'd rather have hit," said Murdoch coldly. "I hope I missed by plenty."

"Why?"

"If we scorched their tails any, there'll be embarrassing questions asked."

"So?"

"So nothing until we're asked. Even then, you know nothing."

In the *Relay Girl,* Channing mopped his forehead. "That was Hell itself," he said.

Arden laughed uncertainly. "I thought that it would wait until we got there; I didn't expect Hell to come after us."

"What—exactly—happened?" Walt asked, coming into the scanning room.

"*That* was a spaceship."

"One of this System's?"

"I wonder," said Don honestly. "It makes a guy wonder. It was gone too fast to make certain. It probably was Solarian, but they tried to burn us with something . . ."

"That makes it sound like something alien," Walt admitted. "But that doesn't make a good sense."

"It makes good reading," laughed Channing. "Walt, you're the Boy Edison. Have you been tinkering with anything of lethal learnings?"

"You think there may be something powerful afloat?"

"Could be. We don't know everything."

"I've toyed with the idea of coupling a solar intake beam with one of those tubes that Baler and Carroll found. Recall, they smashed up quite a bit of Lincoln Head before they uncovered the secret of how to handle it. Now that we have unlimited power—or are limited only by the losses in our own system—we could, or should be able to, make something raw-ther tough."

"You've toyed with the idea, hey?"

"Uh-huh."

"Of course, you haven't really tried it?"

"Of course not."

"How did it work?"

"Fair," grinned Walt. "I did it with miniatures only, of course, since I couldn't get my hooks on a full-grown tube."

"Say," asked Arden, "how did you birds arrive at this idea so suddenly? I got lost at the first premise."

"We passed a strange ship. We heated up to uncomfortable temperatures in a matter of nine seconds flat. They didn't warn us with thought waves or vector invectives. Sheer dislike wouldn't do it alone. I guess that someone is trying to do the trick started by our esteemed Mr. Franks here a year or so ago. Only with something practical, instead of an electron beam. Honest-to-goodness energy, right from Sol himself, funneled through some tricky inventions. What about that experiment of yours? Did you bring it along?"

Walt looked downcast. "No," he said. "It was another one."

"Let's see."

"It's not too good."

"Same idea?"

Walt went to get his experiment. He returned with a tray full of laboratory glassware, all wired into a maze of electronic equipment.

Channing went white. "You, too?" he yelled.

"Take it easy, sport. This charges only to a hundred volts. We get thirteen hundred microfarads at one hundred volts. Then we drain off the dielectric fluid, and get one billion three hundred million volts' charge into a condenser of only one hundred micromicrofarads. It's an idea for the nuclear physics boys. I think it may tend to solidify some of the uncontrollables in the present system of developing high electron velocities."

"That thirteen-million-dielectric-constant stuff is strictly electrodynamic, I think," said Channing. "Farrell may have developed it as a byproduct, but I have a hunch that it will replace some heretofore valuable equipment. The Franks-Farrell generator will outdo Van de Graaff's little job, I think."

"Franks-Farrell?"

"Sure. He thunk up the dielectric. You thunk up the

application. He won't care, and you couldn't have done it without. Follow?"

"Oh, sure. I was just trying to figure out a more generic term for it."

"Don't. Let it go as it is for now. It's slick, Walt, but there's no weapon in it."

"You're looking for a weapon?"

"Uh-huh. Ever since Murdoch took a swing at Venus Equilateral, I've been sort of wishing that we could concoct something big enough and dangerous enough to keep us free from any other wiseacres. Remember, we stand out there like a sore thumb. We're as vulnerable as a half-pound of butter at a banquet for starving Armenians. The next screwball who wants to control the System will have to control Venus Equilateral first. And the best things we can concoct to date include projectile-tossing guns at velocities less than the speed of our ships, and an electron shooter than can be overcome by coating the ship with any of the metal salts that enhance secondary transmission."

"Remind me to requisition a set of full-sized tubes when we return. Might as well have some fun."

"O.K., you can have 'em. Which brings us back to the present. Question: was that an abortive attempt upon our ship, or was that a mistaken try at melting a meteor?"

"I know how to find out. Let's call Chuck Thomas and have him get on the rails. We can have him request Terran Electric to give us any information they may have on energy beams to date."

"They'd tell you?" scorned Arden.

"If they write 'No' and we find out that they did, we'll sue them dead. They're too shaky to try anything deep right now."

"Going to make it an official request, hey?"

"Right. From the station, it'll go out in print, and their answer will be on the 'type, too, since business etiquette requires it. They'll get the implication if they're on the losing end. That'll make them try something slick. If they're honest, they'll tell all."

"That'll do it, all right," said Walt. "They're too shaky to buck us anymore. And if they are trying anything, it'll show."

The rest of the trip was without incident. They put in at Canalopsis and found Keg Johnson with an official 'gram waiting for them.

Don Channing ripped it open and read:

VENUS EQUILATERAL
ATTENTION DR. CHANNING:

NO PROJECT FOR ENERGY BEAM CAPABLE OF REMOVING METEORS UNDER WAY AT TERRAN ELECTRIC, OR AT ANY OF THE SUBSIDIARY COMPANIES. IDEAS SUGGESTED ALONG THESE LINES HAVE BEEN DISPROVEN BY YOUR ABORTIVE ATTEMPT OF A YEAR AGO, AND WILL NOT BE CONSIDERED UNLESS THEORY IS SUBSTANTIATED IN EVERY WAY BY PRACTICAL EVIDENCE.

IF YOU ARE INTERESTED, WE WILL DELVE INTO THE SUBJECT FROM ALL ANGLES. PLEASE ADVISE.

TERRAN ELECTRIC CO.
BOARD OF LEGAL OPERATIONS
MARK KINGMAN, LL.D.

Channing smiled wryly at Keg Johnson and told him of their trouble.

"Oh?" said Keg with a frown. "Then you haven't heard?"

"Heard what?"

"Hellion Murdoch has been on the loose for weeks."

"Weeks!" Channing yelled.

"Uh-huh. He feigned gangrene, was taken to the base hospital, where he raised hob in his own inimitable way. He blasted the communications setup completely, ruined three spaceships, and made off with the fourth. The contact ship just touched there recently and found hell brewing. If they hadn't had a load of supplies and prisoners for the place, they wouldn't have known about it for months, perhaps."

"So! Brother Murdoch is loose again. Well! The story dovetails in nicely."

"You think that was Hellion himself?"

"I'd bet money on it. The official report on Hellion Murdoch said that he was suffering from a persecution complex, and that he was capable of making something of it if he got the chance. He's slightly whacky—dangerously so."

"He's a brilliant man, isn't he?"

"Quite. His name is well known in the circles of neurosurgery. He is also known to be an excellent research worker in applied physics."

"Nuts, hey?" asked Walt.

"Yeah, he's nuts. But only in one way, Walt. He's nuts to think that he is smarter than the entire Solar System all put together. Well, what do we do now?"

"Butter ourselves well and start scratching for the answer. That betatron trick will not work twice. There must be something."

"O.K., Walt, we'll all help you think. I'm wondering how much research he had to do to develop that beam. After all, we were five thousand miles away, and he heated us up. He must've thought that we were a meteor—and another thing, too: he must've thought that his beam was capable of doing something at five thousand miles' distance or he wouldn't have tried. Ergo, he must have beaten that two-hundred-mile bugaboo."

"We don't know that the two-hundred-mile bugaboo is still bugging in space," said Walt slowly. "That's set up so that the ionization byproducts are not dangerous. Also, he's not transmitting power from station to station, et cetera. He's ramming power into some sort of beam and to the devil with losses external to his equipment. The trouble is, damn it, that we'll have to spend a month just building a large copy of my miniature setup."

"A month is not too much time," Channing agreed. "And Murdoch will take a swing at us as soon as he gets ready to reach. We can have Chuck start building the big tubes immediately, can't we?"

"Just one will be needed. We'll use one of the standard solar intake tubes that we're running the station from. There's spare equipment aplenty. But the transmitter-terminal tube will take some building."

"Can we buy one from Terran Electric?"

"Why not? Get the highest rating we can. That should be plenty. Terran probably has them in stock, and it'll save us building one."

"What is their highest rating?" Don asked.

"Two hundred megawatts."

"O.K. I'll send 'em a coded requisition with my answer to their letter."

"What are you going to tell 'em?"

"Tell 'em not to investigate the energy-gun idea unless they want to for their own reasons," Channing grinned. "They'll probably assume—and correctly—that we're going to tinker, ourselves."

"And?"

"Will do nothing since it is an extraplanetary proposition. Unless it becomes suitable for digging tunnels, or melting the Martian ice cap," laughed Channing.

Mark Kingman took the letter to Murdoch, who was hidden in the depths of the *Black Widow*.

Hellion read it twice, and then growled.

"They smell something sure," he snarled. "Why didn't we make that a perfect hit!"

"What are we going to do now?"

"Step up our plans. They'll have this thing in a few weeks. Hm-m-m. They order a transmitter-terminal tube. Have you got any in stock?"

"Naturally. Not in stock, but available for the Northern Landing power line order."

"You have none, then. You will have some available within a few days. That half-promise will stall them from making their own, and every day that they wait for your shipment is a day in our favor. To keep your own nose clean, I'll tell you when to ship the tube. It'll be a few days before I strike."

"Why bother?" asked Kingman. "They won't be around to call names."

"No, but their friends will, and we want to keep them guessing."

"I see. Those tubes are huge enough to cause comment, and there will be squibs in all papers telling of the giant tube going to Venus Equilateral, and the Sunday supplements will all break out in wild guesses as to the reason why Venus Equilateral wants a two-hundred-megawatt tube. Too bad you couldn't keep your escape a secret a while longer."

"I suppose so. It was bound to be out sooner or later, anyway. A good general, Kingman, is one whose plans may be changed on a moment's notice without sacrificing. We'll win through."

The days wore on, and the big turret on the top of the *Black Widow* took shape. The super-tubes were installed, and Murdoch worked in the bowels of the ship to increase the effectiveness of the course integrators and to accommodate high velocities and to correct for the minute discrepancies that would crop up due to the difference in velocities between light and sub-electronic radiation.

And on Venus Equilateral, the losing end of a war of nerves was taking place. The correspondence by 'type was growing into a reasonable pile, while the telephone conversations between Terran Electric and Venus Equilateral became a daily proposition. The big tubes were not finished; the big tubes were finished, but rejected because of electrode misalignments; the big tubes were in the rework department; the big tubes were on Luna for their testing. And again they were not met. They were returned to Evanston and were once more in the rework department. You have no idea how difficult the manufacture of two-hundred-megawatt tubes really is . . .

So the days passed, and no tubes were available. The date passed which marked the mythical date of "if"—*if* Venus Equilateral had started their own manufacturing on the day they were first ordered from Terran Electric, they would have been finished and available.

Then, one day, word was passed along that the big tubes were shipped. They were on their way, tested and approved, and would be at Venus Equilateral within two days. In the due course of time, they arrived, and the gang at the relay station went to work on them.

But Walt Franks shook his head. "Don, we'll be caught like a sitting rabbit."

"I know. But?" answered Channing.

There was no answer to that question, so they went to work again.

The news of Murdoch's first blow came that day. It was a news report from the Interplanetary Network that the Titan Penal Colony had been attacked by a huge black ship of space that carried a dome-shaped turret on the top. Beams of invisible energy burned furrows in the frozen ground, and the official buildings melted and exploded from the air pressure within them. The Titan station went off the ether with a roar, and the theorists believed that Murdoch's gang had been augmented by four hundred and nineteen of the Solar System's most vicious criminals.

"That rips it wide open," said Channing. "Better get the folks to withstand a siege. I don't think they can take us."

"That devil might turn his beams on the station itself, though," said Walt.

"He wants to control communications."

"With the sub-electron beams we now have, he could do it on a mere piece of the station. Not perfectly, but he'd get along."

"Fine future," gritted Channing. "This is a good time to let this project coast, Walt. We've got to start in from the beginning and walk down another track."

"It's easy to say, chum."

"I know it. So far, all we've been able to do is take energy from the solar intake beams and spray it out into space. It goes like the arrow that went—we know not where."

"So?"

"Forget these gadgets. Have Chuck hook up the solar intake tubes to the spotter and replace the cathodes with pure thorium. I've got another idea."

"O.K., but it sounds foolish to me."

Channing laughed. "We'll stalemate him," he said bitterly, and explained it to Walt. Then: "I wonder when Murdoch will come this way?"

"It's but a matter of time," said Walt. "My bet is, as soon as he can get here with that batch of fresh rats he's collected."

Walt's bet would have collected. Two days later, Hellion Murdoch flashed a signal into Venus Equilateral and asked for Channing.

"Hello, Hellion," Channing answered. "Haven't you learned to keep out of our way?"

"Not at all," answered Murdoch. "You won't try that betatron on me again. This ship is coated with four-tenths of an inch of lithium metal, which according to the books will produce the maximum quantity of electrons under secondary emission. If not the absolute maximum, it is high enough to prevent your action."

"No," agreed Channing. "We won't try the betatron again. But, Murdoch, there are other things."

"Can they withstand these," asked Murdoch. The turret swiveled until the triple mount of tubes looked at Venus Equilateral.

"Might try," said Channing.

"Any particular place?" countered Murdoch.

"Hit the south end. We can best afford to lose that," answered Channing.

"You're either guessing, or hoping I won't fire, or perhaps praying that whatever you have for protection will work," said Murdoch flatly. "Otherwise you wouldn't talk so smooth."

"You blackhearted baby-killing rotter," Channing snarled. "I'm not chinning with you for the fun of it. You'll shoot anyway, and I want to see how good you are. Get it over with, Murdoch."

"What I have here is plenty good," said Murdoch. "Good enough. Do you know about it?"

"I can guess, but you tell me."

"Naturally," said Hellion. He explained in detail. "Can you beat that?"

"We may not be able to outfire you," gritted Channing, "but we may be able to nullify your beam."

"Nonsense!" roared Murdoch. "Look, Channing, you'd best surrender."

"Never!"

"You'd rather die?"

"We'd rather fight it out. Come in and get us."

"Oh, no. We'll just shoot your little station full of holes. Like the average spaceship, your station will be quite capable of handling communications even though the air is all gone. Filling us full of holes wouldn't do a thing; you see, we're wearing spacesuits."

"I guessed that. No, Murdoch, we have nothing to shoot at you this time. All we can do is hold you off until you get hungry. *You'll* get hungry first, since we're self-sufficient."

"And in the meantime?"

"In the meantime we're going to try a few things out

on your hull. I rather guess that you'll try out a few things on the station. But at the present, you can't harm us and we can't harm you. Stalemate, Murdoch!"

"You're bluffing!" stormed Murdoch.

"Are you afraid to squirt that beam this way?" asked Channing tauntingly. "Or do you know it will not work?"

"Why are you so anxious to get killed?"

We're very practical, out here on Venus Equilateral," said Don. "There's no use in our working further if you have something that is really good. We'd like to know our chances before we expend more effort along another line."

"That's not all—?"

"No. Frankly, I'm almost certain that your beam won't do a thing to Venus Equilateral."

"We'll see. Listen! Turretman! Are you ready?"

Faintly the reply came, and Channing could hear it. "Ready!"

"Then fire all three. Pick your targets at will. One blast!"

The light in Venus Equilateral brightened. The thousands of line-voltage meters went from one hundred and twenty-five to one hundred and forty volts, and the line frequency struggled with the crystal control and succeeded in making a ragged increase from sixty to sixty point one five cycles per second. The power-output meters on the transmitting equipment went up briefly, and in the few remaining battery supply rooms, the overload and overcharge alarms clanged until the automatic adjusters justified the input against the constant load. One of the ten-kilowatt modulator tubes flashed over in the audio room and was immediately cut from the operating circuit; the recording meters indicated that the tube had gone west forty-seven hours prior to its expiration date, due to filament overload. A series of fluorescent lighting fixtures in a corridor of the station that should have been dark because of the working hours of that section flickered into life and woke several of the workers, and down in the laboratory Wes Farrell swore because the fluctuating line had disrupted one of his experiments, giving him reason to doubt the result. He tore the thing down, and began once more; seventy days' work had been ruined.

"Well," Channing said cockily, "is that the best you can do?"

"You!"

"You forgot," reminded Channing, "that we have been working with solar power, too. In fact, we discovered the means to get it. Go ahead and shoot at us, Murdoch. You're just giving us more power."

"Cease firing!" Murdoch exploded.

"Oh, don't," cheered Don. "You forgot that those tubes, if aligned properly, will actually cause bending of the energy beam. We've got load-terminal tubes pointing at you, and your power beam is bending to enter them. You did well, though. You were running the whole station with plenty to spare. We had to squirt some excess into space. Your beams aren't worth the glass that's in them!"

"Stalemate, then," snarled Murdoch. "Now *you* come and get *us*. We'll leave. But we'll be back. Meanwhile, we can have our way with the shipping. Pilot! Course for Mars! Start when ready!"

The *Black Widow* turned and streaked from Venus Equilateral as Don Channing mopped his forehead. "Walt," he said, "that's once I was scared to death."

"Me, too. Well, we got a respite. Now what?"

"We start thinking."

"Right. But of what?"

"Ways and— Hello, Wes. What's the matter?"

Farrell entered and said: "They broke up my job. I had to set it up again, and I'm temporarily free. Anything I can do to help?"

"Can you dream up a space gun?"

Farrell laughed. "That's problematical. Energy guns are something strange. Their output can be trapped and used to good advantage. What you need is some sort of projectile, I think."

"But what kind of projectile would do damage to a spaceship?"

"Obviously the normal kinds are useless. Fragmentation shells would pelt the exterior of the hull with metallic rain—if and providing you could get them that close. Armor-piercing would work, possibly, but their damage would be negligible since hitting a spacecraft with a shell is impossible if the ship is moving at anything at all like the usual velocities. Detonation shells are a waste of energy, since there is not atmosphere to expand and contract. They'd blossom like roses and do as much damage as a tossed rose."

"No projectiles, then."

"If you could build a super-heavy fragmentation and detonation shell, and combine it with armor-piercing qualities, and could hit the ship, you might be able to stop them. You'd have to pierce the ship, and have the thing explode with a terrific blast. It would crack the ship because of the atmosphere trapped in the hull—and should be fast enough to exceed the compressibility of air. Also, it should happen so fast that the air leaving the hole made would not have a chance to decrease the pressure. The detonation would crack the ship, and the fragmentation would mess up the insides to boot, giving two possibilities. But if both failed and the ship became airless, they would fear no more detonation shells. Fragments would always be dangerous, however."

"So now we must devise some sort of shell—"

"More than that. The meteor circuits would intercept the incoming shell and it would never get there. What you'd need is a few hundred pounds of 'window.' You know, strips of tin foil cut to roughly a quarter-wavelength of the meteor detecting radar. That'll completely foul up his directors and drive couplers. Then the big one, coming in at terrific velocity."

"And speaking of velocity," said Walt Franks, "the projectile and the rifle are out. We can get better velocity with a constant-acceleration drive. I say torpedoes!"

"Naturally. But the aiming? Remember, even though we crank up the drive to fifty G, it takes time to get to several thousand miles per second. The integration of a course would be hard enough, but add to it the desire of men to evade torpedoes—and the aiming job is impossible."

"We may be able to aim them with a device similar to the one Chuck Thomas is working with. Murdoch said his hull was made with lithium?"

"Coated with," Channing corrected.

"Well. Set the alloy-selectivity disk to pure lithium,

and use the output to steer the torpedo right down to the bitter end."

"Fine. Now the armor-piercing qualities."

"Can we drill?"

"Nope. At those velocities, impact would cause detonation, the combined velocities would look like a detonation wave to the explosive. After all, damn few explosives can stand shock waves that propagate through them at a few thousand miles per second."

"O.K. How do we drill?"

"We might drill electrically," suggested Farrell. "Put a beam in front?"

"Not a chance," said Channing. "The next time we meet up with Hellion Murdoch, he'll have absorbers ready for use. We taught him that one, and Murdoch is not slow to learn."

"So how do we drill?"

"Wes, is that non-arcing alloy of yours very conductive?"

"Slightly better than aluminum."

"Then I've got it! We mount two electrodes of the non-arcing alloy in front. Make 'em heavy and of monstrous current-carrying capacity. Then we connect them to a condenser made of Farrell's super-dooper dielectric."

"You bet," said Walt, grinning. "We put a ten-microfarad condenser in front. only it'll be one hundred and thirty farads when we soak it in Farrell's super-dielectric. We charge it to ten thousand volts, and let it go."

"We've got a few experimental jobs," said Channing. "Those inerts. The drones we were using for experimental purposes. They were radio-controlled, and can be easily converted to the aiming circuits."

"Explosives?"

"We'll get the chemistry boys to brew us a batch."

"Hm-m-m. Remind me to quit Saturday," said Walt. "I wonder how a ten-farad condenser would drive one of those miniatures . . ."

"Pretty well, I should imagine. Why?"

"Why not mount one of the miniatures on a gunstock and put a ten-farad condenser in the handle. Make a nice side arm."

"Good for one shot, and not permanently charged. You'd have to cut your leakage down plenty."

"Could be. Well, we'll work on that one afterward. Let's get that drone fixed."

"Let's fix up all the drones we have. And we'll have the boys load up as many as they can of the little message canisters with the windows. The whole works go at once with the same acceleration, with the little ones running interference for the big boy."

"Murdoch invited us to 'come and get him,' " said Channing in a hard voice. "That, I think we'll do!"

Four smoldering derelicts lay in absolute wreckage on or near the four great spaceports of the Solar System. Shipping was at an unequaled standstill, and the communications beams were loaded with argument and recriminations and pleas as needed material did not arrive as per agreement. Three ships paid out one dollar each gross ton in order to take vital merchandise to needy parties, but the mine run of shipping was unable to justify the terrific cost.

And then Don Channing had a long talk with Keg Johnson of Interplanetary Transport.

One day later, one of Interplanetary's larger ships took off from Canalopsis without having paid tribute to Murdoch. It went free—completely automatic—into the Martian sky and right into Murdoch's hands. The pirate gunned it into a molten mass and hurled his demands at the system once more, then left for Venus, since another ship would be taking off from there.

In the *Relay Girl,* Don Channing smiled. "That finds Murdoch," he told Walt. "He's on the standard course for Venus from Mars."

"Bright thinking," commented Walt. "Bait him on Mars and then offer him a bite at Venus. When'll we catch him?"

"He's running, or will be, at about three G, I guess. We're roaring along at five and will pass Mars at better than four thousand miles per second. I think we'll catch and pass the *Black Widow* at the quarter-point, and Murdoch will be going at about nine hundred miles per. We'll zoom past, and set the finder on him, and then continue until we're safely away. If he gets tough, we'll absorb his output. Though he's stepped it up to the point where a spacecraft can't take too much concentrated input."

"That's how he's been able to blast those who went out with absorbers?"

"Right. The stuff on the station was adequate to protect, but an ordinary ship couldn't handle it unless the ship were designed to absorb and dissipate that energy. The beam tubes would occupy the entire ship, leaving no place for cargo. Result: a toss-up between paying off and not carrying enough to make up the difference."

"This is Freddie," spoke the communicator. "The celestial globe has just come up with a target at eight hundred thousand miles."

"O.K., Freddie. That must be the *Black Widow*. How'll we pass her?"

"About thirty thousand miles."

"Then get the finders set on that lithium-coated hull as we pass."

"Hold it," said Walt. "Our velocity with respect to his is about three thousand. We can be certain of the ship by checking the finder response on the lithium coating. If so, she's the *Black Widow*. Right from here, we can be assured. Jimmy! Check the finders in the torpedoes on that target!"

"Did," said Jimmy. "They're on and it is."

"Launch 'em all!" yelled Franks.

"Are you nuts?" asked Channing.

"Why give him a chance to guess what's happening? Launch 'em!"

"Freddie, drop two of the torpedoes and half the 'window.' Send 'em out at ten G. We'll not put all our eggs in one basket," Channing said to Walt. "There might be a slipup. It'll sort of spoil the effect," said Don. "But we're not here for effect."

"What effect?"

"That explosive will be as useless as a slab of soap," Don explained. "Explosive depends for its action upon velocity—brother, there ain't no explosive built that will propagate at the velocity of our torpedo against Murdoch."

"I know," said Franks, smiling.

"Shall I yell 'Bombs away' in a dramatic voice?" asked Freddie Thomas.

"Are they?"

"Yep."

"Then yell," grinned Walt. "Look, Don, this should be pretty. Let's hike to the star-camera above and watch. We can use the double-telescope finder and take pix, too."

"It won't be long," said Channing grimly. "And we'll be safe, since the interferers will keep Murdoch's gadget so busy he won't have time to worry us. Let's go."

The sky above became filled with myriad flashing spots as the rapidly working meteor spotters coupled to the big turret and began to punch at the interferers.

The clangor of the alarm made Murdoch curse. He looked at the celestial globe and his heart knew real fear for the first time. This was no meteor shower, he knew from the random pattern. Something was after him, and Murdoch knew who and what it was. He cursed Channing and Venus Equilateral in a loud voice.

It did no good, that cursing. Above his head, the triply mounted turret danced back and forth, freeing a triple needle of Sol's energy. At each pause another bit of tin foil went out in a blaze of fire. And as the turret destroyed the little dancing motes, more came speeding into range to replace them, ten to one.

And then it happened. The finder circuit fell into mechanical indecision as two of the canisters of window burst at angles, each with the same intensity. The integrators ground together, and the forces they loosed struggled for control.

Beset by opposing impulses, the amplidyne in the turret stuttered, smoked, and then went out in a pungent stream of yellowish smoke that poured from its dust cover in a high-velocity stream. The dancing of the turret stopped, and the flashing motes in the sky stopped with the turret's death.

One hundred and thirty farads, charged to ten thousand volts, touched the lithium-coated, aluminum side of Murdoch's *Black Widow*. Thirteen billion joules of electrical energy, thirty-six hundred kilowatt hours went against two inches of aluminum. At the three-thousand-miles-per-second relative velocity of the torpedo, contact was immediate and perfect. The aluminum hull vaporized under the million upon million of kilovolt-amperes of the discharge. The vaporized hull tried to explode, but was hit by the unthinkable velocity of the torpedo's warhead.

The torpedo itself crushed in front. It mushroomed under the millions of degrees Kelvin developed by the energy release caused by the cessation of velocity, for at this velocity the atmosphere within the *Black Widow* was as immobile and as hard as tungsten steel at its best.

The very molecules themselves could not move fast enough. They crushed together and in compressing brought incandescence.

The energy of the incoming torpedo raced through the *Black Widow* in a velocity wave that blasted the ship itself into incandescence. In a steep wave front, the vaporized ship exploded in space like a super-nova.

It blinded the eyes of those who watched. It overexposed the camera film, and the expected pictures came out with one single frame a pure, seared black. The piffling, comparatively ladylike detonation of the System's best and most terrible explosive was completely covered in the blast.

Seconds later, the *Relay Girl* hurtled through the sky three thousand miles to one side of the blast. The driven gases caught the *Girl* and stove in the upper observation tower like an eggshell. The *Relay Girl* strained at her girders, and sprung leaks all through the rigid ship, and after rescuing Don Channing and Walt Franks from the wreckage of the observation dome, the men spent their time welding cracks until the *Relay Girl* landed.

It was Walt who put his finger on the trouble. "That was period for Murdoch," he said. "But, Don, the stooge still runs loose. We're going to be forced to take over Mark Kingman before we're a foot taller. He includes Terran Electric, you know. That's where Murdoch got his machine work done."

"Without Murdoch, Kingman is fairly harmless," said Don, objecting. "We'll have no more trouble from him."

"You're a sucker, Don. Kingman will still be after your scalp. You mark my words."

"Well, what are you going to do about it?"

"Nothing for the present. I've still got that date with Christine at Lincoln Head. Mind?"

Interlude

Not all inventions and discoveries need be deadly. Yet if the matter is considered deeply enough, inventions and discoveries are, in a sense, deadly to something. The automobile sounded the knell of the blacksmith. Gutenberg stopped the widespread trade of the official scribes, who spent their working day writing books by hand.

It is also safe to assume that inventors themselves seldom realize the effect their contributions will have upon the future. Did the Wright brothers ever stand upon that hill near Dayton, Ohio, where they flew box kites, and believe that within the span of a lifetime that hill would be surrounded on all sides by the solid acres of land that now bears their name—Wright Field? Did James Clerk Maxwell, in postulating his electromagnetic equations, ever conceive of the massive industry that was to grow around the art of radio transmission? Did Thomas Alva Edison contemplate Times Square when he was seeking a more efficient means of illumination?

Yes, inventions are all deadly in one sense or another. They are openly considered so when their effect kills human beings. Few inventions are conceived with the intent of producing murder, the atomic bomb notwithstanding.

That little fiendish device was the accumulation of knowledges and sciences gathered by men who were seeking knowledge for the sake of knowledge, and it was not until the need arose and the facts became clear that the idea of atomic power for military purposes became fact.

Similarly, Walt Franks didn't really know what he was

starting when he began to think about the next big project for Venus Equilateral.

You see, by reasoning, Walt assumed that if men could send intelligence and energy by beam transmission, there was no reason why men couldn't send—THINGS.

SPECIAL DELIVERY

Don Channing grinned at his wife knowingly. Arden caught his glance and then laughed.

Walt Franks leaned back and looked highly superior. "Go ahead and laugh, damn you. I tell you it can be done."

"Walt, ever since you tried that stunt of aerating soap with hydrogen to make a floating soap for shower baths, I've been wondering about your kind of genius."

"Oh, no," objected Arden.

"Well, he wondered about it after nearly breaking his neck one morning."

"That I did," grinned Walt. "It's still a good idea."

"But the idea of transmitting matter is fantastic."

"Agreed," Walt admitted. "But so is the idea of transmitting power."

"It would come in handy, if possible," remarked Don. "At slightly under two G, it takes only four hours to make Luna from Terra. On the other hand, shipping stuff from Melbourne, Australia, to New York City, or to the Mojave Spaceport takes considerably longer. Spacecraft as super stratosphere carriers aren't too good, because you've got to run in a circle. In space you run at constant acceleration to midpoint and then decelerate the rest of the way. Fine for mile-eating, but not too hot for cutting circles."

"Well, having established the need of a matter transmitter, now what?"

"Go on, Walt. You're telling us."

"Well," said Walt, penciling some notes on the tablecloth, "it's like this. The Carroll-Baler power-transmission tube will carry energy. According to their initial experiments, they had some trouble."

"They had one large amount, if I recall."

"Specifically, I recall the incident of the hammer. Remember?"

"Barney Carroll got mad and swung a hammer at the tube, didn't he?"

"It was one of them. I don't recall which."

"No matter of importance," said Don. "I think I know what you mean. He hit the intake end—or tried to. The hammer was cut neatly and precisely off, and the energy of the blow was transmitted, somehow, to the wall."

"Through the wall," Walt corrected. "It cracked the plaster, but it went through so fast that it merely cracked it. The main blow succeeded in breaking the marble façade of the city hall."

"Um. Now bring us up-to-date. What have you in mind?"

"A tube which scans matter, atom by atom, line by line and plane by plane. The matter is removed, atom by atom, and transmitted by a sort of matter bank in the instrument."

"A what?"

"Matter bank," said Walt. "We can't transmit the stuff itself. That's out. We can't dissipate the atomic energy or whatever effect we might get. We can establish a balance locally by using the energy release to drive the restorer. According to some initial experiments, it can be done. We take something fairly complex and break it down. We use the energy of destruction to re-create the matter in the bank, or solid block of local stuff. Let it be a mass of stuff if it wants to; at any rate, the signal impulses from the breakdown will be transmitted, scanned if you will, and transmitted to a receiver which reverses the process. It scans, and the matter bank is broken down and the object is reconstructed."

"I hope we can get free and unrestricted transmutation," offered Don. "You can't send a steel spring out and get one back made of copper."

"I get your point."

"The space lines will hate you," said Arden.

"Too bad. I wonder if it'll carry people."

"Darling," Arden drawled, "don't you think you'd better catch your rabbit first?"

"Not too bad a thought," agreed Don. "Walt, have you got any rabbit traps out?"

"A couple. I've been tinkering a bit. I know we can disintegrate matter through a power tube of slight modification, and reintegrate it with another. At the present state of the art, it is a mess."

"A nice mess," laughed Don. "Go ahead, though. We'll pitch in when the going gets hard."

"That's where I stand now. The going is tough."

"What's the trouble?"

"Getting a perfect focus. I want it good enough so that we can scan a polished sheet of steel—and it'll come out as slick as the original."

"Naturally. We'd better get Wes Farrell on the job."

"I wonder what byproduct he'll get this time?"

"Look, Walt. Quit hoping. If you get this thing running right, it'll put your name in history."

"After all," Walt grinned, "I've got to do something good enough to make up for that Channing Layer."

"Kingman is still fuming over the Channing Layer. Sometimes I feel sorry that I did it to him like that."

"Wasn't your fault, Don. You didn't hand him the thing knowing that the Channing Layer would inhibit the transmission of energy. It happened. We get power out of Sol—why wouldn't they? They would, except for the Channing Layer."

"Wonder what your idea will do."

"About the Channing Layer? Maybe your spaceline competition is not as good as it sounds."

"Well, they use the power-transmission tubes all over the face of the Solar System. I can't see any reason why they couldn't ship stuff from Sydney to Mojave and then space it out from there."

"What an itinerary! By Franks' matter transmitter to Mojave. Spacecraft to Luna. More matter transmission from Luna to Phobos. Then transshipped down to Lincoln Head, and by matter transmitter to Canalopsis. *Whoosh!*"

"Do we have time to go into the old yarn about the guy who listened in and got replicas?" asked Arden.

"That's a woman's mind for you," said Channing. "Always making things complicated. Arden, my lovely but devious-minded woman, let's wait until we have the spry beastie by the ears before we start to make rabbit pie."

"It's not as simple as it sounds," Walt warned. "But it's there to worry about."

"But later. I doubt that we can reason that angle out."

"I can," said Arden. "Can we tap the power beams?"

"Wonderful is the mind of woman," Don praised. "Positively wonderful! Arden, you have earned your next fur coat. Here I've been thinking of radio transmission all this time. No, Arden, when you're set up for sheer energy transmission, it's strictly no dice. The crimped-up jobs we use for communications can be tapped—but not the power-transmission beams. If you can keep the gadget working on that line, Walt, we're in and solid."

"I predict there'll be a battle. Are we shipping energy or communications?"

"Let Kingman try and find a precedent for that. Brother Blackstone himself would be stumped to make a ruling. We'll have to go to work with the evidence as soon as we get a glimmer of the possibilities. But I think we have a good chance. We can diddle up the focus, I'm certain."

Arden glowered. "Go ahead—have your fun. I see another couple of weeks of being a gadgeteer's widow." She looked at Walt Franks. "I could stand it if the big lug only didn't call every tool, every part, and every effect either *she* or *baby*!"

Walt grinned. "I'd try to keep you from being lonely, but I'm in this, too, and besides, you're my friend's best wife."

"Shall we drag that around a bit? I think we could kill a couple of hours with it sometime."

"Let it lie there and rot," snorted Channing cheerfully. "We'll pick it up later. Come on, Walt. We've got work to do."

Mark Kingman glowered at the 'gram and swore under his breath. He wondered whether he might be developing a persecution complex; it seemed as though every time he turned around, Venus Equilateral was in his hair, asking for something or other. And he was not in any position to quibble about it.

Kingman was smart enough to carry his tray very level. Knowing that they were waiting for a chance to prove that he had been connected with the late Hellion Murdoch made him very cautious. There was no doubt in any mind that Murdoch was written off the books, but whether Murdoch had made a sufficiently large impression on the books of Terran Electric to have the connection become evident—that worried Kingman.

So he swore at each telegram that came in, but quietly, and followed each request to the letter. Compared to his former attitude toward Venus Equilateral, Mark Kingman was behaving like an honor student in a Sunday school.

Furthermore, behaving himself did not make him feel good.

He punched the buzzer, told his secretary to call in the shop foreman, and then sat back and wondered about the 'gram.

He was still wondering when the man entered. Kingman looked up and fixed his superintendent with a fishy glance. "Horman, can you guess why the Venus Equilateral crowd would want two dozen gauge blocks?"

"Sure. We use Johannson blocks all the time."

"Channing wants twenty-four blocks. All three inches on a side—cubes. Square to within thirty seconds of angle, and each of the six faces optically flat to one-quarter wavelength of cadmium light."

"Whoosh!" said Horman. "I presume the three-inch dimension must be within a half-wavelength?"

"They're quite lenient," said Kingman bitterly. "A full wavelength!"

"White of them," Horman grunted. "I suppose the same thing applies?"

"We're running over thin ice," said Kingman reflectively. "I can't afford to play rough. We'll make up their blocks."

"I wonder what they want 'em for?"

"Something tricky, I'll bet."

"But what could you use two dozen gauge blocks for? All the same size."

"Inspection standards?" asked Kingman.

"Not unless they're just being difficult. You don't put primary blocks on any production line. You make secondary gauges for production line use and keep a couple of primaries in the check room to try the secondaries on. In fact, you usually have a whole set of gauge blocks to build up to any desired dimension so that you don't have to stock a half-million of different sizes."

"It's possible that they may be doing something extremely delicate?"

"Possible," said Horman slowly. "But not too probable. On the other hand, I may be one-hundred-percent wrong. I don't know all the different stuff a man can make, by far. My own experience indicates that nothing like that would be needed. But that's just one man's experience."

"Channing and that gang of roughneck scientists have been known to make some fancy gadgets," said Kingman grudgingly.

"If you'll pardon my mentioning the subject," said Horman in a scathing tone, "you'd have been far better off to tag along with 'em instead of fighting 'em."

"I'll get 'em yet."

"What's it got you so far?"

"I'm not too bad off. I've come up from the Chief Attorney of Terran Electric to controlling the company."

"And Terran Electric has slid down from the topmost outfit in the System to a seventh-rater."

"We'll climb back. At any rate, I'm better off personally. You're better off personally. In fact, everybody that had enough guts to stay with us is better off."

"Yeah, I know. It sounds good on paper. But make a bum move again, Kingman, and we'll all be in jail. You'd better forget that hatred against Venus Equilateral and come down to earth."

"Well, I've been a good boy for them once. After all, I did point out the error in their patent on the solar beam."

"That isn't all. Don't forget that Terran Electric's patent was at error, too."

"Frankly, it was a minor error. It's one of those things that is easy to get caught on. You know how it came about?"

"Nope. I accepted it just like everybody else. It took some outsider to laugh at me and tell me why."

Kingman smiled. "It's easy to get into easy thinking. They took power from Sirius—believe it or not—and then made some there-and-back time measurements and came up with a figure that was about the square of one hundred eighty-six thousand miles per second. But you know that you can't square a velocity and come up with anything that looks sensible. The square of a velocity must be some concept like an expanding area."

"Or would it be two spots diverging along the sides of a right angle?" queried Horman idly. "What was their final answer?"

"The velocity of light is a concept. It is based on the flexibility of space—its physical constants, so to speak. Channing claims that the sub-etheric radiation bands of what we have learned to call the driver radiation propagate along some other medium than space itself. I think they were trying to establish some mathematical relation—which might be all right, but you can't establish that kind of relation and hope to hold it. The square of C in meters comes out differently than the square of C in miles, inches, or a little-used standard, the light-second—in which the velocity of light is unity, or One. Follow? Anyway, they made modulation equipment of some sort and measured the velocity and came up with a finite figure which is slightly less than the square of one hundred eighty-six thousand miles per second. Their original idea was wrong. It was just coincidence that the two figures came out that way. Anyway," Kingman smiled, "I pointed it out to them and they quickly changed their patent letters. So, you see, I've been of some help."

"Nice going. Well, I'm going to make those gauges. It'll take us one long time, too. Johannson blocks aren't the easiest things in the world to make."

"What would you make secondary standards out of?"

"We use glass gauges, mostly. They don't dinge or

bend when dropped—they go to pieces or not at all. We can't have a bent gauge rejecting production parts, you know, and steel gauges can be bent. Besides, you can grind glass to a half-wavelength of light with ease, but polishing steel is another item entirely."

"I'm going to call Channing and ask him about glass blocks. It may be that he might use them. Plus the fact that I may get an inkling of the ultimate use. They have no production lines running on Venus Equilateral, have they?"

"Nope. Not at all. They're not a manufacturing company."

"Well, I'm going to call."

Kingman's voice raced across Terra to Hawaii, went on the communications beams of the sky-pointing reflectors, and rammed through the Heaviside Layer to Luna. At the Lunar station, his voice was mingled in multiplex with a thousand others and placed on the sub-ether beams to Venus Equilateral.

Don Channing answered the 'phone. "Yes?"

"Kingman, Dr. Channing."

Don grunted. He did not like to be addressed by title when someone who disliked him did it. His friends did not; Kingman's use of the title made it an insult.

"Look," said Kingman, "what do you want to use those blocks for?"

"We've got a job of checking dimensions."

"Nothing more? Do you need the metal for electrical reasons?"

"No," said Don. "What have you in mind?"

"Our tool shop is nicely equipped to grind glass gauges. We can do that better than grinding Jo-blocks. Can you use glass ones?"

"Hang on a minute." Channing turned to Walt. "Kingman says his outfit uses glass gauges. Any reason why we can't?"

"See no reason why not. I've heard of using glass gauges, and they've got some good reasons, too. Tell him to go ahead."

"Kingman? How soon can we get glass ones?"

"Horman, how soon on the glass blocks?"

"Two dozen? About a week."

"We'll have your blocks on the way within four days,

Channing. Four days minimum, plus whatever wait is necessary to get 'em aboard a spacer."

"We'll check from this end on schedules. We need the blocks, and if the wait is too long, we'll send the *Relay Girl* in for 'em."

Don hung up and then said: "Glass ones might be a good idea. We can check the transmission characteristics optically. I think we can check more, quicker, than by running analysis on steel."

"Plus the fact that you can get the blocks back after test," grinned Walt. "Once you tear into a steel block to check its insides, you've lost your sample. I don't know any better way to check homogeneity than by optical tests."

"O.K. Well, four days for glass blocks will do better than a couple of months on steel blocks."

"Right. Now let's look up Wes and see what he's come up with."

They found Farrell in one of the blister laboratories, working on a small edition of the power-transmission tubes. He was not dressed in spacesuit, and so they entered the blister and watched him work.

"Have a little trouble getting the focus to stay sharp through the trace," Wes complained. "I can get focus of atomic proportions—the circle of confusion is about the size of the atom nucleus, I mean—at the axis of the tube. But the deflection of the cone of energy produces aberration, which causes coma at the edges. The corners of an area look fierce."

"I wonder if mechanical scanning wouldn't work better."

"Undoubtedly. You don't hope to send life, do you?"

"It would be nice—but no more fantastic than this thing is now. What's your opinion?"

Wes loosened a set screw on the main tube anode and set the anode forward a barely perceptible distance. He checked it with a vernier rule and tightened the screw. He made other adjustments on the works of the tube itself, and then motioned outside. They left the blister, Wes closed the airtight, and cracked the valve that let the air out of the blister. He snapped the switch on the outside panel and then leaned back in his chair while the cathode heated.

"With electrical scanning, you'll have curvature of field with this gadget. That isn't too bad, I suppose, because the restorer will have the same curvature. But you're going to scan three ways, which means correction for the linear distance from the tube as well as the other side deflections and their aberrations. Now if we could scan the gadget mechanically, we'd have absolute flatness of field, perfect focus, and so forth."

Walt grinned. "Thinking of television again? Look, bright fellows, how do you move an assembly of mechanical parts in quanta of one atomic diameter? They've been looking for that kind of gadget for centuries. Dr. Rowland and his gratings would turn over in their graves with a contrivance that could rule lines one atom apart."

"On what?" asked Don.

"If it would rule one-atom lines, brother, you could put a million lines per inch on anything rulable with perfection, ease, eclat, and savoir faire. You follow my argument? Or would you rather take up this slip of my tongue and make something out of it?"

"O.K., fella, I see your point. How about that one, Wes?"

Wes Farrell grinned. "Looks like I'd better be getting perfect focus with the electrical system here. I hadn't considered the other angle at all, but it looks a lot tougher than I thought." He squinted through a wall-mounted telescope at the setup on the inside of the blister. "She's hot," he remarked quietly, and then set to checking the experiment. Fifteen minutes of checking, and making notes, and he turned to the others with a smile. "Not too bad that way," he said.

"What are you doing?"

"I've established a rather complex field. In order to correct the aberrations, I've got non-linear focusing fields in the places where they tend to correct for the off-axis aberrations. To correct for the height effect. I'm putting a variable corrector to control the whole cone of energy, stretching it or shortening it according to the needs. I think if I use a longer focal length I'll be able to get the thing running right. "That'll lessen the need for correction, too," he added, cracking the blister-intake valve and letting the air hiss into the blister. He opened the door and went inside, and began to adjust the electrodes. "You know," he added over his shoulder, "we've got something here that might bring a few dollars on the side. This matter-bank affair produces clean, clear, and practically pure metal. You might be able to sell some metal that was rated 'pure' and mean it."

"You mean absolutely, positively, guaranteed, uncontaminated, unadulterated, perfectly chemically pure?" grinned Don.

"Compared to what 'chemically pure' really means, your selection of adjectives is a masterpiece of understatement," Walt laughed.

"I'm about to make one more try," announced Wes. "Then I'm going to drop this for the time being. I've got to get up to the machine shop and see what they're doing with the rest of the thing."

"We'll take that over if you wish," said Don.

"Will you? I'll appreciate it. I sort of hate to let this thing go when I feel that I'm near an answer."

"We'll do it," said Walt, definitely.

They left the laboratory and made their way to the elevator that would lift them high into the relay station, where the machine shop was located. As they entered the elevator, Don shook his head.

"What's the matter?"

"Well, friend Wes is on the beam again. If he feels that we're close to the answer, I'll bet a hat that we're hanging right on the edge. Also, that kind of work would kill me dead. He likes to stick on one thing till the bitter end, no matter how long it takes. I couldn't do it."

"I know. About three days of this and you're wanting another job to clear your mind. Then you could tackle that one for about three hours and take back on the first."

"Trying to do that to Farrell would kill both him *and* the jobs," said Don. "But you and I can keep two or three projects going strong. Oh, well, Wes is worth a million."

"He's the best we've got," agreed Walt. "Just because he has a peculiar slant on life is no sign he's not brilliant."

"It's you and I that have the cockeyed slant on life." Don grinned. "And frankly, I'm proud of it." He swung the elevator door aside and they walked down the corridor. "This isn't going to be much to see, but we'll take a look."

The machine shop, to the man, was clustered around the one cabinet under construction. They moved aside to permit the entry of Channing and Franks.

"Hm-m-m," said Don. "Looks like a refrigerator and incinerator combined."

It did. It stood five feet tall, three feet square, and was sealed in front by a heavy door. There was a place intended for the tube that Farrell was tinkering with in the blister, and the lines to supply the power were coiled behind the cabinet.

"Partly wired?" asked Don.

"Just the power circuits," answered Michael Warren. "We'll have this finished in a couple of days now. The other one is completed except for Wes Farrell's section."

Channing nodded, and said: "Keep it going." He turned to Walt and, after the passage of a knowing glance, the pair left. "Walt, this is getting on my nerves. I want to go down to Joe's and drink myself into a stupor that will last until they get something cogent to work on."

"I'm with you, but what will Arden say?"

"I'm going to get Arden. Self-protection. She'd cut my feet off at the knees if I went off on a tear without her."

"I have gathered that," grinned Walt. "You're afraid of her."

"Yeah," drawled Don. "After all—she's the cook."

"I'm waiting."

"Waiting for what?"

"If and when. If you two go on as you have for another year without one of you turning up with a black eye, I may be tempted to go forth and track me down a babe of my own."

The cabinet stood in the north end of Venus Equilateral but it was not alone. It may even be the record for all times: certainly no other cabinet three by three by five ever had twenty-seven men all standing in a circle awaiting developments. The cabinet at the south end of Venus Equilateral was no less popular, though the number of watchers was less by one. Here, then, were winner and runner-up of inanimate popularity for the ages. The communicator system set in the walls of the two rooms carried sounds from the north room to the south, and those sounds in the south room could be heard in the north room.

Channing grinned boyishly at Arden.

"This, my love, is a device which may make it quite possible for me to send you back to Mother."

Arden smiled serenely. "No dice," she said. "Mother went back to Grandmother last week. When is this thing going to cook?"

"Directly."

"What are we waiting for?"

"Walt."

"I'm ready," came Walt's voice through the speaker.

"About time, slowpoke."

"Really, it was not his fault," Wes objected. "I wanted to check the scanner synchronization."

"He's precious," chortled Arden in Don's ear. "He wouldn't think of letting Walt, the big bum, take the blame for anything that wasn't Walt's fault."

"That's a good line," grinned Don. "Walt's faults. After we set this thing aside as a finished project, we'll set that 'Walt's Faults' to music. Ready, Walt?"

"Right. I am now slipping the block into the cabinet. The door is closed. Have you got the preliminary synchronizing signal in tick?"

Channing called: "Wait a minute, I'm lagging a whole cycle."

"Cut your synchronization input and let the thing catch up."

"O.K. Um-m-m — Now, Walt."

"Has anyone any last words to say?" asked Walt.

No answer.

"Then since no one has any objections at this time, I

assume that everything may be run off. Silence, people, we are going on the air!"

"There was a very faint odor of corn in Walt's last remark," said Don.

"I think the corn was on his breath," said Arden.

"Done!" Walt announced. "Don, crack the door so that the rest of us can laugh if it don't work."

Channing swaggered over and opened the door. He reached inside and took out the—object.

He held it up.

"Walt," he said, "what are you giving me?"

"Huh?"

"I presume that you shipped me one of the cubes?"

"Right."

"Well, what we got at this end would positively scare the right arm off of a surrealist sculptor."

"Hang on to it. I'll be right up."

"Hang on to it?" laughed Don. "I'm afraid to touch it."

It was three miles from one end of Venus Equilateral to the other and Walt made it in six minutes from the time he stepped into the little runway car to the time he came into the north-end laboratory and looked over Channing's shoulder at the—thing—that stood on the table.

"Um," he said. "Sort of distorted, isn't it?"

"Quite," said Don. "This is glass. It was once a three-inch cube of precision, polish, and beauty. It is now a combination of a circular stairway with round corners and a sort of accordion pleat. Hell's bells!"

"Be not discouraged," gurgled Walt. "No matter what it looks like, we did transmit matter."

Arden tapped Don on the shoulder. "May I say it now?"

"You do!"

"Then I won't say it doesn't matter."

"I'm ignoring your crude remark. Walt, we did accomplish something. It wasn't too good. Now let's figure out why this thing seems to have been run over with a fourth dimensional caterpillar-tread truck."

"Well, I can hazard a guess. The synchronizing circuits were not clamped perfectly. That gives the accordion-pleat effect. The starting of the trace was not made at the same place each time due to slippage. We'll have to beef up the synchronization impulse. The circular-staircase effect was probably due to phase distortion."

"Could be," said Don. "That means we have to beef up the transmission band so it'll carry a higher frequency."

"A lower impedance with corrective elements?"

"Might work. Those will have to be matched closely. We're not transmitting on a line, you know. It's sheer transmission-tube stuff from here to there. Well, gang, we've had our fun. Now let's widen the transmission band and beef up the sync. Then we'll try number two."

Number two was tried the following afternoon. Again, everybody stood around and watched over Don's shoulder as he removed the cube from the cabinet.

"Nice," he said, doing a little war dance.

Franks came in puffing, took the cube from Don's fingers, and inspected it. "Not too bad," he said.

"Perfect."

"Not by a jug full. The index of refraction is higher at this edge than at the other. See?" Walt held the cube before a newspaper and they squinted through the glass block.

"Seems to be. Now why?"

"Second harmonic distortion, if present, would tend to thin out one side and thicken up the other side. A sine-wave transmission would result in even thickness, but if second harmonic distortion is present, the broad *loops* at the top create a condition where the average from zero to top is higher than the average from zero to the other peak. Follow?"

"That would indicate that the distortion was coming in at this end. If both were even, they would cancel."

"Right. Your scanning at one end is regular—at the other end it is irregular, resulting in non-homogeneity."

"The corners aren't sharp," objected Arden.

"That's an easy one. The wavefront isn't sharp either. Instead of clipping sharply at the end of the trace, the signal tapers off. That means higher-frequency response is needed."

"We need a term. Audio for sonics; radio for electronics; video for television signals—"

"Mateo," said Arden.

"Um—sounds sort of silly," Walt grinned.

"That's because it's strange. Mateo it is," said Don. "Our mateo amplifier needs higher-frequency response in order to follow the square wavefront. Might put a clipper circuit in there, too."

"I think a clipper and a sharpener will do more than the higher frequency," said Farrell. He was plying a vernier caliper, and he added: "I'm certain of that second harmonic stuff now. The dimension is cockeyed on this side. Tell you what, Don. I'm going to have the index of refraction measured within an inch of its life. Then we'll check the thing and apply some high-powered math and see if we can come up with the percentage of distortion."

"Go ahead. Meanwhile, *we'll* apply the harmonic analyzer to this thing and see what we find. If we square up the edges and make her homogeneous, we'll be in business."

"The spacelines will hate you to pieces," said Arden.

"Nope. I doubt that we could send anything very large. It might be more bother to run a huge job than the money it costs to send it by spacer. But we have a market for small stuff that is hard to handle in space because of its size."

"I see no reason why Keg Johnson wouldn't go for a hunk of it," Wes Farrell offered.

"I've mentioned it to Keg; the last time I was in Canalopsis," said Walt. "He wasn't too worried—provided he could buy a hunk."

"Interplanet is pretty progressive," mused Don. "There'll be no reason why we can't make some real handy loose change out of this. Well, let's try it again tomorrow."

"O.K. Let's break this up. Will we need any more blocks from Terran Electric?"

It was less than a month later that a newspaper reporter caught the advance patent notice and swallowed hard. He did a double take, shook his head, and then read the names on the patent application and decided that someone was not fooling. He took leave and made the run to Venus Equilateral to interview the officials. He returned not only with a story, but with a sample glass block that he had seen run through the machine.

The news pushed one hatchet murder, a bank robbery, a football upset, and three political harangues all the way back to page seven. In terms more glowing than scientifically accurate, the matter transmitter screamed in three-inch headlines, trailed down across the page in smaller type, and was embellished with pictures, diagrams, and a description of the apparatus. The latter had been furnished by Walt Franks, and had been rewritten by the reporter because Walt's description was too dry.

The following morning Venus Equilateral had nine rush telegrams. Three were from cranks who wanted to go to Sirius and set up a restorer there to take people; four were from superstitious nuts who called Channing's attention to the fact that he was overstepping the rights given to him by his Creator; one was from a gentleman who had a number of ideas, all of which were based on the idea of getting something for nothing and none of which were legal; and the last one was a rather curt note from Terran Electric, pointing out that this device came under the realm of the power-transmission tube and its developments and that they wanted a legal discussion.

"Have they got a leg to stand on?" asked Walt.

"I doubt it."

"Then to the devil with them," Walt snapped. "We'll tell 'em to go jump in the lake."

"Nope. We're going to Terra and slip them the slug. If we clip them now, they'll have nothing to go on. If we wait till they get started, they'll have a fighting chance. Besides, I think that all they want to do is to have the facts brought out. Are we or are we not under the terms of that contract?"

"Are we?"

"We're as safe as Sol. And I know it. That contract pertained to the use of the solar beam only, plus certain other concessions pertaining to the use of the power-transmission tubes and other basic effects as utilized in communications."

"Why can't we tell them that?"

"It's got to be told in a court of law," said Don. "Kingman's mind runs to legal procedure like Blackstone."

"We'll take the gadgets?"

"Right. What are you using for power?"

"What other? Solar beams, of course. We don't bother about running stuff around anymore. We plug it in the 115-volt line, it energizes the little fellows just long enough to make them self-sustaining from Sol. All the 115-volt line does is to act as a starting circuit."

"You and Farrell had better dream up a couple of power supplies then. We can't use the solar beam on Terra."

"I know. We're a little ahead of you on that. Wes and one of the Thomas boys cooked up a beam-transducer power supply that will get its juice from any standard 115-volt, sixty-cycle line socket. We've got two of them—and they run the things easily."

"Good. I'll 'gram Terran Electric and let 'em know we're on our way for the legal tangle. You load up the *Relay Girl* and we'll be on our way. Stock up the usual supply of bars, blocks, gadgets, and traps. Might include a bar magnet. When we show that it's still magnetized, we'll gain a point for sure."

"If we take a magnet, we'd better take the fluxmeter to show that the magnetic field hasn't dropped."

"Right. Take anything you can think of for a good show. We can knock them dead!"

Mark Kingman put his assistant legal counsel on the witness stand. "You will state the intent of the contract signed between Terran Electric and Venus Equilateral."

"The contract holds the following intent: 'Use of the power-transmission tubes for communications purposes shall fall under the jurisdiction of Venus Equilateral. For power transmission, the tubes and associated equipment shall be under the control of Terran Electric. In the matter of the solar beam tubes, the contract is as follows: Venus Equilateral holds the control of the solar beam in space, on man-made bodies in space, and upon those natural bodies in space where Venus Equilateral requires the solar power to maintain subsidiary relay stations.' "

"Please clarify the latter," said Kingman. "Unless it is your intent to imply that Terra, Mars, and Mercury fall under the classification of 'places where Venus Equilateral requires power.' "

"Their control on natural celestial objects extends only to their own installations and requirements. Basically, aside from their own power requirements, Venus Equilateral is not authorized to sell power. In short, the contract implies that the use of the sub-etheric phenomena is divided so that Venus Equilateral may use this region for communications, while Terran Electric uses the sub-ether for power. In space, however, Venus Equilateral holds the rights to the power beam."

Frank Tinken, head legal man of Venus Equilateral, turned to Don and said: "We should have this in a technical court."

Don turned his attention from the long discussion of the contract and asked: "Why not change?"

"Judges hate people who ask for changes of court. It is bad for the requestee—and is only done when the judge's disinterest is open to question, and also when the suspicion of dislike is less dangerous than the judge himself."

"Well, this should be in a technical court."

"Want to chance it?"

"I think so. This is more than likely to turn up with differential equations, physics experts, and perhaps a demonstration of atom-smashing."

Kingman finished his examination and turned away. The judge nodded sourly at Tinken. "Cross-examination?"

Tinken faced the witness, nodded, and then faced the court.

"The witness' statements regarding the contract are true. However, Judge Hamilton, I will attempt to show that this case is highly technical in nature and as such falls under the jurisdiction of the Technical Court. May I proceed?"

"Counsel for the plaintiff assures me that this is not truly a technical case," snapped Hamilton. "However, if you can definitely prove that the case in point hinges on purely technical matters, what you say may be instrumental in having this hearing changed. Proceed."

"Thank you." Tinken turned to the witness. "Exactly what is the point in question?"

"The point in question," said the witness, "is whether or not the matter transmitter falls under Terran Electric's contract or Venus Equilateral's contract."

"Isn't the question really a matter of whether the basic effect is technically communication or power transmission?"

"Objection!" Kingman barked. "The counsel is leading the witness."

"Objection permitted—strike the question from the record."

"I was merely trying to bring out the technical aspect of the case," explained Tinken. "I'll rephrase the question. Is it not true that the contract between Terran Electric and Venus Equilateral is based upon a certain technology?"

"Certainly."

"Then if the case is based upon technical aspects—"

"Objection!" Kingman interrupted. "More than half of all manufacturing contracts are based upon technical background. I quote the case of Hines versus Ingall, in which the subject matter was the development of a new type of calculating machine. This case was heard in a legal court and disposed of in the same."

"Objection permitted."

"No further examination," said Tinken. He sat down and turned to Don. "We're in trouble. Hamilton does not like us."

"Well, we still have the whip hand."

"Right, but before we get done we'll have trouble with Hamilton."

"Before we get done, Kingman will have trouble with us," said Don.

Terran Electric's lawyer called Wes Farrell to the stand. "Mr. Farrell, you are employed by Venus Equilateral?"

"Yes."

"In what capacity?"

"As an experimental physicist."

"And as such, you were involved in some phases of the device under discussion?"

"I was," said Farrell.

"Does the device make use of the solar beam?"

"It does, but—"

"Thank you," interrupted Kingman.

"I'm not through," snapped Farrell. "The solar beam is not integral."

"It is used, though."

"It may be removed. If necessary, we can have hand-generators supplied to generate the operating power."

"I see," said Kingman sourly. "The device itself is entirely new and basic?"

"Not entirely. The main components are developments of existing parts, specialized to fit the requirements."

"They are based on specifically what?"

"Certain effects noted in the power-transmission tubes plus certain effects noted in the solar beam tubes."

"And which of these effects is more contributory?"

"Both are about equally responsible. One will be useless without the other."

Kingman turned to the judge. "I intend to show that the use of these effects is stated in the contract."

"Proceed."

"Was there anytime during the development of the device any question of jurisdiction?"

"None whatever," said Farrell. "We knew how we stood."

"The statement is hearsay and prejudiced," stated Kingman.

"Strike it from the record," Hamilton snapped.

"It stands at 'none whatever,' " said Kingman.

The secretary nodded.

"Since absolutely no attention was paid to the terms of the contract, doesn't that imply that a certain ignorance of the terms might prevail?"

"Objection!" shouted Tinken. "Counsel's question implies legal carelessness on the part of his opponent."

"How can you be aware of the ramifications of a contract that you do not read?" Kingman stormed.

"Objection overruled."

"May I take exception?" requested Tinken.

"Exception noted. Counsel, will you rephrase your question so that no lack of foresight is implied?"

"Certainly," smiled Kingman. "How were you certain that you were within your rights?"

"If this plan had been open to any question, my superiors would not have permitted me—"

"That will not serve!" snapped Kingman. "You are making an implication. Your testimony is biased."

"Naturally," Farrell barked. "No one but an idiot would claim to have no opinion."

"Does that include the court?" asked Kingman suavely.

"Naturally not," retorted Farrell. "I was speaking of interested parties."

"Let it pass. In other words, Dr. Farrell, you were never sure that you were within your rights?"

"I object!" exploded Tinken. "Counsel is questioning a witness whose business is not legal matters on a subject which is legal in every phase."

"Objection sustained," said Hamilton wearily.

The matter was dropped, but Kingman had gained his point. The item might never appear in the records, but it was present in the judge's mind.

"Dr. Farrell," said Kingman, "since you have no legal training, precisely what has been your education and background?"

"I hold a few degrees in physics, one in mathematics, and also in physical chemistry." Farrell turned to the judge. "Judge Hamilton, may I explain my position here?"

"You may."

"I have spent thirteen years studying physics and allied sciences. I believe that I stand fairly high among my fellows. Since no man may be capable in many arts, I believe that I have not been lax in not seeking degrees in law."

"No objection," said Kingman. "Dr. Farrell, in order that the process be properly outlined in the record, I am going to ask you to explain it in brief. How does your matter transmitter work?"

Farrell nodded, and took time to think.

Tinken whispered in Don's ear: "The stinker! He

knows Hamilton hates anything more complex than a can opener!"

"What can we do?"

"Hope that our demonstration blasts them loose. That's our best bet, plus fighting for every inch."

Farrell moistened his lips and said: "Utilizing certain effects noted with earlier experimentation, we have achieved the following effects: the matter to be transmitted is placed *in situ,* where it is scanned by an atom scanner. This removes the substance, atom by atom, converting the atoms to energy. This energy is then reconverted into atoms and stored in a matter bank as matter again. The energy of disintegration is utilized in reintegration at the matter bank with but small losses. Since some atoms have higher energy than others, the matter bank's composition will depend upon the scanned substance."

"The matter bank is composed of the same elements as the matter for transmission?" asked Kingman.

"No. Some elements release more energy than others. It is desirable that the energy transfer be slightly negative. That is to say, that additional energy must be used in order to make the thing work."

"Why?"

"All power lines and other devices are developed for delivering energy, not receiving it. It is less disastrous to take energy from a power line than to try to drive it back in—and the energy must be dissipated somehow."

"Then the matter bank is not the same material."

"No," said Farrell. "The substance of the matter bank is non-homogeneous. Simultaneously, it will be whatever element is necessary to maintain the fine balance of energy—and it is in constant change."

"Proceed," said Kingman.

"In passing from the disintegrator tube to the reintegrator tube, the energy impresses its characteristic signal on a sub-ether transmission system. Radio might work, except that the signal is unbelievably complex. Wired communications—"

"Objection to the term," said Kingman.

"Sustained."

"Wired—transfer—might work, but probably would not, due to this same high complexity in transmitted signal. At any rate, upon reception, the signal is used to influence or modulate the energy passing from a disintegrator tube in the receiver. But this time the tube is tearing down the matter bank and restoring the object. Follow?"

"I believe so. Does the court understand?"

"This court can follow the technical terms."

"Now, Dr. Farrell, the matter transmitter does actually transmit over a power-transmission tube?"

"Yes. Of the type developed by us for communications."

"But it is a power tube?"

"Yes."

"Then are you certain that you are sending no energy?"

"I object!" shouted Tinken. "The question has no answer."

"Hasn't it?" Kingman queried. "My worthy opponent, all questions have an answer."

"Objection overruled," snapped Hamilton sourly. "Let the witness answer."

"It is impossible to send communications without sending some energy. It is the intent to which the energy is put that determines the classification," Farrell continued.

"Explain further."

"You must send energy when you communicate with a light blinker." Farrell grinned. "The receiving party receives the energy, but couldn't possibly read a newspaper with it. The beams at Venus Equilateral send out several million watts—and by the time they get to Luna, they require amplifications bordering on the million times before they are usable. The intent is clear: we are not supplying power, we are sending intelligence."

"I contend," said Kingman to the judge, "that the contract states clearly that developments of this device are to be used for communications only when operated by Venus Equilateral. I further contend that the transmission of matter does not constitute a communication, but rather a transfer of energy."

"I object," said Tinken. "If this statement was objectionable to the learned counsel before, it is equally objectionable to me now."

"Previously," said Kingman suavely, "counsel was trying to influence a witness. I am merely trying to explain my point."

Hamilton cleared his throat. "Counsel is merely trying to influence the court; the same privilege will be available to his opponent at the proper time. That is why we have courts."

Tinken sat down.

"I maintain that the concept of communication precludes matter transmission," stormed Kingman. "Matter transmission becomes a problem for the transportation companies and the power of companies. *Matter, your honor, is energy*. They are transmitting energy!"

He stalked over to Tinken and smiled affably. "Cross-examination?" he offered.

"No questions," said Tinken.

Hamilton rapped on the bench. "Court is adjourned for ten minutes."

"Looking for something?" Don asked.

Arden turned from the window and faced him.

"I was trying to see Niagara Falls," she smiled. "I've heard that you could see it from Buffalo."

"What do you want to see Niagara Falls for, anyway? Just a lot of water falling over a cliff at two pints to the quart."

"If you recall, chum, we went to Mars, not Niagara. There wasn't two pints of water on the whole planet, let alone a thing like Niagara."

Don nodded. "At the risk of offending a lot of Buffalonians, I'm beginning to dislike the place."

"It isn't the people," said Arden. "It's the position we're in. Bad, huh?"

"Not going too good at all. Kingman slips in a sly dig every now and then. Frankly, I am getting worried. He's got a few points that really hit close to home. If he can sell the judge on a couple more of them, we'll be under the sod."

"You won't be out entirely, will you?"

"Not entirely. He'll have to use the beams of Venus Equilateral to operate, but he'll be collecting all the real gravy. We'll just be leasing our beams to him."

"Well, don't go down without a fight, chum."

"I won't. I really hate to see Kingman get ahead of this, though." Don stretched, took another look out across the city of Buffalo, and then said: "We'd best be getting back. We'll be late . . . He said ten minutes."

They went down the staircase slowly, and at the courtroom door they met Keg Johnson. The latter smiled wearily. "Not too good?"

"Nope."

"Don, if you lose, then what?"

"Appeal, I guess."

"That isn't too good. Judges do not reverse lower courts unless a real miscarriage of justice takes place."

"I know, but that's our only chance."

"What would you advise me to do?"

"Meaning?" asked Don.

"Interplanet. We'll be run right out of business if this thing goes over to Kingman and that bunch."

"I know."

"Look, Don, have you tried living matter?"

"Plants go through with no ill effects. Microscopic life does, too. Animals we have tried died because of internal disorders—they move while being scanned, and their bodies come out looking rather ugly. An anaesthetized mouse went through all right—lived for several hours. Died because the breathing function made a microscopic rift in the lungs, and the beating heart didn't quite meet true. We must speed up the scanning time to a matter of microseconds and then we can send living bodies with no harm."

"That would clean out the spacelines," said Keg. "I think I'll offer that bird a slice of Interplanet for an interest if he wins. We've got to have it, Don."

"I know, Keg. No hard feelings."

"Of course," said Keg wistfully. "We'll be across a barrel if you win, too. But the barrel will be less painful with you holding the handles than if Terran Electric holds them. The same offer goes for you, too."

"O.K." Channing nodded. He returned and entered the courtroom.

Tinken called Don Channing to the stand as his first witness. Don explained the function of Venus Equilateral, the job of interplanetary communications, and their work along other lines of endeavor.

Then Tinken said to the judge: "I have here a glass cube, three inches on a side. This cube was transmitted from Venus Equilateral to the Lunar station. I offer it as Exhibit A. It was a test sample and, as you see, it emerged from the test absolutely perfect."

The judge took the cube, examined it with some interest, and then set it down on the desk.

"Now," said Tinken, "if you do not object, I should like to present a demonstration of the matter transmitter. May I?"

Hamilton brightened slightly. "Permission is granted."

"Thank you."

Tinken made motions and technicians came in with the two cabinets.

"This isn't good," said Kingman's assistant to the lawyer. "The old goat looks interested."

"Don't worry," said Kingman. "This'll take a long time, and by the time they get done, Hamilton will be ready to throw them out. Besides, it will make a good arguing point for my final blast. And, brother, I've got a talking point that will scream for itself."

"But suppose they convince—"

"Look," smiled Kingman, "this is really an argument as to whether matter or intelligence is carried. Believe me, that has everything to do with it. I'm keeping one idea under the wraps until shooting time, so they won't be able to get an argument against it. We're a cinch. That's why I kept it in a legal court instead of a technical court. The Techs would award it to Channing on a technical basis, but the legal boys have got to follow my argument."

"How about an appeal?"

"The record of this court is still a very heavy argument. Look, they're about to start."

The racket and hubbub died, and Tinken faced the judge.

"These are plainly labeled. They are matter transmitter and matter receiver. We have here a set of metal bars. They are made of copper, steel, aluminum, some complex alloys, and the brother to that glass cube you have before you. We will transmit this set of objects from here to there. Have you any suggestions?"

"A matter of control and identity. What have you for control?"

"Nothing that is outside of our hands." Tinken smiled. "Would you care to send something of your own? Your gavel? Inkwell? Marked coin? Anything?"

"I'd offer my glasses except for the fact that I cannot see without them," said Judge Hamilton.

"We wouldn't break them or damage them a bit."

"I know—that much faith I do have—but I'd not see the experiment."

"A good point. Anything else?"

"My watch. It is unique enough for me." He handed over the watch, which was quite sizable.

Tinken inspected the watch and smiled. "Very old, isn't it? A real collector's item, I dare say."

Hamilton beamed. "There are nine of them in the Solar System," he said. "And I know where the other eight are."

"O.K., we'll put it on the top. I'll have to stop it, because the movement of the balance wheel would cause a rift during transmission."

"How about the spring tension?"

"No need to worry about that. We've sent loaded springs before. Now, people, stand back and we'll go on the air."

Don Channing himself inspected the machinery to see that nothing was wrong. He nodded at Walt Franks at the receiver, and then started the initial operations.

"We are synchronizing the two machines," he said. "Absolute synchronization is necessary. Ready, Walt?"

"Right!"

Channing pushed a button. There was a minute, whirring hum, a crackle of ozone, very faint, and an almost imperceptible wave of heat from both machines.

"Now," said Walt Franks, "we'll see."

He opened the cabinet and reached in with a flourish.

His face fell. It turned rosy. He opened his mouth to speak, but nothing but choking sounds came forth. He spluttered, took a deep breath, and then shook his head in slow negation. Slowly, like a boy coming in for a whipping, Walt took out the judge's watch. He handed it to Don.

Don, knowing from Walt's expression that something was very, very wrong, took the watch gingerly, but quickly. He hated to look and yet was burning with worried curiosity at the same time.

In all three dimensions the watch had lost its shape. It was no longer a lenticular object, but had a very faint sine wave in its structure. The round case was distorted in this wave, and the face went through the same long swell and ebb as the case. The hands maintained their distance from this wavy face by conforming to the sine-wave contour of the watch. And Channing knew without opening the watch that the insides were all on the sine-wave principle, too. The case wouldn't have opened, Don knew, because it was a screw-on case, and the threads were rippling up and down along with the case and cover. The knurled stem wouldn't have turned, and as Channing shook the watch gently, it gave forth with one—and only one—tick as the slack in the distorted balance wheel went out.

He faced the judge. "We seem—"

"You blasted fools and idiots!" roared the judge. "Nine of them!"

He turned and stiffly went to his seat. Channing returned to the witness chair.

"How do you explain that?" roared Judge Hamilton.

"I can only think of one answer," offered Channing in a low voice. "We made the power supplies out of power and voltage transducers and filtered the output for sixty cycles. Buffalo is still using twenty-five-cycle current. Since the reactances of both capacity and inductance vary according to the—"

"Enough of this!" Hamilton fumed. "I— No, I may not say it. I am on the bench and what I am thinking would bring impeachment. Proceed, Attorney Kingman."

Kingman took the cue, and before anyone realized that it was still Tinken's floor, he opened: "Dr. Channing, you can send a gallon of gasoline through this, ah, so-called matter transmitter?"

"Naturally."

"Then, your honor, it is my contention that no matter what the means or the intent, this instrument utilizes the sub-etheric effects to transmit energy! It is seldom possible to transmit power over the same carriers that carry communications—only very specialized cases prevail, and they are converted to the job. But this thing is universal. Perhaps it does transmit intelligence. It will and can be used to transmit energy! *Matter, your honor, is energy!* That, even the learned opponent will admit. We have our own means of transmitting power—this is another—and no matter what is intended, power and energy will be transmitted over its instruments. Since this machine transmits energy, I ask that you rule that it fall under the classification. I rest my case."

Hamilton nodded glumly. Then he fixed Tinken with an ice-cold stare. "Have you anything to offer that may possibly be of any interest to me?"

Tinken shook his head. He was still stunned.

"I shall deliver my ruling in the morning. I am overwrought and must rest. Adjourned until tomorrow morning."

The only sounds in the room were the tinkle of glassware and the occasional moan of utter self-dislike. Channing sat with the glass in his hand and made faces as he lifted it. Franks matched his mood. Both of them were of the type that drinks only when feeling good because it makes them feel better. When they drank while feeling low, it made them feel lower, and at the present time they were about as far down as they could get. They knew it; they took the liquor more as a local anaesthetic than anything else. Arden, whose disappointment was not quite as personal as theirs, was not following them drink for drink, but she knew how they felt and was busying herself with glass, ice, and bottle as they needed it.

It was hours since the final letdown in the court. They knew that they could appeal the case, and probably after a hard fight they would win. It might be a year or so before they did, and in the meantime they would lose the initial control over the matter transmitter. They both felt that having the initial introduction in their hands would mean less headache than having Terran Electric exploit the thing to the bitter end as quickly as possible.

The fact of sunrise—something they never saw on

Venus Equilateral—did not interest them one bit. It grew light outside, and as the first glimmerings of sunrise came, a knock on their door came also.

"Mice," hissed Walt.

"S'nock on door."

"Mice knocking on door?"

"Naw!"

"Mice gnawing on door?"

"It's Wes Farrell," announced Arden, opening the door.

"Let'm in. S'all right, Wes. Anyone c'n make mishtake."

"He's sober."

"Gettum drink," said Don. "Gettum drink—gettum drunk."

"Look fellows, I'm sorry about that fool mistake. I've been working on the judge's ticker. I've fixed it."

"Fitched it?" asked Walt, opening his eyes wide.

"Close 'em—y'll bleed t'death," Don gurgled.

Farrell dangled the judge's watch before them. It was perfect. It ticked, it ran, and though they couldn't possibly have seen the hands from a distance of more than nine inches, it was keeping perfect time.

Don shook his head, moaned at the result of the shaking, put both hands on his head to hold it down, and looked again. "How'ja do it?"

"Made a recording of the transmitted signal. Fixed the power supply filters first. Then took the recording—"

"On whut?" spluttered Walt.

"On a disk like the alloy tuners in the communications beams. Worked fine. Anyway, I recorded the signal, and then started to buck out the ripple by adding some out-of-phase hum to cancel the ripple."

"Shounds reas'n'ble."

"Worked. I had a couple of messes, though."

"Messessessessss?" Walt hissed, losing control over his tongue.

"Yes. Had a bit of trouble making the ripple match." Farrell pulled several watches from his pocket. "This one added ripple. It's quite cockeyed. This one had cross-ripple and it's really a mess. It sort of looks like you feel, Walt. I've got 'em with double ripples, triple ripples, phase distortion, over-correction, and one that reminds me of a pancake run through a frilling machine."

Channing looked at the collection of scrambled watches and shuddered. "Take 'em away. *Brrrrr.*"

Arden covered the uninspiring things with a tablecloth.

"Thanks," said Don.

"Do you think the judge'll forgive us?" asked Farrell.

"Don' say it," said Walt, bursting with laughter.

"I don' have to," chortled Don.

"They're both hysterical," Arden explained.

"Carbogen and Turkish bath," roared Don. "And quick! Arden, call us a taxi."

"You're a taxi," giggled Arden. "O.K., fellows. Can do." She went to the phone and started to call.

Farrell looked uncomprehendingly at Walt and then at Don, and shook his head. "Mind telling me?" he pleaded.

"Wes, you're a million!" Channing roared, rolling on the floor.

Farrell turned to Arden.

"Let them alone," she said. "Something probably pleases them highly. We'll find out later— Yes? Operator? Will you call a cab for room 719? Thanks."

Attorney Tinken faced Judge Hamilton with a slight smile. "Prior to your ruling, I wish to present you with your watch. Also I ask permission to sum up my case—an act which I was unprepared to do last evening."

Hamilton reached for the watch, but Tinken kept it.

"You may state your case—but it will make little difference in my ruling unless you can offer better evidence than your opponent."

"Thank you," said Tinken. He made a show of winding the watch, and he set it accurately to the court clock on the wall. "Your honor, a telegram is a message. It requires energy for transmission. A letter also requires energy for carrying and delivery. A spacegram requires the expenditure of great energy to get the message across. The case in hand is this: if the energy is expended in maintaining the contact, then communications are involved. But when the energy is expected to be used on the other side—and the energies transmitted are far above and beyond those necessary for mere maintenance of contact—it may then be construed that not the contact but the transmittal of energy is desired, and power transmission is in force."

Tinken swung Hamilton's watch by the chain.

"The matter of sending flowers by telegram is not a matter of taking a bouquet to the office and having the items sent by electricity to Northern Landing. A message is sent—an order to ship or deliver. It makes no difference whether the order be given in person or sent by spacegram. It is a communication that counts. In this device, a communication is sent which directs the device to produce a replica of the transmitted object. Ergo, it must fall under the realm of communications. I will now demonstrate this effect, and also one other effect which is similar to telegraphic communications."

Tinken ignored Hamilton's outstretched hand, and put the watch in the cabinet. Hamilton roared, but Tinken put up a hand to stop him. "I assure you that this will cause no ill effects. We have repaired the damage."

"For every minute of delay between now and the moment I receive my watch, I shall fine you one hundred dollars for contempt of court," Hamilton stormed.

"Well worth it," smiled Tinken.

Channing pressed the switch.

Click! went the receiver, and from a slide Channing removed the judge's watch. With a flourish he started it, and handed it to the judge, who glared.

"Now," added Tinken, "I wish to add—

CLICK!

"—two objects may be similar in form—

Click!

"—but can not be identities!

Click!

"However, two communications—

Click!

"—may be dissimilar in form—

Click!

"—but identical in meaning!

Click!

"We have before us—

Click!

"—a condition where—

Click!

"—identical messages are—

Click!

"—being reproduced in identical form—

Click!

"—just like a bunch of—

Click!

"—carbon copies!

Click!

"The production rate of which—

Click!

"—will be high enough—

Click!

"—to lower the cost—

Click!

"—of this previously rare item—

Click!

"—until it is well within the reach of us all.

Click!

"Just as in communications—

Click!

"—we may send an order—

Click!

"—directing the fabrication—

Click!

"—of several hundred similar items!

Click!

"And our supplier will bill us—

Click!

"—for them later!"

Brrr-rup!

"That last buzz or burp was a signal that we have reached the end of our matter bank, your honor. Our credit, for example, has run out. However, Dr. Channing is about to make a substantial deposit with the manufacturer, and we will resume operations later. I ask you—

Click!

"—can you do this with energy?"

Click!

"Stop that infernal—

Click!

"—machine before I have you all held for disrespect, perjury, contempt of court, and grand larceny!" yelled the judge.

Channing stopped the machine and started to hand out the carbon-copy watches to the audience, who received them with much glee.

Kingman came to life at this point. He rose from his chair and started to object, but he was stopped by Tinken who leaned over and whispered: "My worthy and no doubt learned opponent, I'd advise you to keep your magnificent oratory buttoned tight in those flapping front teeth of yours. If we all get into that gadget—how would you like to fight ten or twelve of us?"

Interlude

Don Channing turned from the court and made his way through the room to the hallway. In his hand he bore one of the judge's watch replicas. In his mind he had the world by the tail.

He was going to leave the court, make his way to Venus Equilateral, and launch a new era.

He didn't know that he had launched one already.

PANDORA'S MILLIONS

"A lot has been written about mankind starving amid plenty. But never before was a civilization confronted with the prospect of luxury amid bankruptcy—"

Keg Johnson was the executive type. He was the chief executive of Interplanetary Transport, a position of no mean height. Keg had become the chief executive by sheer guts, excellent judgment, and the ability to gamble and win.

Like any high executive in a culture based on a technical background, Keg was well aware of science. He was no master of the scientific method nor of laboratory technique. He was able to understand most of the long-haired concepts if they were presented in words of less than nine syllables, and he was more than anxious to make use of any scientific discovery that came from the laboratory. He knew that the laboratory paid off in the long run.

Keg Johnson was strictly a good businessman. He played a good game and usually won because he could size up any situation at a glance and prepare his next move while his opponent was finishing his preparatory speech.

So when Keg met Don Channing in the hallway of the courtroom in Buffalo, he was dangling an exact replica of the judge's watch—a timepiece no longer a rare collector's item.

He waved the watch before Channing's face.

"Brother," he said with a worried smile, "what have you done!"

"We won," said Channing cheerfully.

"You've lost!" said Keg.

"Lost?"

Keg's eyes followed the Terran Electric lawyer, Mark Kingman, as he left the courtroom.

"He's been trying to put you out of business for a couple of years, Don, without any success. But you just put your own self out of comish. Venus Equilateral is done for, Channing."

"Meaning?" Don asked, lowering his eyebrows. "Seems to me that you're the one who should worry. As I said, we'll give you your opportunity to buy in."

"Interplanetary Transport is finished," Johnson agreed. He did not seem overly worried about the prospect of tossing a triplanetary corporation into the furnace. "So is Venus Equilateral."

"Do go on," snapped Don. "It seems to me that we've just begun. We can take over the job of shipping on the beams. The matter-transmitter will take anything but life, so far. Pick it up here, shove it down the communications beams, and get it over there. Just like that."

"That's wonderful," said Keg in a scathing voice. "But who and why will ship what?"

"Huh?"

"Once they get recordings of Palanortis whitewood logs on Mars, will we ship? Once they get recordings of the Martian lagel to Northern Landing, who will take the time to make the run by ship?"

"Right," agreed Channing.

"The bulk of your business, my brilliant friend, comes not from lovesick swains calling up their gal friends across a hundred million miles of space. It comes from men sending orders to ship thirty thousand tons of Venusian Arachniaweb to Terra, and to ship ten thousand fliers to Southern Point, Venus, and to send fifty thousand cylinders of acetylene to the solar observatory on Mercury, and so forth. Follow me?"

"I think so," said Channing slowly. "There'll still be need for communications, though."

"Sure. And also spacelines. But there's one more item, fella."

"Yes?"

"You've got a terrific laboratory job ahead of you, Don. It is one that must be done—and quick! You owe it to the world, and to yourself, and to your children. You've brought forth the possibility of a system of plenty, Don, and left it without one very necessary item. *"Channing, can you make one item that cannot be duplicated?"*

"No, but—"

"Uh-huh. Now we go back to the barter and exchange."

"Golly!"

"Furthermore, chum, what are you going to barter with? A ton of pure gold is the same value as a ton of pure silver. That is, aside from their relative technical values. A ton of pure radium won't bother us at all, and if we want Uranium 235, we make it by the ton also. *Oh, brother, you've really screwed the works this time."*

"Now what?"

"You and your crew start looking for something that is absolutely un-reproducible. It should be a light, metalloid substance of readily identifiable nature, and it should be ductile and workable. We need a coin metal, Channing, that cannot be counterfeited!"

"Yum. That's one for the book. Meanwhile, we'll retrench on Venus Equilateral and get set for a long, long drought."

"Check. I'm about to do likewise with Interplanetary Transport. You don't know anybody who'd like to buy the major holdings in a spaceline, do you. It's on the market, cheap. In fine condition, too, in spite of the depredations of Hellion Murdoch."

"Might swap you a communications company for your spaceline, Keg."

Johnson smiled. "No dice. I'm looking for a specialized business, Don. One that will pay off in a world where there is no money!"

"What are you going to sell—and for what?"

"I'm going to sell security—for service!"

"So?"

"Those are items that your devil gadget won't duplicate, Channing. Barter and exchange on the basis of a washed car's worth of dug postholes."

Linna Johnson looked up with some annoyance as Keg entered her room. She was a tall woman, lissome in spite of her fifty years, but the artificial stamp of the "woman of fashion" spoke louder than her natural charm.

"Yes?" she asked without waiting for salutation.

"Linna, I need a hundred and seventy thousand dollars."

"Remarkable. What do you want me to do about it?"

"You've got a quarter of a million tied up in baubles. I want 'em."

"Give up my jewelry?" scoffed Linna. "What sort of a tramp deal have you got into this time, Keg?"

"No tramp deal, Linna," he said. "I've just sold the spaceline."

"So, you've sold your spaceline. That should have brought you in a pretty penny. What do you need more for?"

"I want to buy Fabriville."

"Who or what is Frabri . . . what-is-it?"

"Fabriville. A fairly large manufacturing village south of Canalopsis here. They have a complete village, assembly plant, stores, and all that's needed to be self-sufficient, if you permit a thorough income and outgo of fabricated articles."

"Never heard of it."

"Well," said Keg dourly, "there are a lot of things you have never heard of nor taken the interest to find out, Linna. Better shell out the baubles. They won't be worth an exhausted cathode inside of a year."

"Why?"

"The economic structure of the system is about to be shot to pieces in a box. Nothing will be worth anything in money. A diamond as big as your fist will be just so much carbon crystal. I want to butter us up, Linna, before the crash. That's the way to do it."

"What is this crash coming from?"

"Don Channing and Walt Franks have just developed a gadget that will transmit articles any distance. That shoots Interplanetary. The articles—or the signal impulses from them—can be recorded, and the recording can be used to duplicate, exactly, the same thing as many times as you want it."

"You idiot," said Linna, "why not just get one and duplicate your present money?"

"Merely because an operator as large as myself cannot palm off two hundred one-thousand-dollar bills with the serial number AG334557990HHL-6. Counterfeiting will become a simple art soon enough, Linna, but until it is accepted, I'm not going to break any laws. I can't, if I'm going to shove ahead."

"But my jewels."

"So much junk."

"But everything I have is tied up in jewelry.

"Still so much junk."

"Then we're bankrupt?"

"We're broke."

"But the house . . . the cars . . ."

"Not worth a farthing. We'll keep 'em, but their trade-in value will be zero."

"If we have no money," said Linna, "how are we going to pay for them?"

"Not going to. They'll pay for themselves. We'll send 'em back and keep duplicates which we'll make."

"But—"

"Look, Linna. Shell out. I've got to hit the market this afternoon if I'm going to grab Fabriville."

"Seems to me that getting that place is slightly foolish," Linna objected. "If nothing will have any value, why bother?"

"Oh, certain items will have value, Linna. That's what I'm working on."

"I still do not like the idea of giving up my jewels."

"If the junk is that important," Keg exploded, "I'll promise to replace them all with interest as soon as we get running."

"Promise?" whined Linna.

"Yes," said Keg wearily. "It's a promise. I've got to make an option payment immediately. From then on in, the place will be mine."

"But if you gamble and lose?" Linna asked worriedly. "I'll lose my jewelry."

"I can't lose."

"But if the economic structure falls?"

"It can't miss. All I want to do is get out what I need before the bottom falls out. Inflation of the worst kind will set in, and the wheels will stop dead—except at Fabriville. That's where *I* enter the picture."

"Good," said Linna in a bored voice. "As long as I am assured of my jewelry, I don't care how you play the market. Run along, Keg. I've got a dinner engagement. May I have just a few, though? I'll feel naked without at least a ring."

"Take what you need," said Keg, and was immediately appalled at the necessities of life.

An hour later, Keg Johnson was making some quiet trading and slowly but surely gaining control over the manufacturing village of Fabriville. The market was steady and strong. The traders worked noisily and eagerly, tossing millions back and forth with the flick of a finger. It was a normal scene, this work of theirs, and when it was done they would make their usual way home to a quiet evening beside a roaring fireplace.

But this was a surface quiet. Deep down below was a minuscule vortex that churned and throbbed, and other equally minute forces fought the vortex—and strove in a battle that was lost before it began.

Terran Electric bought a full-page advertisement in every paper. A five-minute commercial assailed the ears from every radio that listened to the Interplanetary Network. A full column emerged from the morning newsfacsimile machines. Terran Electric, it said, was announcing the most modern line of household electrical appliances. Everything from deep-freezers to supercookers. Everything from cigarette lighters to doorbell chimes.

The prices they quoted were devastating.

But on page seventeen, hidden among the financial and labor-situation news, was a tiny, three-line squib that told the story to those who knew the truth. Terran Electric had just released sixty percent of their production-line labor.

Don Channing caught the squib, and headed for Evanston less than fifteen minutes after reading it.

Unannounced, Channing entered Kingman's office and perched himself on the end of Kingman's desk. His bright blue eyes met Kingman's lowering brown eyes in a challenge.

"Meaning?" asked Kingman.

"You utter fool," snapped Don. He lit a cigarette and blew a cloud of smoke at Kingman, making the other cough.

"Am I?"

"You idiot. How long do you think this will last?"

"Not long," Kingman admitted, "but while it does, I'm going to get mine."

"What good will it do you?"

"Plenty. Until the crash comes, I'm laying in a stock of stuff for my personal use."

"Lovely setup," grunted Channing. "Have you started duplicating the duplicating machines yet?"

"Just today."

"Don't do it, Kingman. Venus Equilateral has all the rights sewed up tight."

"What shall I do, Dr. Channing?" Kingman asked sourly. The title grated on Don's ears, and Kingman knew it.

"Stop the whole thing."

"And what are you going to do about it?" asked Kingman. "Take me to court, Channing. Go ahead. Get some litigation started."

"Oh, sure. And you'll tie the thing up for seventy years. And all the time, the plant here will be duplicating the whole Solar System into the worst mess it ever got itself into. Better stop until we can get something figured out to take care of the conversion."

"That in itself will take ten years," said Kingman. "Meanwhile, money is still of value because the thing is not widespread. People will buy and sell, and I'm going to buy up enough to keep me and mine in the running until things settle down. You have no idea how much stuff is needed to keep a man running ten years, Channing. Especially when you try to store it all away at once. Oh, sure. Recordings. I know, I'm making them. Also making recordings of everything that I can think of that I might like. But getting originals takes money at the present time, and I'm going to ride the inflation market right up to the peak by being one step ahead, all the way."

"How?"

"When butter is ten dollars a pound, Channing, I'll be producing and selling its equivalent at fifteen."

"Very nice gesture, Kingman. But it doesn't work that way. You're licked."

"Am I?"

"You're licked. You'll be no better off than any of us in the long run. What happens when everyone has duplicators in their own homes and are having their Sunday dinner coming out of the gadget complete; hot, delicious, and costlessly complete—from the saltcellar to the butter square? What price butter?"

"That'll happen," admitted Kingman. "But by the time it does, I'll be able to weather the storm."

"You make it sound very easy, Mark. But it isn't going to work that way."

"This is going to be a nice, level civilization by the time we get through with it," said Kingman. "There'll be no more shopping for food. No more working thirty hours a week for your pay so that you can buy the niceties of life. With your household duplicator, you can make everything you need for life, Channing. The Terran Electric label on your duplicator is the label of the New Way of Living."

Channing snorted, and crushed out his cigarette with a vicious gesture. "You've been reading your own advertising," he gritted. "Kingman, what do you hope to gain?"

Kingman leaned back in his chair and put both of his feet on the desk. "I don't mind telling you," he said gloatingly. "Venus Equilateral is going to have the name of having invented and developed the matter transmitter and matter duplicator. That's fine. It will carry quite an honor, that reputation, up to the time that the big crash comes, when people realize they're being trapped. Terran Electric, selling duplicators for home use at a song, will emerge as the savior of mankind. All I'm going to gain out of this is security for Mark Kingman and a big black eye for Venus Equilateral."

Channing swore. He stood up. "You fool," he snapped, "you blind, bigoted fool. A little cooperation on your part would save a lot of trouble, but you prefer to let a petty quarrel ruin the entire economic system immediately. We could work this out sensibly, Kingman. Will you help?"

"No. Nothing you can say will convince me that I'm doing wrong."

"But why fire your help? That's what is going to hurt."

"I don't need a production line full of people, Channing, to sit around and watch a duplicator turn out vacuum cleaners, complete in their packing cartons."

Channing took Kingman's under ankle where they were crossed on the edge of the desk. He lifted, and the pudgy attorney went over backwards with a roaring crash, hitting his head on the carpet and spilling backward out of the chair onto the floor behind his desk. He arose with a roar of hate, but the door slammed behind Channing before he could become coherent.

Channing returned to Venus Equilateral immediately, a trip that took four days. In touch with events by driver beam, Don heard the news-advertising agencies announcing the Terran Electric Duplicator of a size suitable for a medium home, complete with a recording attachment and a supply of disks. He gritted his teeth and stepped up the drive of the *Relay Girl* another notch.

His first query upon reaching the station was to Wes Farrell.

"Nothing yet, Don," answered Wes. "We've been running some very interesting experiments, though."

Channing was interested in nothing but the non-duplicatable material, but he nodded. Wes Farrell's sideline experiments often paid off more than the main line of research.

"By inserting a filter circuit in the transmission beam, we can filter out other responses," said Wes. "Meaning that we can take a cube of regular iron, for instance, and run it through. The integrated iron in the receiver is pure iron, the purity of which is dependent upon the band pass of the filter. Using alloy-selectivity disks for filters in the circuits, we can make iron that is 99.99997 percent pure."

"Might be useful for metallurgical work, and so forth," Don mused. "Nine-nines iron is valuable and almost impossible—and it takes a gadget that destroys value to make it. Nice paradox, that."

"Another thing," said Wes. "We re-transmit the pure

iron and heterodyne the impulses into other elements. We can start with iron and end up with any of the other elements, merely by introducing the proper heterodyning impulse."

"That's not bad."

"I've got several elements that start off where the Periodic Chart ends. The boys in the chemistry lab are investigating the properties of Venium, Channium, Frankine, Ardenium, and Farrelline right now."

"Who picked the names?" grinned Don.

"Arden."

"O.K., Wes, but keep looking for that non-reproducible substance."

"I will. It may be—"

Farrell was interrupted by the insistent call on the station intercom for Don Channing. Don went to his office to find the Terran beam awaiting his presence. He lifted the phone and identified himself.

"This is P. L. Hughes of the Interplanetary Criminal Office," came the answer.

"I didn't do it," grinned Channing. "Besides, I gotta alibi."

"O.K.," came the amused answer. "No use talking then."

"Just a minute," said Don. "I might as well know what I'm being suspected of. Whom have I murdered?"

"No one, yet. Look, Channing, we're having a time here."

"What kind?"

"Phoney money."

"So?"

"Yes. The trouble is that it isn't phoney. You can always detect spurious coins and counterfeit bills by some means or another. We have bits of nita-fluorescin in the bills that is printed into the paper in a pattern which is symbolically keyed to the issue—date, the serial number, and the identifying marks on the face of the bill. It takes a bit of doing to duplicate the whole shooting match, but we've been getting stuff that we know is phoney. And, Channing, I have the original and the duplicate here on my desk and I can't tell which is which!"

"Give me more."

"I have a hundred-dollar bill here—two of them, in fact. They're absolutely alike. They are both bona fide as far as I or my men can tell from complete analysis, right down to the bits of stuff that get around into a bill from much handling. I have coinage the same way. Isn't there something that can be done?"

"We are trying to find a substance that cannot be duplicated," explained Channing. "Given time, we will. Until then, I'm helpless."

"What do you suggest?"

"I don't know. I've been hoping that we could control the situation until something sensible could be worked out. It slipped out of hand. I'd suggest that you stop operations because of the absolute impossibility of keeping your thumb on things. I'd forget the counterfeiting angle entirely and start building up a force to guard against riots, mob rule, and minor intercommunity warfare."

"I think you're right," said Hughes, and Channing knew that the head of the Interplanetary Criminal Office was nodding his head.

Channing hung up the telephone and toyed with three copies of the judge's watch that were keeping identical time. He shook his head and wondered how it was all going to end.

Conversion from production line to duplicator came all over the Solar System in about ten days. Terran Electric's own staff fabricated a duplicator capable of handling an object the size of a locomotive, and plant-sized duplicators were formed, one after the other, on flat cars that rolled from the maw of the huge machine. For payment, Terran Electric accepted blocks of stock in the purchasing companies, and the wealth and holdings of Terran Electric mounted high and began to look like the major company that would ultimately control all merchandising and manufacture in the System.

And thirty days after the conversion came, the wheels ground to a stop. Industry was finished. Work had ceased. Plants lay idle, nothing to do—and no one to do it for them.

Keg Johnson looked up as Linna entered. There was

a worried look on her face that caused Keg to inquire immediately as to its cause.

She tossed a diamond bracelet on the desk and snorted: "That!"

Keg picked it up. "Looks all right to me," he said. "Like the real article. What's wrong with it?"

"Nothing that I can tell," his wife grumbled. "Excepting that my maid has one like it. Exactly."

"I'm not too surprised," laughed Keg. "I've been warning you of that."

"But what's the world coming to? If my maid can afford a diamond bracelet like this, she won't be working for me very long."

"At that, you're probably right. I'd treat her with the most delicate of care," said Keg.

"She's my maid!"

"Look, Linna. You're not up-to-date. I can predict people sleeping in gold beds and eating from solid-platinum dishes before the hysteria dies out. The economic setup has gone to pot, Linna, and we're trying to work it out."

"But what's the world coming to?"

"It isn't a matter of what it's coming to, it's a matter of where it has gone. My technicians tell me metals will be rated in value as per their atomic number. Uranium is more expensive than lithium because the transmutation factor is higher. It takes a little more power and more matter from the matter bank in the instrument to make uranium than lithium; ergo, uranium will cost more."

"Then if this diamond bracelet is worthless, can't we get some uranium jewelry?"

"Sure—if you want it. But remember it is radioactive and therefore not to be worn too close to the skin. It isn't as bad as radium, for instance, but it's bad enough. Besides, Linna, the matter of uranium's value over lithium is a matter of a few tenths of a percent."

"Um. And how much is a pound of uranium worth, these days?"

"In Terran dollars about forty-seven million, six hundred fifty-thousand, three hundred and eight."

"Are you kidding?" demanded Linna. "How can Marie afford—"

"Linna, dollars are worthless these days. Monetary holdings are worthless. Stocks and bonds are likewise useless. Interplanetary isn't shipping a thing. Venus Equilateral is handling sentimental messages only, and they'd be running at a loss if it weren't for the fact that they're out in space, where power comes from Sol."

"But what is going on?"

"The death of an economic system."

"But why? Keg, you know I've never questioned your ability. You have always enjoyed the run of big business. Whenever I've needed or wanted anything, it has been available. I write checks and never question the balance. But this has me stopped. What has happened, specifically?"

"Channing and Franks invented a gadget that will reproduce anything."

"It is just that?"

"That and only that," said Keg.

"But it seems to me that this would make everybody live in a world of plenty."

"It will. That's why we'll have people sleeping in solid-gold beds, and enjoying silver plumbing. Platinum will have no more value than a slab of lead of the same weight. You see, Linna, when they can duplicate anything—in quantity—it includes money, stocks, bonds, and jewelry as well as radio receivers, automobiles, refrigerators, and table lamps. No one will take one dime's worth of money because it is valueless. Why should I sell my fountain pen for fifty dollars when I can make fifty dollars by pushing a button? Or the other guy can make a fountain pen by pushing a button? Follow?"

"But the public utilities? What of them?"

"That's the cinder in the eye, Linna. Somebody's got to work!"

"Well, I've heard it said that someone will like to do everything—someone will find pleasure in digging latrines, if you look for him long enough."

"Not good enough. Barney Carroll likes to tinker with radio. He's good, too. But it's a hobby, and Barney's tinkering will not produce anything like a commercial receiver. Oh, it'll work, and as good as any set, but no one would have the thing in the living room because it has no artistic appeal. But say it did. Fine. Then what about the automobile boys? Has anyone ever tried to make his own automobile? Can you see yourself trusting a homemade flier? On the other hand, why should an aeronautical engineer exist? Study is difficult, and study alone is not sufficient. It takes years of practical experience to make a good aeronautical engineer. If your man can push buttons for his living, why shouldn't he relax?"

"But what are we going to do?"

"Linna, I bought this place so that we could work it out. There is one thing that cannot be duplicated."

"Yes?"

"Service."

"Meaning?"

"You can't machine-clean the house. You can't machine-write books, music, or moving pictures. You can't machine-maintain machinery. You can't machine-doctor a burst appendix. And so forth. You can duplicate antiques until they have no value. Rembrandt is going to be a household word. The day of the antique is gone, Linna, and the eventual trend will be toward the *unique*. Mark my words, there will one day be 'unique shops' that deal in nothing but items which they can certify as never having been duplicated."

"But if service is of value," said Linna doubtfully, "how am I going to get along?"

"You'll be of service," Keg said harshly, "or you'll not get along."

"So?"

"Look, Linna. You're my wife. As my wife, you've been spoiled. That's my fault. I liked to spoil you. In the early days I couldn't spoil you because we were in no financial position to do any spoiling, but now you've become a parasite, Linna. You and your dinners and your jewels and your cars and your sleek, vacuum-brained friends. Patron of the arts! Nuts. Bum poetry, slapdash canvases, weird discordant music. No, it's not entirely your fault. I've sponsored it because I thought it gave you pleasure.

"But we're all on the same level now," he continued reflectively. "No one is any better than his brains. I've been graced. It has been my very lucky lot to be in a position where I can sway men to my will. Fabriville is mine—and yet it belongs to every man in it equally. I can't get along without them, and they can't get along without Fabriville."

"But how is it going to work out?"

"I don't know. It's tough. We have three physicians and two surgeons and a couple of high-powered diagnosticians. The question is this: how much time should Mrs. Jones desire of Dr. Hansen? She has a bit of rheumatism. Larkin, on the other hand, has a bad case of gallstones. Obviously, these two must not enjoy equal call upon Dr. Hansen. Furthermore, these two must not be expected to pay the same figure."

"Pay the same figure?"

"In service, Linna. The board of strategy sits for several hours each day deciding upon things like this—and it is not simple. How many hours of gardening is worth removing gallstones? And what happens to Dr. Hansen when he has seventeen gardeners, four butlers, nine chauffeurs, fifteen cooks, and twelve of each of the rest?"

"Um. I see."

"But how do we tackle it? Until someone gets a medium of exchange, we're forced to go on the barter-and-trade basis. Fabriville will toss out anyone who isn't paying his way by working. In return, he has free call upon the market, the manufacturing center, and the professionals. Thank God that hoarding is silly in a realm of plenty."

"But what can I do?" Linna wailed.

"Help. Go out and help in the hospital."

"But I'm your wife."

"So what?" said Keg flatly. "I'm working. I get no more for this than Joe Doakes, who is out there painting the flagpole."

"But—"

"Sure, I like to do this. But Joe Doakes always wanted to run up a flagpole on a bosun's chair and paint it. We're exactly even. At least in Fabriville we aren't doing without anything. Eventually the rest of the worlds will fall in line and there will be enough of stuff for everyone, but until that time arrives we'll be seeing trouble."

"The rest of the worlds?"

"There'll be riots and small-town wars. I only hope we can get our fence up before they decide to call on us."

"You've sort of created an oasis here," said Linna. "But how long will it last?"

"Until Channing and Franks come up with some substance that cannot be run through their own duplicator. I hope it will not be too long."

Out in the Trojan position ahead of Venus, Venus Equilateral moved in its quiet way. Like Fabriville, Venus Equilateral was self-sufficient. Furthermore, Don Channing had declared a closed corporation, and the three thousand inhabitants of the relay station were all in accord.

Business was running low. Yet the salaries went on, even increased, while prices went dropping to ridiculously low levels.

With a closed system such as Venus Equilateral, such an artificial economy was possible by mere basic control. The crime angle was nil on Venus Equilateral. With three thousand people living in a cylinder of steel three miles long and a mile in diameter, crime and general nastiness were eradicated by the simple means of making it too hard to conduct anything illegal. The citizens of Venus Equilateral were patriotic to the nth degree.

So the situation was less strained than in Fabriville. Though work moved slowly, there was still more than plenty for everyone, and the people were satisfied.

They were an unsuspicious lot and so they did not think it off-color when a small spacecraft of the plutocrat class came circling up to the south end landing stage. The craft landed, and a tall, broad-shouldered man emerged and asked for Channing. He was escorted along a mile of car-way in the outer skin of the station and then whipped up toward the center of the station for five hundred feet. He was led along the broad corridor and shown the main office of the Director of Communications.

Don Channing's secretary opened the door and said: "A Mr. Laurus Towle to see you, Dr. Channing."

Don nodded.

Towle entered behind the girl, who introduced him to Don and to Walt Franks. Then she left.

And as the door closed, Towle whipped out a revolver and pointed it at Channing. Walt slid forward off his chair and brought the chair around over his head with a single, flowing motion. Towle ducked the thrown chair, faded backward, and fired at Don.

The shot pinged against the steel wall, flaking off some of the plastic covering.

Don dropped to the floor and came up with his wastepaper basket, which he hurled at Towle. Towle ducked, fended it aside with his left hand, and tried to level the gun again. Walt Franks reached into an open file drawer and grabbed a large handful of papers, which he threw at Towle. They fluttered and filled the air for a moment, which distracted Towle long enough for Channing to leap over the desk.

Don and Walt closed on Towle in a high-low tackle, Don jumping at the man's head and shoulders from the desk top, while Franks hit Towle sidewise at thigh level in a crashing tackle. They rolled over and over and Towle lost his revolver.

The papers were still fluttering to the floor when they came to rest with Towle neatly squelched beneath Channing and Franks. Towle tried to heave them off.

Don almost knocked Towle's jaw loose with a stinging backhand slap. "Don't try," snarled Don, "you're had—right now!"

"You stinking—"

"Shaddup," growled Channing, "and start explaining what this is for."

"I'm ruined!"

"Try it again and we'll ruin you some more," Don promised. "I have an aversion to being shot at.'

"So have I," said Walt.

"He wasn't shooting at you," said Don.

"No, but I'd have been next, wouldn't I, Lazarus?"

"Laurus," Towle snarled.

"Now look," said Don in a voice that gave no idea of softness, "you're licked from here on in. This weapon of yours is now ours, and we'll hang it in the museum with other mementoes of our having been shot at. Luckily, this makes the first time that it has been close. Say—you aren't an old crony of Hellion Murdoch?"

"Never heard of him."

"Good. Now, as I was saying, we've disarmed you—Walt, take a prowl of his person and see if he has any more lethal instruments concealed thereupon—and we're inclined to get up off the floor and resume our roles as gentlemen. Besides, I want to know what you had in mind besides assassination."

They lifted the man from his supine position and planted him roughly in an overstuffed chair. Don and Walt sat on one edge of the desk, ready to move in with the first wrong move.

Don snapped the communicator and spoke to the girl outside. "Mr. Towle had an accident with an exploding cigar, Lorraine. No one need enter."

"Now," he said to Towle, "precisely what gives?"

"I'm ruined."

"Yep. You are. But why?"

"You ruined me."

"Me?" asked Channing. "Not that I know of."

"I'm bankrupt."

"Bankrupt?" Channing laughed.

Towle bristled at the laugh. "It's no laughing matter, Channing. For most of my life I've been saving to retire. In the turn of a wrist, you've made all my savings useless."

"Are you starving?"

"No."

"Are you homeless?"

"No."

"Are you being deprived of anything?"

"Um—no."

"Then what's all the shooting for?"

"But my savings?"

"Look, Towle, you worked hard for them, I do not doubt. But you've got just what you wanted, anyway. You have a duplicator?"

"Of course. I bought it early."

"Good. Then use it and quit worrying about your savings."

"But the years of deprivation to build up that fortune."

"Tough," said Channing. "I suppose you're mad because the foolish grasshopper is now enjoying the same benefits as the ambitious ant. That's not right, I suppose. But on the other hand, why should any man be a slave to toil?"

" 'Man shall earn his bread by the sweat of his brow.' "

"Baloney. Next you'll be telling me that men were better off with a ten-hour day and a six-day week."

"They didn't seem to get into as much trouble."

"Nor did they have as much fun," said Channing. "Nor were there as many developments made in the fields of science and industry. Men slaved and worked and lived and died without ever seeing the pleasure of the country sky. The radio would have been useless without leisure to enjoy its offerings. And who will say that radio is a useless science?"

"But it's not right that I should have slaved to acquire a retirement fortune only to have it wiped out."

"Look, Towle, the whole system is undergoing a radical change in the economic structure. By the same token, Venus Equilateral is a ruined concern. We've dropped from ten million paid messages per day to a mere handful. Those we send through because we are bound by agreement to maintain service at all costs. We aren't making expenses, if you feel like hollering about money. Would you like a few million?" Channing asked suddenly.

"I have—"

"And you used your duplicator to run up your fortune, first thing, didn't you?" asked Channing scathingly.

"Naturally."

"And you're sore because everyone else did the same thing. Towle, you're a dope. You've been feeling very virtuous about working like a slave for your fortune, which would probably keep you in cakes and lodging for the rest of your life. You've been promising starvation and pauperism to anyone who bought anything that seemed the slightest bit frivolous to you. Now that the ax has slipped, you're mad because the guy who liked to ramble amid the roses is not going to starve to death as per schedule. What's wrong with you? You're not going hungry. You'll be better off than before. As soon as we get this mess ironed out, you'll be able to enjoy life as before. Your savings are safe. As soon as we get a medium of exchange that works, you'll be credited—the government took care of that as soon as the bottom fell out of the monetary system. Call 'em dollars, credits, or whathaveyou's, they'll all be prorated and you'll then enjoy your fortune—though it won't be as much fun because no man is going to have to slave again. You're a crazy man, Towle, and as such I'm sending you back to Terra under guard. We'll let the psychologists work over you. Maybe they can make you behave."

They stood Towle up, rang and waited for a guard, and then saw the man off under the guard's eye.

And Don Channing said to Walt Franks: "Until we find a medium of exchange, there'll be the devil to pay and no pitch hot."

Walt nodded. "I'm glad we're out here with our little colony, instead of where lots and lots of people can come storming at the gates demanding that we *do* something. Hope Keg Johnson is holding his own at Fabriville."

It was a growling mob that tramped across the desert toward Fabriville. A growling, quarreling mob, which fought in its own ranks and stole from its own men. A hungry, cold, and frightened mob, which followed a blustering man named Norton, who had promised them peace and plenty if they did his bidding. His law did not include sharing among themselves, and so men fought and stole food and clothing and women.

Had the mob been anything but a shaggy, travel-weary band, Fabriville might have been wiped from the face of Mars.

It swept forward without form and like an ocean wave, it laved against the cyclone fencing that surrounded that part of Fabriville, and was repulsed. A determined, well-fed band would have crushed the fencing, but this was a dispirited mob that would have sold its leader for a square meal and would have worked for the promise of a second meal in a row.

Keg Johnson came to the edge of Fabriville in a medium-sized tank that could withstand the entire mob to the last man. He ran the tank out of the gate and right to the edge of the mob, which shrank back to permit the thundering monster to pass. He stopped the tank and stood up in the top turret and spoke.

A built-in amplifier carried his voice to the edge of the mob.

"Who is your leader?"

Norton came forward boldly. "I am."

"What do you intend?"

"We want a haven. We are cold and hungry and needy."

Johnson nodded. "I can see that," he said dryly. "How did you collect this gang?"

"Most of this outfit were caught in the crash. Their incomes did not permit them to buy duplicators, and their friends were too busy running up their money to hand any out."

"Fine friends."

"And in the smaller cities, the attendants at the power stations left. There are a horde of dead towns on Mars today. That's why we have come here. We know that Fabriville is self-sufficient. We intend to join you."

"Sorry," said Keg. "We have no openings."

"We'll join you by force, if need be."

"Want to try it?" asked Keg, patting the twin 105-mm. short rifles that looked out over the mob.

No answer for a moment.

"I'll try appealing to your better nature," said Norton softly. "Shall we starve and shiver while Fabriville eats and is warm?"

"How willing are you to take part?" asked Keg.

"Name it."

"Then listen. We need a more sturdy fence around Fabriville. We have the materials—who hasn't?—but we haven't the manpower. Get your mob to run up this fence, Norton, and I'll see that you are paid by giving each and every man a household-size duplicator complete with a set of household recordings. Is that a deal?"

Norton smiled wryly. "And what good is a duplicator with no place to plug it in? The power stations are down all over Mars."

"In building this fence," said Keg, "you are working out the value of the duplicators. Now look, Norton, in order to make this thing tick, I want to know whether you and your motley crew are honest. There are enough of you to man every vacant power station on Mars. If you, as leader of this gang, will see to it that the stations are manned and running every minute of the day, I'll see that you are given the benefits of Fabriville's more massive duplicators. That means fliers, and equipment of that size, Norton. Are you game?"

"What are you getting out of this?" Norton asked suspiciously.

"No more than you. I can eat only so much. I can wear only so much. I can use only so much. But it is my pleasure to run things, and I like to do it. Therefore, I shall run things until people decide that they want another man to run things. Until that date, Norton, you'll answer to me."

"And if I do not kowtow?"

"You don't have to. No one is going to kill you for spitting in my eye. But if you have sense, you'll see that working my way will ultimately bring you more reward than going on as an unruly mob. Replace me if you can, Norton, but remember that it cannot be done by force. I have too many real friends out across the face of Mars, who won't let me be shot to pieces. I've done them the same service I'm doing you. Take it or leave it."

"Why can't we remain?"

"We have thirteen thousand people in Fabriville. To take on another ten thousand would complicate our work system to the breaking point. We're running pretty close to chaos as it is, and we couldn't take more. If you'll set up the power stations and start small communities at those points, you'll all be better off."

"And what do I get for all this?"

"Nothing. You'll be fed and clothed and housed. That's all that any of us are. Men out there are all the same, Norton. No one has a dime. They're all bankrupt. There isn't one of them that can buy a thing—even if the stores were open. But not one of them is starving, and not one of them is going unclothed, and not one of them is going without the luxuries of life, except for those communities of which you speak. Take life to them, Norton, and you'll be the ultimate gainer."

"Why do they remain?" Norton wondered.

"The duplicator will run on direct current," said Keg.

"They just have a set of fully charged batteries recorded. They have a set in spare. When battery one runs down, battery two takes its place, and the first thing run off is a spare battery number three, and so on. The exhausted batteries are dumped into the matter bank and reconverted. But it is not a real luxury, running on batteries. They need the high power that your stations will deliver. They need the telephone and the radio which your men can maintain. Go and seek the officials of the various companies, and tell them what you want to do. Work at it, Norton. There will be a lot of men in your gang that would rather do something else. Eventually you will be able to release them to do the jobs they're best fitted for. Until we get a medium of exchange, it is a job proposition. I'll add this inducement: the medical service of Fabriville is yours—providing that you and your men will work with us."

Norton thought for a moment. "Done," he said shortly. "Can you give us warmth and food until we take care of the details?"

"That we can."

A stilted monster ran out from Fabriville under its own power. Four great girdered legs supported a housing the size of a freight car, and the legs moved on small tractor threads. Out it came, and it paused just outside the gate. A faint violet glow emerged from the bottom of the housing, and the whirling-skirling of Martian sands obscured the vastness of the space between the legs of the monster machine.

It moved again, and the original dust settled to disclose a very small but completely finished and furnished house. Around the encircling fence went the monstrous duplicator, and at each stop it dropped the carbon copy of the original house. Hour after hour it hummed, and when it completed the circle, Norton's mob was housed, fed, and clothed.

And Norton knew that the "fence-building" job was but a test. For if the thing could build a house—

Venus Equilateral resounded and re-echoed from the force of the blast. It rocked, and precession tilted it away from its true north and south axial positioning.

Men raced along the car-way to the blister laboratory and Channing led the wild rush.

The blister was gone. A shaken Wes Farrell clung to a stanchion, his face white behind the spacesuit mask. They fished him out of the wreckage and took him inside.

"What happened?" asked Don.

"Was making artificial elements," Wes explained. "Far outside of the Periodic Chart. I'd been stacking them over in a corner—they come in six-inch cubes, you know. But the last one— *Bang!*"

Channing shook his head. "That's dangerous," he said solemnly. "If you had a six-inch cube of every known element, would you stack 'em all side by side?"

"It might be all right—until you came to putting phosphorus on top of a hunk of iodin," said Walt.

"There's no reason to suppose that Wes didn't get a couple of very active elements side by each. We know nothing of the extra-charted elements. We can make 'em, but until we do, what can we know about them?"

"Well, we didn't lose the station," said Walt. "And business is so punk that tossing the beams won't harm us much; we'll have to spend some time aligning the place again."

"We're all here, anyway," agreed Don, looking over the ruined blister laboratory. "But look, Wes, I think you're running on the wrong gear. Anything that can be made with this gadget can be duplicated. Right?"

"I guess so."

"What we need is a substance that will be stabilized under some sort of electronic pressure. Then it might come unglued when the matter-dingbat beam hit it. Follow?"

Wes Farrell thought for a few seconds. "We might make an electronic alloy," he said.

"A what?"

"A substance that is overbalanced as goes electrons. They will be inserted by concocting the stuff under extremely high electron pressure. Make it on some sort of station that has an intrinsic charge of ten-to-the-fiftieth electron volts or so; that'll make queer alloys, I'll bet. Then it can be stabilized by inter-alloying something with a dearth of electrons. The two metals will be miscible, say, when liquid, and so their electron balance will come out even. They are cooled under this stress, and so forth. When the disintegrator beam hits them, it will liberate the electrons and the whole thing will go plooey."

"Looks like a matter of finding the right stuff," said Walt. "Don, what about running the station charge up, as Wes says?"

"No dice. The station is too big. Besides, the charge-changing gear would be overworked all over the station to maintain the charge, once made."

"Take the *Relay Girl* out and try it, Wes."

"Come along?"

"We don't mind if we do," grinned Walt, winking at Don. "There'll be nothing didding about business until we get a medium of exchange."

The Reverend Thomas Doylen speared Keg Johnson with a fishy glance and thundered: " 'A plague on both your houses!' "

Johnson grinned unmercifully. "You didn't get that one out of the Bible," he said.

"But it is nonetheless true," came the booming reply.

"So what? Mind telling me what I'm doomed to eternal damnation for?"

"Sacrilege and blasphemy," exploded Doylen. "I came to plead with you. I wanted to bring you into the fold—to show you the error of your sinful way. And what do I find? I find, guarding the city, a massive façade of mother-of-pearl and platinum. Solid-gold bars on gates which swing wide at the approach. A bearded man in a white cloak recording those who enter. Once inside—"

"You find a broad street paved with gold. Diamonds in profusion stud the street for traction, since gold is somewhat slippery as a pavement. The sidewalks are pure silver and the street stoplights are composed of green emeralds, red rubies, and amber topaz. They got sort of practical at that point, Reverend. Oh, I also see that you have taken your sample."

Doylen looked down at the brick. It was the size of a housebrick—but of pure gold. Stamped in the top surface were the words:

99.99% PURE GOLD. A SOUVENIR OF FABRIVILLE.

"What means all this?" stormed the Reverend, waving the brick.

"My very good friend, it is intended to prove only one thing. Nothing—absolutely nothing—is worth anything. The psychological impact of the pearly gate and the street of gold tends to strike home the fact that here in Fabriville nothing of material substance is of value. Service, which cannot be duplicated, is the medium of exchange in Fabriville. Have you anything to offer, Reverend?"

"The Lord saith: 'Six days shalt thou labor—' You have destroyed the law, Johnson."

"That's no law. That's an admonition not to overdo your labor. He didn't want us laboring seven days per. If He were running things under the present setup, He'd be tickled pink to see people taking it easy five days per week, believe me."

"Sacrilege!"

"Is it? Am I being sacrilegious to believe that He has a sense of humor and a load more common sense than you and I?"

"To speak familiarly—"

"If I've offended Him, let Him strike me where I stand," smiled Keg.

"He is far too busy to hear the voice of an agnostic."

"Then He is far too busy to have heard that I mentioned Him in familiar terms. What is your point, Reverend? What do you want?"

"A return to religion."

"Good. Start it."

"People will not come to church. They are too busy satiating themselves with the worldly goods and luxuries."

"Your particular private sect, like a lot of others," said Keg Johnson harshly, "has been catering to the wishful thinking of the have-nots. That used to be all right, I suppose. You gave them hope that in the next life they could live in peace, quiet, and also in luxury, believe it or not. You call down the troubles of Hell upon the shoulders of the ambitious, and squall that it is impossible for a rich man to get ahead in Heaven. Nuts,

Reverend. You've been getting your flock from people who have no chance to have the pleasure of fine homes and good friends. You've been promising them streets of gold, pearly gates, and the sound of angelic music. Fine. Now we have a condition where people *can* have those—worldly goods—right here on earth and without waiting for death to take them there. If you want to start a Return to Church movement, Reverend, you might start it by making your particular outfit one of the first to eschew all this palaver about streets of gold. Start being a spiritual organization, try to uplift the poor in spirit, instead of telling them that they will be blessed because of it. Don't ever hope to keep your position by telling people that material made with a duplicator is a product of Hell, Devil & Co., because they won't believe it in the first place and there won't be anything manufactured by any other means in the second place."

"And yet you have all of Mars under your thumb," scolded the Reverend Thomas Doylen. "Of what value is it to 'gain the whole world and lose your soul'?"

"My soul isn't in bad shape," responded Keg cheerfully. "I think I may have done as much toward lifting civilization out of the mire as you have."

"Sacril—"

"Careful, Reverend. It is *you* that I am criticizing now, not God. Just remember this: people are not going to fall for a bit of salving talk when they want nothing. You promise them anything you like in the way of fancy embroidery, but they'll have it at home now instead of getting it in Heaven. Give 'em something to hope for in the way of greater intelligence, or finer personality, or better friends, and they'll eat it up.

"As far as having all of Mars under my thumb, someone had to straighten out this mess. I gave them the only thing I had worth giving. I gave them the product of my ability to organize; to operate under any conditions; and to serve them as I can. I'm no better off than I would have been to sit at home and watch the rest run wild. They'd have done it, too, if there hadn't been a strong hand on their shoulder. Where were you when the bottom fell out? Were you trying to help them or were you telling them that this was the result of their sinful way of life?"

The Reverend flushed. "They wouldn't listen to my pleas that they forsake this Devil's invention."

"Naturally not. Work *with* this thing and you'll come out all right. But you've got to revise your thinking, as well as the rest of the world has had to revise theirs, or you'll fall by the wayside. Now good day, Reverend, and I wish you luck."

"Your argument may have merit," said the Reverend, "though it is against the nature of things to fall in with any scheme without considerable thought."

"Think it over, then, and see if I'm not correct. I don't expect any immediate change, though, until you find that your former doctrines do not fit the people's wants now."

The Reverend left, and as the door closed a wave of pain swept through Keg Johnson's body. He reached for the telephone painfully and put a call through for the doctor.

"It's here again," he said.

"O.K., Keg. You're it."

"I'm licked, all right. Can I be back in seven days?"

"Make it three days with no mention of work. In five days you can have official visitors for three hours. In seven you may be up and around the hospital. You'll not be back there for eleven days."

"I'll have to put it off."

"Put it off another day and you'll not be back at all," snapped Dr. Hansen. "Take it or leave it!"

"How do I pay?"

"We'll take it out of your hide," said Hansen. "You're under the same rules as the rest of us. You do your day's work, and you receive the same medical blessing. Do you want to hoe the garden, or will you wash my car?"

"I'll wash the car."

"That's what *you* say. Get over here in an hour—and bring Linna with you."

"What for?"

"Someone's got to drive—and it shouldn't be you."

"That an order?"

"Nothing else but. Official order from the Medical Council. You'll play, or else we'll have an intern take out that appendix."

Keg realized the sageness of the doctor's order by the

time he reached the hospital. He was doubled over with agony and they did not permit him to walk from the car to the front door, but came out and got him on a stretcher. He was whisked inside, leaving Linna to straighten out the details at the incoming desk.

He went up to the operating room immediately, and the anaesthetic blacked him out from both pain and consciousness.

The days that followed were hazy; they kept him drugged because his energetic nature would have prevented rapid healing. It was four days after the operation that they gave him a quick shot of counter-drug that brought him out of the fog immediately.

There were people there.

Don Channing, Walt Franks, Wes Farrell, and Dr. Hansen.

"Hello," he said, looking up with a wry smile. "How many car washings do I owe you?"

"Plenty, brother. I tinkered for three hours over that frame of yours. Why did they have to run through an engineering change when they got to hanging your appendix in? I had to dig for it."

"That's the trouble with this system," Keg mumbled to Don. "He'll get the same credit for tinkering with me as he would for removing the cat's appendix."

"Well, you're worth the same as any cat," grinned Walt.

"Thanks," grunted Keg. "Don't tell me that you guys were worried?"

"Nope. We came to give you a hunk of something interesting. Wes Farrell hauled it out of space, electrons, and considerable high-powered theory. *Identium.* Corrosion-proof, inert, malleable, but hard enough for coins, and you can roll it out into ten-thousandths sheets and use it for paper money. But don't ever put it into a duplicator. It'll blow the top right off of your roof if you do. There's our medium of exchange, Keg."

"Now," breathed Keg, "we can all get back to normal. Thanks, fellows."

"The government is making the stuff in reams," said Don. "It won't be too long before you'll be able to pay Hansen what he's really worth, as well as the rest of your crew. But in spite of this trinket, Life has still made a big change. I can foresee the four-hour week right now."

"It's here and been here for some time," said Keg. "But— Hey! Linna!"

Keg's wife entered. She was clad in hospital whites and was carrying a tray.

"Hello, Keg," she said solemnly. Keg hadn't heard that tone of voice for years.

"What happened?" he asked.

"Someone had to help. I was doing nothing, and so I pitched in to help Dr. Hansen when he worked on you. He said I did fine."

"Linna is a good nurse's aid," responded Hansen. "Mind if we keep her on a bit?"

"Not if she minds staying."

"I want to, Keg," she said quietly. "With Marie wearing a platinum-mounted diamond tiara to dust the house, and Briggs coming to work in a limousine—imagine the idea of a butler's chauffeur!—and, as you said, people eating from gold plates and using iridium tableware, there's nothing to get long-nosed about but one's inventiveness, talent, or uniqueness."

"Linna, you're an ace," grinned Keg. He smiled up at her and said, while waving the sheet of identium before their faces, "Do me a job, Linna. Go out and buy me back the spaceline."

"Huh?" blurted Channing, Franks, and Hansen. "What for?"

"When the tumult and the shouting dies, fellers, we'll all be back in business again. Identium! The only thing you can write a contract on and not have it fouled or duplicated. The only thing you can write a check on, or use for credit. Identium—the first page of the new era. And when we get the mess cleared up Keg Johnson and Company will be carrying the mail! Linna, go out and buy me back my spaceline!"

Interlude

An era of absolutely no wqnt may give rise to concern about the ambitions of the race. Those who may wonder why the Period of Duplication did not weed all ambition out and leave the race decadent are missing one vital point. They should ask themselves to consider the many reasons why men work.

Keg Johnson himself can supply one line of reasoning—as follows:

Why do men work? Men often work because they must work in order to live. Then why do many men work hard, at long hours, when there are easier ways of getting along? Because they have the desire to provide the best they can for their families. It is necessary to them to feel proud of the fact that they can do as well as they do. But remove the sheer necessity of toiling for food, clothing, and shelter, and you make all men equally capable of supporting a family. Then come the ambitious ones who would appear a little better, a little more desirable, a little cleverer than their fellow man. This is not odious; it is the essence of ambition, even though it sounds egotistic when mentioned in cold print.

And so when people all are well clad, well housed, and well fed, there arises an almost universal ambition to become clever; to produce things that have not been duplicated by the machine. For, in a culture in which fifty thousand copies of Leonardo da Vinci's *Last Supper* hang in theaters, churches, schools, and living rooms, he who possesses a handmade chromo painted by his own hand owns a true *Unique*, to which he can point with pride.

So once the flurry was over and the tumult gone, men took a deep breath—

And went back to work.

On Venus Equilateral they worked, too. Given more

time for leisure, they took more time for study and experiment.

Of course, it was only a matter of time before someone came up with something that would put Venus Equilateral on the obsolete list. Venus Equilateral had been instrumental in putting a number of other things on the retired list—and the relay station itself was long overdue.

And, too, there was still one man who would give his black soul to see Venus Equilateral lose out . . .

MAD HOLIDAY

"Yeah," Wes Farrell drawled, "but what makes it vibrate?"

Don Channing looked down at the crystal. "Where did you get it?" he asked.

Walt Franks chuckled. "I bet you've been making synthetic elements again with the heterodyned duplicator."

Farrell nodded. "I've found a new series sort of like the iron-nickel-cobalt group."

Channing shook his head. There was a huge permanent magnet that poured a couple of million gauss across its gap, and in this magnetic field Farrell had the crystal supported. A bank of storage batteries drove several hundred amperes—by the meter—through the crystal from face to face on another axis, and down from above poured an intense monochromatic light.

"Trouble is," complained Wes, "that there isn't a trace of a ripple in any of the three factors that work on the thing. Permanent magnet, battery current, and continuous gas-arc discharge. Yet—"

"It vibrates," nodded Channing. "Faintly, but definitely it is vibrating."

Walt Franks disappeared for a moment. He returned with a portable phonograph, which caused Don Channing to grin and ask, "Walt, are you going to make a recording of this conversation, or do you think it will dance to a Strauss waltz?"

"It's slightly bats, so I brought the overture to *Die Fledermaus* for it," snorted Franks.

As he spoke, he removed the pickup from the instrument and added a length of shielded wire. Then he set the stylus of the phonograph against the faintly vibrating crystal and turned up the gain.

At once a whining hum came from the loudspeaker.

"Loud, isn't it?" he grinned. "Can you identify that any better?"

Wes Farrell threw up his hands. "I can state with positiveness that there isn't any varying field of anything that I know of that is at that frequency."

Channing just grinned. "Maybe it's just normal for that thing to vibrate."

"Like an aspen leaf?" Walt asked.

Channing nodded. "Or like my wife's Jell-O."

Walt turned the dial of an audio generator until the note was beating at zero with the vibrating crystal. "What frequency does Arden's Jell-O work at?" he asked. "I've got about four-fifty per second."

"Arden's Jell-O isn't quite that nervous," said Don, puzzling.

"Taking my name in vain?" asked a cool and cheerful contralto.

Don whirled and demanded, "How long have you been keyhole-listening?"

Arden smiled. "When Walt Franks nearly runs me down without seeing me—and in his great clutching hands is a portable phonograph but no records—and in his eye there is that wild Captain Lightning glint—I find my curiosity aroused to the point of visible eruption. Interesting, fellers?"

"Baffling," admitted Channing. "But what were you doing standing on odd corners waiting for Walt to run you down for?"

"My feminine intuition told me that eventually one of you would do something that will wreck the station. When that happens, my sweet, I want to be among the focus of trouble so that I can say I told you so."

Walt grunted. "Sort of a nice epitaph," he said.

"We'll have them words 'I tole ya so' engraved on the largest fragment of Venus Equilateral when we do."

Don grinned. "Walt, don't you like women?"

Franks swelled visibly and pompously. "Why, of course," he said with emphasis. "Some of my best friends are women!"

Arden stuck her tongue out at him. "I like you, too," she said. "But you wait—I'll fix you!"

"How?" Walt asked idly.

"Oh, go freeze," she told him.

"Freeze?" chuckled Walt. "Now, that's an idea."

"Idea?" asked Don, seeing the look on Walt's face. "What kind of idea?"

Walt thought seriously for a moment. "The drinks are on me," he said. "And I'll explain when we get there. Game? This is good."

Insistent, Walt led them from Wes Farrell's laboratory near the south end skin of Venus Equilateral to Joe's, which was up nine levels and in the central portion of the station.

"Y'know," Walt said, "women aren't so bad after all. But I've got this feminine intuition business all figured out. Since women are illogical in the first place, they are inclined to think illogical things and to say what they think. Then if it should happen to make sense, they apply it. I used to know an experimenter who tried everything he could think of on the theory that someday he'd hit upon something valuable. Well—this is it, good people."

Walter shoved the door open and Wes Farrell grinned as he always did at the sign that read:

JOE'S
The Best Bar
in
Twenty-Seven Million Miles
(Minimum)

Arden entered and found a place at the long bar. The three men lined up on either side of her and Joe automatically reached for the Scotch and glasses.

"Now," said Channing, "what is it?"

Walt lifted his glass. "I drink to the Gods of Coincidence," he chanted, "and the Laws of Improbability. 'Twas here that I learned that which makes me master of the situation now."

Arden clinked her glass against his. "Walt, I'll drink to the Gods of Propinquity. Just how many problems have you solved in your life by looking through the bottom of a glass—darkly?"

"Ah! Many," he said, taking a sip of the drink.

He swallowed.

A strange look came over his face. He sputtered. He grew a bit ruddy of face, made a strangling noise, and then choked.

"Migawd, Joe! What have you mixed this with, shoe polish?"

"Just made it this afternoon," replied Joe.

"Then throw it back in the matter bank and do it again," said Walt.

Don took a very cautious sip and made a painfully wry face. "The SPCS—Society for the Prevention of Cruelty to Scotch—should dip their tongue in this," he said.

Joe shrugged. "It's from your own pet brand," he told Channing.

Arden smelled gingerly. "Don," she asked him seriously, "have you been petting dragons?"

Wes, chemist-like, dipped his forefinger in the drink, diluted it in a glass of water, and touched it to his tongue. "It'll never be popular," he said.

Joe turned back to his duplicator and shoved a recording into the slot. The machine whirred for a few seconds, and Joe opened the door and took out the new bottle, which he handed to Walt. Walt cut the seal and pulled the cork, and poured. He tasted gingerly and made the same wry face.

"What in the name of hell could have happened?" he asked.

"It's the same recording," asserted Joe.

"But what happened to it?"

"Well," admitted Joe, "it was dropped this morning."

"In what?" Walt demanded.

"Just on the floor."

Wes Farrell nodded. "Probably rearranged some of the molecular patterns in the recording," he said.

Joe put both bottles in the duplicator and turned the switch. They disappeared in seconds, and then Joe took another recording and made a bottle of a different brand.

Again Walt tasted gingerly, smiled hugely, and took a full swallow. "Whew," he said. "That was almost enough to make a man give up liquor entirely."

"And now," said Don Channing. "Let us in on your big secret—or was this just a ruse to get us in this gilded bistro?"

Walt nodded. He led them to the back of the bar and into the back room. "Refrigerator," he said.

Arden took his arm with affected sympathy. "I know it's big enough, but—"

Walt swung the huge door open and stepped in.

"I didn't really mean—" continued Arden, but her voice died off, trailing away into silence as Walt, motioning them to come in, also put his finger on his lips.

"Are you going to beef?" demanded Channing.

"No, you big ham," snorted Walt. "Just listen!"

Wes blinked and slammed the door shut behind them.

And then in the deep silence caused when the heavy door shut off the incident sounds from Joe's restaurant and bar, there came a faint, high-pitched hum.

Don turned to Arden. "That it?" he asked. "You've got better pitch sense than I have."

"Sounds like it," Arden admitted.

"Cold in here," said Wes. He swung open the door and they returned to the bar for their drink. "We can establish its identity easily enough," he told them. He finished the drink, and turned from the bar. "Walt, you bring the pickup and amplifier; Don, you carry the audio generator; and I'll bring up the rear with the rest of the gadget."

They left, and Joe threw his hands out in a gesture of complete helplessness.

"Trouble?" Arden asked cheerfully.

"I didn't mind when they used the tablecloths to draw on," he said. "I didn't really object when they took the tablecloths and made Warren use 'em as engineering sketches to make things from. But now, dammit, it looks like they're going to move into my refrigerator, and for God knows what! I give up!"

"Joe," said Arden sympathetically, "have one on me."

"Don't mind if I do," chuckled Joe laconically. "If I'm to be shoved out of mine own bailiwick, I might as well enjoy these last few days."

He was finishing the drink as the technical section of Venus Equilateral returned, laden with equipment.

Arden shrugged. "Here we go again," she said. "Once more I am a gadget widow. What do you recommend, Joe? Knitting—or shall I become a dipsomaniac?"

Joe grinned. "Why not present Don with a son and heir?"

Arden finished her glass in one draught, and a horrified expression came over her face. "*One* like Don is all I can stand," she said in a scared voice. Then she smiled. "It's the glimmering of an idea, though," she added with brightening face. "It stands a fifty-fifty chance that it might turn out to be a girl—which would scare Don to death, having to live with two like me."

"Twins," suggested Joe.

"You stay the hell out of this," said Arden good-naturedly.

Walt Franks reappeared, headed out of the restaurant, and returned a few minutes later with another small case full of measuring equipment.

"And this," said Arden as Walt vanished into the refrigerator once again, "will be known as the first time Walt Franks ever spent so much time in here without a drink!"

"Time," said Joe, "will tell."

Halfway between Lincoln Head and Canalopsis, Barney Carroll was examining a calendar. "Christmas," he said absently.

Christine Baler stretched slender arms. "Yeah," she drawled, "and on Mars."

Her brother Jim smiled. "Rather be elsewhere?"

"Uh-huh," she said.

"On Terra, where Christmas originated? Where

Christmas trees adorn every home, and the street corners are loaded with Santa Clauses? Where—?"

"Christmas is a time for joy," said Christine. "Also, to the average party Christmas means snow, wassail, and friends dropping in. Me, I'm acclimated—almost—to this chilly Martian climate. Cold weather has no charm for your little sister, James."

"Oh," said Barney.

"Oh," Jim echoed, winking at his sidekick.

"Don't you 'Oh' me," snorted Christine.

"Oh?" Barney repeated. "Okay, woman, we get it. Instead of the cold and the storm, you'd prefer a nice warm climate like Venus?"

"It might be fun," she said evasively.

"Or even better," said Jim Baler to Barney Carroll, "we might visit Venus Equilateral."

Christine's evasive manner died. "Now," she said, "you've come up with a bright idea!"

Barney chuckled. "Jim," he said, "call Walt Franks and ask him if he has a girl for us?"

"He has quite a stock in his little black book," remarked Jim.

"We'll drop in quietly, surprise-like," announced Christine. "And if there's any little black book, I'll see that you two Martian wolves divide 'em evenly."

"Walt is going to hate us for this," Jim chuckled. "Accessories to the fact of his lost bachelorhood. Okay, Chris, pack and we'll—"

"Pack, nothing," laughed Christine. "I've packed. For all three of us. All we need is our furs until we get to Canalopsis. Then," she added happily, "we can dress in light clothing. I'm beginning to hate cold weather."

"How about passage?" asked Barney. "Or did you—"

Christine nodded. "The *Martian Girl* leaves Canalopsis in about three hours. We pause at Mojave, Terra, for six hours; and thence to Venus Equilateral on the special trip that takes Christmas stuff out there."

Jim Baler shrugged. "I think we've been jockeyed," he said. "Come on, Barney, 'needs must when a woman drives.' "

"The quotation pertains to the devil," objected Barney.

"No difference," said Jim, and then he ducked the pillow that Christine threw at him.

A half-hour later they were heading for Canalopsis.

"Walt?" smiled Arden. "Oh, sure. Walt's fine."

"Then?"

"Yeah," Barney added good-naturedly, "do we find 'em in Joe's or elsewhere?"

"The Joe-Section of the engineering has been completed," said Arden with a grin. "They nearly drove Joe nuts for about a week."

"What were they doing?" asked Jim. "Building an electronically operated martini?"

"When I tell you, you won't believe me," said Arden. "But they've been living in Joe's refrigerator."

"Refrigerator?" gasped Christine.

"Just like a gang of unhung hams," said Arden. "But they're out now."

"Well! That's good."

Arden paused in front of three doors on the residence level near her apartment. Jim, Christine, and Barney each put their traveling bags inside. Then Arden led them high into the station, where they came to a huge bulkhead in which was a heavy door.

Arden opened the door and an icy blast came out.

"Jeepers!" Christine exploded.

"Hey! Icemen!" called Arden.

From the inside of the vast room came Don, Walt, and Wes. They were clad in heavy furs and thick gloves. Channing was carrying a small pair of cutters that looked a bit ridiculous in the great gloves.

"Well, holy rockets!" asked Channing, "what gives?"

"Merry pre-Christmas," said Jim.

Don whipped off a glove and Jim wrung his hand unmercifully. Wes Farrell greeted Barney Carroll jovially, while Walt Franks stood foolishly and gaped at Christine Baler.

Christine looked the heavy clothing over and shook her head. "And I came here to be warm," she said. "Come out from behind that fur, Walt Franks. I know you!"

"What is going on?" asked Barney.

"It all started in Joe's refrigerator," said Wes. "We

found that the cold had crystallized a bit of metal in the compressor. We discovered that it was radiating one of the super-frequencies of the crystal-alloy level. When warm, it didn't. So we've set up this super-cooler to make checks on it. Looks big."

Channing waved toward the door. "We've got the ultimate in super-coolers in there," he said. "Remember the principle of the sun power tube—that it will drain power out of anything that it's attuned to? Well, we're draining the latent heat energy out of that room with a power-beam tube—actually we're transmitting it across space to Pluto."

"Pluto?"

"Uh-huh. In effect, it is like trying to warm Pluto from the energy contained in that room. Obviously we aren't going to melt much of the solid-frozen atmosphere of Pluto nor create a warm and habitable planet of it. We can run the temperature down to damn near Nothing Kelvin without doing much of anything to Pluto."

"We're below the black-body temperature of Mars right now," said Walt. "And the gadgetry is working so much better that we're going to run it down to as far as we can get it."

"What do you hope to find?" asked Barney.

"Why, it looks as though we can make a set of crystals that will permit instantaneous communication from one to the other."

"Sounds good."

"Looks good, so far," said Channing. "Want to see it?"

Christine looked at the thermometer set in the face of the door. She turned back to the others and shook her head vehemently.

"Not for all the ice in Siberia," she said fervently.

Walt brightened. "How about some ice in a glass," he said.

"For medical purposes only," agreed Barney. "It's been deadly cold on Mars—about a quart and a half of sheer and utter cold."

"Been cold in there, too," said Don. "Arden, you're out of luck—you've stayed out of the cold."

"You try to freeze me out of this session," said Arden, "and you'll find that I have the coldest shoulder in the Solar System."

As the party from Mars had left the platform of the spacecraft poised on the landing stage of Venus Equilateral, another landing was made. This landing came from the same ship, but unlike the arrival of the Balers and Barney Carroll, the later landing was unseen, unknown, and unwanted.

Mark Kingman had been a stowaway.

Now, most stowaways are apprehended because success in such a venture is difficult. To properly stow away, it is calculated that more than the nominal cost of the trip must be spent in planning and preparation. Also, there is the most difficult of all problems—that of stepping blithely ashore under the watchful eye of purser or authority whose business it is to see that all the passengers who embarked ultimately disembark—no more and no less; plus or minus zero. (It is considered that an infant born aboard ship is a legal passenger and not a stowaway. This is a magnanimity on the part of the transportation companies, who understand that they might have difficulty in persuading any court that the will exists to defraud the company of rightful revenues, etc. A death and burial at sea is also ignored; the transportation company has already collected for a full fare!)

But Mark Kingman had done it. He had come aboard in a large packing case, labeled:

CERTIFIED UNIQUE!
(Identium Protected)
Under NO Circumstances
Will
DUPLICATOR
or
MATTER TRANSMITTER
Be Tolerated

With magnificent sophistry, Kingman was within the letter of the law that did not permit false representation of contained merchandise. For he, a human being, was a certified unique, he having never been under the beam of the integrator scanning beam of the matter duplicator or transmitter. Nor had any other living human, for that matter. The identium protection was insurance on all such cargoes; it prevented some overly—or underly—bright clerk from slipping the package into a duplicator to make shipping easier. Identium exploded rather violently under the impact of the scanner beam, it will be recalled.

Along with Kingman was a small battery-operated duplicator, and a set of recordings. The duplicator produced fresh air as needed, water, food, and even books, games, and puzzles for solitary entertainment. Waste material went into the matter bank, proving the earlier statements that with a well-equipped duplicator and a set of recordings, any man can establish a completely closed system that will be valid for any length of time desired.

When the ship landed, Kingman tossed all the loose material into the duplicator and reduced it to non-homogenous matter in the matter bank. Then he turned the duplicator beam against the sidewall of the huge box and watched the sidewall disappear into the machine.

He stepped out through the opening, which was calculated to miss the concealed plates of identium installed to prevent just this very thing. Kingman, of course, had planned it that way.

Once outside, Kingman set the duplicator on the deck between other cases and snapped the switch. The scanner beam produced books from Kingman's own library which he packed in the case. Then, by reversing the direction of depth scan without changing the vertical or horizontal travel, Kingman effected a completed reversal of the restoration. The side of the packing case was re-established from the inside out, from the original recording, which, of course, was made from the other side. It re-formed perfectly, leaving no seam.

Kingman went down an unused shaft to the bottom of the ship, where he drilled down with the duplicator through the bottom of the ship where it stood upon the landing stage. Down through the stage he went and into a between-deck volume that was filled with girders.

He re-set the duplicator and replaced landing stage and the ship's hull.

By the time the party had adjourned to Joe's, Mark Kingman was high in the relay station, near the center line and a full mile and a half from the landing stage. He was not far from the vast room that once contained a lush growth of Martian sawgrass, used before the advent of the duplicator for the purification of the atmosphere in Venus Equilateral.

He was reasonably safe. He knew that the former vast storages of food and supply were no longer present and, that being the case, that few people would be coming up to this out-of-the-way place almost a third of a mile above the outer radius of the station, where the personnel of Venus Equilateral lived and worked.

He started his duplicator and produced a newly charged battery first. He tossed the old one into the matter bank. He'd have preferred a solar energy tube, but he was not too certain of Sol's position from there and so he had to forego that.

Next, he used the duplicator to produce a larger duplicator, and that duplicator to make a truly vast one. The smaller numbers he shoved into the larger one.

From the huge duplicator, Kingman made great energy-beam tubes and the equipment to run them. Taking his time, Kingman set them up and adjusted them carefully.

He pressed the starting button.

Then a complete connection was established between an area high in the station but a good many thousand feet away—and on the other side of the central axis—through the energy-beam tubes, and a very distant receptor tube on the planet Pluto.

"This," punned Kingman, "will freeze 'em out!"

His final act before relaxing completely was to have the huge duplicator build a small but comfortable house, complete with furniture and an efficient heating plant. Then he settled down to wait for developments.

"So what brings you out to Venus Equilateral?" asked Don.

"Christmas," said Barney. "We—Christine—thought that it might be nice to spend Christmas with old friends in a climate less violent than Mars."

"Well, we're all tickled pink," nodded Arden.

"Frankly," Jim Baler grinned, "my charming sister has set her sights on your bachelor playmate."

"I think it is mutual," said Arden. "After all, Walt has had a lot of business to tend to on Mars. He used to use the beams to conduct business—in fact, he still does most of it by communications when it isn't Mars—but give him three ten-thousandths of an excuse and he's heading for Canalopsis."

"I noted with interest that Christine was quite willing to help him work."

"Fat lot of work they'll accomplish."

"Speaking of work, Wes, what goes on right now in this deal?" Don asked.

"We've just set up a modulator," said Wes. "I'm modulating the current since the magnetic field is supplied by a permanent magnet and the monochromatic light comes from an ion arc. Using varying light seems to widen the response band with a loss in transmission intensity. This way, you see, all the energy going into the crystal is transmitted on a single band, which is of course a matter of concentrated transmission."

"That sounds sensible. Also, if this gets to sounding practical, it is quite simple to establish and maintain a high-charge permanent magnet field, and also a monochromatic light from a continuous gas arc. Easier, I'd say, than making ammeters all read alike."

"Utopia," said Wes Farrell, "is where you can use any handy meter and find it within one-tenth of one percent of any other—including the Interplanetary Standard."

Channing observed that Utopia was far from achieved. Then he said: "You've got the Thomas gents out in a ship with another crystal setup?"

"*Anopheles,*" said Farrell, "will shortly head for Mars with the other half of the gear in another refrigerated compartment. If this proves practical, Pluto is going to become useful."

Arden nodded absently. "I've always claimed that there is a practical use for everything."

Channing opened his mouth to say something and had it neatly plugged by Arden's small hand. "No, you don't," she said. "We've all heard that one."

"Which one?" asked Farrell.

"The one about the navel being a fine place to hold the salt when you're eating celery in bed," said Arden.

Channing removed Arden's hand from his mouth and placed it in hers. "You done it," he told her ungrammatically. "For which I'll not tell you what Walt and Christine are doing right now."

Arden's attempt to say, "Pooh. I know," was thoroughly stifled and it came out as a muffled mumble.

Channing turned to Wes and asked: "Have any good theories on this thing?"

Farrell nodded. "I noted that the energy entering the crystal was not dissipated as heat. Yet there was quite a bit of energy going in, and I wanted to know where it was going. Apparently the energy going into the crystal will only enter under the influence of a magnetic field. Changing the field strength of the magnet changes the band, for the transmission to the similar crystal ceases until the other one has had its magnetic field reduced in synchronous amount. Also, no energy is taken by the crystal unless there is an attuned crystal. The power just generates heat, then, as should be normal.

"So," said Wes thoughtfully, "the propagation of this communicable medium is powered by the energy going into the crystal. Crystals tend to vibrate in sympathy with one another: hitting one with a light hammer will make the other one ring, and vice versa. I've tried it with three of them, and it makes a complete three-way hookup. As soon as Chuck and Freddie Thomas get out a good way, we'll be able to estimate the velocity of propagation, though I think it is the same as that other alloy-transmission band we've been using."

Channing grinned. "The speed of light, squared?"

Farrell winced. *That* argument was still going on, whether or not you could square a velocity. "We'll know," he said quietly.

The loudspeaker above Farrell's desk hissed slightly, and the voice of Freddie Thomas came in: "I'm about to trust my precious life once more to the tender care of the harebrained piloting of my semi-idiot brother. Any last words you'd like to have uttered?"

Wes picked up a microphone and said: "Nothing that will bear transmission under the rules. If there's anything I want to tell you, I'll call you on this—and if this doesn't work, we'll try the standard. They're on your course?"

"On the button all the way—they tell me."

"Well, if you jiggle any, call us," said Farrell, "either on the standard space phone or this coupled-crystal setup."

Channing grinned. "So it has a name?"

Freddie laughed. "We never did settle on a name for the driver-radiation communication system. So we're starting this one off right. It's the Coupled-Crystal Communicator. For short, 'Seesee,' see?"

Channing returned the laugh. " 'Seeseesee,' or 'Seesee' understand?"

Chuck Thomas chimed in. "My semi-moronic brother will delay this takeoff if he doesn't sharpen up," he said. "What he means is: Seesee, or Get it?"

"I get it," replied Channing.

And they did get it. Hour followed hour and day followed day from takeoff to turnover, where there was no Doppler effect even though the velocity of the ship was fiercely high.

The hours fled by in a working flurry of tests and experiments and almost constant talk between the arrowing ship and Venus Equilateral . . .

"It doesn't add up," Walt Franks complained.

Christine looked up from her book and waited.

"Something's more'n we bargained for," he said.

"What?" asked Christine.

"Why, that area we're chilling off is cooling far too fast."

"I should think that would be an advantage," said Christine.

"Maybe—and maybe not," said Walt. "The big thing is that things should behave according to rules. When they do not, then's when people make discoveries that lead to new rules."

"That, I don't follow," said Christine.

"Well, in this case we know to several decimal places the heat equivalent of electrical energy. Three thousand, four hundred thirteen kilowatt hours equals one BTU—a British Thermal Unit. We know the quantity of electrical power—the number of kilowatts—being coursed through the tubes en route to Pluto. We know by calculation just how many calories of heat there are in the area we're cooling off—and therefore we can calculate the time it will take to reduce the temperature of that area a given number of degrees Centigrade. We're about double."

"And—you were starting to explain something different," said Christine.

"Oh. Yes. Well, for a number of years—several thousand, in fact—it was taught that a heavy mass falls faster than a light mass. Then Galileo tossed rocks off the Tower of Pisa and showed that a small stone and a large stone fall equally fast. That was a case where definitely provable evidence was at variance with the rules. They couldn't revise the actuality, so they had to revise the rules."

"I see. And now because that area is cooling off much faster than anticipated, you anticipate that something is not behaving according to the rules?"

"Bright girl," chuckled Walt.

"Thank you, kind sir." Christine laughed. "But remember that I was raised in a bright family."

"Come on," said Walt. "We're going to investigate."

"In that cold room?" Christine asked with some concern.

Walt nodded. "You'll get used to it," he said absently, collecting a few instruments.

"Look, Walt," said Christine in a scathing tone, "I *am* used to it! That's why I came to Venus Equilateral from Mars. Remember?"

Walt looked at her, wondering. But Christine wore a smile that took most of the sting out of her words.

"Lead on, Walt. I can take a bit of chill. In fact," she said with a half-smile, "under the proper circumstances, a bit of chill is fun."

Walt finished collecting his equipment and packed it into two carrying cases. Then, from a closet, he took electrically warmed clothing, helped Christine into hers, climbed into his own, and they took the long trek along corridors and up elevators to the cold room.

"It's cold even here," said Christine.

"The room leaks bad," said Walt. "Wes Farrell's hobby these days is making synthetic elements on the duplicator—he uses a filter to get a mono-atomic pattern and then heterodynes the resulting signal to atomic patterns above the transuranic system. But in all of Wes Farrell's playing at making synthetic transuranic elements, he hasn't come up with anything like a good heat insulator yet. We did toy with the idea of hermetically sealing in a double wall and piping some of the vacuum of interstellar space in there. But it was too vast a project. So we let some heat leak, and to hell with it."

Christine shuddered. "I've never really appreciated the fact that Venus Equilateral is really just a big steel capsule immersed in the vacuum of interplanetary space," she said. "It's so much like a town on Terra."

"Inside, that is," grinned Walt. "There's nice queasy thrill awaiting you when first you stand in an observation blister made of plastiglass."

"Why," she asked.

"Because first you're terrified because you are standing on a bubble that is eminently transparent and looking down beneath your feet, you see the stars in the sky. You know that 'down' to the working and residence section of the station is actually 'out and away' from the axis of the station, since it revolves about the long axis to provide a simulated gravity plus gyroscopic action to stabilize the beam stage and pointers. Well, when you go down—and again 'down' is a relative term, meaning the direction of gravitic thrust—into one of the blisters, your mind is appalled at the fact that your feet are pressing against something that your eyes have always told you is 'up.' The stars. And then you realize that between you and the awesome void of space is just that thin glass.

"You end up," he grinned, "being very careful about banging your heels on the floor of the station for about a week."

"Well thanks for the preparation," said Christine.

"You'll still go through it," he told her. "But just remember that anybody on the other side of the station, standing in a similar blister a mile 'above' your head, is standing feet 'upward' with respect to you. But he, too, is being thrown out and away by centrifugal force."

Walt put his equipment down and rummaged through it. He selected a supersensitive thermocouple and bridge and fixed the couple to one of the fixtures in the room. He balanced the bridge after the swinging needle came to a halt—when the thermocouple junction had assumed the temperature of the fixture.

"Now," he said, "we'll read that at the end of a half-hour and we'll then calculate the caloric outgo and balance it against the kilowatts heading out through the energy beam."

"And in the meantime?" asked Christine.

"In the meantime, we measure the electrical constants to within an inch of their lives," he told her. "I've got a couple of real fancy meters here—this one that I'm hooking across the original wattmeter in the circuit measures the wattages in the region between one hundred thousand kilowatts and one hundred ten thousand kilowatts. Designed especially as a high-level meter."

Walt clipped the portable meters in place and made recordings. Finally he nodded. "Right on the button," he said. "Just what the meters should read."

The crystal began to vibrate faintly, and Walt mentioned that either Wes Farrell was calling Freddie Thomas or vice versa. "Can't hear it very well," complained Walt, "because Wes has the amplifiers downstairs, both incoming amplifier from the dynamic pickup—we had to give up the standard crystal because it is expected to get cold enough to make the crystal too brittle—to the modulating equipment. The monitor-speaker is outside—we haven't been in here enough to make use of it since our first tries."

Walt took a look at the bridge on the thermocouple and nodded vaguely. He killed more time by showing Christine the huge tube that drained the latent heat out of the room and hurled it across the Solar System to Pluto.

"Y'know," he grinned as a thought struck him, "I think we've licked the Channing Layer that so neatly foiled Mark Kingman and Terran Electric on that solar power project."

"Yes?"

"Sure," he said. "All we do is set up a real beam-input device on the moon, for instance, and then use a batch of these things to draw the power from there."

"But how about the formation of ozone?"

"That'll have to be checked," said Walt. "For Pluto hasn't got a Channing Layer, of course, and our station out there is no criterion. But you note there is no smell of ozone in here. That leads me to think that we've given Terran Electric the runaround once more. Funny thing about Kingman. If someone gave him this development, he'd never think of reversing it to bring energy in."

"From what I know of the man," said Christine, "he'd not think of reversing, but he would think of perverting."

"Christine!" Walt shouted.

"Huh?" asked the bewildered girl.

"You may have had your thought for the week!"

Walt tried a bit of Indian war dance, but failed because the pseudo-gravitic force was too light to hold him down. They were too close to the axis for full force.

"But I don't understand."

Walt laughed hugely and hugged her. Christine was lissome in the curve of his arm as she relaxed against him.

Walt looked down at her for what seemed to be a long time, while the stream of highly technical thinking and deduction gave way to a series of more fundamental thoughts. Then he added his other arm to the embrace, and Christine turned to face him. He kissed her gently, experimentally—and discovered instead of resistance there was cooperation. His kiss became fervent and Christine's lips parted beneath his.

Some minutes later, Christine leaned back in his arms and smiled at him affectionately. "I was wondering if you'd ever get around to that," she said softly.

Walt grinned. "Have I been had?"

"I had Jim pack the all-white shotgun," she told him.

"Shucks, why not just have him threaten to sit on me?" asked Walt.

He kissed her again.

"Now," she said, after an appropriate and pleasant interval, "just what was my 'thought for the week'?"

"Kingman," he said, his forehead creasing in a frown.

"Kingman?"

"We've no corner on brains," said Walt. "Anybody tinkering with these energy tubes might easily devise the same thing. Kingman's immediate thought would be to freeze us out, I betcha."

Walt kissed her again and then let her go. "Let's do some juggling with figures," he said.

"What kind of?"

"The Laws of Probability, aided by a bit of sheer guesswork and some shrewd evaluation of the barrister's mind."

Christine smiled. "You can speak plainer than that," she said.

"I know," he replied, reaching for his bag of gear, "but there's a lady present."

"You forget that the lady thought of it," Christine pointed out. "So let's go and find the—barrister."

"It ought to show, though," observed Walt. "And yet, my lady, we can check whether there has been cross-duggery at the skull-roads by making a brief observation along here somewhere."

"How?"

"Well, about fifty yards up this corridor there is a wall thermostat."

"You think that if Kingman were trying to chill off the place, he'd have bollixed the thermostats so they can't heat up the place and compensate?"

Walt nodded. "He'd do it, not knowing that we had all the nearby circuits shut off for our own experiment, no doubt."

"You don't suppose Kingman knew about this idea and decided to add to the general effect?" asked Christine.

Walt shook his head. "He would assume that someone would be rambling up here, off and on, to look at the works. He'd automatically choose another place if he thought we had this one under observation."

Walt stopped at the thermostat and with a screwdriver he removed the face of the instrument. He reached down into his tool pocket and took out a long, slender pair of tweezers. He probed in the depths of the thermostat and came out with a tiny square of paper.

He held it up for Christine to see.

"Stickum on one side held it until the contacts

closed," he said. "Then it made a damned good insulator. Betcha this slip of paper came from Terran Electric!"

"Now what?" Christine asked.

"I'm going to call Don," said Walt. "Iffen and providen we can find a live jack."

He took a handset from his tools and plugged it into the jack below the thermostat. He jiggled a tiny switch and pressed a little red button, and after a full three minutes, he said, "Damn," under his breath and dropped the handset back into his tool kit.

"Nobody's paying much attention to the telephone from this section of Venus Equilateral anymore," he said. "There's a live one in the cold room, though. Let's take a look around first."

"Which way?"

Walt thought for a moment. "We set the cold room about one-third of the way from the north end because it was as far from the rest of the station's operating and living section as possible while commensurable with being reasonably close to the labs," he said. "We're not very far—perhaps a hundred yards—from the axis. We're about a mile from the north end.

"Now, if I were Kingman, I'd set up shop in some place as far from the operating section as possible, commensurable with an out-of-the-way place—and definitely far from the laboratories. Then I'd select a place as far from me as I could get without too much danger of having the effect detected."

Christine nodded. "If Venus Equilateral were a cube, you'd take one corner and chill off the opposite corner."

"Venus Equilateral is a cylinder, and the skin is filled with people. However, you can set up an equation in differential calculus that will give you two spots as far from one another as possible, with the least danger of detection from the ends or skin of a cylinder. The answer will give you two toroidal volumes located inside of the cylinder. You set your workshop in one and start the chill-off in the other—and right across the center from you."

"And?" Christine prompted with a smile.

"We used the same equation to locate the least dangerous place. Predicated on the theory that if the personnel need be protected from the danger area as much as the danger area need be concealed from people, we can assume the use of the same constants. Now, since by sheer coincidence Markus the Kingman selected a spot in the toroid that we also selected, it narrows our search considerably."

"In other words, we chase down the length of the station, cross the axis, and knock on Kingman's door."

"Right," said Walt.

And being firmly convinced that mixing pleasure with business often makes the business less objectionable, Walt kissed Christine once more before they started toward the place where they expected to find their troublemaker.

"About here," said Walt, looking up at a smooth bulkhead.

"How are we going to find him?" asked Christine.

The corridor was long and die-straight, but both walls were sheer for thirty feet and unbroken.

"Look, I guess," said Walt uncertainly. "I'm not too familiar with this section of the station. When I was first here—many years ago—I spent a lot of spare time roaming and exploring these seldom-used corridors. But my Boy Scout hatchet wouldn't cut trail blazes on the steel walls." He laughed a bit thoughtfully, and then he put his hands to his mouth, cupping them like a megaphone, and yelled: "Hey! Kingman! We're on to you!"

"But what good will that do?" asked Christine doubtfully.

"Might scare him into action," said Walt. "Easiest way to shoot pa'tridge is to flush it into the open. Otherwise you might walk over a nest and never see it. I—Holy grease!"

A four-foot section of the wall beside them flashed into nothingness with neither sound nor light nor motion. It just disappeared. And as they goggled at the vacant square, an ugly round circle glinted in the light and a sourly familiar voice invited them in—or else!

"Well," said Walt Franks, exhaling deeply. "If it isn't Our Legal Lamp himself!"

Kingman nodded snappishly. "You were looking for me?"

"We were."

"It's too bad you found me," said Kingman.

"It was just a matter of time before you dropped all pretense of being thinly legal," said Walt scathingly. "I'll give you credit, Kingman, for conducting yourself as close to the line without stepping over for a long time. But now you can add breaking and entering and kidnaping to whatever other crimes you have committed."

Kingman smiled in a superior manner. "I might," he said suavely, "add murder. There would be no corpus delecti if both of you were fed into the duplicator."

"You can't record a human being," said Walt.

"Don't be stupid," said Kingman. "Who said anything about making a record?"

Walt admitted that this was so.

Kingman snapped the switch on the duplicator and the wall was re-established. Then he forced Christine to tie Walt, after which he tied Christine and then checked and added to Walt's bonds from a large roll of friction tape. He dropped them side by side in chairs, and taped them thoroughly.

"You are a damned nuisance," he said. "Having to eliminate you tends to decrease my enjoyment at seeing the failure of Venus Equilateral. I'd have preferred to watch all of you suffer the hardest way. Killing you leaves fewer to gloat over, but it must be done. Once you found me, there is no other way."

"Walt," pleaded Christine, "won't the others find the same thing and follow us?"

Walt wanted to lie—wanted desperately to lie, if for no other reason than to spare Christine the mental anguish of expecting death. But Walt was not a good liar.

He gave up and said: "I happen to be the guy who rigged the thermal-energy tube—and I'm the only guy who knows about the too-fast drop. All I hope for is that we'll be missed."

"We will," said Christine.

Kingman laughed nastily and began to fiddle with the scanning-rate controls on his duplicator.

Arden came running into her husband's office breathlessly. She was waving a sheet of paper and there was mingled anger and pleasure on her face as she shoved the paper under Don's eyes and waggled it.

"Look!" she commanded.

"Stop fanning me with that," said Channing, "and let me see it if it's so all-fired important."

"I'll murder 'em in cold blood," Arden swore.

Channing pried his wife's fingers apart and took the paper. He read—and his eyes bulged with amused concern:

Dear Characters:

When we were giving Venus Equilateral's advantages the up and down a coupla years ago after the sudden and warranted departure of Director Francis Burbank, we forgot one important item—a justice of the peace.

So Christine and I are eloping in a time-honored fashion.

Neither of us have any desire to get wedded in the midst of a Roman holiday, even though it does deprive a lot of guys the right to kiss the bride.

You may give my Little Black Book to Jim Baler, Barney Carroll, and Wes—and have Arden see that they divide 'em up proportionately.

Your ex-bachelor chum(p)
Walt.

PS: He chased me 'til I caught him—
Christine.

"Well," chuckled Don good-naturedly, "that's our Walt. He never did do anything the slow-and-easy way. Does Jim know?"

"I dunno. Let's find him and ask."

They found Jim and Barney in Farrell's laboratory discussing the theories of operating a gigantic matter-transmitter affair to excavate sand from a cliff. Channing handed the note to Jim, who read it with a half-smile and handed it to Barney, who shared it with Wes while they read it together.

Jim said, "I'm not surprised; Christine could have been talked into wedlock—holy or unholy—by a mere wink from Walt."

"I hope she'll be kind to our little bucket-headed idiot," said Arden, making to wipe tears with a large sheet of emery paper from Farrell's workbench. "He's been slightly soft-skulled ever since he set eye on that scheming hussy you have for a sister."

Barney shook his head sadly. "Poor guy."

"We ought to toast 'em though they aren't here," suggested Farrell.

"A requiem toast."

"This," chuckled Don Channing, "is one mess that Walt will have to get out of himself."

"Mess, is it?" Arden demanded with a glint in her eye. "Come, husband, I would have words with thee."

Don reached in his hip pocket. "Here," he said, "just take my checkbook."

"I'd rather have words with you."

Don shook his head. "If I just give you the checkbook, you'll use it reasonably sparingly, all things feminine considered. But gawd help the balance, once you get to talking me into writing the check myself. Besides, we're about to hear from the Thomas boys again. They're about to land at Canalopsis."

"I'll wait," said Arden, settling on a tall stool and lighting a cigarette.

It took about ten minutes, and then Freddie Thomas' voice came from the speaker, loud and clear. "Well, we've landed. We're here. And where are you?"

"Hang on, Freddie," replied Farrell. "And we've some news for you. Walt Franks and Christine Baler have just committed matrimony."

"That's fine— What? Who? When?"

"They eloped; left a note; took the *Relay Girl* unbeknownst to all and sundry. Left their damned note right where the *Relay Girl*'s landing space was."

"Well I'll be—"

Chuck's voice came in. "He probably will," he observed. "And you know, when I think of spending eternity with my brother, it's enough to make a guy spend an exemplary life in the hope of going to Heaven so we can be apart. But I've got another guy here that might be interested."

"Hello, Channing?"

"Well, if it ain't Keg Johnson. Own Mars yet?"

"No, but I'm damned interested in this coupled-crystal gadget of yours. Mind if I bring Linna out for a few days?"

"Come ahead. Coming on *Anopheles*?" asked Don.

Keg Johnson laughed. "Not a chance, Don. I own a spaceline, remember? And not wanting to cast disparagement at your type of genius, I'll prefer riding in style at two gravities instead of blatting all over the sky at five; ducking meters and festoons of cable; eating canned beans off a relay-rack shelf standing up; and waking up in the morning to the tune of Chuck Thomas carving a hole through the bedroom wall to make a straight-line half-wave dipole that won't quite fit in otherwise."

"I'd send the *Relay Girl,*" said Don, "but it seems as how my old sidekick, Walt Franks, swiped it to locate a justice of the peace in the company of a young and impressionable gal named Christine."

"Nuts?"

"If so, happy about it. Hope he'll be home by Christmas, anyway."

"Well, we'll be arriving in about ten days. See you then, Don."

"Right," answered Channing, and Wes Farrell took the microphone to give the Thomas boys some information.

Mark Kingman emerged from his tiny house in the huge storeroom and his breath blew out in a white cloud. He went to the couple tied to their chairs and said: "Cold, isn't it?"

Franks swore. Christine shivered despite the electrically heated clothing.

"You know," said Kingman, "those batteries are going to wear out sooner or later. I'd remove them and let the cold do its work, except for the fact that I'd have to loose you and get into the inside pocket of the suits. You stay tied!"

"Having nothing to eat but your words is beginning to undermine my health," snapped Walt. "Gonna starve us to death, too?"

"Oh," said Kingman expansively, "I've been devising a machine for you. As an inventor of note, you will appreciate little Joe. He will take care of you both, to keep you alive until the cold gets you."

He returned to his little house and emerged with a large, complicated gadget that he trundled to position in front of Walt and Christine. There was a large hopper above and a wild assortment of levers and gears interlocked in the body of the mechanism.

Kingman pressed a button, and the gears whirled and the levers flashed—

And from the insides of the thing a lever speared forward. A spoon was welded to the fore end, and it carried a heaping load of mushy something-or-other.

Walt blinked and tried to duck, but his bindings wouldn't permit too much freedom of motion. The spoon hit him on the cheek, cutting him and spilling the food on his chest. The spoon disappeared back into the machine.

It reappeared on the other side and sliced toward Christine, who screamed in fright. The spoon entered her opened mouth, and the stuff it hurled into her throat nearly strangled her. It came again at Walt, who miscalculated slightly and received a cut lip and a mouth full of heavy gruel.

"You have to get set just so," explained Kingman, "then you'll not be cut."

"Damn you— *Glub!*" Walt snapped.

Christine waited and caught the next spoonful neatly.

And then the thing accelerated. The velocity of repetition increased by double—then decreased again—and then started on random intervals. They could never be certain when the knifing spoon would come hurtling out of the machine to plunge into the position where their mouths should be. They were forced to swallow quickly and then sit there with mouth wide open to keep from getting clipped. With the randomness of interval there came another randomness. One spoonful would be mush; the next ice cream; followed by a cube of rare steak. The latter was tough, which demanded jaw-aching rapid chewing to get set for the next possible thrust.

"A balanced diet," chortled Kingman, rolling his eyes in laughter. He held his stomach at the sight.

"You—*glub!*—devil!—*glub!*"

"It won't be long now," said Kingman. "Your cold room is down to almost absolute zero now. You know what that means?"

"—*glub!*—you—"

"When the metal reaches absolute zero, as it will with the thermal beam, the spread of cooling will accelerate. The metal will become a superconductor—which will superconduct heat as well as electricity. The chill area is spreading rapidly now, and once this cold-room section reaches absolute zero, the chill will spread like wildfire and the famous Venus Equilateral Relay Station will experience a killing freeze."

Walt glared. There was nothing else he could do. He was being fed at a rapid rate that left him no time for other occupations. It was ignominious to be so treated, but Walt consoled himself with the fact that he was being fed—even though gulps of scalding-hot coffee drenched spoons of ice cream that came after mashed potatoes (with lumps, and where did Kingman get *that* duplicator recording?). The final blow was a one-inch tube that nearly knocked their teeth out in arriving. It poured a half-pint of Benedictine and brandy down their throats which made them cough—and which almost immediately left them with their senses reeling.

Kingman enjoyed this immensely, roaring with laughter at his "feeding machine" as he called it.

Then he sobered as Walt's eyes refused to focus. He stepped to a place behind Walt and unbound him quickly. Walt tried to stand, but reeled, and Kingman pointed his heavy rifle at Walt from a very safe distance and urged him to go and enter the small metal house. Walt did. Then Kingman transferred Christine to the house in the same way.

He sealed the only door with the duplicator and, from a small opening in the wall, he spoke to them.

"I'm leaving," he said. "You'll find everything in there to set up light housekeeping but food and heat. There'll be no heat, for I've removed the heating plant. You can see it through this hole, but the hole will soon be closed by the feeding machine, which I'm fixing so that you can eat when hungry. I'd prefer that you stay alive while you slowly freeze. Eventually your batteries will give out, and then—curtains. But I've got to leave because things are running my way and I've got to be in a place to cash in on it. I'll be seeing you."

Keg Johnson greeted Don warmly. Then he said, "I knew you'd do it sooner or later," with a grin.

Don blinked. "The last time you said that was in the courtroom in Buffalo, after we wrecked the economic system with the matter duplicator. What is it this time?"

"According to the guys I've had investigating your coupled-crystal effect, it is quite simple. The effect will obtain with any crystalline substance—so long as they are absolutely identical! It took the duplicator to do it right to the atomic lattice structure. You'll get any royalties, Channing, but I'm getting all my ships talking from ship to ship direct, and from Canalopsis direct to any ship. You've just invented Venus Equilateral out of business!"

"Good!" exclaimed Don.

"Good?"

Don nodded. "Venus Equilateral is fun—and always has been. But, damn it, here we are out here in space lacking the free sky and the fresh natural air. We'd never abandon it so long as Venus Equilateral had a shred of necessity. But now we can all go home to man's natural environment: a natural planet."

"So what are we going to do?"

"Furnish the communications stations at Northern Landing, at Canalopsis, and on Terra with coupled-crystal equipments. Then we abandon Venus Equilateral in one grand celebration."

Arden smiled. "Walt and Christine will be wild. Serves 'em right."

Farrell shrugged. "Going to tell 'em?"

"Nope. For one thing, they're honeymooning no one knows where. And so we'll just leave quietly and when they come back, they'll find that Venus Equilateral is a large empty house. Run off on us, will they!"

"Making any public announcements?" asked Keg.

Don shook his head. "Why bother?" he asked. "People will know sooner or later, and besides, these days I'd prefer to keep the coupled-crystal idea secret as long as possible. We'll get more royalty, because once it is known the duplicators will go crazy again. So long as

Venus Equilateral—the generic term—maintains interplanetary communications, that's all that is necessary. Though Venus Equilateral as an identity is no more, the name of the Interplanetary Communications Company shall be known as Venus Equilateral as a fond tribute to a happy memory of a fine place. And—"

"And now we can haul off and have a four-alarm holiday brawl," said Arden.

Farrell noted the thermometers that measured the temperature of the cold room. "About all we'd have to do is to hold the door open and Venus Equilateral will have its first snowstorm."

"Just like Mars," said Jim. "No wonder Christine eloped with Walt. Bet they're honeymooning on Venus."

"Well," said Channing, "turn up the gain on that ice-cream freezer of Walt's, and we'll have our winter snowstorm. A white Christmas, by all that's good and holy!"

Farrell grinned widely and reached up to the servo panel. He twisted the master control dial all the way clockwise and the indicators read high on their scales. Imperceptibly, the recording thermometers started to creep downward—though it would take a day or so before the drop became evident.

"Get everything in motion," said Channing. "Arden, make plans to clean out about an acre of former living space—make a one-room apartment out of it. Get the gals a-decorating like mad. Wes, get someone to make a firebrick and duplicate it into enough to build a fireplace. Then make enough fireplaces to go around to all as wants 'em. For draft, we'll tie the chimneys together and let it blow out into space at fourteen pounds per square inch of draft. Better get some good dampers, too. We'll get some crude logs—duplicate us a dozen cords of wood for firewood. Tell the shopkeepers down on the Mall that the lid is off and the Devil's out for breakfast! We'll want sleds, fur coats, holly and mistletoe by the acres. And to hell with the Lucite icicles they hang from the corridor cornices. This year we have real ones.

"Oh," he added, "better make some small heating units for living rooms. We can freeze up the hall and 'outdoor' areas, but people want to come back into a warm room, shuck their earmuffs and overcoats, and soak up a cup of Tom and Jerry. Let's go, gang. Prepare to abandon ship! And let's abandon ship with a party that will go down in history—and make every man, woman, and child on Venus Equilateral remember it to the end of their days!"

"Poor Walt," said Arden. "I wish he could be here. Let's hope he'll come back to us by Christmas."

For the ten thousandth time Walt inspected the little metal house. It was made of two courses of metal held together with an insulating connector, but these metal walls had been coupled with water now, and they were bitter cold to the touch.

Lights were furnished from outside somewhere, there was but a switch in the wall and a lamp in the ceiling. Walt thought that he might be able to raise some sort of electrical disturbance with the lighting plan, but found it impossible from the construction of the house. And obviously Kingman had done the best he could to filter and isolate any electrical fixtures against radio interference that would tell the men in Venus Equilateral that funnywork was afoot. Kingman's duplicator had been removed along with anything else that would give Walt a single item that he could view with a technical eye.

Otherwise, it was a miniature model of a small three-room house; not much larger than a "playhouse" for a wealthy child, but completely equipped for living, since Kingman planned it that way and lived in it, needing nothing.

"Where do we go from here?" Walt asked in an angry tone.

Christine shuddered. "What I'm wondering is when these batteries will run out," she said.

"Kingman has a horse-and-buggy mind," said Walt. "He can't understand that we'd use miniature beam-energy tubes. They won't give out for about a year."

"But we can't hold out that long."

"No, we damn well can't," grunted Franks unhappily. "These suits aren't designed for anything but a severe cold. Not a viciously killing kind. At best, they'll keep up fairly well at minus forty degrees, but below that they lose ground degree for degree."

Christine yawned sleepily.

"Don't let that get you," said Walt nervously. "That's the first sign of cold adaptation."

"I know," she answered. "I've seen enough of it on Mars. You lose the feeling of cold eventually, and then you die."

Walt held his forehead in his hands. "I should have made an effort," he said in a hollow voice. "At least, if I'd started a ruckus, Kingman might have been baffled enough to let you run for it."

"You'd have been shot."

"But you'd not be in this damned place slowly freezing to death," he argued.

"Walt," she said quietly, "remember? Kingman had that gun pointed at me when you surrendered."

"Well, damn it. I'd rather have gone ahead, anyway. You'd have been—"

"No better off. We're still alive."

"Fine prospect. No one knows we're here; they think we're honeymooning. The place is chilling off rapidly and will really slide like hell once that room and the original tube reaches absolute zero. The gang below us don't really know what's going on because they left the refrigerator tube to my care—and Channing knows that I'd not go rambling off on a honeymoon without leaving instructions, unless I was certain without a doubt that the thing would run without trouble until I returned. I'm impulsive, but not forgetful. As for making any kind of racket in here—we're licked."

"Can't you do something with the miniature power tubes that run these suits?"

"Not a chance—at least nothing that I know I can do between the removal of the suit and the making of communications. They're just power-intake tubes tuned to the big solar beam jobs that run the station. I—"

"Walt, please. No reproach."

He looked at her. "I think you mean that," he said.

"I do."

He nodded unhappily. "But it still obtains that it's my fault."

Christine put cold hands on his cheeks. "Walt, what would have happened if I'd not been along?"

"I'd have been trapped alone," he told her.

"And if I'd come alone?"

"But you wouldn't have—"

"Walt, I would have. You couldn't have kept me. So, regardless of whether you blame yourself, you need not. If anybody is to blame, call it Kingman. And Walt, remember? I've just found you. Can you imagine—well, put yourself in my place—how would you feel if I'd walked out of your office and dropped out of sight? I'm going to say it once and only once, because it sounds corny, Walt, but I'd rather be here and knowing than to be safe and forever wondering. And so long as there is the breath of life in us, I'll go on praying for help."

Walt put his arms around her and held her gently.

Christine kissed him lightly. "Now I'm going to curl up on that couch," she said. "Don't dare let me sleep more than six hours."

"I'll watch."

"And I'll measure time for you. Once we start sleeping the clock around, we're goners."

Christine went to the couch and Walt piled the available covers on after he checked the operation of the power tube that furnished heat for her suit. He turned it up a bit, and then dimmed the light.

For Walt there was no sleep. He wandered from room to room in sheer frustration. Given anything of a partially technical nature, and he could have made something of it. Given a tool or two or even a few items of kitchen cutlery, and he might have quelled his restlessness in working toward some end. But to be imprisoned in a small house that was rapidly dropping toward Zero degrees Kelvin without a book, without a knife or fork or loose bit of metal anywhere, was frustration for the technical mind.

Mark Kingman, of course, had been quite afraid of just that and he had skinned the place bare of everything that could possibly be used. Kingman even feared a loose bit of metal, because metal struck against metal can produce sparks that will light a fire.

There was nothing at all but himself—and Christine.

And Walt knew that it would take only a few more days before that, too, would end.

For the metal of the house was getting to the point where he stuck to it if he touched it. The suits kept them warm—to take them off would have been sheer folly.

So from kitchenette to bathroom to living room prowled Walt. He swore at the neat little shower—the water was frozen, even had anybody wanted to take a bath.

Kingman entered the conference room of the Interplanetary Communications Commission with confidence. He knew his ground and he knew his rights, and it had been none other than he who had managed to call this meeting together. With a bland smile, Kingman faced the members of the commission.

"I wish to state that the establishment known as Venus Equilateral has forfeited its license," he said.

This was intended to be a bombshell, and it did create a goodly amount of surprise on the part of the commission.

The chairman, Lewis Hollister, shook his head in wonder. "I have this morning received a message from Mars."

"It did not go through Venus Equilateral," stated Kingman.

"I'm not acquainted with the present celestial positions," said Hollister. "However, there are many periods during which time the communications are made direct from planet to planet—when Terra and Mars are on line-of-sight to Venus and one another."

"The celestial positions are such that relay through Venus Equilateral is necessary," said Kingman.

"Indeed?"

Kingman unrolled a chart showing the location of the planets of the inner Solar System: Mars, Terra, Venus—and Venus Equilateral. According to the lines-of-sight drawn on the map, the use of the relay station was definitely desirable.

"Conceded," said Hollister. "Now may I ask you to bring your complaint?"

"The Research Services Corporation of Northern Landing, Venus, have for years been official monitors for the Interplanetary Communications Commission," Kingman explained. "I happen to be a director of that corporation, which has research offices on Terra and Mars and is, of course, admirably fitted to serve as official monitor. I make this explanation because I feel it desirable to explain how I know about this. After all, an unofficial monitor is a lawbreaker for making use of confidential messages to enhance his own position. As an official monitor, I may observe and also make suggestions pertaining to the best interests of interplanetary communications.

"It has been reported along official channels that the relaying of messages through the Venus Equilateral Relay Station ceased as of twelve hundred hours Terran mean time on twenty December."

"Then where are they relaying their messages?" asked Hollister. "Or are they?"

"They must," said Kingman. "Whether they use radio or the sub-electronic energy bands, they cannot drive a beam direct from Terra to Mars without coming too close to the sun. Ergo, they must be relaying."

"Perhaps they are using their ship beams."

"Perhaps—and of course, the use of a secondary medium is undesirable. This matter of interrupted or uninterrupted service is not the major point, however. The major point is that their license to operate as a major monopoly under the Communications Act insists that one relayed message must pass through their station—Venus Equilateral—during every twenty-four-hour period. This is a safety measure, to ensure that their equipment is always ready to run—even in periods when relaying is not necessary."

"Venus Equilateral has been off the air before this."

Kingman cleared his throat. "A number of times," he agreed. "But each time that discontinuance of service occurred, it was during a period of emergency—and in each instance this emergency was great enough to demand leniency. Most of the times an explanation was instantly forthcoming; the other times were after seeking and receiving permission to suspend operations during the emergency period. This, gentlemen, is twenty-three December and no message has passed through

Venus Equilateral Relay Station since noon on twenty December."

"Your statements, if true, indicate that Venus Equilateral has violated its license," Hollister nodded. "However, we are inclined to be lenient with them because they have been exemplary in the past and—"

"And," interrupted Kingman, "they are overconfident. They think that they're big enough and clever enough to do as they damn well please!"

"Indeed?"

"Well, they've been doing it, haven't they?"

"We've seen no reason for interfering with their operations. And they are getting the messages through."

Kingman smiled. "How?"

Hollister shrugged. "If you claim they aren't using the station, I wouldn't know."

"And if the government were to ask, you would be quite embarrassed."

"Then what do you suggest?" asked Hollister.

"Venus Equilateral has failed to live up to the letter of its license, regardless of what medium they are using to relay communications around Sol," said Kingman. "Therefore, I recommend that you suspend their license."

"And then who will run Venus Equilateral?" asked Hollister.

"As of three years ago, the Terran Electric Company of Evanston, Illinois, received an option on the operation of an interplanetary communications company," said Kingman. "This option was to operate at such a time as Venus Equilateral ceased operating. Now, since Venus Equilateral has failed, I suggest that we show them that their high-handedness will not be condoned. I recommend that this option be fulfilled; that the license now held by Venus Equilateral be suspended and turned over to Terran Electric."

Hollister nodded vaguely. "You understand that Venus Equilateral has posted as bond the holdings of the company. This of course will be forfeit if we choose to act. Now, Mr. Kingman, is the Terran Electric Company prepared to post a bond equivalent to the value of Venus Equilateral? Obviously we cannot wrest holdings from one company and turn them over to another company free of bond. We must have bond—assurance that Terran Electric will fulfill the letter of the license."

"Naturally we cannot post full bond," replied Kingman stiffly. "But we will post sufficient bond to make the transfer possible. The remainder of the evaluation will revert to the Commission—as it was previously. I might point out that had Venus Equilateral kept their inventiveness and efforts directed only at communications, they would not be now in this position. It was their side interests that made their unsubsidized and free incorporation possible. I promise you that Terran Electric will never stoop to making a rubber-stamp group out of the Interplanetary Communications Commission."

Hollister thought for a moment. But instead of thinking of the ramifications of the deal, he was remembering that in his home was a medium-sized duplicator made by Terran Electric. It had a very low serial number and it had been delivered on consignment. It had been sent to him not as a gift, but as a customer-use research—to be paid for only if the customer were satisfied. Not only had Terran Electric been happy to accept the thousand-dollar bill made in the duplicator, but it had happilly returned three hundred dollars' worth of change—all with the same serial number. But since Hollister received his consignment along with the very first of such deliveries, he had prospered very well and had been very neatly situated by the time the desperate times of the Period of Duplication took place. Hollister recalled that Venus Equilateral wanted to suppress the duplicator. Hollister recalled also that Venus Equilateral had been rather tough on a certain magistrate in Buffalo, and though he thought that it was only a just treatment, it was nevertheless a deep and burning disrespect for the law.

Besides, if this deal went through, Hollister would once more be a guiding hand in the operation of Venus Equilateral. He did believe that Channing and Franks could outdo Terran Electric any day in the week, but business is business. And if Kingman failed, the license could always be turned back to Channing & Co.—with himself still holding a large hunk of the pie.

"You will post bond by certified identium check,"

said Hollister. "And as the new holder of the license, we will tender you papers that will direct Venus Equilateral to hand over to you, as representative of Terran Electric, the holdings necessary to operate the Venus Equilateral Relay Station and other outlying equipments and stations."

Kingman nodded happily. His bit of personal graft had begun to pay off—though he of course did not consider his gift anything but a matter of furnishing to a deserving person a gratuity that worked no hardship on the giver.

The bond annoyed Kingman. Even in an era when material holdings had little value, the posting of such securities as demanded left Kingman a poor man. Money, of course, was not wanted nor expected. What he handed over was a statement of the equivalent value on an identium check of the Terran Electric Company, his holdings in the Research Services Corporation, and just about everything he had in the way of items that could not be handled readily by the normal-sized duplicator. At Terran Electric, for instance, they had duplicators that could build a complete spacecraft if done in sections, and these monstrous machines were what kept Terran Electric from the cobweb-growing stage. A man could not build a house with the average household-sized duplicator, and to own one large enough to build automobiles and the like was foolish for they were not needed that often. Kingman didn't like to post that size of bond, but he felt certain that within a year he would be able to re-establish his free holdings in Terran Electric because of revenues from Venus Equilateral. Doubtless, too, there were many people on Venus Equilateral that he could hire—that he would need desperately.

For Kingman had no intention of losing.

A duplicator produced snowflakes by the myriad and hurled them into the corridor ventilators. They swirled ad skirled and piled into deep drifts at the corners and in cul-de-sacs along the way. A faint odor of pine needles went with the air, and from newly installed water pipes along the cornices long icicles were forming. There was the faint sound of sleigh bells along the corridors, but this was obviously synthetic since Venus Equilateral had little use for a horse.

Kids who had never seen snow nor known a cold snap reveled in their new snowsuits and built a huge snowman along the Mall. One long ramp that led into a snaky corridor was taken over by squatter's—or rather "sledder's"—rights and it became downright dangerous for a pedestrian to try to keep his ankles away from the speeding sleds. Snow forts were erected on either side of one wide corridor and the air was filled with flying snowballs.

And from the station-wide public announcement system came the crooned strains of "Adeste Fideles" and "White Christmas."

A snowball hissed past Arden's ear and she turned abruptly to give argument. She was met by another that caught her full in the face—after which it was wiped off by her husband.

"Merry Christmas," he chuckled.

"Not very," she said, but she could not help but smile back at him. When he finished wiping her face Arden neatly dropped a handful of snow down his collar. He retaliated by scooping a huge block out of a nearby drift and letting it drape over her head. Arden pushed him backward into a snowbank and leaped on him and shoveled snow with both hands until her hands stung with cold and Don was completely covered.

Channing climbed out of the drift as Arden raced away. He gave chase, though both of them were laughing too much to do much running. He caught her a few hundred feet down the hall and tackled her, bringing her down in another drift. As he was piling snow on her, he became the focal point of a veritable barrage from behind, which drove him to cover behind a girder. His assailants deployed and flushed him from behind his cover, and he stood in the center of a large square area being pelted from all sides.

Channing found a handkerchief and waved it as surrender.

The pelting slowed a bit, and Channing took that time to race to one side, join Jim Baler, and hurl some snowballs at Barney Carroll across the square. That evened things, and the snow fight was joined by Arden, who arose from her snowdrift to join Barney Carroll and Keg Johnson.

"We used to freeze 'em," grunted Don.

"Me too," Jim agreed. "These things wouldn't stop a fly."

Then down the corridor there hurtled a snowball a good two feet in diameter. It caught Channing between the shoulder blades and flattened him completely. Baler turned just in time to stop another one with the pit of his stomach. He went *"Oooof!"* and landed in the drift beside Don. Another huge one went over their heads as Don was arising, and he saw it splat against a wall to shower Barney Carroll and Arden with bits.

"Those would," remarked Don. "And if Walt weren't honeymooning somewhere, I'd suspect that our Captain Lightning had just hauled off and re-invented the ancient Roman catapult."

"There's always Wes Farrell, or does the physicist in him make him eschew such anachronisms?" asked Jim.

Arden scurried across the square in time to hear him, and she replied: "Not at all. So long as the thing is powered by a new spring alloy and charged by a servomechanism run by a beam-energy tube. Bet he packs 'em with an automatic packing gadget, too."

Barney caught one across the knees that tripped him headlong as he crossed the square. He arrived grunting and grinning. "We can either take it idly," he said, "or retreat in disorder, or storm whatever ramparts he has back there."

"I dislike to retreat in disorder," said Channing. "Seems to me that we can get under that siege gun of his. He must take time to reload. Keep low, fellers, and pack yourself a goodly load of snowballs as we go."

"How to carry 'em?" Arden asked.

Don stripped off his muffler, and made a sling of it. Then down the corridor they went, dodging the huge snowballs that came flying over at regular intervals. Channing finally timed the interval, and they raced forward in clear periods and took cover when fire was expected.

They came upon Farrell eventually. He was "dug in" behind a huge drift over which the big missiles came looping. Farrell had obviously cut the power of his catapult to take care of the short-range trajectory, but his aim was still excellent.

With as many snowballs as they could carry, the attackers stormed the drift, pelting without aim until their supply was gone and then scooping snow up and throwing without much packing.

Behind the rampart was Farrell with a trough-shaped gadget and a pair of heavy coil springs. Above the rear end of the trough was a duplicator. It dropped a snowball on the trough and the springs snapped forward.

The flying ball caught Don Channing in the pit of the stomach just as he attained the top of the rampart.

When he regained the top once more, the festivities were about over. The shooting was stopped, and the others of his side had Farrell held face upward on the trough while the duplicator dropped snowball after snowball on him.

"Wonder how far we could shoot him," suggested Jim Baler.

Farrell did not think that funny. He struggled to his feet and then grinned. "Fine war," he told them. "Anybody ready for a bit of hot toddy?"

Channing grunted. "Yeah, and a hot bath and a hearty dinner and a seven-hour sleep. So you've taken over Walt's job of making weapons, huh?"

"Walt will be green with envy," said Arden.

Don sobered. "He's missing plenty. I've got all the word out that if he's seen, get here quick. He must have dropped the *Relay Girl* in some out-of-the-way place. He hasn't landed on any regular spaceport."

"There's lots of room for that in the Palanortis Country," said Farrell.

"We've got likker and wassail and turkey," said Arden. "Also mistletoe. Let's go to our place and drink Walt's health and Christine's happiness."

"And that's appropriately apportioned," remarked Don with a grin. "Walt's health and Christine's happiness. But I'll bet a hat that they'd not mind being cold if they knew what fun this is." He brushed snow from the back of his neck and grinned. "Let's add fuel for the inner man," he suggested, leading the way to the Channing apartment.

Walt Franks sat dully in a chair, his eyes glazed over and but half open. Through them dimly, and out of focus, he could see Christine, who was huddled and quiet under the blankets. Her lips were blue and Walt felt dully that this should not be so but had trouble remembering why. There was but one thought in his mind, and that was to awaken Christine before he himself fell asleep. They'd been doing that for—for—for years? No, that was not right. It must have been days, because he hadn't been living with Christine for years. Fact, he hadn't really lived with Christine at all; he'd just found her when this all happened—and—and—

He shook himself, and the motion hurt inside and outside. His muscles ached and where his skin touched a bit of clothing that hadn't been against his skin before, it was bitterly cold. Quickly Walt opened his hands and then drew out his left hand from the pocket and took a quick look at his wristwatch. He stuffed his hand back in again quickly and tried to stand up.

His legs were numb and he almost fell forward, which carried him where he wanted to go anyway, so he just let himself stumble forward heartlessly until he fell on his knees beside the couch.

"Christine," he mumbled.

To himself his voice sounded loud, but it was faint and cracked. It hurt his lips to move, but he moved them for Christine, where he would have moved them for no one else.

"Christine," he said, a bit more clearly and loudly on the second attempt. "Christine!"

Dull eyes opened and cracked lips smiled faintly and painfully.

"Mus' wake up," he warned.

She nodded—painfully slowly. She made no effort to move.

Walt stood up and made his way to the accursed feeding machine. He pressed the button and collected dollops of hot food in a shallow bowl. It was a mess because coffee mingled with the many other items of a fine balanced diet, including appetizer and dessert, made just that—a mess. But it was hot and it was food, and though there was not a single bit of silverware in the place, Walt managed. He carried the bowl to the couch and offered it to Christine, who protestingly permitted Walt to feed her with his fingers. She did not eat much, but it did warm her. Then Walt finished the plate.

Christine shuddered under the blankets. "Suits losing ground?" she asked.

Walt nodded pitifully.

Christine thought that over for a full minute. Then she said: "Must get up, Walt."

Walt wanted to let her stay there, but he knew that she must arise and move in order to keep from freezing. He nodded dumbly.

"Losing ground," he said, meaning the heated suits. Minutes he considered it. Long minutes . . .

There was suddenly a faint crackling noise, and a pungent odor. It increased without either of them noticing it because their senses were numbed. A curl of smoke wreathed Walt's chest and rose above his face and got into his eyes. He coughed and tears came, and the salty water dribbled down his cheeks, dropped to his suit, and froze.

"Something burning," he mumbled, looking around to see what it was.

"It's you!" cried Christine.

Walt looked down at his hip, where the tiny power tube was, and saw it smoking. As he watched, flame burst from the inside and came through.

He shucked the suit just as it burst into open flames, and watched it burn on the metal floor. He warmed himself against the flames, but they were too meager to really help, and five minutes later all that was left of the heated suit was a still-operating power tube and a tangled maze of red-hot heater-resistance wire.

Walt shivered. Beneath the suit he wore the usual slacks and short-sleeved shirt, and it was pitifully inadequate. The dullness that had been assailing him for hours reasserted itself—strengthened by the exertion of removing the suit—and helped not at all by the scant warmth from the charred remains.

He reeled dizzily, his eyes half closed; beads of ice from the tears on his lashes gave the scene a dazzlingly sparkling tone that prevented him from seeing clearly.

He fell forward and his body twitched violently as his skin touched the viciously cold metal of the floor.

Christine hurled the covers back and with great effort pulled and lifted Walt onto the couch. She covered him and then leaned down and kissed him with dry, cracked lips. As she stood up, she felt a spear of pain at her side.

Looking, she found her suit on fire as Walt's had been. As she fumbled with cold fingers at the fastenings, she realized that only the added warmth of the blankets had kept both suits from burning out at the same time. For they were duplicated models and were identical; therefore they would burn out at exactly the same temperature.

She shivered in her thin summer frock even though she stood with the flames licking at her sandals.

Then there were two useless tangles of wire on the floor, their red-hot wires struggling hopelessly against the monstrous quantity of cold.

Christine shuddered convulsively, and turned slowly to look at Walt. He was asleep already.

The sleep of frozen death.

Christine's eyes filled with tears, which she brushed away quickly. She smiled faintly.

It seemed warmer under the blankets, or maybe it was warmer there beside him. His arm went around her instinctively, though he slept, and Christine pressed against him partly to gain what warmth there was from him and partly to give him what warmth there was in her.

It was warmer beneath the blankets.

Or, she thought just before the dizzying but welcome waves of black slumber crept over her, this is that feeling of warmth that goes before—

"Now that," said Arden with complimentary tones, "is something that duplicating can't buy."

She meant the twenty-piece orchestra that filled the vast hall with music. It was an immense place, for it contained three thousand people, all talking or dancing. Joe presided over a bowl of punch that would have made Nero die of jealousy—it was platinum, fifteen feet in diameter, studded profusely with huge gold chasings and inlays, and positively alive with diamonds and emeralds. On the edge of the huge bowl hung Joe's original sign, and Joe handled a huge silver ladle to scoop the highly charged punch into small gold cups.

Linna Johnson, she of the formerly bejeweled class, proudly displayed a bit of handmade jewelry and told everybody that Keg had made it for her. Barney Carroll was holding forth at great length to a group of women on the marvels and mysteries of digging in the Martian desert for traces of the lost Martian civilization, while his partner Jim was explaining to Chuck and Freddie Thomas just how they intended to let a matter transmitter do their excavating for them. Wes Farrell was explaining the operation of the element filter and heterodyne gadget that produced pure synthetic elements to a woman who nodded gayly and didn't understand a word he said but would rather be baffled by Farrell than be catered to by anyone else.

"It's quite a sight," Don agreed. "Never before."

Arden sighed. "And never again!"

"It's an occasion to remember," grinned Don. "Christmas Eve at Venus Equilateral! Here's Triplanet Films with their cameramen, and they tell me that the Interplanetary Network has called off all Christmas broadcasts at midnight, Terra Mean Time, to carry the sounds of revelry from Venus Equilateral as a Christmas celebration program."

"Yeah," said Arden, "and tomorrow I've got to go to church and explain to a class of Sunday Schoolsters how and why Santa Claus can make the haul across a hundred million miles of space in an open sleigh powered with a batch of reindeer."

"Some blowout," said Michael Warren, coming up with his wife.

Hilda Warren smiled happily. "I don't think I've ever appreciated how many people really worked here," she said.

"Shucks," grinned Don, "I've been trying to get along by merely mumbling about half of the names myself. And if I may point it out, Hilda, you're standing under a hunk of mistletoe." Before she could say anything, Don had proceeded with great gusto, to the amusement of Warren.

Arden shook her head. "The rascal has been standing there for a half-hour because people are always coming up to tell him it's a fine party."

"Method in my madness," Channing nodded.

A faint tinkle of bells sounded in the distance, and as people became aware of them Keg Johnson tapped Don on the shoulder and said: "The fleet's in, Don. Here comes our professional Santa Claus. And the fleet is going to land and await midnight tomorrow night. The Johnson Spaceline is going to have the honor of hauling bag, baggage, foot, horse, and marines to Terra. Everything ready?"

Don nodded absently. He listened to the sleigh bells for a moment and then said: "Everything of a personal nature is packed. The rest is worthless. How many men have you?"

"About two hundred."

"Then tell 'em to forget the packing and join in. After this mass, we won't even notice a couple of hundred more. But tell me if S. Claus is going to drive that thing right in here?"

Keg nodded. "He's running on snow in the corridor, of course, but he's equipped with wheels for hard sledding."

The orchestra broke into "Jingle Bells" and a full dozen reindeer came prancing in through the large double doors. They came in in a whirl of snow and a blast of icy air from the corridor, and they drew a very traditional Santa Claus behind them in the traditional sleigh laden with great bags.

Before the door was closed on the veritable blizzard in the hallway, several men came in hauling a great log that they placed on the monstrous fireplace at one end of the vast hall.

The only incongruity was the huge spit turned by a gear train from a motor run from a beam-energy tube.

Santa Claus handed out a few gifts to those nearest and then mounted the orchestra platform. He held up his hands for silence.

"Before I perform my usual job of delivering gifts and remembrances," he said, "I want you to hear a word or two from your friend and mine—Don Channing!"

This brought a roar. And Channing went to the platform slowly.

"My friends," said Don, "I've very little to say and I'm not going to take a lot of time in saying it. We've had a lot of hard work on Venus Equilateral and we've had a lot of fun. Venus Equilateral has been our home—and leaving our home tomorrow night will be as great a wrench as was the leaving of our original homes so many years ago to come to Venus Equilateral. It will for me. I shall darned well be homesick.

"Yet—this job is finished. And well done. Frankly," he grinned cheerfully, "we started out just covering the planet-to-planet job. We extended that to include planet-to-ship, and then when they added ship-to-planet, it automatically made it ship-to-ship. Well, we've got it all set now to make it anywhere-at-all without relay. People speak of Venus Equilateral and forget the 'Relay Station' part of the name. A relay station is no darned good without something to relay—and you know, good people, I'm completely baffled as of now for a communications project. I can't conceive of a problem in communications that would be at all urgent. But . . ."

A loop of the maze of heater wire from the fire-ruined suit twisted on the bare metal floor. The bare metal shorted part of the long loop and the remaining section grew hotter as a consequence. The expansion caused by heat made the tangle of wire writhe slowly, and two crossing lines touched, shorting the overheated loop still more. It flared incandescent and blew like a fuse and showered the room with minute droplets of molten metal that landed on wall and floor solid, but yet warm.

A tiny stinging rain of them pelted Walt's face. This penetrated when few other things would have. Walt stirred coldly painful, and his eyes struggled against a slightly frozen rim that tried to hold eyelash to cheek.

It took minutes for the idea to filter through his mind: *What woke me?*

He could not know that it had been his subconscious mind. To the trained electronics technician the arc discharge of a shorted circuit has a special meaning whereas to the untrained it may be but an ambiguous *"Splat!"* The blowing of a fuse penetrates the subconscious and brings to that part of the brain a realization of the facts in the case, just as a trained musician will wince when the third violin strikes a sour note in the midst of full orchestration.

Instinctively, Walt's trained brain considered the source. Ponderously slow, he turned a painful head to look on the floor at the remains of the ruined suits. As he watched, the still writhing metal shorted again and a loop glowed brightly, then died as the additional heat expanded it away from its short circuit.

Walt wondered about the time.

He found his left arm trapped beneath Christine and he turned from one side to the other and he considered her dully. She slept, and was as still as death itself.

Walt released his arm, and the motion beneath the blankets pumped viciously cold air under the covers and chilled his already stiff body. He looked at his watch; it was nine hours since he'd awakened Christine before.

Walt felt no pain, really. He wanted desperately to snuggle down under the covers once more and return to oblivion, where it was warmer and pleasant. But there was something—

Something—

Taking his nerve in his teeth, Walt forced his brain to clear. Christine didn't deserve this.

Yet if he got out from beneath those covers he would most certainly freeze in a matter of minutes. Yet he must—do—something.

He considered the tubes and their tangles of wire through puffed, half-closed eyes. He thought he was moving with lightning rapidity when he leapt out of the bed, but his motion was insufferably slow. He dropped on his knees beside the tubes and with his bare hands fumbled for the hot wires. They seared his fingers and sent pungent curls of smoke up to torture his nose, but his fingers felt no pain and his olfactory sense did not register the nauseous odor of burning flesh.

He found the switch and turned off the tiny tubes.

He collected loop after loop and shorted them close to the terminals of the two cubes. A hundred feet of wire looped back and forth in a one-inch span across the terminal lugs would produce a mighty overload. It made a bulky bundle of wire, the very mass of which would prevent it from heating to incandescence and blowing out in a shower of droplets.

One chance in a million!

Just one!

Walt snapped the switches on.

For to the trained technician, a blown fuse is not an ill. It is a symptom of an ill, and no trained technician ever replaced a blown fuse without attempting to find out why and where the overload occurred.

Walt crept painfully back to bed and huddled under the blankets against Christine.

"Kiddo," he said in a dry, cracked voice, "I did what I could! Honest."

The oblivion of cold claimed Walt again . . .

". . . there is but one unhappy note in this scene of revelry," continued Don Channing a bit soberly. "We're sorry that Walt Franks took this opportunity of rushing off to get matrimonially involved with Christine Baler. He didn't know this bash was imminent, of course, otherwise he'd have been here. We all love Walt and he'll be unhappy that he missed the blowout here. Fact is, fellers, I'd give eight years off of the end of my life to get any kind of word from Walt—"

An alarm clamored in the hallway and Wes Farrell jumped a foot. He headed for the door, but Channing stopped him with a gesture.

"Friend Farrell forgets that we no longer care," laughed Channing. "That was the main fuse in the solar energy tubes blowing out and we won't be needing them anymore. It is sort of pleasant to know that a fuse blew—a thing that was formerly master and we the slave—and that we don't have to give a hoot whether it blew or not. Let it blow, Wes. We don't need power anymore!

"So I suggest that we all have a quick one on Walt Franks, wishing him health and happiness for the rest of his life with Christine née Baler, even though the big bum did cheat us out of the privilege of kissing his bride.

"And now, I'm going to step aside and let Santa Claus take over."

There was a thunderous roar of applause, and Channing rejoined Arden and the rest of them, who had sort of gravitated together.

"Merry Christmas," he grinned at them.

Keg Johnson nodded. "Merry Christmas—and on to Terra for your Happy New Year!"

They raised their glasses, and it was Wes Farrell who said: "To Walt—and may he be as happy as we are!"

Arden chuckled. "We used to sing a song about 'Walt's Faults,' but there's one thing: Walt would have replaced that fuse even though we didn't need it. The old string saver!"

A messenger came up and tapped Don on the shoulder. Channing turned with an apologetic smile to his guests and said: "I get more damned interruptions. They tell me that someone is knocking on the spacelock door. If anyone here knows any prayers, let 'em make with a short one. Pray this—whoever it is—knows something about Walt."

Don left the party and went along the cold, snow-filled corridor to his office. As one of the few remaining places where operations were in full tilt, Channing's office was where any visitor would be conducted. Once the business was finished, Channing could hurl the guest into the middle of the big party, but the party was no place to try to conduct business in the first place.

So, with heels on desk, and a glass of Scotch from his favorite file drawer, Don Channing idled and waited for the visitor.

The knock came and Channing said: "Come in!"

Two policemen—the Terran Police—entered quietly and stood aside as the third man entered cautiously.

Channing's feet came off the desk and hit the floor with a crash.

"The specter at the feast," snorted Channing. "Of all the people I know, I least expected you—and wanted to see you least. I hope it is a mutual affection, Kingman."

"Don't be godlike, Channing," said Kingman coldly. "You may think you're running things all your way, but some people object to being made a rubber stamp."

"Look, Kingman, get whatever is on that little mind of yours damn well off it, so I can continue as I was."

"Channing, I have here papers of disenfranchisement."

"In-deed?"

"Right."

Channing smiled.

"Don't be so damned superior," Kingman snapped.

"Tell me, Markus, just why this disenchantment takes place?"

"Venus Equilateral suspended operations on twenty December," said Kingman. "Without notice nor permission nor explanation. Since the relay beams of Venus Equilateral have carried nothing for a period beyond that permitted for suspension of operations by the Interplanetary Communications Commission, they have seen fit to revoke your license."

"Well! And after all I've done," said Channing.

"You see—you think you can get away with anything. Doubtless this ultra-frigid condition was the cause of failure?"

"Possibly. And then again, maybe someone wanted to make ice cream."

"Don't be flippant. You'll find these papers are final and complete. You'll not be able to talk your way out of it."

"Tell me, O Learned Legal Light, who is going to run Venus Equilateral when I am far away?"

"Some time ago Terran Electric applied for a franchise and took an option pending failure at Venus Equilateral. This failure has taken place and Terran Electric now controls—"

"I gather that you've been forced to put Terran Electric up as bail for the license?"

Kingman flushed.

"Find that Terran Electric wasn't worth much?" Channing jeered.

"Sufficient," said Kingman.

"Did it ever occur to you that maybe Venus Equilateral wasn't worth much either?" asked Channing.

"I'll make it work for me. And I'll also report that one of your wild experiments got loose and nearly froze the station out completely. I still say that if you'd stopped toying around with everything that came along, Venus Equilateral would still be a running corporation."

"I daresay you're right. But the Devil finds work for idle hands, you know. So just what is the future holding?"

"Channing, your attitude is entirely frivolous, and unconvinced that I mean business. To convince you, I'm going to give you twelve hours to relinquish the station and be on your way from here!"

"May I point out that this is Christmas?"

"I've investigated that," returned Kingman. "I find that Christmas is a completely Terran date and is therefore legal for any and all legal action on any planet or place removed from the interplanetary boundary of the planet Terra. That, Channing, has been established to the Channing Layer."

"And how about the personnel? Must they get the hell off, too?" Channing asked loftily.

"You and your managerial cohorts must leave. Those upon whom the continued service of communications depends are requested to remain—under new management."

"You're taking on a big bite," grinned Channing. "I trust you can chew it."

"I need no help from the likes of you."

"Good. And now that you've had your say, I'll return to my own affairs. Make yourself at home; you'll not be bothered here."

Kingman nodded slowly. He'd expected a battle, and he believed that Channing did not think it true. Channing would damn well find out once he appeared before the Interplanetary Communications Commission. In the meantime, of course, he might as well remain in the office. There was an apartment next door, and it was comfortable.

He did not notice that every very personal thing had been removed from Channing's office. Frankly, Kingman did not care. He had had everything his own way.

The senior officer spoke. "You need us anymore, Mr. Kingman?"

"No," replied the new owner of Venus Equilateral.

"Then we'll return to duty on Terra," said the officer.

Channing went back to the party and spent ten minutes telling his friends what had happened. Then he forgot about it and joined in the merrymaking, which was growing more boisterous and uninhibited by the moment. It was in the wee small hours of the clock—though not necessarily the night, for there is no such thing on Venus Equilateral—when the party broke up and people bundled up and braved the howling blizzard that raged up and down the halls.

Home to warmth and cheer—and bed.

Arden sat up in bed and looked sleepily around the dark bedroom. "Don," she asked with some concern, "you're not sick?"

"Nope," he replied.

Arden pursed her lips. She snapped the light on and saw that Don was half dressed.

"What gives?" she demanded, slipping out of bed and reaching for a robe.

"Frankly—"

"You've been stewing over that blown-out fuse."

He nodded sheepishly.

"I knew it. Why?"

"Those tubes have been running on a maintenance load for days. They shouldn't blow out."

"Critter of habit, aren't you?" Arden grinned.

Don nodded. "A consuming curiosity, I guess."

Arden smiled as she continued to climb into her clothing. "You're not the only one in this family who has a lump of curiosity," she told him.

"But it's—"

"Don," said his wife seriously, "rules is rules and electricity and energy are things I'm none too clear on. But I do know my husband. And when he gets up out of a warm bed in the middle of the night to go roaming through a frozen world, it's urgent. And since the man in question has been married to me for a number of years, getting up out of a warm bed and going out into snow and ice means that the urgency angle is directed at whatever lies at the other end. I want to go see—and I'm going to!"

Channing nodded absently. "Probably a wild-goose chase," he said. "Ready?"

Arden nodded. "Lead on, curious one."

Channing blinked when he saw the light in the room where the solar intake tubes were. He hastened forward to find Wes Farrell making some complex measurements and juggling a large page of equations.

Farrell looked up and grinned sheepishly. "Couldn't sleep," he explained. "Wanted to do just one more job, I guess."

Channing nodded silently.

Arden said: "Don't kid anybody. Both of you want to know why a fuse should blow on a dead line."

Farrell grinned and Channing nodded again. "I—" Don started, but turned as the door opened.

"Thought we'd find you here," said Barney Carroll. Jim Baler added: "We got to arguing as to how and why a fuse should blow on an empty line and decided to ask you."

Arden squinted at Jim. "Did it ever occur to you that we might have been in bed?"

Barney grinned. "I figured if *we* were awake from wondering about it, so would *you-all*. So—"

Jim interrupted. "So what have you found?"

Channing shook his head. "Ask Wes," he said. "He got here first and was measuring the deflecting electrode voltages when I arrived. I note that he has a hunk of copper busbar across the main fuse terminals."

Wes smiled sheepishly. "Had to," he said. "Short was really shorted!"

"So what have you found?"

Farrell pointed to a place on a chart of the station. "About here."

"Spinach!" said Channing. "There isn't anything there!"

Farrell handed the figures to Don. "That's where the short-circuit load is coming from," he said.

"Up there," said Channing, "I'll bet it's hitting close to seventy or eighty degrees below zero. A supercold condition—" He paused and shook his head. "The tube room reached absolute zero some time ago," he said, "and there's no heavy drain to that position."

"Well?" demanded Arden, yawning. "Do we wait until tomorrow morning or go up there now?"

Channing thought for a moment. "We're due to leave in the morning," he said. "Yet I think that the question of why anything up in an empty section of Venus Equilateral should be blowing fuses would belabor us all of our lives if we didn't make this last screwball search. Let's go. Wes, get your portable sun finder, huh?"

"His what?" Arden asked.

"Figger of speech, sweet. We mean a small portable relay tube that we can stick in series with his gawdawful drain and use for a direction finder. I have no intention of trying to scour every storeroom in that area for that which I don't really believe is there."

The main deterrent to swift action was the bitter, bitter cold that stabbed at their faces and hands, which were not enclosed in the electrically heated suits—of which each one of them wore three against the ultraviolent chill.

"There should be a door here," objected Don, reading a blueprint from the large roll he carried under his arm. "Fact is, this series of rooms seems to have been sealed off entirely though the blueprint calls for a door, about here!"

"How would anybody re-seal a doorway?" asked Barney.

"Duplicator," Don said thoughtfully. "And I smell rats!"

"So. And how do we get in?" demanded Arden.

"We break in," said Channing harshly. "Come along, gang. We're going back downstairs to get us a cutter!"

The cutter consisted of a single-focus scanner beam that Don wielded like an acetylene torch. Clean and silently it cut through the metal wall and the section fell inward with a slight crash.

They stepped in through the opening.

"Someone has been homesteading," said Channing in a gritty voice. "Nice prefab home, hey? Let's add housebreaking to our other crimes. I'd like to singe the heels off the character that did this. And I think I'll let the main one simmer."

"Who?" asked Arden.

Channing pointed to the huge energy tube at one end of the room. It bore the imprint of Terran Electric.

"Kingman," he said drily.

Applying his cutter to the wall of the cottage, he burned his way through. "No one living here," he said. "Colder than Pluto in here, too. Look, Wes, here's your short circuit. Tubes from—"

"And here," said Farrell quickly, "are your missing chums!"

Channing came over to stand beside Farrell, looking down at the too-still forms. Baler looked at Channing with a puzzled glance, and Channing shook his head quietly.

Then he said: "I may be wrong, but it strikes me that Walt and Christine interrupted skullduggery at work and were trapped as a consequence. No man, no matter how insane, would ever enter a trap like this willingly. This is neither a love nest nor a honeymoon cottage, Jim. This is a death trap!"

Channing turned from the place and left on a dead run. He paused at the door to the huge room and yelled: "Don't touch 'em till I get Doc!"

By the clock, Christmas Day dawned bright and clear. The strip fluorescents came on in the corridors of Venus Equilateral and there began the inexorable flow of people toward the south end landing stage.

Each man or woman carried a small bag. In this were the several *uniques* he or she possessed and a complete set of recordings on the rest of his personal possessions. Moving was as easy as that—and once they reached Terra, everything they owned could be reproduced at will. It was both glad and sad, the thrill of a new experience to come balancing the loss of the comfortable routine of the old. Friends, however, managed to get aboard the same spacecraft as a general rule and so the pain of parting was spared them.

One by one, the huge ships dropped south and then headed for Terra. One by one, until the three thousand-odd people who lived on, loved, and operated Venus Equilateral through its working years had embarked.

Channing shook hands with Captain Johannson as he got aboard the last remaining ship. Behind Channing came Keg Johnson, who supervised the carrying aboard of Walt Franks and Christine Baler. They were seated side by side in deck chairs on the operating bridge of the spacecraft and Arden came up to stand beside her husband as she asked: "Captain Johannson, you are empowered to perform matrimony?"

Johannson nodded.

"Well," she said, "I'm the matron of honor and this husband of mine intends to be best man. We agree that the couple there have spent too much time living with one another—"

"If she says 'sin' I'll strangle her," groaned Walt.

Christine reached over and took her hand. "She doesn't dare," she said. "She knows it was ah—er—colder than sin!"

Big Jim Baler clenched and unclenched his hands. "I still think we should have called on Mark Kingman," he said in a growl.

Channing shook his head. "And spoil the fine end of a fine holiday? Nope. And also spoil a fine bit of retribution?"

Linna Johnson smiled. "A man of action like Jim finds the finer points of retribution a bit too smooth," she said. "But it'll be plenty rough on Kingman."

"To the devil with Kingman," said Barney Carroll. "I say we ought to commit this ceremony at once and then repair to the bar—or have the bar repair here—and have a last drink to Venus Equilateral."

Walt Franks stood up. "I'm still stiff," he said. "But I'll be damned if I'm going to sit down at my own wedding."

Christine stood beside him. "You're thinking about that 'repair to the bar' and don't want to get left," she told him. "Well, frozen solid or not, I'm sticking tight."

Johannson turned to the pilot and gave the order. The big ship dropped from the platform and they all looked down through the glass dome at the diminishing view of Venus Equilateral.

The captain turned to Channing and asked: "Just what did happen to Mark Kingman?"

"Mark has mortgaged his everlasting black soul to the hilt to maintain communications under the standard franchise. For a period of five years, Mark Kingman must live on that damned station alone in the cold and the loneliness, maintaining once each day a relay contact, or lose his shirt. And because he dropped the *Relay Girl* into the sun when he planned that 'elopement,' we've just confiscated his ship. That leaves Kingman aboard a practically frozen relay station with neither the means to get away nor the ability to handle the situation at all. He must stay, because when he puts a foot on any planet we clap him in jail for kidnapping. He's lost his financial shirt because Venus Equilateral is an obsolete commodity and he'll never regain enough of his personal financial standing to fight such a case. If I were Mark Kingman, about now I'd—"

Channing shook his head, leaving the sentence unfinished. He turned to Walt. "Got a ring handy?"

Wes Farrell held up a greenish metal ring that glinted iridescent colors. "Y'might try this new synthetic," he offered.

Walt shook his head. He fumbled in an inner pocket and came up with a small band that was very plain. "This is a certified unique," he said proudly. "It was my mother's, and grandmother's, too."

Then, with Venus Equilateral still visible in the port below and a whole sky above, Captain Johannson opened his book and started to read. Behind them was work and fun and pain, and before them—

Was the exciting, unchartered future.

Interlude

Twenty-seven years have passed since Don Channing and his merry men invented Venus Equilateral out of a job, and closed the relay station after one last bash. The matter transmitter, which turned out to be a matter duplicator as well, not only brought chaos to the economy, but brought to conclusion the communications industry as an interplane-

tary business. It also made "work" a nasty, four-letter word.

But if one expects chaos to last indefinitely in the face of plenty, one does not understand human nature. For the household duplicator and its file of recordings became a way of life. So, with its belly filled, its back clothed, and its person housed, the human race cast about for new mountains to climb, new follies to indulge, new mischief to get into, and new happiness to pursue. New problems arose. When the maw of the home duplicator needed only to be filled with rubbish when its owner wanted something, it is true that the trash piles were recycled, but it is also true that backyards and the landscape began to look like strip mines.

Ecology, this time in favor of beauty, arose and pointed a bony finger to Outer Space where there was plenty of rubbish—that could be converted as easily into hot water, warm air, and rich topsoil as it was to manufacture bricks, gold, or transactinide elements. So, with the duplicator to provide and maintain a habitable environment, the satellites of the Outer Planets, and Pluto itself, were Terra-Converted and colonized.

THE EXTERNAL TRIANGLE

Some miles south of Bifrost Bridge, which spans the River Styx between the twin cities of Mephisto and Hell, on the newly transformed and settled Pluto, there is an island some acres in area. Upon it is a gracious house, flanked on one side by a low building that is obviously a workshop, and on the other side by the tall and unmistakable form of an aging spacecraft, the *Relay Girl II*, a replacement after Mark Kingman's destruction of the original at the closing of Venus Equilateral Relay Station.

The house belongs to Don and Arden Channing.

The years have been fairly kind to Don. He retains most of his teeth and his hair, and by a combination of luck and good management he has avoided that malady euphemistically called "Falling arches of the chest." His hair is gray, but he is cheerful. But if the years have been kind to Don, they have been even more so to Arden. Hers is the beauty of maturity, assisted by more than a quarter of a century of a well-mated marriage and the secure knowledge that their daughter appears to be facing a repetition.

The unmistakable sound of a jet-helicopter making an approach caught Arden's attention, but not Don's, for he was at his usual task of drawing diagrams on a pad of quadrille paper (Arden had cured him of using the tablecloth) and discarding them in disgust. She caught his attention by saying, "We seem to have company."

He looked at the 'copter. "That ain't company, that's the whole damn Franks family."

First out, while the blades were still awhirl, came Jeffrey Franks, followed by Diane Franks, née Channing. They raced for the house, leaving Walt and Christine to follow.

The years have been kind to Walt Franks, but the combination of Christine's cooking and his own nature have contributed to a spare tire which, in combination with a rotund face and a bald scalp, make him resemble a Santa Claus during the off-duty season. He climbed out slowly, then paused to assist his wife, whose main change in the passing years has been hair turned ashen. Neither of them were inclined to make a mad dash; they sauntered slowly toward the Channing home, hand in hand.

Diane Franks burst in first. "It's true!" she cried. "Confirmed."

Don Channing looked up at her. "You'll simply have to put a stop to it. I'm much too young to be a grandfather."

"The facts say otherwise," said his wife.

"I'll leave home."

"Running out isn't going to change anything. Why not get used to the idea? Then when it happens, it won't be such a shock."

Walt came in with Christine. The three women immediately clustered together.

Don eyeballed Walt and said, "Do you realize what your son has been doing to my daughter?"

"All very legal," asserted Walt. "Been going on in the Franks family ever since a couple of amoebae named Frank and Francine climbed out of the primordial swamp and decided to try fusion instead of fission. How does the Channing Tribe increase?"

"Telepathy," said Don, "modified by some ground rules to include hand-holding and an occasional peck on the cheek."

"Yeah, I'll bet," Walt chuckled. "So, okay—break out the champagne, gran'pa."

"Don't call me gran'pa!" yelped Don.

"If I can take it so can you," Walt laughed.

Don turned and called to Jeffrey Franks, "You young despoiler of my daughter's virtue, go run the special recording, kept for special occasions, through the duplicator. Your father thinks champagne is in order."

Arden looked at him. "Gee," she said. "We thought you'd never ask."

Jeffrey exited willingly upon his errand, and as he left, Walt looked down at some of the drawings strewn around Don's chair. "What's all this, Don?"

"Puzzle I've been working on for some time."

"Puzzle? What's it about?"

"Something that has been bugging me for quite a while. Way back when we invented us out of the economic mess that we had duplicated ourselves into, why, that old bigmouth Keg Johnson told me that the matter transmitter we'd invented wasn't that at all. We scan a solid, send a signal analog of the thing, particle by particle, then reconstitute it at the receiving end. That's why we can record the signal and make a million duplicates. Keg wants something that will transmit a certified 'unique' and keep it certifiable as a unique, since it will be the same object—not a faithful replica."

"Some problem," Walt said, his eyes going out of focus as he mused over it.

Jeffrey returned with the champagne bucket and, after expertly twirling the bottle, he as efficiently extracted the cork and topped up glasses all around, the ladies included.

Handing out the glasses, Jeffrey paused to look at the

diagram as Don proposed a toast to the imminent, and inescapable, event.

After the first polite sip, Jeffrey said, "I hate to sound rash, but—er—you—er—were all born too early."

"Meaning what?" demanded his father.

"Well, Dad, you and Mr. Channing were running Venus Equilateral on *vacuum tubes*. Thermionic devices. Power klystrons and wide-band traveling wave tubes, and things like that. Why, you didn't even know about parametric amplifiers."

"So?"

"Look," said Jeffrey, "back in those olden days, when you started to design some doodad, you went out and got tubes and resistors and capacitors and all sorts of junk. You actually *built* flipflops, and/or gates and monostable multivibrators. You're still thinking that way."

Don shook his head. "I'm afraid so. We dogs are both too old to be taught a lot of new tricks. So, you tell us what you are thinking about."

"Well, the advent of the solid-state device opened up a whole new concept. The old electron tube was as crude as opening an oyster with a hammer. But once the semi-conductor came in, quantum mechanics stuck its nose in the tent like the proverbial camel, and like the camel it took over the tent. Now, let's review what we know about the tunnel diode."

"You tell us."

"Well, sir, Werner Heisenberg once pointed out that under some circumstances the exact position of the electron can be determined, but not its energy, and under other conditions the exact energy can be measured, but then its position becomes uncertain. Between these extremes, the laws of probability take over, and if the conditions are right, one can assume with some degree of confidence that the electron has as probable a chance of existing on the mythical planet of Aldebaran as it has of being in this living room.

"In the tunnel diode," he went on, "there is the interface between the two terminals, and for some small distance across this interface there is a so-called forbidden gap, in which the electron cannot exist. But bias the tunnel diode properly, and the electrons will slyly disappear from one side and reappear on the other—as if they'd passed through a tunnel—hence the name. In other words, there is a flow of current across the gap."

"And you're suggesting that if this can take place with electrons, we ought to make out with heavier stuff?"

"Yes."

Don eyed his son-in-law with amusement. "There is a lot of your old man in you, Jeff. No man but a Franks could cross the credibility gap by leaping from a hare-brained idea to a foregone conclusion."

Christine Franks looked at Arden and pointed at the men. "I think we've lost our husbands for another session."

"Not for a while," replied Arden. "They're still babbling about it. We can enjoy their company through the first phase, which always begins with the old hackneyed phrase 'Let us repair to the bar,' where there are always new tablecloths and nice black pencils."

The first operation, once the tablecloth session closed, was a bit of hardware-building in the workshop. This produced a large model of the tunnel diode—which is usually quite small—made with the terminals movable and constructed of coupled crystals.

Now, the undoing of Venus Equilateral as a communications relay had been the coupled-crystal effect. With the matter duplicator, exactly identical replicas of anything could be produced. By the philosophy of Einsteinian reasoning that argues that if no measurement can be made to show a difference between two things, they are then manifestations of the same thing, two identically duplicated crystals are one and the same. Twitch one and the other says, "Ouch!"

Progress was slow. The tunnel diode as conceived, and built by the tens of millions, is a solid-state device, meaning that it comes in one chunk. The problem was to separate the terminal semiconducting elements at their interface—the forbidden gap—and do what was necessary to keep the flow of tunneling electrons across it.

There was a minor celebration when their meters registered the trickle of a current across a gap of a thousandth of a millimeter.

The celebration was minor, because the thing worked as predicted. Since the theory of the tunnel diode is sound, they all *knew* that the Heisenberg Uncertainty Principle ruled over electrons crossing a physical gap, as it did over electrons crossing a mere forbidden gap at the interface between two semiconductors in physical contact.

Then the gap was increased to a millimeter, to a centimeter, and finally the micrometer screw was removed, the two terminals remounted on separated stands, and separated by meters. It was unnerving, at first, to walk between the two, knowing that there was a statistical flow of electrons passing, hidden, from one to the other. But they were not only hidden from sight or detection, they disappeared physically from one terminal and reappeared physically at the other. The men felt nothing: nothing but uneasiness.

Then the "other" terminal—that is, the receptor—was moved from the Channing workshop to the Franks attic, some eight kilometers distant.

Next came nuclei. Protons and deuterons are easy to come by; the ion source has been known since long before the cyclotron. They are also easy to detect and to identify; the Aston mass spectrograph was a commercially available instrument in the middle of the twentieth century. And after protons and deuterons came helium nuclei, and then the heavier ions: singly ionized oxygen and nitrogen.

Carbon dioxide was the first molecule to tunnel the gap. And at this point, Don Channing said, "We may be overlooking something."

"You mean that everything that goes over has to be ionized?"

"No," said Don. "That doesn't bother me. Once we get to trying gross matter, we can simply slap an electrostatic charge on it. What bothers me is that we're not really zapping something solid over there. So far as I know, it still may be 'flowing' as a stream of electrons flow. In fact, I'm sure of it."

"What have you in mind?" asked Franks.

"Well, we're about to rebuild these things, anyway.

Let's put a couple of small cabinets at either end and try an all-at-once zap of a gas volume."

"How small?" Walt asked quietly.

"Couple of cubic centimeters."

"Shucks. Why not a full cubic meter?"

"I'm a little concerned—"

"Let's compromise," suggested Walt.

Don eyed his lifelong friend. "From long years of close experience," he said, "I think I'm about to be outmaneuvered. Walter, what, for example, is the size of the cabinet you've been building in your attic?"

"Twenty by thirty by forty centimeters. And—"

"It just so happens that you have it in your 'copter?"

"I did want to show it to you, Don. It's an heirloom. Dad used to use it to keep the beer cold. Great fisherman, my father."

"And you've been cherishing Father's ice chest all these decades so we could use it for our matter transporter? Wonderful! How sentimental! How truly thoughtful! And, I suppose, the scion of the Franks family, that despoiler of my daughter's innocence, is now connecting its duplicate to the receiving terminal at your place."

"Why, yes. It just so happens—"

"Walt, less circumlocution and more action. Go bring in Pappy's ice chest."

Walt went out; he reappeared a moment later with a metal cabinet complete with door and latch. "Connecting it up is no problem, Don. Father, you see, had plans to convert it to an electric refrigerator, so he equipped it with connectors."

"And so thoughtful of him to use those high-voltage insulators for the feet. That's what I call foresight."

"One more point," said Walt. "Let's toss this in for good old empirical information."

He held up a large, sixty-degree prism of some transparent material that he identified as one of the synthetic glasses with a high index of refraction.

"Jeff has measured everything about this to fifteen or twenty decimal places," he said. "If we zap it over there in one piece, he can measure it, and if it goes all right, we're several steps ahead."

"Okay," said Don with a shrug. "Here goes."

"You push the button."

"Nope," said Don. "It's *your* father's ice chest. *You* push."

"Okay. One! Two! Three! *Fire!*"

At the word, all hell broke out. The cabinet imploded with an ear-shattering, high-pitched *Crack* and for a moment there came the whistling screech of air rushing in through jagged cracks in metal.

Over at the Franks place, the receiving cabinet exploded with an equally shattering blast that ripped the cabinet apart along the corners and seams and bulged the flat surfaces outward. A roughly rectangular hole marked the exit of the cabinet door through the wall, and every window in the room was shattered outward.

They were surveying the ruin when Arden came rushing in. "Migawd," she blurted. "What happened?"

"My dear," said Don. "At this end, Walter has just demonstrated that old Torricellian remark that 'Nature abhors a vacuum.' At the other end, our son-in-law has most likely been observing the truth of that statement that two things cannot occupy the same place at the same time."

"I have the unpleasant notion that someone is going to be pessimistic," Walt said. "I'm about to be lectured about safety and about looking ahead, and about planning, when the important point—being grossly overlooked if not blatantly ignored—is that we did indeed transmit matter."

"Arden, get on the pipe and ask Jeff if we did indeed zap that prism over there."

"One problem I foresee," said Walt. "Are we going to have to pull a hard vacuum on these cabinets, or conduct all transport operations from the surface of airless satellites?"

"Neither sounds eminently acceptable," said Don. "But I think we can make it run quietly by arranging a double switch, swapping what's in that cabinet for what's in this."

"Jeff's on the intercom," said Arden.

She flipped a switch, and the loudspeaker said, "I'm half deaf. Someone blew the roof off the joint."

"Forget the roof," said his father. "We needed a new

one, anyway. The important thing is that prism. Did it come over?"

There were rummaging sounds on the intercom, and then Jeff returned. "If someone likes solid-problem jigsaws made of cut glass, and doesn't mind a few hundred missing pieces, and has a lot of time and infinite patience, one might be able to restore it—partially. It sort of got fractured."

"Okay, Jeff," said Don. "Call in the cleanup crew and the roofing contractor, and then let's all have lunch. Walt, you get out the crystal ball and make contact with Madame Ouija and ask her to get the specifications for that ice chest from your father's blithe spirit."

"Oh," said Walt airily, "those were duplicates. I have a lot of them. Thought they might come in handy. Now, about that lunch?"

The economy had been ruined by the matter duplicator; when the turn of a switch, using the proper recording, can produce anything from Sunday dinner, steaming hot, to a new tire for the family wagon, not only does man get lazy, but nothing remains worth anything. No, Hilda the maid doesn't wear faithful replicas of the crown jewels; Hilda just isn't the maid anymore.

And nothing is worth anything as a medium of exchange.

Then Wes Farrell discovered the synthetic element called identium, which exploded with ruinous violence when it was touched by the scanning beam of the matter transmitter-duplicator. Identium became the medium of exchange, and the stuff upon which contracts and binding agreements were inscribed.

Of course, once something is uncovered to the amazement of all, the next thing is to find it on every hand. On the satellites of the outer planets and upon Pluto itself, crystals and minerals born of extreme cold and lack of pressure—the opposite of the diamond—were discovered, and many of these refused dissection under the scanning beam.

Keg Johnson's spaceline carried humans, and as he put it, "the mail" and then these precious minerals that could not be scanned and transmitted, nor recorded and reproduced; and Life Went On in an oddball economy. But then, all economy is oddball.

So, with the success at zapping solid matter across the forbidden gap of about eight kilometers, Channing contacted Keg Johnson over the coupled-crystal communicator.

"Keg?" asked Channing. "Brace yourself. We're about to bankrupt you again."

"I'm scared," said Keg cheerfully. "Don, you and your crew could always solve problems, but you always waited until they hit you between the eyes before you bent a brain cell. Singly or collectively, you fellows couldn't program a fight in an Irish bar on Boylston Street in Boston on the Eve of Saint Patrick. Now, what have you blithering geniuses cooked up, and why do you think I'm ruined?"

"You chided me, twenty-five years ago, for not building a *real* matter transmitter," Don said with some pleasure. "Keg, we're going to transmit not only identium, but any other certified unique. Not a facsimile, nor the analog-scan signal, but the item itself. Once you get your receiver plugged in, we can pour anything into the hopper and zap it across the Solar System. The *thing*, the *stuff*, the *artifact*, itself."

"Well, I knew you'd do it sometime," Keg said. "But have you taken the Walt Franks habit of extreme extrapolation? How do you know your devil machine will cross space?"

"Oh, we set up a station on Neptune's moon, Triton. Neptune, you'll recall, has been the outermost planet since Pluto crossed its orbit in the Seventies, but Neptune is a goodly heliocentric angle ahead of Pluto—like fifty-five degrees."

"Damned near libration point," Keg chuckled. "Tell me, Don, is Pluto going to be 'Neptune Equilateral' or is Neptune going to be 'Pluto Equilateral'?"

"You ground-gripping administrative types always have the quaint notion that the libration points are some sort of four-space gravitational cusp, or a detent stop," said Don. "The celestial object that passes through one of them doesn't go *'Zock!'* into lock-tight position. They stay in the libration point only when they're moving along the orbit where the libration point is. Anyway, we've zapped stuff over to Triton. Now we intend to zap some over to Earth. Okay?"

"Sure—and will you wager against me that it won't put me out of business?"

"Nope. I've seen you at work, Keg. So—"

"Whoa, fellow! There's more important information missing."

"But—"

"Why, you supreme egotist, you. Goddammit, Donald, it's known all over that your daughter is great with child. How're they doing?"

"The proper phrase is 'Great with children.' Doctor says it's twins."

"Take courage, Don. I think the maternity folks may have lost a father once about four hundred years ago—but there is no record in history of losing a grandfather. Kiss Arden for me, Don, and we'll be a-seein' you."

Walt Franks entered with a wire cage containing three small field mice. "These animals are hard to find on Pluto," he said. "I think when we zap these micers to Wes Farrell, on Triton, we'll be cutting the mice population of Pluto by half."

Don chuckled. "Keg is going to get a shock when he finds out that his spaceline isn't going to have anything to carry."

"Still don't bet against Keg," said Walt. "Communication takes two terminals, and Keg's spaceline may be the last means by which we can plant a receiver on Ugggthubbbb."

"On what?"

"The only colonizable planet in the Alpha Centauri System. Now, which of these little fellows do you like for the first?"

"Walt, when you've seen one mouse, you've seen 'em all. Sashay that cage to the cabinet door and let the most curious mouser venture forth. I—"

Channing was interrupted by a screech that might have been heard on Uranus if interplanetary space hadn't existed.

The screecher was Arden, who ran out of breath, inhaled deeply, and then said, "Get those things out of here!"

"This we propose to do—via tunnel transport."

"Well, so long as you get rid of them. And who's going to be on the receiving end?" she asked suspiciously. "Diane?"

"No, we're not about to relieve me of this gran'pa kick by scaring her out of—of—of— Forget it. We're zapping these small rodents over to Triton, where our old pal Wes Farrell is running the receiving end."

Channing poked the intercom button and said, "Wes? Stand by for the live one. Ready?"

"Ready," replied Farrell.

The mouse, running aimlessly about the floor of the transmitting cabinet in the way of mice, quietly disappeared, and reappeared roaming about the receiving cabinet.

"Live one received," reported Wes Farrell. "I doubt that he can appreciate being the first live one to be zapped across about twenty-eight astronomical units of wide-open interplanetary space."

"Okay. Give me a minute-by-minute report."

At the end of the first minute, Farrell reported that the mouse was still acting typically mouselike. At minute two, the mouse had been proffered a bit of fairly high cheese, and had taken it in with mouselike enthusiasm. At minute three, the mouse had relieved himself—in one end and out the other. At four, no change. But at the end of five minutes—

"Don, our mouse friend has suddenly slowed down. He's not squealing as if in pain, it's more like he just simply got tired. Run out of energy. Now he's stopped cold; lain down. Flat. I've nudged him with a stick, but he didn't respond. I'm little judge of mice life, Don, and wouldn't know what to do with a mouse-sized stethoscope if I had one, but I'm very much inclined to think that we have one dead mouse on our hands."

"We'll zap him back," said Don, "and have Mephisto Medical take a look. Stand by for Number Two."

An ordinary citizen, entering a large medical clinic with three very deceased mice and asking that they examine the trio of specimens for the cause of death, would either be curtly invited to leave or quietly invited to become a member of the smile-in ward. But when the citizen bearing the specimens happens to be a well-known scientific type, the director of any such clinic knows that something is going on over and above the development of a new way to dispose of the rodent menace.

His report, made the following morning, was negative. "Mr. Channing," said the director, "there is absolutely no reason for these mice to die. There are signs of anoxia, but no apparent cause."

"Now, since I can carve my medical knowledge on the head of a pin with a dull hatchet, you'll have to explain."

"Suffocation," said the doctor, "to the layman implies fighting for breath in a smoke-filled room or having his windpipe plugged by a blanket. Drowning means gurgling water and not being able to breathe. Fact is, suffocation is a failure of the blood to carry oxygen in and carbon out of the body. So far okay?"

"Yes. Go on."

"First, there is no trace of poison. Your associate on Triton reported that he fed these mice some of the cheese left over from a sandwich, and that the water was from the drinking-water supply. Scratch out poison, Mr. Channing.

"But let's consider suffocation. Veinous blood is notably blue; arterial blood is bright red. Laymen seldom observe veinous blood because hemoglobin acts so fast that if a vein is cut, it reacts with the oxygen of the air and instantly turns red. In monoxide poisoning, for example, the carbon monoxide molecule latches on with—so to speak—both hands, and the veinous blood from the victim is bright red. In cases of oxygen shut off, there is no supply and arterial blood runs blue. That's oversimplified, of course, but your mice show no such anomalies."

"Just like hell," mumbled Channing.

"What was that?" the doctor asked sharply.

"Oh, in the technical world, hell is where all the parts function properly but nothing works. Well, back to the old drawing board."

It was, indeed, back to the old drawing board, but this problem was not to be solved. Animals flipped over to the station on Triton all died, in about the same mysterious pattern. Upon their return, when they could be compared in autopsy to the carefully made pre-trip examinations, no reason could be found.

But in the three weeks that followed the first failure, the old drawing board brought forth a new success. A large packing case was deposited on the lawn of Keg Johnson's new Terran domicile, with an ornate label carrying his name as the addressee. On the six flat sides was a large, two-colored stencil that couldn't have been missed at ninety meters in a high fog:

CERTIFIED UNIQUES

In the case was a batch of smaller boxes, each containing some real or synthetic mineral—including a sheaf of identium documents—that either refused or reacted violently to the matter-scanning beam. The sheaf of identium documents was, upon examination, the certification papers and a copy of an application for a patent for a true artifact transmitter.

As Keg Johnson was reading the details, Walt Franks entered. "How do you like these apples?" he asked Keg.

"Looks like you fellows did it," Keg nodded. "Only two things bother me. First, how much is it going to cost me to buy a piece of this action; and second, do humans merely walk into a booth and dial their destination, or do we go through that old 'Fasten Seat Belts, No Smoking' routine?"

Walt shook his head. "First, we haven't formed any company yet; and second, while getting there may be half the fun, staying alive once you've arrived is more so." Walt explained in some detail. "So until we lick this problem, we're not going to offer passenger service."

"Well, let me know when you begin to get these two things off and running. I want in. Now to other items: how come an old duffer like you came a-spacing across the System?"

"I was elected by default." Walt chuckled. "Don's busy with the experimental work. Since Neptune is at about fifty-five degrees heliocentric from Pluto, it would take Wes Farrell the same time to cross the arc as it takes to run from Pluto to Earth. So I took the good old *Relay Girl* and loaded up with parts for a one-cubic-meter transporter, built the thing here on Earth, and received that humble package for you. I'm expendable in this imminent maternity case, you know. Grandfathers are less important than fathers."

Keg laughed. "Actually, the father isn't important at the time, but none of them believe it. How's things going?"

"Routine, if you believe the medico. Says it's a shame to take his valuable time."

"Sounds fine. We'll keep in touch, Walt. I think I am about to draw up a proposal to incorporate. Both you and Channing are too interested in playing with the nuts and bolts to give serious thought to business. There's always that one way to become useful: be very adept at something distasteful to the other guy."

"I'd be in favor of it," said Walt. "All you can get is a refusal, and what you say about our interest is true. Try it for size."

On the link between Pluto and Triton, Don Channing said, "Wes, we're slowly running the mice population to zero over here. How're they on Triton?"

"Oh, we can catch a few."

"Okay, go catch, and we'll zap a few this direction. Send their examination records along. I think we'd best keep the same autopsy crew operating."

"Will do," replied Farrell on Triton.

Channing had never observed the death of a transported animal. He was a fairly gentle man who had no cruel streak; he felt it deplorable that things should cease to live after being transported, and felt it necessary to continue until they found out why. But there was not enough morbid interest in him to suggest—until now—that the transport process be reversed.

So he watched with as near to a clinical interest as his training for electronics and hardware permitted, ran off the by-now-customary reel of videotape, and then packaged the dead mouse, videotape, and the reel of examination records and headed for the 'copter parked in his heliport. Halfway to the machine, he was stopped by a hail from the house: Arden, dressed for the city, on a stiff walk.

"What gives?" he asked.

"Where are you heading?"

"Mephisto Medical. Got another dead one."

"I hate to use the old cliché—'Killing two birds' makes me nervous. But we're all heading for the same hospital."

"Great! When did the word come, and how far along?"

"Jeffrey called about ten minutes ago. He's been wearing a course in the carpet for about three hours. Delivery-room attendants say it might be within the hour."

Don landed on the hospital roof, although the heliport there was supposed to be for special equipment and emergencies. His small helicopter was immediately hauled over to a far corner, and he and Arden parted, she toward Maternity and he toward Analysis with his package.

When he was finished with his business, he went to Maternity, where he found Arden, Jeffrey, and the family doctor, Farnum, in a three-way.

Farnum turned to Don. "Channing," he asked, "has any of your family any record of Rh negative blood?"

"Not that I know of."

"Well, we've a problem. It's turned up. The kids—fraternal twins, one of each—are Rh negative."

"How serious is this?"

"For the immediate instant, no more than mildly serious. But as time wears on, and nothing is done, it becomes terminal."

"So what must be done?"

"The standard practice is to give the infant a complete, whole blood replacement with a compatible type."

"So let's go," said Don impatiently. "We don't need a high-level conference to come to a sensible decision."

"The decision has been made," said Doctor Farnum. "The problem is implementing it. First, compatible whole blood of their type is fairly rare, but there is a reasonable probability that, by a general broadcast plea, we can get enough to do the trick. Second, we are set up to do it, but it's a process that we seldom face because the incidence of Rh negative offspring from a positive mother is low; and further, there is usually a history of mixed Rh in the family to make plans beforehand—such cases usually are sent early enough in their terms to make preparation."

"Well, if we have time enough, I can get a spacecraft from Keg Johnson."

"How long will it take?"

"Pluto is thirty astronomical units out," said Don, pulling his mini-computer out. "Under one G drive, it would take about eight and a half days to midflight and another eight and a half to the Inner System."

"That's seventeen days. Out of the question."

"Well, if we double the drive to two G, we—"

"Halve the time," finished Doctor Farnum for him, "and also halve the survival time, since higher G force means greater strain on the breathing and blood systems."

"When we're really in a hurry," said Don, "we load up on gravanol and take it at five or six G."

"And suffer the pangs of hell for a week afterward," the doctor added. "But we're not dealing with hardy adults, especially those kept in fair training." He eyed the perceptible bulge around Channing's midsection. "We're dealing with two newly born infants and one mother who's still dopey and pardonably weak."

Distantly, a telephone rang, and an attendant came up. "Mr. Channing? Doctor Wilburs in Analysis would like to speak to you."

"Apologize to Doctor Wilburs for me," said Don. "We've a more personal problem than a dead mouse."

"Dead mouse," said Doctor Farnum. "I've been hearing waiting-room tales about this. What is with this matter transmitter of yours?"

"It does fine on minerals and the like, but kills life."

"I wonder—would that include whole blood?"

"I don't know at what level one can say, 'Here life begins.' But I do know that all of our experiments end the same way. Appearance of anoxia but no evidence of any change in the blood."

"I'll make the arrangements," said Doctor Farnum. "You get your crew alert."

Arrangements.

First was a full hour of wide-band transmission of every characteristic of the compatible blood type that was, to date, known to medical science. Next, the word was broadcast, and whole-blood banks were shipping that blood type to Central Medical Center on Terra. Helicopters especially contrived to transport whole blood carried the precious fluid to the transporting station built by Walter Franks.

A Doctor Knowles was in charge. "First, we test for compatibility," he explained. "We'll do this two ways. They're sending a sample this way, and we're sending a sample from the banks that way. We'll test on either end for compatibility before we risk this many canisters."

"Okay," said Franks nervously.

He put the sample in the chamber and pressed the button. The transfer was instantaneous, and a second later, he handed the sample from Pluto to Doctor Knowles.

"Got it, Don," said Franks.

"Ditto," replied Channing on Pluto.

"My God!" Doctor Knowles exploded. "Compatible? This reacts as if they weren't even within the same gross blood types. Quick coagulation. Odd—"

He deposited a small drop on either end of a slide, one from the sample from Pluto, the other from the banks on Terra.

"Observe," he said tensely. "The whole blood from our banks here on Terra is red—veinous blood turned red upon contact with atmospheric oxygen. The sample from Pluto remains blue. It is not reacting with atmospheric oxygen."

He reached for the telephone; it rang as his hand touched it. The caller was from Doctor Farnum on Pluto.

"Doctor," Farnum said, "we've an odd incompatibility here—and the sample from your blood banks does not react—"

"No," said Doctor Knowles, "it's the sample from Pluto that remains blue."

"Let's both check this."

The samples were reswapped, and as they were all waiting for the result, Don Channing's hand strayed into his side pocket. An envelope. He'd been handed it as he left Maternity, his mind awhirl with plans to set up this blood transmission, and he'd abruptly shoved it in his pocket. With nothing else to do, and with nervous tension making his hands itch, he opened the envelope and read:

> Channing:
>
> The last mouse also died of anoxia—but with this difference: the hemoglobin did not react with oxygen. How do you explain this? None of the others acted that way.
>
> Finholdt—Analysis.

The speaker blurted into life.

"Farnum? Hate to question you, but there is not only complete compatibility, but that sample you alleged to be inert is nicely red when exposed."

Doctor Farnum looked up from his test table. "I was about to report the same thing."

Channing whistled. "Walt—you heard that?"

"Yes. And if you're thinking what I'm thinking, then we've got the problem licked. Both problems."

Channing poked another button. "Stand by, Walt. Conference call." Wes Farrell's voice came in to confirm. "Wes, we think we're on to something. Stand by five."

Don went to a wall plate and began to unscrew it.

Doctor Farnum asked, "What are you up to, Channing?"

"I've got us an idea," said Don. He returned to the machine with two small machine screws in his hand. "Now," he said, "I have two standard wall-plate machine screws, here and ready to go. The first goes direct to Terra. While I'm zapping it off, Wes, I'm sending the other to you. Take a look at it, and then fire it off to Walt."

"I hear you, but I don't understand."

"Wes, in all our experiments—except the last—we returned the dead ones to the point of origin for examination. Making a two-trip each?"

"Yes, now that you mention it. But—"

"Here she goes."

On Terra, Walt Franks said, "It's here—but left-hand threaded."

On Triton, Wes Farrell said, "She's here, but left-hand threaded."

On Terra, Walt said, "The second one arrived. It's as natural as anyone rolling a three-and-four."

"All right," said Don, with a smile. "Walt, get another blood sample, and *transport it to Triton.* Wes, when it arrives, waste no time, but re-zap it over here."

"I still don't follow."

Don said, "Somewhere I've heard that there are more than forty times ten to the six-hundredth power ways of arranging the components that compose the hemoglobin molecule—and of that monstrous figure, only one way has even been found in life. Mightn't a mirror image of the real thing be equal to one of the wrong ways?"

"We'll look into that when we have better time," said Doctor Farnum. "But since we now have complete compatibility"—he held up the blood sample under test—"let's get along with this."

"One moment," Jeffrey Franks interrupted. "You claim the facilities are superior on Terra?"

"That's undeniably true."

"Then think of this," said Jeffrey slowly and calmly. "I'm the only one present that has total authority. No matter what you decide to do for the twins, my permission must be received. It is to my best interest to see them alive and healthy, and it is your medical opinion that they'll receive superior care on Terra. We'll take the chance. Double-zap the twins to Terra."

And so the first to survive the zap from Pluto to Triton to Earth were the twin grandchildren of the men and women who once manned the Venus Equilateral Relay Station, beaming radio communications among the inner planets. To do so, they traversed two nearly equal legs of what Keg Johnson promptly called "The External Triangle."

Interlude

The true matter transmitter, better called a "teleport," changed the mass-transportation habits of the Solar System, just as the matter duplicator had during the days of Venus Equilateral. But the changing life-style caused by the duplicator was still in change: the work started by the duplicator had not quite been completed. There was still to come a changed attitude in the thinking habits of the human race.

Indeed, the change continued for decades, so long indeed that historians misplaced the discovery of identium into a span of years called the "Period of Duplication," during which it became evident that a person's own unique personality was the most important thing in life.

EPILOGUE

IDENTITY

Cal Blair paused at the threshold of the Solarian Medical Association and held the door while four people came out. He entered, and gave his name to the girl at the reception desk and then, though he had the run of the place on a visitor basis, he waited until the girl nodded that he should go on into the laboratories.

Cal's nose wrinkled with the smell of neoform, and he shuddered at the white plastic walls. He came to the proper door and entered without knocking. He stood in the center of the room, as far from the shelves of dangerous-looking bottles on one wall as he could get—without getting too close to the preserved specimens of human viscera on the other wall. A cabinet, with its glint of chrome-iridium surgical tools, seemed to be like a monster loaded to the vanishing point with glittering teeth.

In here, the odor of neoform was slightly tainted with a gentle aroma of perfume.

Cal looked around at the empty room and then opened the tiny door at one side. He had to pass between a portable radiology machine and a case of anatomical charts, both of which made his hackles tingle. Then he was inside the smaller room, and the sight of

Tinker Elliott's small, desirable head bent over the binocular microscope made him forget his fears. He stepped forward and kissed her on the ear.

She gasped, startled, and squinted at him through half-closed eyelids.

"Nice going," she said sharply.

"Thought you liked it," he said.

"I do. Want to try it again?"

"Sure."

"Then don't bother going out and coming in again. Just stay here."

Cal listened to the words but not the tone.

"Don't mind if I do. Shall we neck in earnest?"

"I'd as soon that as having you pop in and out, getting my nerves all upended by kissing me on the ear."

"I like kissing you on the ear."

Tinker came forward and shoved him onto a tall laboratory chair. "Good. But you'll do it at my convenience, next time."

"I'd rather surprise you."

"So I gathered. Why did you change your suit?"

"Change my suit?"

"Certainly."

"I haven't changed my suit."

"Well! I suppose that's the one you were wearing before."

"Look, Tinker, I don't usually wear a suit for three months. I think it was about time I changed. In fact, this one is about done for."

"The one you had on before looked all right to me."

"So? How long do you expect a suit to last, anyway?"

"Certainly as long as an hour."

"Hour?"

"Yes. Say, what's this?"

Cal Blair shook his head. "Are you all right?"

"Of course. Are you?"

"I think so. What were you getting at, Tinker. Let's start all over again."

"You were here an hour ago to bid me hello. We enjoyed our reunion immensely and affectionately. Then you said you were going home to change your suit—which you have done. Now you come in, acting as though this were the first time you'd seen me since Tony and I took off for Titan three months ago."

Cal growled in his throat.

"What did you say?" asked Tinker.

"Benj."

"Benj! Oh no!"

"I haven't been here before. He's my . . . my—"

"I know," said Tinker softly, putting a hand on his. "But no one would dream of masquerading as anyone else. That's unspeakable!"

"It's ghastly! The idea is beyond revolting. But, Tinker, Benj Blair is revolting—or worse. We hate each other—"

"I know." Tinker shuddered and made a face that might have resulted from tasting something brackish and foul. "*Ugh!* I'm sorry, Cal."

"I'm raving mad! That dupe!"

"Cal, never say that word again. Not about your twin brother."

"Look, my neuropsychiatristic female, I'm as stable as any twin could be. Dwelling on the subject of duplication is something I won't do. But the foul, rotten trick. What was he after, Tink?"

"Nothing, apparently. Just up to deviltry."

"Deviltry is fun. He was up to something foul. Imagine anyone trying to take another's identity. That's almost as bad as persona duplication."

Tinker went pale, and agreed. "Theft of identity— I imagine that Benj was only trying to be the stinker he is supposed to be. That was a rotten trick"—Tinker wiped her lips, applied neoform on a cello-cotton pad, and sterilized them thoroughly—"to play on a girl." She looked at the pad and tossed it into the converter chute. "A lot of good that will do. Like washing your hands after touching a criminal. Symbolic—"

"Tinker, I feel cheated."

"And I feel defiled. Come here, Cal."

The result of his approach was enough to wipe almost anything from the minds of both. It went a long way toward righting things, but it was not enough to cover the depths of their mental nausea at the foul trick. That would take years—and perhaps blood—to wash away.

"Hello, Cal," she said as they parted.

"I'm glad you're back."

"I know," she laughed. "Only Dr. Tinker Elliott could drag Specialist Calvin Blair into anything resembling a hospital, let alone a neurosurgical laboratory."

"Wild horses couldn't," he admitted.

"That's a left-handed compliment, but I'll treasure it—with my left hand," she promised.

"Benj—and I can speak without foaming at the mouth now—couldn't have played that trick on you if you'd seen me during the last three months."

"True. Three months' absence from you made his disguise perfect. I'd forgotten just enough. The rotter must have studied— No, he's an identical twin, isn't he?"

"Right," Cal gritted. "But look, Tinker. This is no place to propose. But why not have me around all the time?"

"Nice idea," said Tinker dreamily. "You'll come along with us on the next expedition, of course?"

"You'll not go," said Cal.

"Now we're at the same old impasse. We've come up against it for three years, Cal."

"But why?"

"Tony and I promised ourselves that we'd solve this mystery before we quit."

Cal snorted. "You've been following in the footsteps of medical men who haven't solved Makin's Disease in the last hundred years. You might never solve it."

"Then you'll have to play my way, Cal."

"You know my opinion on that."

"You persist in putting me over a barrel, Cal. I think a lot of you. Enough—and forgive me for thinking it—to ignore the fact that you are a twin. But I'll not marry you unless we can be together—somehow. I love surgery and medical research. I like adventuring into strange places and seeking the answer to strange things. Tony is my ideal and he loves this life, too, as did our father. It's in our blood, Tony's and mine, and saying it isn't going to remove it."

Cal nodded glumly. "Don't change," he said firmly. "Not willingly. I'm not going to be the guy to send someone to a psychiatrist to have his identity worked over. I've been hoping that you'd get your fill of roistering all over the Solar System, looking for rare bugs and viruses. I've almost been willing to get some conditioning myself so that I could join you—but you know what that would mean."

"Poor Cal," said Tinker softly, "you do love me. But Cal, don't you change either! Understand? If you change your identity, you'll not be the Cal I love. If the change comes normally, good and well, but I'll not have an altered personality for my husband. You love your ciphers and your codes and your cryptograms. You're a romanticist, Cal, and you stick to the rapier and the foil."

"Excepting that I get accused of cowardice every now and then," Blair snorted.

"Cowardice?"

"I've a rather quiet nature, you know. Nothing really roils me except Benj and his tricks. So I don't go around insulting people. I've been able to talk a lot of fights away by sheer reasoning, and when the battle is thrust upon me I choose the rapier. There's been criticism, Tink, because some have backed out rather than cross rapiers with me, and those that do usually get pinked. I've been accused of fighting my own game."

"That's smart. That's your identity, Cal, and don't let them ridicule you into trying drillers."

"I won't. I can't shoot the side of a wall with a needle beam."

"Stay as you are, Cal."

"But that's no answer. You like space flying. I hate space flying. You love medicine and neurosurgery. I hate the smell of neoform. I hate space and I hate surgery—and you love 'em both. To combine them? To call them Life? No man in his right mind would do that. No, Tinker, I'll have nothing to do with either!"

The ghost of Hellion Murdoch—pirate, adventurer, and neurosurgeon—stirred in his long, long sleep. Pirates never die, they merely join their fellows in legend and in myth; and through their minions—the historians and novelists—their heinous crimes are smoothed over, and they become uninhibited souls that fought against the fool restrictions placed upon them by a rotten society.

Hellion Murdoch had joined his fellows, Captain Kidd, Henry Morgan, Dick Turpin, and Robin Hood three hundred and fifty years before. And, like them, he went leaving a fabulous treasure buried somewhere. This came to be known to all as Murdoch's Hoard, and men sought up and down the Solar System for it, but it was never found.

But the words of Cal Blair aroused the ghost of Hellion Murdoch. He listened again as the words echoed and re-echoed through the halls of his pirate's citadel in the Hereafter. The same halls rang with his roaring laughter as he heard Calvin Blair's words. He sprang to his feet, and raced with the speed of thought to a mail chute.

With his toe, the ghost of Hellion Murdoch dislodged a small package from where it had lain for years. With his ghostly pencil, he strengthened certain marks, plying the pencil with the skill of a master counterfeiter. The stamp was almost obliterated by the smudged and unreadable cancellation. The addressee was scrawled and illegible, but the address was still readable. Water had done its job of work on the almost imperishable wrapper and ink of the original, and when the ghostly fingers of Murdoch were through, the package looked like a well-battered bundle, treated roughly by today's mail.

With his toe, he kicked it, and watched it run through the automatic carrier along the way to an operating post office. It came to light, and the delivery chute in Cal Blair's apartment received the package in the due course of time.

Cal looked at the package curiously. He hadn't ordered anything. He was expecting nothing by mail. The postmark—completely smudged. He paid no attention to the stamp, which might have given him to think. The address? The numbers were fairly plain and they were his, Cal Blair's. The name was scrawled, and the wrapping was scratched across the name. Obviously some sharp corner of another package had scratched it off.

He inspected the package with the interest of a master cryptologist, and then decided that opening the package was the only way to discover the identity of the owner. Perhaps inside would be a packing slip or something that might be traced—

Paper hadn't changed much in the last five hundred years, he thought ruefully. At least, not the kind of paper this was wrapped in.

No store, of course. Someone sending something almost worthless, no doubt, and wrapping it in the first piece of paper that was handy. He tore the wrapping carefully and set it aside for future study.

Inside the package was a tin box, and inside the box was a small cross standing on a toroidal base. The whole trinket stood two inches tall, and the crossarms were proportional—though they were cylindrical in cross-section instead of rectangular.

It would have made a nice ornament for an altar, or a religious person's desk, except for the tiny screw stud that projected out of the center of the bottom. That prevented it from standing. Other taped holes in this flat base aroused his attention.

"This is no ornament," said Cal Blair, aloud. "No mere ornament would require that rugged mounting."

There seemed to be some microscopic engravings around the surface of the toroid. Cal set up the microscope and looked. Characters in the solarian were there, micro-engraved to perfection. But they were in no order. They had a randomness that would have made no sense to any but a master cryptologist—a specialist. To Cal they took on a vague pattern that might be wishful thinking, and yet his reason told him that men do not micro-engrave things just to ornament them. A cipher it must be, by all logic.

He was about to take it into the matter converter and enlarge it mechanically, when he decided that it might spoil the things for the owner if he did and was not able to return it to the exact size. He decided on photographs.

Fully three hours later, Cal Blair had a complete set of photographic enlargements of the micro-engravings.

Then, with the patience and skill of the specialist cryptologist, Blair started to work on the characters.

The hours passed laboriously. The wastebasket filled with scrawled sheets of paper, and mathematical sequences. Letters and patterns grew beneath his pencil, and were discarded. Night passed, and the dawn grayed in the east. The sun rose, and cast its rays over Cal's desk, and still he worked on, completely lost in his work.

And then he looked startled, snapped his fingers, and headed across the room for an old book. It was a worthless antique, made by the reproducer in quantity. It was a Latin dictionary.

Latin. A dead and forgotten language.

Only his acquaintance with the folks at the Solarian Medical Association could have given him the key to recognition. He saw one word there, and it clicked. And then for four solid hours he cross-checked and fought the Latin like a man working a crossword puzzle in an unknown language, matching the characters with those in the dictionary.

But finally the message was there before him in characters that he could read. It was clear and startling.

"The Key to Murdoch's Hoard!" he breathed. "The fabulous treasure of the past! This trinket is the Key to Murdoch's Hoard!"

A cavity resonator and antenna system, it was. The toroid base was the cavity resonator, and the cross was the feedline and dipole antenna. Fitted into the proper parabolic reflector and shock-excited periodically, it would excite a similar antenna at the site of Murdoch's Hoard. This would continue to oscillate for many milliseconds after the shock-excitation. If the Key were switched to a receiving system—a detector—the answering oscillation of the sympathetic system would act as a radiator. Directive operation—scanning—of the parabolic reflector would give directive response, leading the user to the site of Murdoch's Hoard.

How men must have fought to find Murdoch's Hoard in the days long past!

Cal Blair considered the Key. It would lead him to nothing but roistering and space travel, and the result would be no gain. Yet there was a certain scientific curiosity in seeing whether his deciphering had been correct. Not that he doubted it, but the idea sort of intrigued him.

The project was at least *unique*.

He looked up the history of the gadget in an ancient issue of the *Interplanetary Encyclopaedia* and came up with the following description:

> **Murdoch's Hoard:** An unknown treasure said to be cached by the pirate Hellion Murdoch. This treasure is supposed to have been collected by Murdoch during his years as an illegal neurosurgeon. For listings of Murdoch's better-known contributions to medicine, see . . . [A list of items filled half a page at this point, which Cal Blair skipped.]
>
> Murdoch's Hoard is concealed well, and has never been found. The Key to Murdoch's Hoard was a minute cavity resonator and antenna system which would lead the user to the cache. No one has been able to make the Key function properly, and no one was ever able to break the code, which was engraved around the base.
>
> The value of the Key is doubtful. Though thousands of identical Keys were made on the Channing-Franks matter reproducer, no scientist has ever succeeded in getting a response. Engravings on the base are obviously a code of some sort giving instructions as to the use of the Key, but the secret of the code is no less obscure than the use of the Key itself. The original may be identified by a threaded stud protruding from the bottom. This stud was eliminated in the reproduction since it interfered with the upright position of the Key when used as an ornament. The original was turned over to the Interplanetary Museum at the time of Channing's death, from which place it has disappeared and has been rediscovered several times. At the present time, the original Key to Murdoch's Hoard is again missing, it having been stolen out of the museum for the seventeenth time in three hundred years.

Cal smiled at the directions again. He envisioned the years of experimentation that had gone on with no results. The directions told why. Without them, its operation was impossible. And yet it was so simple.

The idea of owning contraband bothered Cal. The Key belonged to the Interplanetary Museum, by rights. It would be returned. Of that, Cal was definite. But some little spark of curiosity urged him not to return it right away. He would return it, but it had been gone for several years, and a few days more would make no difference. He was far from a brilliant scientist—any of the engineers of the long-gone Venus Equilateral Relay Station would have shone like a super-nova against his own dim light. But he, Cal Blair, had the answer and they did not.

But it was more to prove the correctness of his own ability as cryptographer that he took on the job of making the little Key work.

The job took him six weeks. An expert electronics engineer would have done it in three days, but Cal had no laboratory filled with equipment. He had neither laboratory technique nor instruments nor a great store of experience. He studied books. He extracted a mite of information here and a smidgin there, and when he completed the job, his equipment was a mad scramble of parts. Precision rubbed elbows with sloppiness, for unlike the trained technician Cal did not know which circuits to let fly and which circuits needed precise placing. He found out by sheer cut-and-try and by finally placing everything with care. The latter did not work too well, but continuous delving into the apparatus disrupted some of the lesser-important lines to the point where their randomness did not cause coupling. The more important lines complained in squeals of oscillation when displaced, and Cal was continually probing into the gear to find out which wire was out of place.

He snapped the main switch one evening six weeks later. With childlike enthusiasm he watched the meters register, compared notes, and decided that everything was working properly. His testing equipment indicated that he was operating the thing properly—at least in accordance with the minute engravings on the side.

But with that discovery—that his rig functioned—there came a letdown. It was singularly unexciting. Meters indicated; the filaments of the driver tubes cast a ruddy glow behind the cabinet panel; a few ill-positioned pilot lamps winked; and the meter at the far end of the room registered the fact that he was transmitting and was being detected. It was a healthy signal, too, according to the meter, but it was both invisible and inaudible as well as not affecting the other senses in any way.

Now that he had it, what could he use it for?

Treasure? Of what use could treasure be in this day and age? With the Channing-Franks matter reproducer, gold or any rare element could be synthesized by merely introducing the proper heterodyning signal. Money was not metal anymore. Gold was in extensive use in electrical works and platinum came in standard bars at a solarian credit each. Stable elements up to atomic weights of six or seven hundred had been made and investigated. A treasure trove was ridiculous. Of absolutely no value.

The day of the Channing-Franks development was after the demise of Hellion Murdoch. And it was after the Period of Duplication that identium was synthesized and became the medium of exchange. Since identium came after Murdoch's demise, obviously Murdoch's Hoard could only be a matter of worthless coin, worthless jewels, or equally worthless securities.

Money had again become a real medium of exchange. Now it was something that did away with going to the store for an egg's worth of mustard.

So Cal Blair felt a letdown. With his problem solved, there was no more to it, and that was that. He smiled. He'd send the Key to Murdoch's Hoard to the museum.

And furthermore, let them seek Murdoch's Hoard, if they wanted to. Doubtless they would find some "uniques" there. A pile of ancient coins would be uniques, all right. But the ancient papers and coins and jewels would not be detectable from any of the duplicates of other jewels and coins of that period that glutted the almost-abandoned museum.

Benj Blair snarled at the man in front of him. "You slinking dupe! You can't get away with that!"

The man addressed blanched at the epithet and hurled himself headlong at Benj. Cal's twin brother callously slipped a knife out of his belt and stabbed down on the back of his attacker. It was brutal and bloody. Benj kicked the dead man back with a lifted knee and addressed the rest of the mob.

"Now look," he snarled, "it is not smart. This loke thought he could counterfeit. He's a dead idiot now. And anybody that tries to make identium in this station or any place that can be traced to any one of us will be treated likewise. Get me?"

There was a growl of absolute assent from the rest.

"Is there anyone who doesn't know why?"

"I'm dumb," grinned a man in the rear. "Make talk, Benj."

"O.K.," answered Benj. "Identium is a synthetic element. It is composed of a strictly unstable atom that is stabilized electronically. It starts off all right, but at the first touch of the scanning beam in the matter converter, it becomes unstable and blows in a fission-reaction. Limpy, there, tried it once and it took his arm and leg. The trouble with identium explosions is the fact that the torn flesh is sort of seared, and limb-grafting isn't perfect. That's why Limpy is Limpy. Then, to make identium, you require a space station in the outer region. The manufacture of the stuff puts a hellish positive charge on the station, which is equalized by solar radiation in time. But the station must be far enough out so that the surge inward from Sol isn't so high that the inhabitants are electrocuted by the change in charge.

"Any detector worthy of the name will pick it up when in operation at a half light-year—and the Patrol keeps their detectors running. That, plus the almost impossible job of getting the equipment to perform the operation. I'll have no identium experiments here."

A tiny light winked briefly above his head. It came from a dusty piece of equipment on a shelf. Benj blinked, looked up at the winking light, and swore.

"Tom!" he snorted. "What in the name of the devil are you doing?"

The technician put his head out of the laboratory door. "Nothing."

"You're making this detector blink."

"I'm trying to duplicate an experiment."

"Trying?"

Tom grinned. "I'm performing the actual operation of the distillation of alcohol."

"That shouldn't make the detector blink."

"There's only one thing that will do that!"

"Not after all this time."

"It's not been long. About ten years," Tom objected. "Look, Benj. Someone has found the Key. And not only that, but they've made it work."

"I'd like to argue the point with you," said Benj pointedly. "Why couldn't you make it tick when we had it seven years ago? You were sharp enough to make a detector, later."

"Detecting is a lot different from generating, Benj. Come on, let's get going. I want to see the dupe that's got the Key."

Had Cal Blair been really satisfied just to make his gadget work, he might never have been bothered. But he tinkered with it, measured it, and toyed with it. He called Tinker Elliott to boast, and found that she had gone off to Northern Landing with her illustrious brother to speak at a medical convention, and so he returned to his toy. Effectively, his toying with the Key gave off enough radiation to follow. And it was followed by two parties.

The first one arrived about midnight.

The doorbell rang, and Cal opened it to look into the glittering lens of a needle beam. He went white and retreated backward until he felt a chair behind his knees. He collapsed into the chair.

"P-p-p-put that thing away."

"This?" grinned the man, waving the needle beam.

"Shut up, Logy," the other snapped. To Cal, he said: "Where is it?"

"W-w-w-where is w-w-w-what?"

"The Key."

"Key?"

"Don't be an idiot!" snarled the first man, slapping Cal across the face with the back of his hand.

Cal went white. "Better kill me," he said coldly, "or I'll see your identity taken!"

"Cut it, Jake. Look, wiseacre, where did you get it?"

"The Key? It came in the mail."

"Mail, hell! That was mailed ten years ago!"

"It got here six weeks ago."

"Musta got lost, Logy," offered Jake. "After all, Gadget's been gone about that long."

"That's so. Those things do happen. Poor Gadg. An' we cooled him for playing smart."

"We wuz wrong."

"Yep. So we wuz. Too bad. But Gadget wasn't too bright—not like this egg. He's made it work."

"Logy, you're a genius."

"So we chilled Gadget because we thought he was playin' smart by tryin' to swipe the pitch. He didn't lam wit' the Key at all."

"How about this one?" asked Jake.

"He ain't going to yodel. Better grab him and that pile of gewgaws. The rest of the lads'll be here too soon."

"Rest?"

"Sure. The whole universe is filled wit' detectors ever since Ellswort' made the first one."

"Git up, dope," snapped Jake. motioning to the door with his beam.

Blair walked to the door with rubber joints in his knees. Logy lifted the equipment from the table and followed Jake. "He ain't made no notebook," Jake complained.

"He had some plans," said Logy, "but the fool set the stuff on 'em and they're all chewed up. He can make 'em over."

"O.K. Git goin', loke."

Blair could not have protested against the pair unarmed. With two needle beams trained on his back, he was helpless. He went as they directed, and found that his helplessness could be increased. They forced him into a spacecraft that was parked on the roof.

The autopilot was set, and the spacecraft headed across the sky, not into space, but making a high trajectory over Terra itself. Once into the black of the superstratosphere, they turned their attention back to Cal.

"Gonna talk?"

"W-w-w-what do you w-w-want me to s-s-say?" Cal chattered.

"Dumb, isn't he?"

"Look, sweety, tell us what's with this thing."

"It's a c-c-cavity resonator."

"Yeah, so we've been told," growled Logy. "What makes?"

"B-b-b-but look," stammered Cal. "W-w-what good'll it do you?"

"Meaning?" Jake snarled.

"Whatever treasure might be there is useless now."

Jake and Logy split the air with peals of raw laughter.

Jake said: "He is dumb, all right."

"Just tell us, bright-eyes. We'll decide," snapped Logy.

"W-w-well, you send out a signal with it and then stop it and switch it to the detecting circuit. You listen, and the signal goes out and starts the other one going like tapping a bell. It resonates for some time after the initial impulse. It returns the signal, and by using the directional qualities, you can follow the shock-excited second resonator right down to it. Follow?"

"Yeah. That we all know," Jake drawled in a bored voice. His tone took on that razor edge again and he snarled: "What we're after is the *how,* get me? How?"

"Oh, w-w-w-well, the trick is—"

"Creeps!" Logy exploded. He crossed the cabin in almost nothing flat and jerked upward on the power lever.

The little ship surged upward at six gravities, making speech impossible. Blair wondered about this, sitting there helpless and scared green, until a blast of heat came from behind and the ship lost drive. A tractor beam flashed upward, catching the ship and hurling it backward. The reaction threw all three up against the ceiling with considerable force, and the reverse acceleration generated by the tractor's pull kept them pasted to the ceiling. Another ship was beside them in a matter of seconds, and four space-suited men breached the air lock and entered, throwing their helmets back.

"Jake Jackson and Freddy Logan," laughed the foremost of the newcomers. "How nerce of you to meet us here."

"Grab the blinkers," said the one behind.

"Naturally. Naturally. Pete and Wally take Blair. Jim and I'll muscle the gripper."

Two of them carried Cal to the larger ship. The other two scooped up the equipment and carried it behind them. Once inside, the tractors were cut and the smaller ship plummeted toward Terra. With no concern over the other ship and its two occupants, the newcomers hurled Cal back against the wall and put his apparatus on the navigator's table.

"Very nice and timely rescue, eh, Cal?"

Cal whirled. "Benj," he snarled. "Might have known—"

He started forward, but was stopped by the ugly muzzles of three needle beams that waggled disconcertingly at the pit of his stomach. He laughed, but it had a wild tone. "Go ahead and blast! Then run the Key yourselves!" he hurled at them. But he stopped, and the waggling of the three weapons became uncertain.

"Hellfire," Pete snorted, looking from one to the other. "They're duplicates!"

Cal leaped forward, smashed Pete's beam up, where it furrowed the ceiling. His fist came forward and his knee came up. Beneath Cal's arm flashed a streak of white. It caught Pete in the stomach and passed down to the knee, trailing a bit of smoke and a terrible odor. Cal dropped the lifeless form and whirled. Benji stood there, his needle beam held rock-steady on the form that lay crumpled beneath his brother's feet.

Benj addressed the other two. "My brother and I have one thing in common," he said coolly. "Neither of us cares to be called a duplicate!" He holstered his weapon and addressed Cal. "Where is it?"

"Where is what?" asked Cal quietly.

"Murdoch's Hoard."

"I haven't had time to find out."

"O.K. So tell us how to make this thing run."

"I'll be psyched if I do."

"You'll be dead if you don't," Benj warned.

"Someday, you stinker, I'll take the satisfaction of killing you."

"I'll never give you cause," sneered Benj.

"Stealing my identity is plenty of cause."

"You won't take satisfaction on that," taunted Benj.

"Because *you'd* have to call *me*, and I'll only accept battle with beams."

Cal considered. Normally, he would have been glad to demonstrate to anyone the secret of the Key. But he would have died before he told Benj the time of day. Then another consideration came. The Key was worthless—and less valuable would be the vast treasures of Murdoch's Hoard. Why not give him the Key and let him go hunting for the useless stuff?

Wally waved an instant-welder in front of Cal's nose. The tip glowed like a white-hot stylus. "Might singe him a bit," Wally offered.

"Put the iron down," snapped Benji. Wally laid the three-foot shaft on its stand, where it cooled slowly. "Cal wouldn't talk. I know. That thing would only make him madder than a hornet."

"So what do we do with the loke?" asked Wally.

"Take him home and work on him there," said Benj. "Trap his hands."

No more was said until they dropped onto Cal's rooftop. He was ushered down the same way he had gone up—with beams looking at his backbone. They carried his equipment down, and set it carefully on the table.

"Now," said Benj. "Make with the talk."

"O.K.," said Cal. "This is a cavity resonator—"

"This is too easy," Wally objected. "Something's fishy."

Cal looked at the speaker with scorn. "You imbecile. You've been reading about Murdoch's Hoard. Vast treasure. Money, jewels, and securities. Valuable as hell three hundred and fifty years ago, but not worth a mouthful of ashes today. Why shouldn't I tell you about it?"

"That right, boss?" asked Wally.

"He's wishful thinking," snorted Benj.

Cal smiled inwardly. His protestation of what he knew to be the truth was working. The desire to work on Benj was running high, now, and Cal was reconsidering his idea of handing the thing to Benj scot-free.

"Let me loose. I'll show you how it works," he said.

"Not a peep out of it," warned Benj. "Wally, if he

touches that switch before he takes the Key out of the reflector, drill him low and safe—but drill him!"

Cal knew the value of that order.

His hands were freed, and he stepped forward with tools and removed the Key. "Now?" he asked sarcastically.

"Go ahead," said Benj.

"Thanks," he grinned. "That I will."

He took three steps forward and went out of the open window like a running jackrabbit. His strong fencer's wrists caught the trellis at the edge and he swung wide before he dropped to the ground several feet below. He landed running, and though the flashes of the needle beams scored the ground ahead of him, none caught him. Plowing through a hedge, he jumped into his car and drove off with a swaying drive that would disrupt any aim.

He drove to the Solarian Medical Association, where he found Dr. Lange in charge. In spite of the hour of the morning, he went in and spoke to the doctor.

Lange looked up, surprised. "What are you doing here at this hour?" he asked with a smile.

"I've got a few skinned knuckles that hurt," said Cal, showing the bruises.

"Who did you hit?" asked Lange. "Fisticuffs isn't exactly your style, Cal."

"I know. But I was angry."

Lange inspected Cal's frame. "Wouldn't like to be the other guy," he laughed. "But look, Cal. Tinker will be more than pleased."

"That I was fighting? Why?"

"You're a sort of placid fellow, normally. If you could only stir up a few pounds of blood pressure more frequently, you'd be quite a fellow."

"So I'm passive. I like peace and quiet. You don't see me running wild, do you?"

"Nope. Tell me, what happened?"

Cal explained in sketchy form, omitting the details about Benj.

"The Key to Murdoch's Hoard?" asked Lange, opening his eyes.

"Sure."

"What are you going to do with it?"

"Send it back to the museum. They're the ones that own it."

"You'll give them Murdoch's Hoard, if you do."

"Granting for the moment that the Hoard is valuable," laughed Cal, "it is still the property of the museum."

"Wrong. The law is a thousand years old and still working. Buried treasure is his who finds it. The hoard is yours, Cal."

"Wonderful. About as valuable as a gallon of lake water in Chicago. And about as plentiful."

"May I have the Key?" asked Lange eagerly.

Cal stopped. This was getting him down. First, that pair of ignorant crooks. Then his brother, trying to steal from him something that both knew was worthless—just for the plain fun of stealing, he believed. But now this man. Dr. Lange was advanced in years, a brilliant and stable surgeon.

Was he wrong? Did the Key really represent something worthwhile? If so, what on earth could it be? A hoard of treasure in a worthless medium of exchange and with duplicates all over the System? What could Murdoch's Hoard be that it made men fight for it even in this day?

"Sorry," said Cal. "This is my baby." He said no more about it.

Whatever the Hoard might be, it was getting Cal curious. That and the desire to get the best of Benj worked on him night and day during the next week. He was forced to hide out all of that time, for Benj was looking for him. The equipment still required a knowing hand to run it—any number of technicians had concocted the same circuit to drive the Key—but it was the technique, not the equipment, that made it function properly.

He toyed with the idea for some time. The desire to go and see for himself, however, was not greater than his aversion to space travel. Cal had an honest dislike; he had tried space travel three times when business demanded it. He'd hated it all three times.

But there it was—and there it stayed. The whole affair peaked and then died into a stasis. Murdoch's

Hoard was something that Cal Blair would eventually look into—someday.

The one thing that bothered him was his hiding out. He hated that. But he remained under cover until Tinker Elliott returned, and then sought her advice. She made a date to meet him at a nearby refreshment place later that afternoon.

The major-domo came up with a cheerful smile as Cal sauntered into the chromium-and-crimson establishment. "At your service," the major-domo greeted him.

"I'm meeting a friend."

"A table will be reserved. Meanwhile, will you avail yourself of our service in the bar?"

Cal nodded and entered the bar. He climbed up on a stool and took cigarettes from his pocket.

The bartender came over immediately. "Your service?"

"Palan and ginger," said Cal. He was still working on the dregs of his first glass when Tinker came up behind him and seated herself on the stool beside.

"Hi, Tink," he smiled.

"Hello. What are you drinking?"

"Palan and ginger."

"Me, too," she said to the bartender. "Cal, you are a queer duck. Your favorite liquors come from Venus and Mars. You seem to thrive on those foul-tasting lichens from Titan as appetizers. You gorge yourself on Callistan loganberry, and your most-ordered dinner is knolla. Yet you hate space travel."

"Sure," he grinned. "I know it. After all, there's nothing that says that I have to go and get it. Four hundred years ago, Tink, there were people who ate all manner of food that they never saw in the growing stage. And a lot of people lived and died without ever seeing certain of their meat animals."

"I know. Gosh. They used to kill animals for meat back then. Imagine!"

Cal looked sour-faced, and silence ensued for a moment. Then Tinker's face took on a self-horror.

"Hey. That look isn't natural. What's up?" Cal asked.

"Order me a big, powerful, hardy, pick-me-up," said Tinker, "and I'll tell you—if you really want to know."

"I do and I will," said Cal, wonderingly.

He ordered straight palan, which Tinker took neat. She coughed, and then brightened somewhat.

"Now?" asked Cal.

"Better order another one for you," said Tinker. "Anyway, we had one of those jobs last night."

"What jobs?"

"An almost-incurable."

"Oh," said Cal with a shiver. He ordered two more straight drinks, in preparation. "Go ahead and tell, Tink. You won't be free of it until you spill it."

"It was a last-resort case and everybody knew it. Even the patient—that's what made it so tough. It's distasteful enough to consider a duplicate when you're well. But to be lying on the brink and then know that they're going to make a duplicate of you for experimental surgery—I can't begin to tell. The patient took it, though.

"And even that wouldn't be too bad. We made our duplicates and went to work on one immediately. We operated, located the trouble, and corrected it. The third duplicate lived. Then we operated on the patient successfully. I didn't mind the first two dupes, Cal. It was the disposing of the cured duplicate that got me. It was like— No, it *was* disposing of an identity." Tink shuddered, and then drained her second shot of palan simultaneously with Cal.

"And you wonder why I dislike medicine," he said flatly.

"I know—or try to. But look, Cal. Aside from the distaste, look at what medicine has been able to accomplish."

"Sure," he said without enthusiasm.

"Well, it has."

"But at what a cost."

"Cost? Very little cost," snapped Tinker. "After all, once one has the stomach to dispose of a duplicate, what's the cost? Doctors bury their mistakes just as always, but the mistake is a duplicate. The sentience remains."

"How can you tell the real article from the duplicate?"

"We keep track."

"I know that. What I mean is this: a man is born, lives thirty years as an identity. He is duplicated for surgical purposes at age thirty. All duplicates and the original are he—complete with thought and habit patterns of thirty years. They are identical in every way, right down to the dirt on their hands and the subconscious thoughts that pass inside of their brains. Their egoes are all identical. When you kill the duplicate, you might as well kill the identity. The duplicate is as much an identity as the original."

"True," said Tinker. "However, once a duplicate is made, the identities begin to differ. One will have different experiences and different ideas and thoughts. Eventually the two duplicates are separate characters. But in deference to the identity, it *is* he that we must cure and preserve. For the instant that the duplication takes place, the character starts to differ. We cannot destroy the original. The duplicate is not real. It—how can I say it?—hasn't enjoyed— Yes it has, too. It was once the original. Cal, you're getting me all balled up."

"Why not let them both live?"

Tinker looked at Cal with wonder. "Inspect your life," she said sharply. "You and Benj. How do I know right now that you are not Benj?"

Cal recoiled as though he had been struck.

"You're Cal, I know. That distaste was not acting. It was too quick and too good, Cal. But can you see what would happen? What is a dupe's lot?"

Cal nodded slowly. "He's scorned, taunted, and hated. He cannot masquerade too well—that in itself is a loss in identity. Yes, it is a matter of mercy to dispose of the duplicate. The whole thing is wrong. Can't something be done about it?"

"Not until you change human nature," smiled Tinker.

"It's been done before."

"I know. But not a thing as ingrained as this."

"Ingrained? Look, Tinker Elliott, up to the Period of Duplication, three hundred years ago, twins and multiple-births used to dress and act as near alike as possible."

"Hm-m-m. That was before a duplicate could be made. Double birth was something exceptional, and unique. The distaste against duplicates bred the hatred between twins, I know. We might be able to change human nature, then."

"Not in our lifetime."

"I guess not. What was the big kicker, Cal?"

"About duplication? Well, there was a war in Europe and both warring countries put armies of duplicates into the field. The weapons, of course, were manufactured right along with the troops. There were armies of about nineteen million men on each side, composed of about a thousand different originals. They took the best airmen, the best gunners, the best rangers, the best officers, the best navigators, and the best of every branch of fighting, and ran them into vast armies. It was stalemate until the rest of the world stepped in and put a stop to it. Then there were thirty-eight million men, all duplicates, running around. The mess that ensued when several thousand men tried to live in one old familiar haunt . . . It was seventy years before things ran down."

"That would send public opinion reeling back," Tinker smiled. "But do you mind if we change the subject? I think that I've gotten last night's experience out of my system. What was all this wild story you were telling me?"

"Let's stroll toward food," he said. "I'll tell you then."

Cal dropped some coins on the bar to take care of the check and they went into the dining room. The waiter led them to their table and handed them menus.

"This isn't needed," he told the waiter. "I want roast knolla."

"Please accept the apology of the management," said the waiter sorrowfully. "Today we have no knolla."

"None?" asked Cal in surprise. "That's strange. Every restaurant has knolla."

"Not this one," the waiter apologized. "An accident, sir. The alloy disk containing the recording of the roast knolla dinner slipped from the chef's hands less than an hour ago and fell to the floor. It was thought to be undamaged, close inspection showed it all right. But it was tried, and the knolla came out with the most peculiar flavor. The master files haven't replaced it yet. It will be four hours before they get to our request for transmission of the disk. The engineer there laughed and said something about molecule displacement when I mentioned the peculiar flavor. It was *most* peculiar. Not distressing, mind, but most alien. We're keeping the damaged disk. It may be a real 'unique.' "

"Good eating?"

"I'll reserve opinion on that until we find out how we like it ourselves," smiled the waiter. "I'd recommend something else, sir."

Cal ordered for both Tinker and himself. Then he leaned forward on his elbows and gave Tinker the highlights of his life for the past few weeks. He finished with the statement: "It's worthless, but somehow I can't see letting Benj get it."

"Worthless? Murdoch's Hoard?"

"Shall I go into that again? Look, Tinker. Murdoch's era was prior to the discovery of the matter duplicator, which followed the Channing-Franks matter transmitter by only a few weeks. Now, anything that Murdoch could cache away would be in currency of that time. The Period of Duplication hadn't come yet, and the eventual invention or discovery of identium as a medium of exchange had not arrived. So what good is Murdoch's Hoard? It must be of some value. But what? I could discount everything as ignorance or hatred except Dr. Lange's quick desire for it. Lange is no fool, Tink. He knew what he was getting. Darn it all, I feel like going out and running the Hoard down myself!"

Tinker's laugh was genuine and spontaneous.

Cal bridled. "Funny? Then tell me why."

"You, who hate roistering, adventure, space, and hell-raising. Going after Murdoch's Hoard! That, I want to see."

"So that you can laugh at my fumbling attempts?"

Tinker sobered. "I've been unkind, Cal. But you aren't equipped to make a search like that."

"No?"

"You, with your quiet disposition and easygoing ways. Yes, Cal, I can be honest with you. Forgive me, but the idea of watching you conduct a wild expedition like that intrigues me." Tinker became serious for a moment. "Besides, I'd like to be there when you open Murdoch's Hoard."

"Hm-m-m. Well, it's just an idea."

"You'll get right back into your rut, Cal. You don't really intend to do anything about it, do you?"

"Well—"

"Cal—would you give me the Key?"

"What!"

"I mean it."

"Tinker! What is Murdoch's Hoard?"

"Not unless you give me the Key," Tinker teased.

"Not a Chinaman's chance," said Cal with finality.

"What are you going to do with it?"

"I'm going after it myself!"

Tinker looked into Cal's face and saw determination there. "I want to go along," she said. "Please?"

Cal shook his head. "Nope. I'm not going to have anyone laughing at me. Tell me what it is."

"Take me along."

Cal thought that one over. The idea of having Tinker Elliott along appealed to him. He'd wanted her for years, and this plea of hers was an admission of surrender. But Cal felt that conditional surrender was not good enough. He didn't like the idea of Tinker's willingness to be bought for a treasure unknown. What was really in the depths of her mind he could not guess—unless she were trying to goad him into making the expedition.

"No," he said.

"Then you'll never go," she taunted him.

"I'll go," he snapped. "And I'll prove that I can take care of myself. I hate space-roving, but I'm big enough to do it despite my distaste. Now, will you tell me what Murdoch's Hoard is that it is so valuable?"

"Not unless you take me along."

Pride is always cropping up in the wrong place. If Cal or Tinker had not taken such a firm stand in the first place, it would have been easier for either one of them to back down. The argument had started in fun, and was now in deadly earnest. How and where the change came Cal did not know. He reviewed the whole thing again. The first pair were ignorant. Benj was vindictive enough to deprive his brother of a useless thing that interested Cal. Dr. Lange was enigmatic. He had neither personal view nor ignorance to draw his desire for Murdoch's worthless Hoard. Tinker Elliott might be goading Cal into making an adventuresome trip for the purpose of bringing him closer to her way of living. He wouldn't put it past her.

But the more he thought about it, the deeper and deeper he was falling into his own bullheadedness. He was going to get Murdoch's Hoard himself, if it turned out to be a bale of one-hundred-dollar bills of the twenty-first century—worth exactly three cents per hundredweight for scrap paper.

Tinker Elliott returned to the Association after the dinner with Cal. She worked diligently for an hour, and loafed luxuriously for another hour. It was just after this that Cal came into her laboratory and grinned sheepishly at her.

"Now what?" she asked. "Changed your mind?"

"Uh-huh," he said.

"Still squeamish about space?"

He nodded.

"Poor Cal," she said, coming over to him. She curled up on his lap and put her head on his shoulder. "What are we going to do about it?"

"I'm going to give you the Key," he said.

She straightened up. "You don't mind if we use it—Tony and I?"

"Not at all."

"I'm going to punish you," she said. "I'm not going to tell what Murdoch's Hoard is until we bring it back."

Cal looked surprised. "All right," he said. "It's worthless, anyway. I'll wait."

"You don't want to go along?"

"If I wanted to go at all, I'd go myself," said Cal.

"O.K. Then wonder about Murdoch's Hoard until we get back. That'll be your punishment."

"Punishment? For what?"

"For not having the kind of personality that would go out and get it."

"All right. Do you want the Key?"

"Sure. Where is it?"

"At home."

"Thought you weren't living at home," said Tinker.

"I haven't been. The Key is there, though. You see,

Tink, it takes the *technique* to make it work rather than the *equipment*. I'll give you both the equipment and the technique as soon as we get there. I'll demonstrate and write out the procedure. Now?"

"The sooner the better." Tinker graced her hair with a wisp of a hat and said: "I'm ready."

Putting her hand in his arm, she followed him to the street and they drove to his cottage. He led her inside, seated her, and offered her a cigarette.

"Now, Tinker," he said seriously, "where is it?"

"Where is what?"

"The Key."

"You have it, as far as I'm concerned."

"You know better than that."

"You had it."

"No, you're wrong. Cal had it."

"I'm wrong— *Who* had it?" Tinker exploded as the words took.

"Cal," he smiled.

"You're Benj."

"Brilliant deduction, Tinker. Now do you get the pitch?"

"No. You're trying to get Murdoch's Hoard, too."

"I haven't your persuasive charm, Tink. The illustrious cryptologist known as my twin brother wouldn't go into space for anything. You want the Key, ergo, unless I miss my guess, you've been talking and using those charms on him. Don't tell me that he didn't give it to you."

"You stinking dupe."

Benj grew white around the mouth. "Your femininity won't keep you alive too long," he gritted.

"I won't steal anyone's identity," she retorted.

"I'll wreck yours," he rasped. "I'll duplicate you!"

"Then I'll be no better than you are," she spat. "Go ahead. You'll get a dead dupe—two or a million of 'em. I can kill myself in the machine—I know how. I'd do it."

"That wouldn't do me any good," Benj snapped. "Otherwise I'd do it now. I may do it later."

"Keep it up—and I'll see that one-half of this duplication is removed. Now, may I leave?"

"No. If you don't know where the Key is—or Cal—

you may come in handy later. I think that I might be able to force the Key away from him. He'd die before he permitted me to work on you."

"You rotten personality stealer. You deserve to lose your identity."

"I've still got Cal's."

"Make a million of you," she taunted, "and they'll still be rotten."

"Well, be that as it may. You and I are going to go to Venus. Murdoch's Hoard is still hidden in the Vilanortis Country. We have detectors. We'll just go and sit on the edge of the fog country and wait until we hear Cal's signal."

"How do you know he's going?"

"Assuming that Tinker Elliott could get more out of him than any other person, it means that he said, 'No,' and is now preparing to make the jaunt himself. That'll be a laugh. The home-and-fireside-loving Cal Blair taking a wild ride through the fog country of Vilanortis. I'd like to be in his crate, just to watch."

"Cal is no imbecile," said Tink stoutly. "He'll get along."

"Sure, he'll get along. But he won't have fun!"

Tinker considered the future. It was not too bright. The thing to do, of course, would be to go along more or less willingly and look for an escape as soon as Benj's suspicions were lulled by her inaction.

Cal boarded the *Lady Unique* at Mohave Spaceport not knowing of Tinker's capture at the hands of Benj. Benj was careful not to let Cal know of this development, since it would have stopped Cal short and would have possibly gotten him into a merry-go-round of officialdom and perhaps fighting, in which the Key would most certainly be publicized and lost to all. Courts were still inclined to view the certified ownership rather than the possessor of an object like the Key in spite of the nine points often quoted. This was a case of the unquoted tenth point of the law. Finders of buried treasure were still keepers, but the use of a stolen museum piece to find it might be questioned. So Cal took off in a commercial liner from Mohave at the same time that Tinker was hustled aboard Benj's sleek black personal craft at Chicago.

Cal, during the trip, underwent only a bit of his previous distaste. His feelings were too mixed up to permit anything as simple as *mal-de-void* to bother him. He was part curiosity, part hatred, part eagerness, and part amazement. He found that he'd had no time to worry about space by the time the *Lady Unique* put down at Northern Landing, Venus.

With his rebuilt equipment in a neater arrangement, and the Key inserted, all packed into a small case, Cal went to the largest dealer in driver-wing fliers and purchased the fastest one he could buy. He then went to the most famous of all the tinker shops in Northern Landing and spoke with the head mechanic.

"Can you soup this up?" he asked.

"About fifty percent," said the mechanic.

"How long will it take?"

"Couple of hours. We've got to beef up the driver cathodes and install a couple of heavier power supplies, as well as tinker with the controls. This thing will be hotter than a welding iron when we get through. Can you handle her?"

"I can handle one like this with ease. I have fast reflexes and quick nerve response."

"It'll take some time before you get all that there is in it out of it," grinned the mechanic. "Mind signing an affidavit to the effect that we are not to be held responsible for anything that happens with the souping up?"

"Not at all."

The mechanic went at the job with interest. His estimate was good, and within two hours the flier was standing on the runway, all ready to go. Cal returned from a shopping trip at about this time and packed his bundles into the baggage compartment. He paid, and then took off at high speed and headed south.

Eight hours later the fog bank that marked the Vilanortis Country came before the nose of Cal's flier. He plunged into the fog at half-speed and continued on for a full five hundred miles.

He was about halfway through the vast fog bank

when he landed and started to install the Key equipment for operation. The job took him a full day, and he slept on the divan in the cabin of the flier that night. He could have used the flier at night, for there was no choice between night operation and the thickness of the eternal fog of the Vilanortis Country. In neither case could he see more than a few yards ahead.

While Cal slept, Benj dropped his flier on the edge of the fog country and waited. The detectors were installed and operating, and the black flier was all ready to surge forward on the trail as soon as Cal's initial signal went forth. Having had more experience in this sort of thing, Benj knew how to go about it. He'd not follow the trail of Cal's signal, but would turn and follow the answering, sympathetic oscillation from the resonant cavity at Murdoch's Hoard. And with that same experience, Benj knew that he could beat Cal to the spot, and possibly be gone with Murdoch's Hoard before his brother got there. He composed a sarcastic sign to leave on the spot for Cal to find. That, he liked. Not only would he have Murdoch's Hoard, but he would be needling his hated brother, too.

Tinker had curbed her tongue. What was going to happen she did not know. Benj was quite intent on the mechanics of the chase, and hadn't paid too much attention to her except to see that she was completely held. The idea of her—a sentient identity—being restrained with heavy handcuffs made her rage inwardly. Yet she kept her peace. She was not going to attract Benj's attention to her.

So she dozed on the divan in Benj's flier while Benj catnapped at the wheel of the flier. He would be up and going at the first wink of the pilot light and the first thrumming whistle that came from the detector. He wanted to waste no time. Running down a source of transmitted signal was a matter of a few hours at most, even though it were halfway around the planet. He chuckled from time to time. He'd had Wally tailing Cal, and had a complete report on the flier and its souping up. His own flier was capable of quite a few more miles per hour than Cal's, and Benj was well used to his.

And so Tinker dozed and Benj catnapped until the

first glimmer of dawn. Benj shook himself wide-awake, and took a caffeine pill to make certain.

Reaching back from the pilot's chair, he shook Tinker. "Pay for your board," he growled. "Breakfast is due."

"I'll poison you," she promised.

"There isn't anything poisonous aboard," he said, roaring with laughter.

It was more self-preservation than his threat that made Tinker prepare coffee and toast. Working with manacles on made it difficult, and she hated him for them again. She was carrying the hot coffee to the fore-cabin when his roar came ringing through the ship.

"Grab on! Here we go!"

The rush of the ship threw her from her feet, and the hot coffee spilled from the pot, scalding her. She screamed.

"Now what?"

"I'm burned."

"Coffee spill? Why didn't you put it down?"

"I wish I'd spilled it on your face," she snapped. "Mind taking these irons off so I can get some isopi-crine for the burn?"

He tossed her the key. "If you run now, you'll starve before you get anywhere," he told her. "But stay out of my way. We're on the trail of Murdoch's Hoard."

The thrumming whistle came in clear and strong as Benj headed into the thick fog. And as they drove forward at a wild speed, Benj tinkered with the detector.

He picked up Cal's emitted signal easily and clearly, but was unable to get a response from the other source. He considered, and came to the conclusion that the other resonator might be outside of Cal's range of transmission and therefore inoperative as yet. Knowing Hellion Murdoch's personality by comparison to his own devious way of thinking, he knew that a worldwide broadcast of the response-signal would have been unnecessary. A general location within a hundred miles would have been good enough.

So, having no goal but Cal's signal, Benj turned the nose of his flier upon Cal's sharp, vibrating tone and drove deeper and deeper into the fog blanket of Vilan-ortis.

As for Cal, he had awakened by the clock and had tuned up his resonator before taking off. Immediately after making the initial adjustments, and tuning the Key a bit, the response came in strong and clear. Cal lifted the flier and began to trace the source. At almost full throttle, he went on a dead-straight line for Murdoch's Hoard. He wondered whether his signal were being followed, and suspected that it was. He knew, however, that no one was in possession of the technique of receiving the response, and therefore he drove at high speed. If he could arrive before the others, he would be able to establish his claim on Murdoch's Hoard, whatever it might be, or perhaps remove it if it were not too bulky.

Once he established the direction of the response, Cal wisely turned his equipment off. That would forestall followers, and he could snap the gear on and off at intervals until he came close to the site of the famous Hoard.

Benj swore as the signal ceased. But prior to its cessation, there had been a strong indication as to the relative motion of Cal's ship. He continued by extrapolation and went across the chord of the curve to intercept the other ship at some position farther along.

Tinker smiled openly. "Cal isn't ignorant," she said.

"Turning that thing off isn't going to help at all," Benj responded. "I've got Cal's original junk in the ship. I don't know the technique of finding the real Hoard, but I've been thinking that following the Key in Cal's ship might be possible. After all, that's a cavity resonator, too, you know."

"Sure it is. But if you can't follow the Hoard resonator, how can you follow Cal's?"

"Murdoch did something to his that makes it different," explained Benj. "What, no one has ever known until that brilliant brother of mine unraveled the code. But if the Hoard had been a standard resonator, people would have uncovered it long years ago. There's nothing tricky about getting a response from a resonant cavity."

Benj set the flier on autopilot and went forward into the nose of the craft with tools. He emerged a moment later with a crooked smile.

"All I had to do was to hitch up Cal's original junk. The detector is running as it always was, but now I can shoot forth a signal from Cal's equipment, stop it, and receive on my own detector. We had a fistful of duplicate Keys around the lab. We can't follow Murdoch's Hoard, but we can follow Cal—who is on the trail of Murdoch's Hoard."

He snapped a switch, and a thrumming whine came immediately.

"That will be Cal's response," said Benj cheerfully. "No matter how he tries, he'll lead us to the spot."

Cal sped along in the thick white blanket of fog, not knowing that his own Key was furnishing a lead spot for another. Had he known, it is possible that he would have stopped and had his argument when the other arrived, or perhaps he could have damped the resonator enough so that its decrement was short enough to prevent any practical detection of the response.

But Cal was admittedly no technician. He did not realize that his own resonator would become a marker. So he sped along through the white at a killing pace. He snapped the switch after some time and listened to the response from Murdoch's Hoard—as well as another signal that blended with his. The latter did not bother him as it might have bothered an engineer. Cal had no way of knowing what the results would be, and so he accepted the dual response as a matter of fact.

It was in the third hour of travel that the inevitable came. By rights, it should have come easily and quietly, but it came with all of the suddenness of two fliers running together at better than five hundred miles per hour.

Out of the whiteness that had blocked his vision all day, Cal saw his brother's black flier. It came through the sky silently, skirling the fog behind it into a spiral whirl. It came at a narrow angle from slightly behind him, and both pilots slammed their wheels over by sheer instinct.

The fliers heeled and cut sweeping arcs in the fog. Inches separated their wingtips and they were gone on divergent courses.

Cal mopped his brow. In the other ship, Benj swore

roundly at Cal, and mopped his brow, too. And Tinker sat on the divan, letting her breath out slowly.

But Benj whipped the wheel around, describing a full, sharp loop in the sky. He crammed a bit of power on, and the tail of Cal's ship came into sight through the fog. Cal saw him coming and whipped his plane aside. Benj anticipated the maneuver and followed Cal around, crowding him close.

"What are you trying to do?" screamed Tinker, white-faced.

"Run him down," gritted Benj.

"Kill him?"

"No. He'll glide out of power if I can ram his tail."

He followed Cal up and over in a tight loop, dropping into an ear-drumming dive instead of completing the loop. Cal pulled out and whipped to the left, and Benj, again trying to anticipate the action, missed and turned right. Cal was lost again in the fog.

Cal waited for several minutes to see if he had really lost Benj, hoping and yet knowing that he had not. Yet there was quite a difference between knowing where he was and being within ten feet of his tail. In ten minutes, and one hundred miles later on the straightaway, Cal opened the throttle to the last notch and by compass streaked directly onto his former course.

Benj streaked after him, the resonator in operation, as soon as enough distance had been put between them for the gadget to function. Then Benj started to overhaul Cal's swift flier.

Meanwhile, Cal tried the Key. The answering signal indicated that he was approaching the site of Murdoch's Hoard, and not more than fifteen minutes later the direction indicator whipped to the rear. Cal had passed directly over it.

He circled in a tight hairpin turn and went back.

He forgot about Benj.

The black ship came hurtling out of the fog just a few feet to his right.

Before, they had been approaching on an angle, which had given both men time to turn. But now they were approaching dead on at better than six hundred miles per hour each. They zoomed out of the fog, brushed wingtips, and were gone into the fog again, but not without damage. At their velocity, the contact smashed the wingtips and whirled them slightly around.

Like falling leaves they came down, and before they could strike the ground with killing crashes, they both regained consciousness.

Benj's ship was beyond repair. It fell suddenly, even though Benj struggled with the controls. It hit ground and skidded madly along the murky swamp, throwing gouts of warm water high and shedding its own parts as it slid. It *whooshed* to a stop, settled a bit into the muddy swamp, and was silent.

Cal had more luck. By straining the wiring in his ship to the burning out point, he fought the even keel back and came down to a slow, side slippage that propelled him crabwise. He dropped lower and lower, and because there was nothing against which to measure his course, he did not know that he was describing a huge circle. His ship came to ground not more than a half-mile from Benj's demolished craft.

He set the master oscillator running in his ship and then put the field locator in his pocket. No matter where he went, he could return to his own craft, at least. Then he stepped out of his flier to inspect the damage.

A roaring went up that attracted Cal's attention.

He turned, and started to beat through the swamp toward the noise.

Light caught his eyes, and he came upon the burning wreckage of Benj's flier. Benj was paying no attention to the burning mass behind him, nor was he interested in Tinker Elliott. He was working over Cal's original equipment furiously, plying tools deftly and making swift tests as he worked.

Tinker was struggling across the ground of the swamp, pulling herself along with her hands. Her hips and legs were following limply as though they had not a bite of life. Her face was strained with the effort, though she seemed to be in no pain.

She saw Cal, and inadvertently cried: "Cal!"

Benj leapt to his feet, his hand swinging one of the three-foot welding irons. He saw Cal, and with his other hand he whipped out the needle beam and fired. The beam seared the air beside Cal's thigh.

Cursing, Benj tried again, but nothing came from the beam. He hurled the useless weapon into the swamp and came forward in a crouch, waving the welding iron before him.

Cal ducked the first swing and caught Benj in the face with a fist. It hurtled Benj back, but he came forward again, waving the white-hot needle-sharp iron before him.

Cal couldn't face that unarmed. He dropped below the thrust, and his hand fastened on the matching iron to the pair that went in every flier repair kit. He flung himself back, and came up in a crouch as his thumb found the switch that heated his own point.

Silently, their feet making soggy sounds in the swamp, Cal and Benj crossed points in a guard of hatred.

Benj lunged in a feint, first. That started it. Cal blocked the feint swiftly and then crossed his iron down to block the real lunge that came low. While Benj recovered, Cal thrust and missed by inches. Benj brought the hot tip up and passed at Cal's face. Cal wiped the iron aside with a circular motion and caught Benj on the crook of the elbow.

Smoke curled from the burn and Benj howled. It infuriated him and he pressed forward, engaging Cal's point. Cal blocked another thrust, parried a low swing, and drove Benj's point high. He dropped under the point and lunged in a thrust that almost went home. Benj dropped his white-hot iron and deflected the thrust. He jabbed forward as Cal regained his balance, and pressed forward again before Cal could get set.

The mugginess caught Benj's feet and slowed him. Cal was slowed, too, but his backward scramble to regain balance was swifter than Benj's advance. The white-hot points made little circles in the foggy murk as they swung and darted.

Benj wound Cal's point in a circular motion and then disengaged to lunge forward. His point caught Cal in the thigh and the scar burned like living flame, laming Cal slightly. Cal parried, and then pressed forward with a bit of the fastest handwork Benj had ever seen. By sheer luck, Benj blocked and parried this encounter. The final lunge found Benj retreating fast enough to evade the thrust that might have caught him fair had he been slow in retreat.

He regained and forced Cal back. His dancing point kept Cal too busy blocking to counterthrust, and Cal fought a stubborn retreat. The ground behind him grew harder as he went back, and so he took a full backward step to get the benefit of hard, dry ground. He made his stand on the bit of dry knoll, and fought Benj to a standstill.

He fought defensively, waiting for Benj to come close enough to hit. Their irons danced in and out, and Benj circled his brother slowly. Partway around, Benj forced Cal's point up and rushed him. Cal backed away three steps—and tripped over Tinker's hips. He went rolling in a heap, curling his feet and legs up into his stomach.

Benj leaped over Tinker and rushed down on Cal, who kicked out with both feet and caught Benj hard enough to send him flying back.

Both men jumped to their feet, circled each other warily, waiting for an opening. Benj rushed forward and Cal went to meet the charge. The ring of the irons came again and the white-hot points fenced in and out.

Benj thrust forward, high, and Cal blocked him with the shaft of the iron. Their arms went up, shaft across shaft, and shoulder to shoulder they strived in a body block.

"Steal my identity, will you?" snarled Cal.

"Destroy it," Benj rasped. "You've been asking for this."

Cal's mind flashed, irrelevantly, to books and pictures he had seen. In such, the villain always spat in the hero's face in such a body block. Cal snarled, pursed his lips, and spat in Benj's face. Then with a mighty effort, he shouldered Benj back a full three feet and crossed points with him again.

Benj wiped his face on his shirtsleeve and, raving mad, drove forward, his point making wicked arcs. Cal parried the dancing point, engaged Benj in a thrust and counterthrust, and then with Benj's point blocked high he drilled forward.

The white-hot point quenched itself in Benj's throat with a nauseating hiss.

Cal stood there, shaking his head at the sight, and

retching slightly. His face, which had been set like granite, softened. He dropped his iron and turned away.

"Tink!" he cried.

"Nice job, Cal," she said with a strained smile.

"But you?"

"I'm in no pain."

"But what's wrong?"

"Fractured vertebrae, I think. I'm paralyzed from the waistline down. That crash—"

"Bad. Now what?"

"Where's your ship?"

"Back there a half-mile or so," said Cal.

"Don't carry me," she warned as he tried to lift her. "Go back there and either bring it here or get something to strap me on."

"It'll take hours. The ship won't fly. I'll have to radio back to Northern Landing for help."

"I . . . won't last."

"You—" The meaning hit him then. "You won't last?"

"Not unless that vertebrae is repaired."

"Then what can we do?"

"Cal . . . where's Murdoch's Hoard?"

"Nearby, but you're more important than anything that might be in Murdoch's Hoard."

"No, Cal. No."

"Look, Tink, you mean more to me than—"

"I know that, Cal. But don't you see?"

"See what?"

"What could possibly be of value?"

"No. Nothing that I have any knowledge of."

"That's it! Knowledge! All of the advanced work in neurosurgery is there. All in colored, detailed three-dimensional pictures with a running comment by Murdoch himself. Things that we cannot do today. Get it, Cal. It'll tell you how to fix this crushed spinal cord."

Cal knew she was right. Murdoch, in his illegal surgery, had advanced a thousand years beyond his fellow surgeons, who could legally work on nothing but cadavers or live primates while Murdoch had worked on the delicate nervous system of mankind itself. Murdoch's Hoard was a hoard of information—invaluable to the finder and completely unique and non-duplicative. At least until it was found.

"I can't leave you."

"You must—if you want me! I'm good for six or seven hours. Go and get that information, Cal."

"But I'm no physician. Much less a surgeon. Even less a neurosurgeon."

"Murdoch's records are such that a deft and responsible child could follow them. According to history, his hoard is filled with instruments and equipment. Cal?"

"Yes?"

"Cal. *This is the place where Murdoch worked on living nerves!*"

Tinker Elliott closed her eyes and tried to rest. She did not sleep, nor did she feel faint. But her closed eyes were a definite argument against objection on Cal's part. Worrying, he left her and went back to his flier. He called for help and then went to work on the Key.

Cal does not remember the next four hours. It was a whirling montage of dismal swamp and winking pilot lights and thrumming whistles. It was a lonely boulder with a handle on it that Cal lifted out of the ground with ease. It was an immaculate hospital driven deep into the murky ground of Venus. Over three hundred years before, Dr. Allison Murdoch worked here, and today his refrigerating plants started to function as soon as Cal snapped the main switch.

On a stretcher that must have held many a torn and mangled set of nerves before, Cal trundled Tinker through the muggy swamp of Venus and lowered her into Murdoch's hospital.

In contrast, the next few hours will live forever in Cal's mind. He came to complete awareness when he realized that he did not know his next move.

"Tinker?" he asked softly.

"Here . . . and still going," she said. "Ready?"

Cal swallowed deep. "Yes," he said hoarsely.

"In that case over there— See it? Take an ampule of local—it's labeled Neo-croalaminol Opium, ten percent. Get a needle and put three cubic centimeters of it into space between the sixth and seventh cervical vertebrae.

Go in between four and five millimeters below the surface of the bone. Can do?"

"I . . . I can't."

"You must! How I wish we had a duplicator."

Cal shuddered. "Never."

"Well, I could show you how it's done on the duplicate, and then the duplicate could fix me up."

Cal gritted his teeth. "And which one would I dispose of? No, Tinker. It's bad enough this way!"

"Well, do it my way, then!"

Cal fumbled for the needle, and then with a steady hand he broke the glass ampule and filled the needle. "Is this still good?"

"It never deteriorates in a vacuum. We must chance everything."

Cal inserted the needle and discharged the contents. His face was gray.

"Now," said Tinker, "I'm immobilized completely from the shoulder blades down and can't harm myself. Cal, find the library and locate the reel that will deal with vertebrae and spinal operations."

"How do you know it's here?" asked Cal.

"It's listed in Murdoch's diary. Now quit arguing and go!"

"How come this diary isn't common knowledge?"

"Because too many prominent people did not want their names mentioned as fostering Murdoch's surgery. Their offspring have never known about it and the medical profession has been keeping it under their hats so long that it has become a habit like the Rx mark."

Cal located the library and consulted the card file. He returned with a reel of film. He inserted the reel into the operating-room projector and focused it on the screen.

As the film progressed, Cal took the proper tools from the boiling water and placed them on a sterilized carrier.

Then, as Tinker instructed him through a system of mirrors, Cal lifted the scalpel and made his first incision.

With increasing skill, Cal applied retractors and hemostats and tweezers. Tinker kept up a running fire of comment, and the motion picture on the screen progressed as he did, with appropriate close-ups to show the condition of the wound during each step. Cal came upon the fractured bone as it said he should, and then, though the fracture was not just like that in the picture, he plied his instruments carefully and lifted the crushed bone away from the spinal cord. With a wide-field microscope, Cal inspected the cord.

"Can't tell, Tinker. I don't know anything about it."

"And I can't see it too well. Look, Cal. Don't touch it. It may be only bruised. Run the projector over to the replacing operation and put the stuff back according to directions. If the cord is damaged, they can repair it at the Association. You'll be responsible for getting me there, anyway."

"All right," said Cal.

With tiny splints, Cal fastened the splintered bone back into place. It was as painstaking a job as putting a fine watch back together again, and as tedious as breaking the worst code in history. But Cal succeeded finally, and the final wrappings were placed by hands that were beginning to shake.

The plane from Northern Landing located them from Cal's master oscillator and came in for a landing. The official in the plane wasted no time. He ordered two of his helpers to install Tinker—stretcher and all—in his flier and they all took off after leaving a guard at Murdoch's Hoard.

Cal Blair headed up the walk from the gate to the front doors of the Solarian Medical Association with a springy step. He headed in with determination, but was hailed by Tony Elliott.

Tinker's brother grinned at Cal and shook his hand. Cal tried to leave, but Tony kept him for a moment.

"For a guy that hates surgery and space-flying and roistering around, Cal, you do all right."

"Look, Tony, I want to see Tink."

"I know. You haven't seen her since you brought her back six weeks ago, have you?"

"No, and I intend to rectify that error right now."

"You could have been here three weeks ago."

"No, I couldn't. I've been in Vilanortis, working with

the fellows on Murdoch's Hoard. After all, I'm not . . . not—"

"Not twins? No, thank the Lord! O.K., Cal. Go on in."

Cal left in a hurry, and Tony said to the receiving clerk: "He's changed."

Cal found Tinker in a wheelchair in the conservatory.

"Tink!" he roared.

"Cal!" she answered. Then she arose from the wheelchair and came toward him with a light, eager step.

Cal was a gentleman: he met her halfway.